WHERE WE COME HOME

a novel

RAINE FRASER

For my darling mother who taught me to love stories.
And my G'pa Fraser, who always believed in me.

Chapter One

CHILDREN TAKE ENCHANTMENT AS writ. By the age of five—weaned on my Irish grandfather's steady diet of stories—Celtic histories and folklore were the same, fable indistinguishable from fact. When, as a tiny girl, I first stood in front of the family cottage, the wild, inexplicable beauty stunned me. Even the unkempt rose bushes leaning against the gray stone walls seemed mystical; their faded petals littered the muddy sod like a carpet for fairies. It took no effort to conjure visions of Fionn mac Cumhaill striding across the surrounding fields, searching for his enchanted wife. Without doubt *aos sí, púcaí,* and other denizens of *Tír na nÓg* were about their ineffable business within the walled garden.

The magical memories never dulled, remaining lovely as a petite china figurine, its charm giving pleasure, even as the onslaught of school and growing up rendered it frivolous. Then, twenty-two years later, Grand-da Seamus, with uncharacteristic abruptness, died and left the cottage to me. Even in my grief I wondered if magic still lived there.

After several months, when shock and loss muted to a dull, though ever-present ache on the heart, I returned to Ireland, ready to discharge the duties set upon me by Grand-da's will.

But while waiting for a ride outside the Dublin airport, an unexpected tsunami of emotion swamped me. Questions, resentment, and confusion tugged in its bruising current. Alone amid tour groups loading onto buses and joyful individuals calling out to loved ones, I sobbed and clamped chilly fingers to my eyes, striving for control over a soul throbbing with grief.

Head hung low, grasping for enough wisps of composure to get through the day, I shuddered several breaths, opened my watery eyes, and glimpsed a pair of polished black wingtips. They belonged to a tall, good-looking man in his late thirties with hands shoved deep in the pockets of a Burberry trench coat. He wore a perplexed, wary expression and asked, "Miss Riordan?"

Cringing I replied, "Clare. Yes. You must be Mr. O'Donnell." Damn. I'd imagined a more dignified introduction to Grand-da's Irish solicitor.

"Ya don't appear well."

I searched my purse for a tissue. "It's nothing. Early onset jet lag."

Dubious, he nodded toward my battered duffle bag. "If you're sure, we can go. Allow me to carry your luggage."

We walked to the parking garage without speaking. I struggled to quiet mortification and pass for a reasonable human while he, no doubt, attempted to deduce the emotional stability of his new client. He halted behind a gray Mercedes and unlocked the trunk.

Distracted by the pristine, expensive vehicle, I blew an appreciative whistle. "Nice car."

He grimaced, defensive. "It's practical."

"Sure." Cowed by his interpretation of the compliment as a judgement, I waited by the passenger side, twisting a stray curl.

With a slam of the trunk and a rattle of keys he said, "We drive on the left here."

Scurrying to the correct side, I slunk in, burning with an embarrassment which only increased with an accidental glimpse of my reflection in the window. Leggings, an oversized hoodie, and a messy bun granted comfort for a long flight, but two minutes spent with a hairbrush would not have gone to waste.

Mr. O'Donnell pulled onto the highway out of Dublin. Scratching at my palms, searching for an ameliorative comment to banish the awkward mood, I said, "Thanks for the ride."

"Ya needn't have come all this way." The clipped remark rang with reproof.

"Grand-da wanted his ashes in Ireland and this is as good a time as any to see the old place." Regret replaced my defensiveness. Grand-da would have brought me along on any of his annual visits but an over-cautious mother thwarted early opportunities, then youthful arrogance deemed summer camp with friends more compelling than a month in a small Irish town. Rather than risk crying again I took refuge in small talk. "Do you live in Dublin?"

"Killarkin," Mr. O'Donnell answered, chipping out the village name between tight lips.

"And you don't mind such a long commute?"

The corner of his eye twitched. "I'm in the city when required; my practice is in the country."

The notion of a well-dressed, Mercedes owning solicitor managing a comfortable living from a handful of sheep farmers and shopkeepers strained credulity. "How do you keep busy enough?"

His mouth twisted in a disdainful smirk. "Sure, ya are an American."

My Yankee patriotism didn't run deep but the insult landed. "What's that supposed to mean?"

He barked a laugh. "Americans love askin' personal questions, even of strangers."

"Oh." Curling like a hedgehog under the cowl of my hoodie, I peered out the window pondering how casual conversation could start an international incident. Letting down my hair to cover heated cheeks and dragging my fingers through snarled curls, I rued not taking the bus.

In a vinegary tone he added, "Most of my work at home is pro bono."

His altruism didn't make me feel less ridiculous about my sloppy appearance, unwelcome curiosity, or propensity for conversational mistakes. Contemplating the landscape, the one Grand-da loved and would never see again, my heart stung like a skinned knee. Determined not to blubber in front of Mr. O'Donnell, I blew my nose with discretion and watched the winter sun refract prisms through fine rain falling from patchy clouds.

We didn't speak again until the car bumped off the highway and onto the road into Killarkin. "Ma and Da are expectin' ya," Mr. O'Donnell said.

"What?" I had little interest in meeting anyone, let alone the parents of my stodgy escort.

"They keep the pub and let rooms."

An exhale of relief accompanied my reply. "Thanks, but the cottage is fine."

"It's not," he replied, with calm authority. "I closed it in September. It'll be baltic." Then, with a condescending tone he added, "Cold."

My shoulders drew up like an offended feline. "I know what you meant."

"You'll want a hot bath and food. The pub will be more comfortable."

Aggravated by his insistence, I pressed my heels into the car mat, fingers clenching the seat. Based on my lousy first impression, he took me for an unfledged waif in need of his guidance. Time to assert myself. "Grand-da left me the cottage and it's where I'll stay."

"You'll find it primitive." A whiff of snobbish patronage blew through his words as if he patted my head and sent me off to play while the grownups talked.

"It's my house."

"Suit yourself." Mr. O'Donnell squeezed shut his mouth and turned onto a twisting road which soon narrowed to two lanes. As we crested a hill, nerves transformed into hopeful anticipation. My profound early memories, enhanced by Grand-da's stories and photos, made Killarkin as familiar as my own Seattle neighborhood. The clustered buildings of the village, surrounded by broad fields garnished with farmhouses, hove into view and nostalgia seized my heart.

We left the road, pulling onto a small lane no longer than a city block, and barely wide enough for two cars to pass. One and two-story buildings stood cheek-by-jowl along brick sidewalks. The cottage slept at the far end of the street, its small windows dark.

Mr. O'Donnell parked his car and retrieved my bag while I snapped a photo, texting it home to announce my arrival. The fresh, grassy scent of the air intoxicated me as if it were a glass of vintage wine. When Mr. O'Donnell rejoined me, I said, "The village hasn't changed much."

"I wasn't aware you'd visited before."

"For great-grand-da Sean's funeral."

"Over twenty years then. Ya would ha' been wee." He turned up his collar against a shifting wind. "Rain's comin'. I'll see ya ta the door."

"Not necessary, thanks. It's a short walk up one street."

"Two. Or one street with two names. This bit is The High. Most folk live in cottages around the bend, on The Low."

The simple, evocative names had always delighted me, but my chuckle made Mr. O'Donnell frown. "It's charming. Like something in a story book."

He harrumphed, and with a smidge of reluctance, handed over my bag and the key to the cottage. "Best we meet soon about the sale as I'm returnin' ta Dublin next week."

Wanting to explore without the weight of business decisions, a twinge of resistance pinged at his presumptive remark. "Could you give me a few days to settle first?"

He loured and consulted the calendar on his phone. "Thursday at ten will do." He jabbed a thumb toward a building. "My office is there."

"OK. Thanks again for the lift." With a nod of obvious annoyance, he marched away, and I drew my first normal breath since meeting him.

Daylight tussled against gathering clouds, glimmering against windowpanes while it could. A woman exited the butcher shop and hurried across the pavement to the post office, leaving me the sole occupant in the street. I headed toward the cottage at a brisk pace, hoping to gain the door before anyone spotted me.

Averting my face, I slipped past the pub, assuming Mr. O'Donnell now sat inside, regaling his parents with stories about the nosy, ungrateful American who wouldn't condescend to their hospitality. After passing the doctor's office and a handful of homes, the cottage came into full view.

Trembling with emotion, I halted at the gate. The house appeared smaller and less whimsical than in childish memory, and in the dim winter light, sadder, too. Moss furred and softened the roofline, chipped paint dulled the window frames, and the naked rose canes scratched the weather-worn walls. Since Great-grand-da's passing no one had occupied her save pilgrims who, charmed by the life of a poet-saint, visited what remained of nearby St. Dallán's Church.

Wet, overgrown grass damped my leggings from the knee down as I approached the house, and my hands shook as the large, old key jiggled in the lock until it hit the sweet spot with a click. Heaving a shoulder against the peeling red door, I entered a silent, murky chill. A press of a button on the brass switch plate released both a dull glow and a concerning trace of ozone. Rain started, tapping the window glass like tossed pebbles.

A beautiful wicker turf basket, dark with age and smoke, sat beside the hearth, empty save for small clumps of earthy peat. Beside it stood Grand-da's chair. Like a peasant daring to take the throne, I hesitated before sitting, then stroked the chocolate brown leather of the rolled arm rests, worn smooth as butter. From this chair, and one like it back home, he entertained my brothers and me with Irish legends and the tapestried stories of our forebears; the jewel-colored warp of familial love and loyalty, the dark weft of loss and sorrow.

Now I possessed the locus of those stories, a fact which confused me. Grand-da always stayed at the pub on his visits, leading us to believe he'd sold the house. Learning he still owned the place and rented it out to tourists came as surprise enough, but why he left it to me, the least reliable of his three grandchildren, baffled.

Everyone expected me to sell it, and on the face, doing so would solve a lot of immediate problems. But an emptiness within wanted filling, and a desperate, anxious part of me hoped the house would again prove itself a well-spring of dreams and possibility. Even if the notion proved foolish, no one would bully me into a hasty decision.

Leaving the chair, I removed the cardboard box of ashes from my bag, then choked up again while placing it on the dusty mantel. "You're home, Grand-da."

Nervous about the state of the electrics, I switched off the lights and lit a candle. The small flame flickered as I climbed the narrow stairs; they groaned under my modest weight with soft exhalations of old oak. The attic door stuck; the frame swollen with damp. Nudging it open, a small gasp escaped as familiarity pricked my soul. Like generations of Riordans before me, I too had slept on one of the iron cots ranged below west facing windows.

Soot smudged the plaster above the plain fireplace; a crucifix hung over the mantel, Jesus' head tarnished black. In the spare, dusty room, the voices of me and my brothers sounded, then American accents faded to the Irish lilt of preceding generations. I roamed the room, sensible of the heft of ancestors.

Excavating a worn quilt from the linen press, I extinguished the candle and curled onto one of the beds. Melancholy came in waves while the long flight, repressed tears, and edgy encounter with Mr. O'Donnell knit into a heavy mantle of weariness.

Obsidian dark obscured all form and seeping cold enveloped me from crown to toes. Leafless tree branches, tossed by howling wind, clawed the windows and broke through my sleepy haze. Then water splattered on my head.

"Shit!" Jumping from the bed, I bashed my shins on the neighboring cot before stumbling to the head of the stairs and finding the light switch by touch. The naked bulb overhead flickered on, confirming a leak. It dribbled from a wet patch on the ceiling, curved like a shallow bowl.

Dragging the bed away from the leak I tromped downstairs, setting the cottage ablaze with electric lights—fire hazards be damned—and curses. A tin basin from the kitchen went under the steady drip and swears lessened to grumbling.

After draping damp linens over dining chairs, I grabbed a paperback from a wobbly bookcase, and stooped over the front room grate, attempting to build a fire with crumbs of peat and torn pages. But the weak flames quivered and hissed, unable to gain purchase for all the water sluicing down the chimney. Huddling under the blanket I glared at the spartan room. Magic my ass.

Furious rain pelted the roof and windows, wind rattled the sashes, and a tiny coil of fear tightened in my belly. The cottage had withstood almost three hundred years of Irish weather, but in the stormy dark, her odds didn't look good. My eyelids felt sandy, and despair clutched my chest.

I dozed, skimming the surface of dreams, until a tremendous noise jolted me awake. Convinced the roof had collapsed, I ran upstairs on chilled feet and made an adrenalin fueled inspection. But other than slow plops from the attic ceiling, the room remained unimpaired. Another slam, less fearful than the first, drew my attention outdoors. The storm still wailed like a banshee, but dawn lightened the view enough to reveal the source of the noise: the door of the garden shed swung in the wind, one hinge ripped loose.

Pulling Wellingtons from my duffle, I went outside to secure it. Wind-whipped hair stung my eyes, and I mumbled impressive swears while wrestling the gale for control. Anger more than upper body strength shifted the door back into place and I shoved the bolt hard enough to bruise my palm.

I sprinted back into the cottage, thoroughly drenched and gut punched. I could have had a wet, crap apartment without leaving Seattle. With balled fists I shouted at the walls, "God dammit, I wanted to love you!" Already hearing Mom's gloats in my head, I stomped to the couch, tented under my coat, and phoned my best friend.

"Hi, hon!" Edie said. "I didn't expect a call so soon. Is it as magical as you remembered?"

"God, no." Purging a bitter litany of complaints about Mr. O'Donnell and the state of the house brought no relief. "Being here is supposed to provide answers about what to do with the cottage and my life, but if there are any signs they're all saying, 'get the hell outta there.'"

In a voice quiet as snowfall she replied, "Don't be so impatient."

Resentment boiled over, my hand tightening on the mobile phone. "I'm not!"

"Beg to differ. You're giving up after mere hours."

I hiccuped on a lash of oncoming tears. "There's nothing special about this place and it pisses me off."

"I'm sorry the cottage isn't what you remembered, but in its defense, it didn't ask for neglect. Hire another lawyer if you don't like O'Donnell. Do whatever you please with the house, look for signs if you want, but for once in your damn life, trust yourself."

"Dammit, Edie—"

Unflappable and honest, she said, "You're a dilettante, hon. You bolt whenever you don't have perfect command of a situation. Jobs, guys, the piano. This reaction is more of the same."

Chastened, I burrowed under the quilt. "I'm lonely, overwhelmed, and the cottage is just a shitty old house." The next words came out weak as a new-born kitten. "What in the world possessed Grand-da?"

"He wanted you to mind the heart and hearth."

"Yeah, well, never trust a crazy old Irishman. If he loved me, he wouldn't have foisted his stupid piece of—"

Edie gasped with genuine horror. "Are you blaspheming the sacred name of Seamus Riordan? Jesus, girl! You hate flying but got on a damn plane to see an old pile of stones. It means something to you. Don't you dare give up this time."

Smacking my forehead in contrition I sat erect, the standard response whenever Edie set me straight. "Come hold my hand."

"You're a big girl, Clare. Besides, I hear your house is crap."

Chapter Two

HITCHING A BLANKET OVER my shoulders, I stumbled into the kitchen, risked using the electric kettle, and ferreted out a cup from a large dresser crammed with crockery. A shelf contained a few pantry items, the remnants of tourists. A tin half-full of black leaves gave off a vague wisp of tea. It wouldn't be strong, but it would be hot.

Edie's patient admonitions did their work. We'd been friends since sixth grade; she knew as well as anyone my propensity for flitting through life like a honeybee, though I lacked the impetus of the noble insect. My bee self would no doubt still lie awake in the night, worrying over the quantity and quality of my honey output before abandoning the hive while the rest of the workers slept. Quitting before failing. My signature move.

But the present situation warranted more. Deciding to keep or sell the cottage involved practical considerations, matters which didn't require a trip to Ireland to resolve. Something more complex and indefinable brought me, and the need to understand it wouldn't allow me to leave.

Hands wrapped around a thick mug—my sole heat source—I explored, cataloguing the assets and deficits of the property. The kitchen comprised half of the cottage. Its beautiful slate floor, large fireplace, and black and white Stanley stove anchored a homey, if chaotic jumble of sagging shelves and mismatched furniture. Mildew wafted from the clothes washer, and I made a mental note to purchase bleach.

The small bedroom could be cozy, if it contained appropriately sized furniture. The bathroom, however, did not impress. The fixtures bore traces of rust and the taps, when opened, gave an anemic display. It would take an hour to fill the tub. I hoped the pub had better water pressure.

Pausing in the hallway, my fingertips searched the paneling of the staircase for a worn brass latch. During our long ago visit, my seven-year-old brother Colin and I discovered a door, disguised by beadboard, and decorated with a row of square cut crosses along the top. It opened to a small space under the stairs, which Col dubbed our "secret chamber". Forced indoors by a week of incessant rain, we spent hours there playing and avoiding our bossy older brother Stephen. I pressed my forehead against the door, recalling the refuge it provided during Great-grand-da Sean's wake.

Everyone from Killarkin, and beyond, crammed into the cottage for the event. The small rooms were stifling and close. Grand-da stood near the fireplace, his broad shoulders, and head of thick white hair towering above the men thronged around him. He beamed when his merry green eyes caught mine. I squeezed through the room, and he lifted me into a tight hug.

After kissing his bristled cheek I'd said, "You need a shave, Grand-da." The men around him roared with laughter while my flaming cheeks hid against his shoulder.

"It's all right, darlin'. Ya didn't do anythin' wrong." He accompanied his words with another reassuring hug and embarrassment faded in the safety of his arms. Then the din of voices hushed as an ancient woman, gnarled like an oak and all in black, glided through the room toward where Grand-da stood. He moved to the old leather chair and settled me on his lap. I snuggled in his embrace, secure and content.

A horrific noise tore out of the woman's mouth, ripping the silence. I sat stock still and clutched Grand-da's arm, unable to tear my eyes from the twisted face of the deranged woman who screamed and wailed, inarticulate and frightening. Astonished when none of the grownups stopped her, I cried, silent and too afraid to move, praying for the awful noise to end.

The woman left off; one last cry settled through the room before the crowd burst into a babble more deafening than before and a fiddle screeched to life. "Up ya go, darlin'," Grand-da said. He set me down and joined a group of drink-flushed men, who clogged with sloppy enthusiasm. Strange women cooed and pinched my cheeks; men patted my head. The loud talk, bellowed laughter, and wild music stomped on my head like a giant in one of Colin's stories.

Overwhelmed, I sidled through the forest of legs and backsides into the hallway, opened the latch, and crept into the secret chamber. The thick oak of the staircase muffled the noise of the wake. Electric light from the hall made the cross shadows more prominent. I scooted to a corner, head on my knees and hands over my ears. Spiders or rats may have lurked in the shadows, but they could not be worse than those loud, crazed Irish.

The door to my hiding place creaked open, and the clamor from the front room rushed in. Flattening myself against the wall, my tummy tightened with a panicked thought of Sean's ghost.

An older boy, his head a thatch of red curls, knelt in the doorway. I knit my brow and put my finger over my lips. The boy smiled, his kind eyes the blue of cornflowers. "You've nothin' ta fear, little Clare. Don't cry."

With defiance I brushed away the evident tears. "I'm not."

He urged me out, his voice a lullaby, but I pursed my lips and shook a stubborn head.

"No, then?" He left but returned a few minutes later. "It'll be a long night, darlin'." He laid a wool blanket over my knees and offered a honey cake. "Yer home here." He grinned and his eyes burned straight into mine, like we shared a deep secret. "I'll keep a watch out." He made his promise and slipped away. Pulling the blanket over my knees, I nibbled the light, sweet cake.

I woke in my cot the next morning, sure the fae had transported me there.

Sentimental at the remembrance and wondering if the same sense of peace still lingered, I opened the secret chamber. Something other than the hinges squeaked and I slammed the door, the hair on my neck standing at full attention.

The rain eased a tad and rather than share the indoors with potential vermin, I pushed out through the back door to the neglected gardens. Winter-naked shrubbery, rangy for want of trimming, crowded the walls. Thigh-high weeds choked the sodden vegetable beds. Twisted rowan and hawthorn branches brushed the cottage roof and spread past the garden wall. To the east stood a dilapidated barn, silvered by weather, and beyond it, pastures stretched seamless toward the distant hills and the crumbled arches and pillars of St. Dallán's Church.

Another torrential onslaught dampened my longing to visit it. Bolting inside, I gathered my bag, and pressed my nose to the front window, squinting into the storm. The tempest made it impossible to define the edges of buildings, but yellow smears of light appeared in what must be windows. If the pub also operated as an inn, surely, they would be open.

I had no umbrella, but in fairness, nothing could offer protection against the fierce, driving elements shrieking outside. The brief distance from the garden gate to the pub—a mere saunter under mild conditions—didn't daunt me. Experienced with precipitation and chilled to the point of numbness, a little wet in exchange for the promise of a hot meal and coffee seemed a small price.

Buttoning my coat to the neck, I stepped into the deluge. Wind blew full in my face, making it hard to catch a breath. Rain like needles pierced my clothes, plastering my curly hair straight. I fought through the storm, puddle water slopping and splashing over my boots, hoping to reach shelter before drowning.

When I pushed into the light and warmth of the pub, a striking gentleman, with a full head of silver hair peered up from behind the bar and flashed a brilliant smile. "Mr. O'Donnell?"

"One of them. I answer ta Eamon. And were a name be put ta ya, I reckon it would be Clare Riordan."

"Yes, sir." I combed away the wet hair clinging to my face like seaweed.

"It's lashin' out, darlin.' Are ya mad?"

"Possibly." I stared at the growing puddle forming at my feet. "Sorry about the mess."

Eamon chuckled with sympathetic amusement, handed me a clean bar towel for my hair, and pushed another across the floor with his foot. "Sit down and warm yourself. My wife will bring ya tea and breakfast, if ya like."

"Please." I slid into a booth and began defrosting, my skin tingling in the snug room. Scrumptious scents of toast and fried meat made my mouth water.

In less than a minute Eamon returned in the company of a plump, sweet-faced woman who danced forward with a pot of tea. "Clare Riordan! A treat it is ta see ya! I hoped ya would come ta supper last night, though I understand ya were eager ta visit the aul cottage again and why wouldn't ya be? Goodness, you're a picture. Ya have Seamus' eyes."

"Thank you, ma'am."

"I'm Maeve, darlin'. You'll not remember me, of course, but I'd know ya anywhere. Such a pretty little thing ya were with your ginger curls and angelic face and you're still lovely as can be, isn't she, Eamon."

The elder O'Donnell grinned and chuckled. "Sure, though I don't remember her quite so damp."

"Jaysus! You're soaked," Maeve said, registering my bedraggled state. "Why ever did ya leave the house?"

"It's none too dry there." Warming my hands against the side of the tea pot, I explained about the leak and general frigidity of the house. "Is there any chance you still have a room available?"

"Sure, and we do, the nicest one, though they're all lovely in their way, and you'll be quite comfortable."

"Anything dry will be perfect."

"Enjoy your cuppa, and I'll fetch a fry up."

Good to her word, Maeve delivered a full Irish breakfast before I'd drained my first cup of tea. Too hungry for scruples, I even ate the savory, earthy black pudding without a thought for its chief ingredient. "This is delicious, Maeve."

"Hunger is the best sauce," she replied, smiling with approval as I wiped my plate with toast. "Now, let's get ya settled. I expect you'd do with a hot bath."

She showed me upstairs to a guest room smelling of lavender and peat, dominated by a large bed covered with a crisp white eiderdown. "There's a robe on the door and you'll find the bath down the hall. There's no one else stayin' at present, it bein' February." She appraised me with a loving eye. "And by the looks of ya, you'll want a good, long rest. Settle yourself, and then, if you're of a mind later, come ta the kitchen for a chat."

I laid my soggy raincoat over a chair and, after a hot, restorative shower, climbed into bed, and fell asleep to the soft hisses and clicks of the radiator.

I woke from my nap in the late afternoon. My eyes no longer skritched when I blinked and though the hands of my internal clock were still set between Seattle and Dublin time, the general sense of heaviness had lifted. The weather had improved somewhat, too. The rain tumbled straight down rather than lashing like a whip.

Pulling on jeans and a fresh t-shirt, I went downstairs. Eamon grinned over the heads of a three older men sitting at the end of the bar and shot a broad thumb over his shoulder. "You'll find her through there."

The kitchen ran the length of the public room and matched it with a timbered ceiling and commodious fireplace. A long deal table stood in the center, surrounded by counters, two industrial stoves, and a bank of refrigerators along the perimeter. A massive hutch, loaded with dishware, filled another wall. The deep windowsill over the sink held a phalanx of votives; tall three-day candles, emblazoned with garish pictures of saints or the Sacred Heart, and myriad tea lights in jam jars with soot smutted rims. The candles flickered or guttered, depending on how long they'd burned. A vase of holly branches occupied the center. I'd never seen a lovelier altar or a room which better mirrored the generous soul of its owner.

"There ya are," Maeve greeted me. "Care for a cuppa?"

"If it's no trouble, do you have coffee?"

"If ya like."

Remembering her son's propensity for umbrage I added, "Your tea is delicious,"

"Ya had Barry's this mornin', it bein' my favorite though there's Lyons, too, for those who prefer it. Still, plenty of folk love their coffee and I'll say nothin' against it." She paused and beamed a gracious smile. "I'll put some on."

Her consideration made me embarrassed I'd even asked. "Please don't bother. Tea is fine."

As if she were sweeping a cobweb, Maeve waved away the suggestion and clicked on the coffee maker. "You're our guest, even if it's for so short a time." She dipped a spoon into a simmering pan and gave the contents a taste. "Come here ta me," she said, reaching for a clean spoon and offering a sample. "I'm of two minds about the seasonin'."

I blew on the rich, dark sauce and sipped it into my mouth. "It's perfect," I said, licking the spoon and peeking into a low-simmering pot full of meat and beautiful vegetables. "Lamb or beef?"

"Beef tonight; I'm usin' Guinness."

"It's the best Irish stew I've ever tasted." My stomach growled in anticipation of supper.

Maeve answered the compliment with a smile. "Now you're more than welcome ta take your meals here, but if ya are wantin' anythin' in the way of groceries—includin' coffee—ya need only pop in ta Fannin's just over the way. Cathleen carries all ya could want. And her mother-in-law Aideen runs The Cosy next door it. Does some lovely baked goods; her biscuits are grand. Oh, what a time she'll have should ya visit." Maeve winked. "A mite sweet on Seamus she was, back in the day."

"Really?" The information startled as we'd never assumed anything but general sentimentality motivated Grand-da's trips.

"Oh, all on her side, ta be sure. I'll tell ya one thing about Seamus Riordan, though ya knew him better than the rest of us, but he only had eyes for his Clare and never took notice of another from the day they met or any time after she passed, so the story goes, and I've heard no one dispute it." All the time Maeve spoke she performed an unceasing dance from table to stove and back again. Now she stopped, placed dumpling-soft hands on both my cheeks and peered into my face. "How are ya farin', child?" Deep concern resonated from the lake-blue pools of her eyes.

"I miss him."

"'Course ya do. Grief is an odd animal. In the beginnin' it sticks close, curlin' 'round ya like a cat, and it's hard ta move. Over time, it gives ya space, though it'll sometimes pounce when you're least prepared. And then, well, it never leaves ya, but it learns some manners."

"I'm still in the curling cat phase and it's worse now. It's awful knowing Grand-da will never come here again. And I wish—well, I wish he'd lived long enough to see me make some sense of my life."

Maeve busied herself slashing crosses in domes of dough, waiting their turn for the oven. "Don't fret on it, darlin'. I reckon aul Seamus is watchin' over ya even now."

I had a less definite theology concerning the afterlife, but if it were true, better he had his attention elsewhere at the moment. "I don't want to disappoint him."

Maeve lowered her knife and stared. "I'm sure there's no way ya could."

Everything held inside since October went limp, released like water through a sluice gate. Maeve's kind presence and the comfort of her kitchen invited confidence. "We hadn't absorbed the shock of Grand-da's passing when we heard the reading of the will. Leaving me the cottage seemed like a joke." I examined a fingernail. "Then I got here and—"

Maeve had listened with rapt interest, but upon my trailing off she issued a tiny puff of air and said, "Ya mustn't take a little leak so ta heart."

"It's not the state of the roof. Well, it is, but only because I hoped the cottage would feel like home. It did at first; a little. But now—" Profound disappointment stopped my words again.

"Ya didn't receive a proper reception, ta be sure."

Maeve touched the core with ninja-like precision. I wanted the cottage to welcome me and instead, its sorry state only proved an apt, if regrettable, metaphor for the nonsense of my life. I dropped into a chair as confusion, my familiar companion, coiled in my belly. "Except for Sean's wake, Grand-da never darkened the cottage door from the day he left Ireland. It's clear he had no idea how it had fallen apart, but, oh Jesus, Maeve. It's in bad shape and I can't fathom what he wants me to do about it."

Maeve responded by setting aside her knife and fetching a bottle. She poured whiskey in two glasses and raised hers. "*Sláinte.*" I returned the toast and sipped, the friendly slide of liquor warming me through. "It's a heavy load for such a young one."

Her simple words uncorked the tears bottled since my arrival. They fell like the beating rain, and with them came all the words dammed inside. I told Maeve everything about Grand-da's sudden death, my unimpressive track record, my anger at the cottage's disrepair, and the conflicting emotions about selling it—all while sopping fat tears with a napkin.

"I lost my job right before Grand-da died, haven't had a boyfriend in nine months, and would like to erase the ones before him. Now I've got this fusty old cottage which everyone—including your son—thinks I should sell, but..." I hiccoughed and snorted. Maeve's warm pudding of a hand covered mine as I gave a final, pitiful sniff and swiped at my nose.

"Let me tell ya a thing or two." Her brogue sounded "thing" like "ting." It made me love her. "If I'm interferin' ya say so, but as my children aren't under my roof at the moment, I'll look after ya, if ya like."

"What should I do, Maeve?"

She rendered a patient smile. "If it's advice you're after, I'd say ya can't decide your future on one roof wot leaks in a hammerin' rain. When it's repaired and the sun is shinin' bright, ya might have another perspective. When ya know your mind, trust it."

I wrinkled my nose, still in despair. "Confidence isn't one of my strong suits."

"Goodness, darlin'! Then I say ya learn it." Maeve stood and smoothed her apron. "And make your decisions irrespective of anyone else, includin' Declan. I love the boy, but he can rub folk wrong, thinkin' he knows best. Sometimes he does and more often he doesn't."

My shoulders tweaked toward my ears. "My mom will be furious if I don't sell."

"And I'm sure ya hate disappointin' her, but it's your choice."

"Daddy said the same."

Maeve fixed me with a look like a pin. "He's as wise as his da, then. Seamus put the cottage in your keepin', knowin' you'd choose right." She glanced at a wall clock and slapped her hands together with a clucking noise. "Goodness! Suppertime." She scampered toward the ovens, pulling out a large sheet pan and replacing it with a tray of fresh dough. From then on the toasty fragrance of fresh-baked bread became the signature of goodness, home, and Maeve. "Would ya mind takin' those napkins out front? Eamon will show ya where they belong. Thank ya, darlin'."

"I'm the one who's grateful, Maeve. You and Eamon have been so hospitable."

"Pft," she said with a flip of her hand. "We wouldn't do much trade if we were anythin' else."

Their occupation had nothing to do with their kindness, but I didn't argue. I delivered the basket of napkins to Eamon and received a heartwarming smile in reward. Even if the cottage were a lost cause, for the duration, the pub provided the comfort I sought.

Chapter Three

Drained by travel and emotion, sleep came quick and deep, and I didn't appear downstairs until near noon the next day. Two young men played darts in the back; Eamon rested elbows against his bar, in conversation with an ancient man who appeared screwed onto his stool. Maeve stood beside a snug, chatting with someone. With a cheerful wave she called me over.

"Clare, darlin', I've been tellin' Paddy here about your roof. Paddy Flannery, meet Clare Riordan."

A tall, broad man with full, apple-red cheeks and short, grizzled beard unfolded from the bench to shake my hand. "Seamus' Clare, is it? Oh, it's grand ta meet ya. We're near ta bein' kin, ya know," he said, with a friendly dig of a meaty elbow in my side. "Me da and Seamus were friends from boyhood, God rest their souls." He and Maeve crossed themselves with solemn expressions before Paddy regained his avuncular spirit. "A shame, about the house. Where 'bouts is she leakin'?"

"The attic roof, Mr. Flannery."

He waggled his head, emphatic as a wet dog. "None of yer formal nonsense," he said. "It's Paddy; Padraig if you're angry. If ya will indulge me dispatchin' my lunch and pint first, ya can show me the trouble after."

Maeve brought lunch without my asking and I fell on it with ravenous furor. Paddy quizzed me on the nature of the leak, its proximity to the chimney and the like. "Now, she'll need inspectin' before I know fer sure, and though it could be some slates blew loose in the wind, my guess is one or more of them chimney caps is banjaxed."

Already expecting the worst, my nerves went on high alert. "Do you mean cursed?"

He roared a laugh and smacked the table. "Nothin' like. Broken, darlin', and we can sort it."

"Excellent."

In acknowledgment he shouted over his shoulder at the men playing darts. "Jamie, lad." A dark head swiveled our direction. "Fetch yer da. Meet us at aul Sean's within the hour. And you, Liam." When he had the attention of the other head he tossed a jangle of keys in its direction. "Take my truck along. We've got a mite a work." Then he returned his focus toward me. "We'll see the job through, and not leave til you're comfortable."

A gut deep certainty assured me Paddy Flannery, more than anyone, could work whatever miracles the cottage required. "Thanks."

"Buildin' is my trade and this time a year I've but odd jobs here and there. It's more than a treat bein' of service ta Seamus Riordan's granddaughter."

By the time we'd finished our lunch and walked to the cottage the other men huddled around an antiquated pickup truck parked near the garden gate. They straightened up as we approached, and Paddy made introductions. "Sorely O'Rourke, here, will see ta the chimneys proper." Short and extremely thin, with bristling black hair, the man resembled one of his brushes. "And these lads are Liam Forsyth and Jamie—Sorley's youngest. You'll find they're mostly good fer nothin'." The young men laughed at the good-natured insult. My offered thanks elicited a wink from the blond, broad-shouldered Liam. His friend, thin and dark as his father, answered with a silent nod and bashful foot shuffle.

"Sorely, if you'll get a start, I'll see ta the trouble above." Jamie spotted the ladder and Paddy nimbly scrambled up, looking like a genial, hunched gargoyle as he inspected the roof. "There's a blessin'," he called down. "I told ya, didn't I, Clare? It's the caps. Lads, fetch new ones from the truck."

He returned to earth; his hands smudged green. Wiping them on his work trousers, he said, "She needs the moss cleared, but a slate roof will last hundreds a years if done right and aul Sean knew his trades." He gave me a broad smile, face florid as beetroot. "The chimneys have a crook in 'em, keeps the rain out, ya see; but when it's lashin' like yesterday, with them caps peeled, it's no surprise ya had a problem. Still, once they're restored, and the chimneys swept, ya should have no further trouble. Mind now, there may be masonry ta repair or such, but Sorely will know soon enough."

Shivering with cold and a surprising sense of relief I asked, "It's really not so bad?"

"The aul girl weren't naught but one room when Sean took her on. Now, she's not seen an upgrade in donkey's years; the wirin' is still knob and tube, for Heaven's sake, but he gave her some of the best bones in the county."

Renewed longing surged; my throat went thick, and so did the space around my heart. The obvious signs of neglect didn't render the cottage hopeless; I had over-dramatized her condition.

The men set to work, and the small house rang with their banter. Huddling close to a radiator in the kitchen, out of their way, I sent email messages back home then thumbed through a book of Irish fairy tales, illustrated by Arthur Rackham. The drawings terrified me as a child; now their lush, complex beauty spoke of magic. An admirable two hours later, Paddy reported the work complete.

"Terrific! What do I owe you?"

He sniffed, as if repairing chimneys and plaster were mere trifles. "Don't ya fret; I'll settle it with Declan."

"No," I said, with some force. "We're meeting tomorrow. I'll take care of it."

In answer, he pulled a twice-folded receipt book from his back pocket, licked the business end of a pencil stub and with a squint, made mental calculations before scribbling the results. He ripped the sheet from the notebook, bestowed it with a flourish, then led me upstairs to show off the fresh plaster patching the site of the former leak.

"The lath is sound so there's a mercy." He swept the musty remains of the old plaster into a bucket and winked. "You'll not have problems from this quarter again."

The men went away after heartfelt and borderline tearful thanks. Sorely had laid a fire to demonstrate the "sweet draw" of the chimneys and I noticed an appreciable lift from the damp. The sun appeared, shining as if the audacious weather of the last two days had never happened, and lured me into the garden. Sunlight met the rain-soaked ground, raising a faint mist over the hills. St. Dallán's Church, broken but still majestic, beckoned. Something charmed ruffled inside, like breeze-tossed bed sheets twitching on a clothesline, drawing me over the garden wall and up.

Upon arriving at the site, pure quiet embraced me. I perched on a wall opposite the remains of the altar and a fine shower fell, slicking the smoky gray stones. Time worn limestone columns picked out the footprint of the old church; one arch remained intact. Tall grasses swayed and moss dug unseen roots into interstices of lichened rock. In time, it would all be dust. The space opened to the sky above and disintegrated below, but a sacred, serene aura breathed through it. For centuries people had gathered in this tranquil place and their prayers had worked into the stones. In the hallowed silence a faint, but profound vibration connected the ancient with the divine.

I trembled with awe. Here mystery seemed like a natural state rather than something fearful. Inhaling deeply, the last snarls in my chest untangled in the hush.

From the hilltop vantage the village lay cradled in velvety folds of malachite, the dark green riven with black shadow. White birds perched on the cottage's dark roof. Small to the point of absurdity—more toy than habitation—it seemed like an abandoned plaything in the expanse of emerald. It stood apart from the rest of the village, like Great-grand-da Sean, who eschewed community in a whiskey-soaked grief. But it remained a testament to his son's devotion.

Grand-da's death darkened the shadows on my life and his gift, especially in the first unmagical hours of my visit, struck as an unwanted burden. But the sight of the cottage quirked my heart. Love and family story whispered, too soft for articulation, but certainty quieted my mind, vitalizing as summer rain on a drought-parched garden. Whatever he became in later years, Sean made her beautiful. Despite the sorrow she'd housed, Grand-da loved her. The leak hadn't been a test but a plea. She wanted to be a home again and who better to make her fit for a new family than another Riordan?

Thursday began with a walking tour of Killarkin. Dampened by a chill light rain, I made circuits of the village, growing more captivated with each pass. Endearing limestone cottages scattered The Low, distinguished by various and vibrant paint on doors and window trims. Foot-worn, unnamed dirt paths tendrilled from the narrow lane to the open fields of the farms beyond. A tall stone and timber building, with boarded windows, stood across the road from Killarkin. Its exclusion from the village proper made me wonder what it had done to offend.

Villagers bustled about The High, busy on their morning errands, popping into shops with baskets and bags. Inured, no doubt, to strangers, they didn't heed a young crimson-haired woman in their midst, though most acknowledged me with a nod and one older man called out a cheerful *"maidin mhaith"* as he passed.

"Good morning!" I answered, pleased I understood him.

My stomach tap-danced with nerves; despite the surety of my decision, I dreaded the impending discussion with Mr. O'Donnell. It required four laps around the village before summoning enough calm to halt before the green door of the narrow two-story building. A simple bronze sign read "D. O'Donnell, Solicitor." Drawing a steadying breath, I pledged to state my intention with dignified firmness while avoiding animosity, snark, or unnecessary questions. Starting on the wrong foot didn't doom us to continued limping. After smoothing the waist of my skirt, I threw back determined shoulders and opened the door.

A clock chimed and Mr. O'Donnell emerged from his office on cue. "Good mornin', Ms. Riordan. Right on time." He steered me into a dark paneled room which held wide bookcases, heavy draperies, and an imposing desk with two deep leather chairs facing it: suitable décor for the irascible Mr. O'Donnell. Once seated, he offered me coffee.

"Please. You're a saint."

"My brother is the holy one," he replied, with a bitter huff. "I've cream and sugar, if ya like."

"Blasphemy." Cradling the cup, I inhaled the rich aroma with gratitude.

Every bit as no-nonsense as he'd presented at the airport, Mr. O'Donnell had no use for further pleasantries. He handed over the most recent financial statements of Grand-da's Irish accounts, along with a list of properties comparable to the cottage, then arranged his tie. "As ya see, even at the lower end, once ya sell, together with the money comin' from the trust, you'll leave here a wealthy young woman."

It might risk his displeasure, but rushing the matter didn't seem prudent. I scanned the numbers which, in my current situation were impressive, although wealthy overstated the case. "Let's back up a moment. The existence of the trust came as a total surprise to us. Could you explain?"

Mr. O'Donnell bristled, as expected, but indulged me. "What do ya know of Seamus and his da?"

"They weren't close. Sean drank too much after his wife died. Grand-da helped with his siblings but left the minute he could, and he blamed Sean when his little sister died of 'flu."

Mr. O'Donnell nodded confirmation. "Despite their disagreements, Seamus loved the aul place and sent a regular stipend for taxes and upkeep. Ta ensure Sean didn't drink or gamble it away, he put the funds in the keepin' of the town solicitor, Fergus Malone. His son Finnin took it over after his da's passin'." He regarded his coffee cup. "Finnin Malone brought me into the practice before he died."

I inclined forward, curiosity piqued. "Grand-da sold his Seattle pub for a tidy profit. But the trust is substantial; unless there's a decimal wrong."

"He sent over money for decades, from the time he left Ireland." Mr. O'Donnell removed a ledger from a shelf, opened the furred gray-green cover, and handed it across the desk. "Through sound investments, and rentin' the cottage after Sean's passin', the amount increased." He ran a long finger down the column of figures. "More than preservin' the cottage; Seamus assured the village around it thrived. He designated part of the income for charitable use—loans and gifts outright—ta folk in the community."

In his adult years, Grand-da lived a comfortable life, but Frugality might have been his middle name. Stunned by his largess, my head bobbled in astonishment. "He never let on."

"He'd have kept it secret altogether, but Killarkin's a small village. Now, I've an appointment with an agent ta discuss the sale—"

A flush of nerves flared, but tamping them down I said, "There's no hurry. My plans have changed."

Mr. O'Donnell looked askance. "The sooner the property is listed the sooner ya—"

I squeezed a thumb, struggling to explain what I didn't fully comprehend myself. "I'm not selling yet."

He sank deep in his chair, stunned. "Ya came here ta do."

"It can't be sold while it's so sad and worn down."

The solicitor's shoulders bunched in offense. "I employed the trust accordin' ta Seamus' terms. The buildin' is sound."

I'd tread on his thin skin again and cursed myself for not speaking with more care. "More or less; but the roof sprang a leak." I handed over the receipt. "Paddy fixed it, but the electrics and plumbing need updates."

Dragging a hand through thick hair Mr. O'Donnell said, "Ms. Riordan, there's no need ta do anythin' prior ta the sale; as-is will suffice."

"That may be how you do it in Europe, but she'll appraise higher if she's fixed up."

"Sure—"

"It's poor stewardship to sell without ensuring she'll last another couple hundred years."

Mr. O'Donnell stared like I'd sprouted a second head. "Ya cannot be serious."

Rising impatience threatened my vow of mature behavior. "You may think it's rash or silly—"

"I didn't say so."

"Mr. O'Donnell, it's the family home." I damned the sudden tightness in my throat. "You are no doubt eager to be shod of the responsibility but—"

He huffed, his cheeks pink with umbrage. "I considered workin' with Seamus an honor."

The statement cut two ways but choosing to believe he wasn't insinuating anything about *our* working relationship, I continued. "We know Grand-da trusted you. There's no higher testament." My words were gentle, but Mr. O'Donnell blanched like they stabbed him through the heart. "The will said the trust is for the cottage's preservation and maintenance; there's plenty to fix it up. Can I live on it, too?"

"Sure. The terms are clear. But ya can't mean you'll stay and do the work yourself." He stared unblinking; watching him made my own eyes dry.

"After all you've done, no one expects you to take on project management, too."

Long fingers tapped against his forehead, as if words stuck there and he meant to tumble them loose. "Ya don't understand. There are good reasons why—" His mouth clamped shut on further words and a nerve ticked in his cheek. "Endeavors like this take any amount of time. Ya have work and family waitin' for ya. Ya can't be too stubborn ta see sense."

My plans were inchoate, but nothing made me feistier than opposition. I straightened my spine, attempting to appear taller than my five feet, six inches and parried his steel with the truth. "My current trajectory is not exactly meteoric. What is certain, though, is how much the cottage, and Killarkin, mattered to Grand-da." I gestured to the ledger. "There's the proof. I don't know what the hell I'm gonna do with a cottage in Ireland, but I'll live with the question and fix it in the meantime."

My conviction should have settled the matter, but Mr. O'Donnell made an admirable, if frustrating, effort to steer me toward his original plan. "Ya must consider your own needs and desires in the matter, no one else's."

"My desire is to restore the cottage. If Grand-da suggested the same would you challenge him?"

"Of course not; he owned it." Recognizing the paucity of his argument, he took another tack. "Then there's the problem of your visa. Anythin' more than fresh paint will take longer than three months."

"Time isn't an issue; I have dual citizenship." The odd slant of Mr. O'Donnell's shoulders, one slumped and the other raised like a hackle, signaled his surprise, so I leapt into the gap. "I intend to contract Paddy for the renovation."

"He's the man for it," Mr. O'Donnell replied, his gaze firm on the ledger. "But Ms. Riordan—" A horrified awe colored his voice, like an honor student informed he'd missed a final exam. "Ya were ta be here a week. Ya can't be mad enough ta think—"

It took everything in me not to shout. "Your objections are noted but my decision is firm. I need a bank account."

Mr. O'Donnell furrowed his brow. "I can draw checks on the trust."

The man got points for tenacity, but my stubborn streak ran deep, too. "I assume the nearest bank is in Tullamore; do you have a bus schedule?"

Mr. O'Donnell's shoulders slouched, and his chair creaked as he rested back in defeat. "I can run ya over."

His pained acquiescence stirred mild sympathy. He'd no doubt envisioned a straightforward end to his management of Grand-da's affairs. "Thank you. May I call you Declan?"

"Sure." He sounded exhausted.

Chapter Four

O N Friday I woke as the first fingers of dawn stretched to lighten the sky. Faint knocks and taps from downstairs indicated Eamon and Maeve prepared for another day. With a languorous stretch I abandoned the plump, cozy bed and unlatched the window. It had rained overnight, but the pale sun pushed through wisps of cloud.

I leaned out the window, overlooking the pub's back garden, and admired the view of a wide lawn, bound by a stone wall, with neat garden beds at one end. Beyond, fields undulated east to the lush hills. White sheep studded the deep green. A tabby cat, tangerine with carrot stripes and a cream muzzle, poised like a sentinel on the eaves. Its tail twitched.

"Here, Puss." With delicate steps, the cat walked across the tiles, leapt onto the windowsill, and examined the view while I stroked under its chin. After a patient receipt of the attention, it returned with nonchalance to its former perch and groomed its paws. Taking her cue, I went down the hall to shower away the film of sleep.

I came downstairs into the near-empty public room and Maeve's cheerful face. She made the requisite inquiries about the quality of my slumber, then hustled off to fetch my breakfast. The woman never walked; she scampered.

When she returned with my plate she stood, hands crossed over her heart. "I swear, you're the spittin' image of your grandma with those curls and darlin' freckles, though aul Clare had the blonde hair. Ya must have some Scots." Maeve patted her own red curls.

"On Mom's side," I said, my mouth full of toast and eggs.

"I couldn't be more delighted about your news. Oh, there's a rightness ta it; I have it here." She touched her heart. "Think on it, Eamon! A Riordan back in the cottage!"

Her husband grinned. "It's a grand notion, indeed."

"The poor old house has been without life so long; save for the French group the one time. Do ya remember, Eamon? Oh, the parties and carryin' on. Ya could hear their accordion all up The High. But most times, even with pilgrims there, the cottage sat dark and woeful. It warms me ta picture it—lace blowin' at the windows by day, all the roses bloomin', and comfortin' lights glowin' of an evenin'." She clasped her hands under a rapturous smile.

Though we shared a similar vision, the circumstances didn't warrant such poetry. "It's temporary; just until the cottage is in better shape."

"And it must be in quite a state after all these months lyin' empty. Should ya need any help, I can spare Eamon. Or ring Declan."

I gulped the last of my coffee and grinned. "I can manage a little housework."

"You'll tell me, though, should ya need anythin'." Maternal concern furrowed her brow. "Oh, and I near forgot! Bide a bit if ya will, darlin'."

As Maeve bustled back into the kitchen Eamon chortled then, in a musical voice, called to the old man hunched over the end of the bar. "Tim Sheenan, see who it is! Seamus' Clare is stayin' in Killarkin a time."

"Sure, look it," Tim said, in a brogue thick as the head on his pint. "*Céad míle fáilte.*"

Maeve reappeared with a basket, stuffed to the brim, and covered with a tea towel. "A small lunch."

"You're too good to me, Maeve. Thank you."

Eamon cast a sly glance around and said, "And take this along." He handed me a bottle of Jameson.

The idea of an evening tot in front of my own hearth warmed me. "It's my favorite."

"The Riordan men are friends of Jamie; no reason their women should be different."

Laden with the basket and my duffle, I exited the pub and rear ended a sheep, who baaed with irritation. A young boy wielding a long stick strode with purpose amid a flock which straggled from one side of the narrow street to the other. A beautiful border collie walked close beside him. The boy regarded me, and I motioned to my burdens. "May I get through?"

"Sure, miss," he said, with a salute. He whistled to the dog; encouraged by her gentle nips and soft prods of the boy's staff, the sheep moved aside. I waved as I passed, my notion of a morning commute forever changed.

The cottage door unlocked with ease, as if to welcome me back. I parked my bag at the foot of the stairs, left Maeve's basket on the dining table, and attempted laying a fire with a bit of peat Sorely left behind. My first attempt produced more smoke than heat, but the cold lessened, and I'd work up a sweat cleaning anyway.

Preferring the light and spaciousness of the leak-free attic to the dark bedroom downstairs, I dragged one of the bedsteads away from the wall to the middle of the room, its foot toward the fireplace, and dressed it with fresh, dry linens. While delighting in the spare, lovely effect, a firm hammering at the door summoned me downstairs.

Paddy waited on the stoop with a bundle perched on his shoulder. "Declan asked me ta bring along fuel." He laid his burden in the wicker basket and grinned. "I understand ya intend ta make the aul girl over."

Eager to set my plans in motion, I didn't spend too much annoyance on Declan announcing my business to all who'd listen. "You heard right. Are you available for the job?"

He grinned like a child at Christmas. "Indeed, I am, darlin'. Now, depends on what ya want done, but if we start soon, me and the crew can give ya a good three months before other jobs interfere. I'll be 'round ta the pub this evenin' and ya can tell me yer thoughts."

With unmitigated glee, I promised to meet him there and with a touch of his cap, he left me to my business. While the kettle heated, my ambitious agenda smacked into a chief flaw: the cottage's sole domestic implements were a manky mop and rotting broom. Abandoning ideas of refreshment I paid my first visit to the corner shop, which wasn't on the corner at all but, as Maeve promised, next door to the tea shop.

A sweet bell announced my entrance. Shelves rose to the ceiling, crammed with every conceivable household item and dry good known to humankind while bins stuffed with fresh foodstuffs waited in front. An older woman with a blonde updo and bright smile came around the counter. "You'll be Miss Riordan. Maeve mentioned ya might come by. I'm Cathleen Fannin. Shame we welcomed ya home with a rotten rain."

"I'm from Seattle; February is the same there."

Mrs. Fannin collected the housewares on my list while I filled a basket with pantry staples. Then, while I scanned the crockery and neat stacks of linens on nearby shelves, the tabby cat, with effortless grace, leapt on the counter, arranged her tail around her feet, and stretched her neck, as if granting me permission to resume my earlier ministrations.

"This cat was at the pub this morning," I said, scratching the animal's belly. "Who owns her?"

"Orla owns herself. But should ya find her on your doorstep, she'll appreciate a saucer of cream or such."

"Noted." The idea of a communal pet appealed to me and a bottle of cream joined the basket of groceries.

Mrs. Fannin piled cleaning supplies and a French press coffee pot on the counter. "Will ya be wantin' anythin' else?"

"Not today, thank you."

"Keep in mind I can order in anythin' ya can't find in the shop," she said, deferential and polite. "Now, how will ya be payin' today?"

My cheeks burned with a blush. I had a handful of euros and next to nothing in my US account, rendering my current bank card useless. "Sorry, Mrs. Fannin. I'll take the mop and broom now and come back when my new debit card arrives."

"No need ta fuss, dear. Gerry, I'm startin' an account for Miss Riordan."

Gerry Fannin emerged from the back room, rubbing his hands on his apron. "It's already in the book, Cathleen. Declan took care of it yesterday. I swear I told ya."

"Ah, well. All's sorted then, isn't it?" she said, pulling a ledger from under the counter.

Mr. Fannin welcomed me with a handshake. "We settle accounts at the end of the month. Declan will see ta yours."

Asserting myself with a warm smile I said, "Send the bill to me, thanks." Under no circumstances would Declan O'Donnell get a scrutinizing peek at my personal expenditures.

I carried my purchases and suspicions next door to The Cosy where a young woman with dark, spiky hair and midnight blue nail polish greeted me. Requesting sugar cookies and jam, I then tested my theory by asking her to charge my account. The woman responded with a nod, wrapped the order, and without asking my name, jotted the amount in a notebook.

Declan had an impressive grasp of details, but given his opposition to my presence, his interference smacked more of condescension than care.

I returned to the cottage bristling with irritation but dusting, sweeping, and scrubbing every surface in the cottage banished it. With robust energy I emptied cupboards and sorted through the dishes and crockery which crammed the huge kitchen dresser. The mess of plastic plates and cheap glasses accumulated during the pilgrim years went into the bin, leaving room for a trove of small found treasures: bone spoons, tarnished bits of silver, and candlesticks. In the bowels of the lower cupboard, in a battered cardboard box and wrapped safe in yellowed tea towels, hid two crystal wine glasses and a lovely Belleek tea pot. Astonished they'd survived at all, they received pride of place on the top shelf.

By the time the dimness of late afternoon prompted me to switch on the lights, I had scoured and buffed the ancestral remnants into new life. Copper pots gleamed from their hooks, and a good dose of bleach mitigated the stench from the washer. With a tremendous sense of well-being, I relaxed in Grand-da's chair with a short pour of whiskey. "A good day's work, Grand-da. *Sláinte.*" Full of contentment, I failed to recognize the irony of wishing health to a box of ashes.

After a shower and a change into clean jeans and a blouse, I strolled up the empty High and entered the pub, jammed and noisy with a Friday night crowd. The patrons all wore eager, inquisitive faces, giving the decided sense I'd crashed a party.

Heads turned when a stocky man left his bar stool and headed toward me calling, "Is it the famous Clare Riordan?"

"Well, I'm Clare, anyway."

The man barked a loud laugh and offered a brisk handshake. "Garbhán Forgaill McAllister." A short man somewhere in his forties, he wore an expensive suit and had wavy dark hair tamed into submission with a thick application of pomade. Defiant curls peeked from behind his ears like tiny devil horns. He reminded me of a glad-handing used car salesman, and I greeted him with wary politeness. "How do you do. Garvan? Forgaill? Like the saints?"

He laughed loudly again. "Ma's wishful thinkin', givin' me godly names; I haven't much use for holiness." A salacious wink accompanied the remark. He led me to the bar and resumed a seat next to Declan. "Join my friend and me for a drink and we'll have the craic."

"I'm meeting someone, thanks." Garbhán might be all right but partying with Declan didn't sound at all like fun. "It looks like the whole village is here."

Declan managed a weak smile and said, "Folk are eager for a glimpse of Seamus Riordan's granddaughter. You're somethin' of a celebrity."

The information provoked a blush. "How disconcerting." He turned his attention back to his pint, signaling disinterest in further conversation, but in a frosty tone I added, "Thanks for the shop accounts."

"I reckoned you'd have needs before the bank card arrived."

"Your consideration is appreciated, but I can manage my own business."

Garbhán chortled at his friend's subdued appearance. "Don't mind him. How are ya findin' Killarkin?"

"Everyone pronounces my name correctly. Americans say 'air' not 'are', so only family and close friends get it right."

"Well, you're with your folk now, and kinder you'll not meet." Garbhán had the aspect of a raptor, with a beaked nose and pointed chin; a generous smile softened his harsh profile. Nose poking toward his pint he said, "Good of ya, comin' all this way ta sell the cottage."

"I'm going to fix it up first."

Garbhán shot Declan a look, then turned back to me all smiles. "Best take as much as ya can for it."

With a pained expression Declan growled. "Leave off, man."

"Don't get chronic, boyo. I'm makin' conversation."

Maeve surged forward with a radiant smile, her presence diffusing the rising tension. "Darlin', I've saved a snug if you're ready for supper."

I waved toward the door as my dinner companion entered. "Thanks, Maeve. Paddy is joining me."

Maeve nodded toward an empty booth. "I'll send 'im over when he's done with Eamon and be out with your plates in two shakes."

Within minutes Paddy joined me, slid a pint glass across the table, and said, "I took the liberty." I thanked him, sipped the thick, nutty Guinness, and set it aside. "I am pleased ya mean ta make the cottage a proper home again."

"It filled with sadness in Sean's lifetime and has been a way station since. No one's loved her in a long time." My nose wrinkled at the over-romantic explanation.

"Right ya are, and I'll be honored ta help."

Maeve arrived with plates of roast lamb, aromatic with rosemary and garlic. Mashed potatoes and Brussels sprouts rounded out the meal. "Eat up; there's treacle pudding for afters. Jaysus, Paddy; ya don't wear a hat when dinin' with a lady!" She snatched the offending cap from his bald head and slapped it against his chest. "I'll fetch ya another pint."

Over our delicious meal we discussed water pressure, the paucity of electrical outlets, and other improvements for the cottage. Assuring me of his credentials Paddy said, "I've been pullin' down and puttin' up everythin' from cottages ta castles since I were the age of them lot." He gestured toward Jamie and Liam who joked with the girl from The Cosy.

Declan moved toward us through the crowd; two pints held safe over his head. He settled beside me. "Plottin' the restoration of a relic, I see."

Straight-faced Paddy replied, "It's holy work."

"A shame Ciarán isn't here." Declan's scowl did not match the joking tone.

"Ah, I do miss your brother." Paddy's voice sang with affection. "The finest carpenter I've had the pleasure ta know. The lad turns poetry on a lathe." He made short work of his meal, all the while extolling the virtues of the younger O'Donnell. Then, with a gentle belch, he pushed away his empty plate. "And now I'll be after a game a darts."

To my dismay, Declan moved his pint, taking Paddy's spot; we'd have to make conversation and inquiring why he disliked his brother didn't strike as a wise opener. Maeve saved me when she bore a round of pints to the table and bestowed them with solemnity. "From Councilman Delaney."

Declan answered my mystified air with a lecture on local politics, giving the impression the councilman served as de facto mayor. Meanwhile, rounds arrived at an alarming rate, prompting a confession. "Beer isn't my favorite."

"Then what the hell are ya doin' in Ireland?" He barked a laugh of genuine amusement, the sort of which I hadn't deemed him capable. He fetched a bottle of wine and returned, still chuckling. Rather than waste the sea of beers, he began inviting people over, offering them a glass, and making introductions.

He presented a pretty woman with a dark bob as Nessa Cassidy, the village doctor, who displayed no enthusiasm and dismissed me with a terse "I know who ya are," before giving Declan her attention. "Maeve mentioned you're goin' ta Dublin next week."

"Leavin' Sunday."

"I'd like ta come along. I've got a conference, and Jamie still has my car up on blocks."

Declan's expression hovered somewhere between shyness and regret. "Ya may, but I'm not sure when I'm returnin'."

Nessa set down her empty glass with a nod. "I can take the bus home."

"Seven o'clock, then."

As she walked away Jamie and Liam joined us, and introduced their friend, Moira Fannin. Conversation with them proved much easier, despite the unnerving realization they, and every other villager, already knew of my plans for the cottage.

Paddy returned to the table; a cluster of darts brandished in his fist. He helped himself to a pint, dispatched it in several large gulps, and belched behind his hand. "Do ya play, Clare?"

I cringed into the bench. "I avoid pointy projectiles."

"Have a go and prove you've Irish blood."

"In the interest of public safety, take my word for it."

"Come on then." Liam tugged me on my feet with a chortle and a nod toward Declan. "Ya have a solicitor should it go amiss."

Chapter Five

Early the next morning, with a knot of dread in my belly, I made a video call home. My parents expected my return in two days, so the time had arrived to stop procrastinating and inform them of my decision. Daddy responded with nothing more than a cockeyed grin, but Mom, who seldom swore, greeted my declaration with a near-hysterical, "Have you lost your damn mind?"

"I'd have to know where it is, first."

Her image jiggled as she stomped her foot. "Don't joke, Clare. Come home and find a job!"

"As soon as the cottage is renovated."

She clapped a hand to her distressed forehead. "You have been reckless before, but this is a whole other level."

Daddy patted Mom's shoulder and winked at me. "Oh, Denise, it's not rash; it's exciting."

"Don't side with her, Ewen!"

"What sides?" In thirty-four years of marriage, Daddy elevated forbearance to an art form. "Da gave her the house and he'd be pleased she cares about it."

I leapt to piggyback on his support. "Mom, the cottage needs me. I want to do this for Grand-da."

She groaned with an all too familiar despair. "Oh, Clare, Ireland is so far away."

"It's not like I'm on a deserted island hunting my own food. Killarkin has running water and Internet. It's for a few months, six tops."

Mom did not come around, nor had I expected she would, given her inability to approve any of my choices. But Daddy's enthusiasm encouraged me, as did Edie's. My other best friend, Joel, who worked as an architect, confirmed his support by offering to draw blueprints. The notion of physical plans breathed additional life into my ideas, inspiring further conversations with Paddy. I emailed Joel photographs and measurements, already seeing the restored cottage shining in my mind's eye.

Then everything went wrong.

The decrepit water tank in the attic gave up the ghost, creating another, worse leak. Paddy shut off the water and helped me mop the flood. "Seems ya arrived in the nick of time," he said.

Moving back into the pub didn't bother me; the trouble lay with starting the project at all. On Declan's advice I'd opened two bank accounts, keeping the reno money separate from my living expenses. It made perfect sense, but a mere five hundred euro stood in the building fund, the minimum balance required. He would transfer the full amount when Paddy provided a budget for the work. But by the time we produced the requisite document, Declan's business in Dublin took priority. Paddy offered to start anyway, knowing the money would be available, but having him and his crew work on credit felt wrong.

Having made a firm, adult decision after years of waffling, I wasn't prepared to wait. Seeking distraction from my disappointment, I passed the mornings in the pub kitchen. While the altar of prayer candles flickered on the windowsill, Maeve undertook the enhancement of my poor culinary skills, peppering my lessons with doses of motherly encouragement. Most evenings the post-supper hours were occupied by attempting to play darts with Moira and the lads. Their camaraderie and banter helped me feel less alone.

The waiting didn't weigh so much as ache and the irony of the situation had not escaped me; after a life of not accepting challenges, this time, I couldn't. At any other point in my history frustration and a sense of impending failure would have sent me scuttling home in defeat. This time, defiance surged and while February and its relentless rain ground to an end, I made my second truly adult decision. As trustee, Declan managed the estate, but nothing granted him control over me. Grand-da charged me with care of the cottage and by god, the renovation would go forward, even if Daddy had to lend me the money. Declan could grumble and delay, but he couldn't stop my plans.

Liberated, I left my room and joined the darts game. My lack of skill entertained the locals and Moira's deft ability to flirt with both Liam and Jamie without distinguishable preference amused me.

"Are ya wool gatherin', Clare?" she asked, with a nudge of my arm.

"Sorry?"

"It's your turn." Jamie and Liam dangled their empty pints for emphasis.

"One sec." My first month in Ireland taught me one important lesson: the Irish track rounds like so many beads on an abacus. It wasn't a debt, but a duty one could not shirk.

When I returned to the game, Liam asked when we'd start work on the cottage. Jamie's eyes glittered, awaiting my answer. Members of Paddy's crew, they had a personal stake in the matter.

The answer flew from my mouth with resolute ease. "Soon, Liam."

I roused early the next morning. Watery gray, like the wash of a pastel crayon, suggested the sun lurked behind the clouds. Layering on denim and thick wool, I shoved Wellingtons over two pairs of socks, and sneaked out the back door before Maeve and Eamon spotted me. Upon gaining

The High my phone pinged with a text from Declan, promising we'd discuss the budget on Monday. With immature, but gratifying pique, I did not reply.

The shepherd boy neared, chirruped to his dog, and called a cheery greeting. Stifling a fresh spurt of Declan-inspired annoyance, I smiled. "Morning, Michael."

"Miss, if ya don't mind, might I take the sheep through yer pasture? It's a straighter shot ta the hills."

I glanced toward the cottage, clear in our line of sight. "I assumed you did."

Michael squinched his face. "Mr. O'Donnell calls it trespassin'."

A possessive anger simmered. "You're welcome to take the sheep through *my* pasture any time you like."

"Thank ya kindly, miss!" The boy beamed a huge smile and all but danced ahead with his flock. It seemed a small gesture to produce such inordinate gratitude, but it cheered me.

The pungent reek of mildew wrinkled my nose as I entered the cottage. This time the culprit proved to be the ratty living room rug, victim of the second leak. A faded, threadbare monstrosity unworthy of salvation, its state still provoked an onslaught of regret. My idleness allowed more neglect to seep into the cottage.

Kicking the disgusting mess into a heap, I shoved it out the kitchen door, then examined the black veins marbling the floorboards. The mildew came up when scrubbed but some of the boards had warped from lying under a soggy rug for three weeks.

I slumped in Grand-da's chair, frigid hands stuck firm under my armpits. The leather creaked as I curled my legs to limit the total surface area available to the chill. The mantel—and the box of ashes—drew my attention. "Sorry, Grand-da. I didn't mean to make the cottage worse."

Light rain pattered a hypnotic tattoo on the roof as I gazed at the cold fireplace, seething with guilt. I remembered the cottage during Sean's wake; the warmth of the hearth, the loud, raucous Irish, and me safe on Grand-da's lap. Then the memory sharpened. The room, people, and noise were the same. But through the slim spaces between the packed bodies, light glinted. It flickered in a roaring fire and danced from the rim of drink glasses. Rings flashed gold, bald foreheads radiated, sparks winked from blonde and bronze curls. Laughter and song held the vitality of sun and shimmered out over the room before shattering into gilt fragments.

Grand-da's laugh rang and its music vibrated through me, warming my heart. His uproarious guffaws never startled, even at his father's wake. Joy was Grand-da's watchword.

Happiness lived here, until a mother's death and a father's despairing addiction chased it away. Sean's passing freed Seamus from the pain of those intervening years. His laughter didn't curse his father; it forgave. "That's when you knew, isn't it?" I addressed the box on the mantel. "That's when you decided."

Nothing changed. Grand-da didn't speak from the heavens. A musty funk still hung faint on the damp air and my fingers ached with cold, but blood and energy had lain shallow too long. The rain stopped and a flicker of morning sun shone a confirmation through beveled glass; I flung open the windows to air the cottage. Shedding the first layer of sweaters, I breakfasted on stale crackers, then bustled through the rooms chasing away dust and cobwebs.

By mid-afternoon I'd erased evidence of the latest neglect, and my aching muscles were nothing to the satisfaction it gave. Limp sunlight glinted through spotless windowpanes, tempting me outdoors. The Irish took advantage whenever the sun made an appearance, and after a month of rain the predilection made perfect sense. With a vow to return soon, I reclaimed my sweaters and boots and strolled up the hill. I had neglected St. Dallán's, too.

I climbed the hill at a slow pace, relishing the clean, fresh air and rich scent of wet earth, and hearing Grand-da in the susurrating grasses. He'd first told me I'd have the keeping of the family's heart and hearth at St. Dallán's. Then, with the scant comprehension of a small child, the phrase struck as another of Grand-da's jokes, and as an adult I dismissed the oft-repeated phrase as his charming but patronizing version of 'a woman's place is in the home.' Now his meaning came clear; he'd always meant a literal fireplace. I paused, turning my face into the breeze, and listened.

It would take consistency and patience to restore the house, and neither were among my strengths, but I'd made a promise to Grand-da and would not disappoint him again. Possessed of both my faculties and my vision, I approached St. Dallán's like a pilgrim, ready to reaffirm there what I'd proved in the cottage.

Eagerness faded as I drew near the ruins. A young man, also bundled and booted, sat on the wall, motionless as the church stones. An open book lay on his knees. Eyes closed, his face lifted toward the sky. Dark ginger hair fell past his chin and the sunlight lit the curls like flames. Other than a short beard, he resembled a pre-Raphaelite angel. With a silent pledge to return tomorrow, even if it rained, I headed back toward the village, leaving the man to his sacred aloneness.

"Howya! Come to worship?"

Still walking, I turned my head, waving a hand in blessing. "Sorry to intrude."

"Ya didn't." The man gestured to the empty wall.

Rather than appear rude, I retraced my steps and joined him. "Are you a pilgrim?"

He answered with a laugh like song. "No more than the next soul." The man had a beautiful face; thin, even a little gaunt, but with fine cheekbones and clear, deep blue eyes which pierced the surface of all they encountered.

I scanned his reading material and giggled. "La Carre?"

He pretended offense. "Nothin' wrong with spy novels."

"I expected an illuminated sheepskin vellum, in Latin. Even sans tonsure, you resemble a monk."

"I considered it once. But Latin, while entertainin', is work. Bought this at the airport." He tucked the book in a pocket of his long navy-blue wool coat.

"Where did you come from?"

"Syria."

"Damn! Not much of a vacation spot these days."

"I've been doin' aid work with an NGO, but the UN brought us out. It's too dangerous for foreigners now." He snorted with derision. "Or Syrians. But the UN couldn't guarantee our safety; even our local counterparts begged us ta leave."

My hands clutched our stone perch as I examined the toes of my Wellies. "It's pretty grim there, isn't it?"

"Worse than whatever you've heard." He tossed a pebble toward the altar. "But I can do no more now." With sadness he contemplated the far-off horizon until his lips again spread into a grin. "It's time for discernin' what's next."

"You've found the perfect spot for contemplation. I had an epiphany here, and I don't do spiritual."

The man quirked his head. "There's an interestin' way of puttin' it. We're none of us mere brains and bodies."

The observation resonated rather than affronted; an influx of pilgrims might do me good. I shivered into my coat but wasn't eager to leave. "My family is Catholic, but it's impossible for me to reconcile the beauty of the tradition with the ugly politics."

My companion chuckled. "I didn't mention religion. We direct all spiritual energy toward the one Divine; makes no difference what ya call it or if ya name it at all." He spoke his conviction with gentleness, and zero hint of dogma.

"You're right. The most spiritual people I know aren't religious."

His point proved, the man contemplated the ruins. "This is a truly ancient site."

"I know it to the bone. Everything inside me hushes here."

"Leavin' Spirit room ta move." He pointed east, passed the pillars, to a semi-circle of large boulders. "Have ya noticed those?"

Nodding, I twisted a stray curl behind my ear. "Yeah. I assumed they fell off the old church."

"They're the remains of a stone circle. The auld ones worshiped here before the Christians came and baptized the old ways."

I snorted with contempt. "More ugly politics."

"Sure. But renamin' deities and feasts couldn't change facts. This is a thin place, one where heaven and earth meet. Those who came before us—pagan and saint—recognized it." He smiled, his azure gaze soft as fine-combed wool. "Ya recognize it, too."

"This is the most sacred place I've ever been."

We sat silent, the absence of words another form of communication. The man scooped a handful of pebbles, chose one, and lobbed it toward the altar. "I trust you're enjoyin' your visit."

We'd just met; no need to bare my soul. "It's nice here. The couple who run the pub have been wonderful. It's rained a lot, though. This is the first time I've been outside longer than ten minutes. But after the Middle East, you probably don't mind a little wet."

"I could do with a good lashin'. My bones are full of dust."

"How long were you over there?"

"A year and a half, near the Turkish border; and Iraq for two years previous."

"Shit!" He laughed while I scrambled to recoup my dignity. "You must be awful brave."

"Not much." Another pebble plinked against the altar.

His visa stamps didn't warrant self-deprecation. "Those are treacherous places."

"Any place is dangerous and safe at once. It's a matter of timin'." He gave me a playful wink and nodded toward the leaning pillars. "No reason one of those couldn't fall on our heads."

"Or rogue sheep could trample us," I said, thinking of Michael and his flock. "But we're not talking about random occurrences; it's courageous going where there are good odds of harm."

"You and I define bravery different, then." The pebbles gone, the man plucked long, thick blades of grass and plaited them with graceful fingers. "I joined Cara avoidin' other risks. I'll hazard drones and IEDs but sweet Jaysus, don't ask me ta confront my own heart." A tiny moan escaped his smiling lips.

His words, not the exhalation, made me grin. "Your NGO work is penance?"

He laughed again. "Sure, though I've too much pride for proper atonement. If I intended ta face myself, I'd have chosen an occupation better suited ta meditation."

"My hamster wheel of a brain makes contemplation a challenge. But St. Dallán's has been a revelation." I studied the man's down-turned face. "This is a good place for answers."

"Chrissake, I'm thirty-two. It's beyond time I find 'em." He twirled the woven grass between his fingers, then handed me the braid. Four arms branched from a square center.

"How pretty!"

"St. Brigid's cross." With a wink he added, "But it's likely a pre-Christian symbol, if ya prefer."

The sun lowered on the horizon and thickening clouds signaled another storm. "I enjoyed our chat. A lot." In truth, it jolted me; our conversation left me joyous, as if I'd been in the ruins alone. "I should get back to the pub before it rains."

"I'll come along, if ya don't mind." He offered a hand, and we rose together. "Besides, ya haven't told me about *your* quest."

"I'm not on one."

"I reck you're seekin' somethin'."

To avoid answering the unanswerable I used his earlier words. "No more than the next soul." His chuckle sang out again. We strolled down the hill and into the village, silent with our own thoughts. Then I said, "It's amazing how a person who's endured war zones can laugh with such ease."

"Someone—can't remember who—said, 'We must laugh or break our hearts in this damnable world.' Life is sorrow and pain mitigated by joy and a great deal of beauty. It's narrow-minded not ta acknowledge the whole."

I observed the man's profile, his hollow cheeks violet in the twilight. "May I buy you a drink?" The natural ease of the impulse surprised me. "I'm Clare Riordan."

He held open the pub door and made a little bow. "I'll have a drink with ya, Clare Riordan. I'm Ciarán O'Donnell."

Chapter Six

MAEVE SKITTERED AWAY FROM the bar with a delighted cry. "Clare! Ya found my other boy! I wondered where you've been, son." She stood on tiptoe and ruffled his hair. "I worried when ya didn't come ta tea."

"Sorry, Ma. I met Clare at St. Dall's and clean lost track of time."

Maeve gave her son a joyful squeeze. "It's of no account. I hope ya had a lovely afternoon."

"Grand."

Maeve squinted into his face. "You're worn out. A kip will set ya right."

"Nappin' won't cure jet lag, Ma. And I promised Clare a drink." He nodded toward me. "What's your poison, miss?"

"I invited you."

"I'll have a pint of black stuff, then."

While Maeve bustled him into a snug, I fetched Ciarán's Guinness and my merlot. Placing his pint before him, I sat opposite and said, "You knew who you were talking to this whole time, didn't you?"

"Simple enough ta deduce; ya matched Ma's description and the accent and questions confirmed your nationality. But there seemed no need ta interrupt our communion for formal introductions."

I groaned with an unwelcome memory. "Your brother tipped me off about the questions. Sorry."

He chuckled. "Americans can't help it. I've spent enough time around them not ta mind. Ask me whatever ya like."

My attempt at an accusatory glare fell short. "I thought you were a legitimate pilgrim."

"Oh, I am, darlin'; make no mistake. I'm always searchin'."

"When did you get back?"

"Arrived in Dublin on Wednesday and came home late last night."

Ciarán's perpetual smile beamed amused delight on everything. But when he grew serious his whole face sobered, from his brow to his lips, like his entire being bore the weight of whatever problem or sadness it addressed. "Ma shared the sad news about Seamus. I am so sorry."

"Thank you." I'd grown accustomed to condolences, but the genuine sorrow inhabiting his features and his words moved me.

"Must have been something titanic ta take out Seamus Riordan."

Bitterness flavored my tone. "He had a mild stroke, fell, and cracked his head. He died from bleeding on the brain and deserved a far better end than he got."

"Indeed, he did." Ciarán touched his glass to mine. "God rest 'im."

Hair fell over my cheeks as I bent forward. "Did you know Grand-da well?"

"All my life. Like part of the family, he was, even joinin' our Sunday suppers." Ciarán nodded and gave me a wink. "He told me stories about his granddaughter; declared her Grainne Mhaol re-incarnate."

Grand-da's oft-stated compliment always made me laugh. "Unfortunately, the only similarities between me and the pirate queen are Celtic blood and red hair."

"Not ta hear Seamus tell it."

I shrank like a sun-drenched violet. "He gave me more credit than I ever deserved."

Ciarán narrowed one eye. "Seamus never deluded himself about someone's character."

"He had a bias. Grand-Nan died right before my birth, so the folks gave me her name."

He abandoned teasing for kindness. "Seamus and ya were close."

"The closest. I could tell him anything, make every mistake, and he still loved me. It may sound sacrilegious, but when people talk about God, I picture Grand-da."

"Knowin' someone's imperfections and lovin' them anyway is a fittin' image of the Creator. Seamus focused on your promise, not your failings."

The pub filled with the supper crowd. Eamon's early evening languor quickened, becoming a balletic performance as he pulled pints, then pirouetted to open bottles of whiskey or wine. He shouted greetings to patrons and handed over their usual libation without consulting more than his memory. Meanwhile, Maeve scurried between tables with plates of chicken and bundles of bread. The darts game in the back of the room added a beat to the clamor of voices and Councilman Delaney—who also owned the butcher shop—and his son Padraic, the village schoolteacher, occupied a corner in the front, playing dulcimer and flute.

The happy magic dimmed when Declan entered with Garbhán and Ciarán hailed them.

"There ya are. I hoped ta see ya again." Garbhán slid into the booth beside me while Declan and his unrelenting scowl shared a bench with Ciarán. The younger brother had more objective beauty; chiseled and graceful, compared to Declan's solid build. But the most profound contrast lay between his sullen disposition and Ciarán's lighthearted ease. They resembled each other when they smiled, but Declan seldom did.

At first, Garbhán's good humor offset his companion's grumpiness. "A pleasure meetin' ya at last, boyo! Your virtuous deeds are legend."

Ciarán flushed at the praise. "It's good bein' home."

"I wonder I don't settle here. Lovely spot with grand people." Garbhán nudged my arm. "What would ya say ta it, Dec?"

Glowering, the solicitor replied, "I'll fetch a round."

"I shouldn't mess with him," Garbhán said with a hoarse laugh. "I'm a Dubliner through and through. Never could leave and be a culchie, though Killarkin has certain charms." Another nudge. "I've got my bits of business here and there and off elsewhere; keeps me on the go, it does. Now, Clare, here's an opportunity ya might consider." Elbows firm on the table, he outlined a speculative and convoluted business plan; I lost the thread early.

Declan returned toward the end of Garbhán's proposal and set down the pints with such firmness the heads threatened to swamp us. "Leave it out; she doesn't care about business."

He correctly assessed my disinterest in Garbhán's schemes, but I could speak for myself. "Thanks for the offer, but the cottage is my focus right now."

Garbhán sat back, swatting my shoulder. "Sure. Settle in and then perhaps you'll fancy my ideas."

News of Ciarán's return had circulated through the village. More people than I recognized flooded the tables and all wanted time with him. "Will ya excuse me a few minutes, Clare? Time ta greet some folk."

My stomach tightened at the thought of only Declan and Garbhán for company but a polite smile masked my discomfort. "Enjoy your reunion."

The Killarkin community's enthusiastic embrace of Ciarán deepened Declan's pout. Garbhán blathered on, heedless, but his boasts wearied me, and my arm ached from his frequent and over-familiar prods. Scooting out of range, I sipped wine, and people-watched, not heeding the conversation.

"Your glass wants fillin'. Have another." Garbhán lifted his hand to get Maeve's attention, spreading his legs until our thighs touched.

The alarm bells in my gut signaled the intimacy wasn't accidental. "It's been a long day, Excuse me."

Garbhán frowned at my announcement. "Don't leave me with this dry shite."

"The lady wants ta go." Declan's voice menaced.

Garbhán grimaced at his friend but relented. "All right then. Hope ta see ya soon." He stood and swaggered toward the bar.

Declan quietly asked for a brief word in private, and without waiting for a reply, exited out the back door. Hoping we could discuss the cottage, I followed. Outside, with the door closed, the roar of the pub muted to a pleasant muffle. A gentle breeze bellied Declan's trench coat as he lit a cigarette. "You're full of surprises."

"Don't tell Ma."

I promised, pleased to discover someone who seemingly cared so little about anyone's opinion, owned enough humanity to fear his mother's disapproval. "I know how moms are."

He drew deep on his cigarette, his gaze toward the darkened hills. "I apologize for Garbhán. He's too eager by half."

The wind picked up, sending tiny daggers of cold through me. I huddled against the wall of the pub; arms crossed. "He's obnoxious but manageable." My gut sent another warning ping. "Is he staying here? In the pub?"

"He has a lady friend in Tullamore. One of many, ta hear him tell it."

"What a relief. I don't want him too close."

"Trust your instincts." Declan stepped back and shuffled his feet. "I'll see you're not bothered."

I kicked at the grass, illuminated by the pale gold of the lights inside. "It's not your fault he's arrogant and presumptuous. Are we outside on a frigid night to talk about him?"

He exhaled a cloud of smoke and warmed breath. "I've drawn a contract for the renovation; ta protect your interests."

Astonishment pulled me away from the wall. "Protect me from Paddy? Don't be ridiculous! He has a sterling reputation and this village is too small for him to get away with shenanigans. I'm not a fool."

"I'm not suggestin' ya are."

Exhausted by his meddling bossiness, I glared while a month's worth of exasperation spilled out. "You've kept me waiting weeks for you to loosen *my* purse strings. You have no right. Don't hover and fuss and set up shop accounts like I'm incapable or send Paddy with fuel while withholding the money necessary for his real help. Gawd! I'm capable of tying my own damn shoelaces!"

He moved toward the garden wall, turning in profile toward the fields beyond the pub. Only the glowing tip of his cigarette fixed his location. I stayed put, refusing to apologize for my warranted indignance.

Cloaked by night, I scoured the sky, searching for calm. A thick carpet of stars hung above, their brilliance unblemished by light pollution. I picked out Orion, an anchor in the spangled sky. Faint music from inside and the soft lowing from nearby farms danced together in the frosty air.

Declan stubbed the cigarette on the sole of his shoe and pocketed it, moving back into the lamplight at a careful distance. "I'm responsible for ya, Clare," he said. "I never meant ta imply anythin' else."

"You aren't! Jesus; I'm not a child. Granted, no one knows better than me how much I have to learn, but don't be such a damn prick about it."

He shoved his hands into his coat pockets, stunned. "I see."

"If your help is needed, I'll ask. Meantime, credit me with an ounce of freaking sense." I shivered. "It's too cold out here." Turning my back, I stomped back into the pub, Declan lagging behind.

Ciarán sat on the end of our snug's bench, chatting with Nessa. They grinned at one another like long-lost siblings. Declan slid onto the seat opposite and acknowledged her with a remorseful smile; her face flickered with sadness before her characteristic brusqueness returned. "I'm glad you're home, man. *Slán,*" she said, and started away.

"*Slán abhaile*, Ness," Ciarán said. Then his eyes met mine. "I feared ya'd disappeared. Sorry for the distractions."

"You've been away three years; it's understandable." My stomach rumbled. "And I should eat."

"Ma is on her way," Ciarán said. He patted the seat beside him, and I accepted the invitation. "What were ya two on about out there? More top-level negotiations?"

My glance traveled from Ciarán's teasing smile to his brother's uncomfortable scowl. "What do you mean?"

"Dec played an instrumental role gettin' us home."

"Stop the lights, man." Declan sniffed, his attention on a hurling poster.

Ciarán clasped his brother's wrist. "I'm not exaggeratin'; don't be modest. They told us in hospital about the back channels, the negotiations between Turkey and the U.S. Ya engineered a grand piece a diplomacy."

"I telephoned embassies, as did many others." Declan shifted his shoulders like they itched.

Realization dawned. "You stayed in Dublin because of Ciarán."

A sneer fanned Declan's mouth. "I hope my brother's wellbein' is a legitimate excuse for delayin' your plans."

"Of course it is," I replied, snippy and irritated. "You could have told me." Then I comprehended Ciarán's words and turned on him with alarm. "Why were you in the hospital?"

"It's standard procedure. I'm fine, darlin'." Maeve appeared with dinner plates and Ciarán exhaled with pleasure. "Ma, I've dreamed about your roast chicken and boxty."

She dabbed tears with an apron corner. "My darlin' boy. Eat up; there's plenty. You're too thin, son."

Ciarán blew her a kiss. "A situation you'll remedy in no time."

She reached across me to run her hand through his long curls. "I'll feed ya, then take a scissor to this mop. Jaysus, ya look like one of the apostles."

Laughing, Ciarán waved her off. "It'll keep, Ma. Let me get back on Irish time."

"Don't matter the hour, ya can't go about lookin' like an urchin. I can't see your darlin' face. The man's a fright, isn't he, Clare?"

Considering how well the curls suited him, I chuckled. "Leave me out of this, Maeve."

"And ya need a shave. You're too young for whiskers." Maeve spun away and into Paddy's arms. "Lord's sake, Padraig Flannery! Haven't ya got eyes in your feckin' head?"

Paddy took a seat beside Declan with a chortle like gravel. "What the hell has her so riled?"

"She disapproves of long hair and beards," Ciarán replied.

"Ah," Paddy said, with a knowing nod. "And she's too pleased you're home ta take it out on ya. Ciarán O'Donnell! Jaysus, it's good havin' ya home!" The men clasped hands across the table. "Are ya stayin' put?"

"I'm not leavin' any time soon."

"Then I'd be terrible grateful for yer help."

"What's the *sceál*, Paddy?" Ciarán asked, gnawing a chicken leg.

"I'll be restorin' the aul Riordan cottage and would love ya ta come on."

Blissful, Ciarán chewed his food, then swallowed. "I worried I'd not have enough ta do. I like buildin'."

"Cottages, if not the Kingdom," Declan said.

Ciarán laughed, ignoring the sarcasm. "When do we start?"

"Next week," I replied, glancing at my contractor, who nodded confirmation.

Paddy slapped the table with vigor. "Indeed. Once Dec trusts our pure intentions."

Thwarted enough for one evening, Declan rose. "We'll finalize everythin' Monday mornin'."

As he walked away, Paddy's face gleamed with mirth. "There's a man wot will be the death of some poor colleen one day." He gave the table a joyful thump. "Ta celebrate yer homecomin' I'll lend me fiddle ta the session."

As he strode off Ciarán called, "Ya never needed an excuse before." Paddy replied by scratching the back of his head with his middle finger. Vibrating with laughter, Ciarán turned toward me. "I'll fetch another round; if anyone intrudes meantime, warn 'em my mood is foul, and they'd best stay clear. More wine?"

With the specter of my solicitor gone and satiated by Maeve's delicious chicken, a considerable lightness restored my mood. "Whiskey, please."

With all the people laying claim to his time, it took Ciarán a few minutes to gain the bar. Liam cocked an arm around his shoulder and gestured toward the dart board; other patrons urged him to empty chairs. There were countless embraces and handshakes, but he eventually returned with our drinks.

"This must be what it's like to date a celebrity."

Ciarán chuckled. "Don't be jealous, darlin'. Ya have your own fans. We're invited ta join the darts match, but I defer ta your wishes."

"Let's take advantage of the relative quiet while we can."

"Agreed. So, ya mean ta restore the cottage ta its former glory."

"Glory is a bit much, but yes." I told him about Grand-da's 'hearth and heart' refrain, the circumstances surrounding my decision, and my frustrations with the delay. Talking to Ciarán felt comfortable, like stepping into a bespoke dress. "First the roof, then the water tank. I can't even manage more than smoke from said hearth yet."

"I'll teach ya," he said, his shoulders set firm. "And we'll put the rest ta rights soon enough."

His confidence reassured me, but my nose wrinkled anyway, a time-honored technique for squeezing back tears. "What's baffled me most is how being here, where Grand-da grew up, is more emotional than expected." I chewed on the nail of my little finger. "He lived in America over seventy years, but never considered himself anything but Irish. He retained his brogue and sang trad tunes in a soft, sweet tenor."

"Ah, his voice could bring tears from a stone."

Sniffing my whiskey, the notes of brown sugar and peat conjured a sweet, painful nostalgia. "His Irishness wasn't mere patriotism; he carried it in his soul and sinew."

Ciarán's eyes were sweet and soft. "And he passed it on ta ya."

"Don't think so. Grand-da nursed a tortured, profound passion for Ireland, speaking of her like a long-lost lover. All I have is a fondness for Jameson and a few Irish toasts."

Ciaran squinted. "His spirit hasn't eluded ya entirely. There's a Celtic stitchin' in your fabric."

"What's certain is he's wanted me here since Sean died, if not before. Mom thinks I'm reckless and for a while I agreed."

"But you're still here. There's nothin' amiss in settin' off on a journey without knowin' the destination. Ya can still end where you're meant ta be."

Blazing sun skewered my eyelids, and I rolled over in bed, scrabbling blind on the night table for my phone. I groaned, possessed of a scratchy thirst, and blurred recollections of Paddy's roared laugh and Ciarán amused expressions, scored by thunking darts. Specific memories were sparse, but I recalled at least one empty whiskey bottle. There were two distinct Riordan legacies: philanthropist and town sot. The latter did not inspire.

Pulling on a robe, I shuffled down the hall. The warm shower didn't mitigate the needle-sharp pain lodged behind my right eye, but I wouldn't stink of roast chicken and humiliation. Wounded, but clean, I emerged from the bathroom, damp towel over my arm.

"No worse for the wear, I see." Ciarán rested against the wall, wearing sweatpants and a faded Soundgarden t-shirt.

My hand flew up to clutch the robe tight at my throat. "Sorry you had to wait. Don't you sleep downstairs?"

"Da wanted a shave so I came up here. I didn't expect ya awake this early."

"You may record my status as bleary, but functioning." My stomach made an indelicate burble. "And hungry."

Ciarán grinned. "I'll join ya, if ya like. Meet downstairs in thirty minutes?"

"Ten, sir." I spun away with an exaggerated head toss which dislodged the eye needle. "Ow!" Ciarán had the decency to not laugh outright and coughed over a snicker.

After donning jeans and a sweater, I held my injured head steady and made a slow descent to the public room. When a damp haired Ciarán loped in a few minutes later he found me presiding over two plates of fry-up and a tea pot.

"I apologize, darlin'. I implied earlier ya required time ta make yourself lovely, a sexist statement on its face and also inaccurate. For a woman in pain, ya look remarkably well."

Elbows on the table and chin in my hands I asked, "Are you flirting with me, Mr. O'Donnell?"

Chuckling, he threw his arms across the chair back. "Could be."

"Taking advantage of a woman with a hangover is poor form." Arched eyebrows accompanied my reply.

Ciarán scowled. "You're not a lick of fun."

"So, despite the evidence of an aching skull, past Clare did not dance on tabletops?"

He folded his hands and smiled, kind and sincere. "She didn't say or do anythin' mortifyin'."

"There's a mercy. Wouldn't want to give you the wrong impression this early in the game."

"Now who's the flirt?"

It hurt to laugh, but I couldn't resist. "You're a pretty decent guy, Ciarán O'Donnell."

"You're not half bad, yourself, Clare Riordan."

"Dorothy L. Sayers, by the way." Ciarán cocked his head like a confused puppy. "Your quote yesterday; I looked it up."

A delighted smile spread across his face. "Sure; from Lord Peter."

My head throbbed with a ghost of pain. "God, I'd kill for coffee, but didn't know your views on the subject."

Ciarán speared an egg, mixing the viscous yolk with baked beans. "I take it with breakfast. Would ya like some?"

"Tea will do; Maeve's food is giving me the will to live."

"And it should fit ya for your appointment with Paddy."

"Excuse me?"

"You're meeting him at the cottage at nine."

"I am?" My phone showed 8:30. "It's almost time now."

"You've time ta finish your sausages." He assessed my dubious state with a squint. "And I'll fetch coffee."

Chapter Seven

THE BUDGET MEETING TOOK place, as promised, on Monday. We met in the pub, during the lull between breakfast and lunch. Paddy and Ciarán were cheerful, I verged on the edge of giddiness, but Declan glowered over the document with the aspect of chief mourner at a wake. Wasting no time in pleasantries he voiced his first concern. "The wages seem high."

Sobering, I examined the numbers and regarded Paddy; chin lifted and mouth stern, like a lawyer interrogating a recalcitrant witness. "It's the going rate, right? And no discounts for Seamus' sake?"

Paddy placed a solemn hand on his heart. "All as ya requested."

Another scan of the figures prompted me to ask, "Is Ciarán working gratis?"

Paddy ran his finger over the crew list. "Oh! But I'm an eejit. He weren't back when I drew this up."

He scribbled an amendment and handed it to Declan, who punched the change into a calculator and reviewed the total with a cavernous, unwavering crease in his forehead. "You're spendin' Clare's money like it's your own."

I groaned, fed to the teeth with his disapproval and gatekeeping. "The cottage won't fix itself and the crew deserve fair compensation. What's the damage?" Declan turned his calculator toward me with a self-satisfied huff.

Though significant, the full renovation costs didn't sway me. They represented a fraction of the amount in the trust. "Not bad at all." My approval elicited a pained noise from Declan, and I snapped. "Gawd! A budget assures we don't go twelve rounds whenever Paddy needs more nails. And please add bonuses for the crew if we finish on schedule."

"Fair play, Lady Bountiful," Ciarán said, with a wink. I blushed and stared into my teacup.

"Aren't ya a generous one," Paddy added.

Outnumbered, Declan held his counsel for the remainder of the meeting. When we concluded, aside from my solicitor, who had taken to puffing like a landed fish, we were in accord. "Are you satisfied, Declan?" With his eyes firm on the table rather than me, he nodded in the affirmative, though another distressed sound escaped his throat.

I grinned at Paddy, unable to contain my eagerness. "When can we start?"

"Seven on the dot tomorrow, if it suits ya."

The presence of witnesses guaranteed Declan couldn't stall any longer. My elated smile met his hang-dog expression. "When can you transfer the money? There are appliances to order."

"I'll do it now." He gathered his papers, pale as someone with a mortal wound.

I all but skipped back to the cottage. With a new month begun and the path forward cleared, all the stormy emotions lifted away. Even the bedraggled garden held a new beauty; her bones were obvious under blackened leaves and twisted vines. Full reclamation of the grounds would wait until the weather warmed, but the vegetable beds were thick with weeds, and I had pent energy to dispel. I found a spade, chopped the muddy ground and, despite the March drizzle, worked up a sweat.

Sun shone wan through chiffon clouds and the digging cleared my head. Declan's decided lack of enthusiasm no longer deterred my mission. Once he funded the account, we could avoid each other until it came time to sell. With the happy thought held close, I abandoned the spade and knelt to pull the loosened weeds.

While collecting an impressive pile of future compost the gate creaked, and I turned to see Ciarán ambling up the walk.

"Howya."

I straightened up, brushing back my hair. "What brings you here?"

"Paddy asked me ta confirm some measurements."

"Liar." I flung a clump of muddy roots toward the wall. "Declan sent you to babysit the village idiot."

"Wrong on both counts, darlin'. I never lie and Dec believes no such thing about ya. Frettin' is his second nature. Understand it and he'll annoy ya less. May I come in?"

He had a smile like firelight; unable to maintain petulance in the warmth of it, I invited him inside. "Let me wash my hands and I'll help."

"I'd be grateful." He grinned, tapped my cheek, and said, "Ya might take a cloth ta your face, too."

"Oh, geez."

I left him in the kitchen and trotted into the bathroom. The wavy glass showed damp, wind-blown hair, and a face streaked with mud. Vanity routed, I washed and returned to the kitchen with a small unit of self-possession. "What are we measuring?"

"The new bathroom." We climbed the stairs and stood in the intended corner. "Hold this, please." He took the business end of the tape measure and paced off the area. "Clever design, this."

"It's all to Joel."

Ciarán made an intent examination of the tape measure. "Is he your fella?"

"Best friend number two. He's doing me a favor."

"Ya miss him." Ciarán's kind eyes operated on a dimmer switch. The standard brilliant twinkle muted to a soft glow. "This must be an adjustment."

"Not a sad or regretful one. It's nice here. But most people treat me with a weird deference. I can't tell if it's genuine kindness or because they feel obligated to Grand-da."

"Bit of both, I expect. Seamus' myth is potent."

I snorted. "Don't confuse the man with the legend."

Ciarán clicked open a pen and noted meters and centimeters on a scrap of paper. "Now if you'll stand on the other wall." After moving as ordered, he took another measurement. "All myths have a kernel of truth. Good reputations, however much deserved, grow larger with time."

"Which probably explains the urge to justify my existence, to live up to the hype."

"Be yourself, darlin'; folks will come ta see ya, not Seamus' shadow. Ya can let go now." I did, and the tape skittered across the floor with a clatter and snicked back into its case.

As Ciarán pocketed the measuring tape I made a meek confession. "About the bonus...it wasn't showing off."

He fixed me with a knowing expression. "Ya were after gettin' one over on Dec."

"Guilty."

The corners of Ciarán's eyes crinkled. "He provokes the instinct in folk."

I squared my shoulders. "I'll try not to let him get to me. Would you like tea?"

"I won't intrude."

"You're not. I planned on having some anyway."

"Sure, but ya have better ta do than entertain me."

"This silly back and forth goes on in Maeve's kitchen all the time. Guests always say yes in the end. What's the point of it?"

He grinned at my exasperated tone. "It's our way of testing the sincerity of the offer. If the host accepts the first refusal it means they're only bein' polite."

I shook my head. "Alrighty then. But between us, if I make the offer, it's sincere."

He answered with a thumbs up, so I left him in charge of the kettle and jogged to The Cosy. Aideen Fannin rocked in a chair behind the counter but set aside her tatting when I entered. "You'll be wantin' somethin' nice for tea."

"Scones, please, Mrs. Fannin. And jam."

She added half a dozen small, golden cakes to the box. "Ciarán is fond of these. I'll put it on account, so ya needn't keep yer guest waitin'."

Ciarán had the tea steeping when I returned. "Ya were quick."

"The advantages of a small village and psychic baker. Mrs. Fannin knew you were here."

Ciarán laughed. "Aideen knows all the news in Killarkin worth knowin' and plenty what's not."

This bit of small-town lore prompted a grimace. "A person should be allowed to entertain without prying neighbors."

"It's not malicious, darlin'. Ya can't help but be a topic of interest."

"It's creepy."

Ciarán bore the teapot to the table, his expression one of sympathetic amusement. "Don't mind it. It'll die down soon enough, or, like the rain, you'll become accustomed."

"Doubtful. On the plus side, Aideen knew you like these cakes."

The next day I met the crew with all the tingly anticipation of a first date. Paddy marshaled his troops with affable efficiency, assigning stations and giving orders. Jamie began opening walls, exposing pipes and wiring, while Liam and Ciarán removed the old water tank and installed a new one. Against the din of hammers and chisels, I asked Paddy for my assignment.

He gave my bicep a gentle pinch. "I don't reckon you'll manage a sledgehammer, though if spirit were muscle, ya wouldn't have a need fer us."

"Please let me help. I can paint and hammer a nail. And I learn fast."

"Yer eager, ain't ya? But it's not glamorous work."

"Glamor is over-rated."

"Help me clear the shed, then."

We stood in the doorway, surveying the interior of the dank outbuilding and regret replaced my enthusiasm. A jumble of miscellany, none of it identifiable in the dingy light, hulked against walls and on deep shelves shrouded with cobwebs. "Let's pretend I don't have a shed."

"We could if we weren't installin' a new service panel." Paddy chewed a thumb, considering the mess before us. "Sing out if ya want any of this; otherwise, I'll haul it off in the truck."

By quitting time, every muscle screamed for relief, but we had the shed cleared, with a small collection of family items and a battered but operational bicycle, stashed in the barn. It would be two weeks, at least, before the house would be habitable, but the open studs and dusty smell of old plaster were signs of progress.

The crew headed over to the pub, but before he left, Ciarán taught me to build a proper fire. "Put fuel on the grate, with plenty of air below so it can draw breath. Then ya lay the turve." Following his instructions to the letter resulted in a glow of pride as the turf lit and grew into a merry blaze. "Fair play! Are ya after a pint?"

"I'll catch up with you later."

I admired my tiny inferno, then walked through the rooms, the quiet more profound after the commotion of workers. The cottage would never know neglect again. The upstairs windows afforded a clear view of the rowans, the once bare limbs now covered with the springtime promise of supple, grey-green leaf buds. From a pocket of my grubby jeans, I pulled out Ciarán's braided grass. Appropriating a small nail from Paddy's toolbox, I tacked Brigid's cross above the bedroom hearth.

❖

"Is it too early?"

Edie snorted. "I've been waking at five since our senior year. What's all the racket?"

"Jamie's on the other side of the wall installing a shower."

"How's it going?"

"Great. These guys work hard every day, all the while laughing and teasing each other like they're in the pub."

"Sounds like indoor plumbing and perky Irishmen have improved your mood. Any of them handsome?"

I peered over my shoulder at Liam and Ciarán in the kitchen, their heads together over Joel's blueprints, hair burnished gold and bronze in the afternoon sun. Ciarán caught me spying and winked. "More than one. It's impossible to choose so I admire them all with objective detachment."

"Shit, Clare. How mature."

"Mock all you want, but frankly, your feminist credentials are in question by even suggesting a man is the source of my happiness."

Snickering Edie replied, "I'll report myself to the committee. So, to what do we attribute your elation?"

"Progress. I get to move back on Friday. And my cooking lessons so far have covered soda bread and griddle scones and soon Maeve's graduating me to stews. Hanging out with her is a lot of fun."

"I like hanging out with Denise."

My shoulders bunched. "You're making me look bad."

"Not my intention, hon. Give her a call; she misses you."

Defiance straightened my back. "We Skype once a week, Edie. After she assures herself her daughter is not malnourished or has otherwise fallen prey to whatever horrors she worries I'll find in a civilized European country, she guilts me until the session ends with one or both of us in tears."

I sidestepped out of Jamie's way as he came through with an armful of pipe fittings. The silence on Edie's end lasted longer than expected. "She didn't mention it. I apologize."

"You damn well should. You know how she is. Mom's still mad at me and the weekly call saps all the emotional fortitude I possess. Don't feel sorry for her."

Edie sighed; something she didn't often do. "I can't help it. I'm pissed she misrepresented the case, but she's your mom and she misses you. Give her a casual call once in a while."

"*You* call her. She likes you better. New subject. How's Aimee?"

"Never better."

"Dig us; I'm a homeowner and you're in love. It's like we're grownups, or something."

"We're unrecognizable," Edie said, laughing.

Laughter returned to my vocabulary, too; my spirits buoyed by the early improvements in the cottage. On Friday afternoon Paddy turned on the water. After only two weeks I had a working laundry, hidden behind an original Ciarán O'Donnell cabinet, and bathrooms with actual water pressure.

"Take out your rubbish, Liam!" Paddy shouted. "People live here! Now, Clare, are ya clear on usin' the immersion? I can run ya through it again."

With a finger on the thermostat I recited his instructions. "The button is here and must be turned on about twenty minutes before I want hot water."

"These new systems are a wonder. Aul immersions don't shut off on their own and if ya forget ta do, yer head will spin when ya get the bill. Now, remember ya can't use the upstairs bathroom until the floor tile sets."

I gave Paddy an indulgent and deserved smile. "Your handiwork is not in peril. Now, I have arrangements to make. You'll bring everyone along?"

He turned toward the crew, voice raised. "I'll be there, but these eejits won't see the inside of the pub until they clean their bleedin' stations!"

I followed a grinding buzz to the barn, where Ciarán guided a thick post through the table saw. His biceps strained with the effort to hold the wood true. His tight t-shirt, covered with sawdust, revealed a more muscled torso than his lean frame suggested. The wood cleaved in two and he pushed safety goggles up on his head.

"You're working hard." The stack of trimmed lumber and dewy glisten of sweat on his arms confirmed the observation.

"It's more meditation than labor."

"We're going to celebrate our accomplishments. Will you come?"

"Almost done." Ciarán winked, pushed down the goggles, and placed another post on the saw.

"Eamon?"

"Clare."

We faced off across the bar with crossed arms and flinty postures. "Answer the question, please. Where's my tab?"

"Why would ya have one?" He chuckled as he pulled a pint and slid it down the bar toward old Tim.

"I've been here seven weeks and haven't seen a bill. It's ridiculous. And when the crew arrives, the first round is on me."

"This is biscuits ta a bear, darlin'. Dec said—"

"Never mind him. No one else eats, drinks, or sleeps here free, do they?" Eamon rubbed a nonexistent spot on his meticulous bar top. Standing on the foot rail to bring my eyes level with his, I tipped closer, determined. "You will accept payment, Eamon O'Donnell. Do you understand?"

"Oh, go on with ya."

My heart welled with gratitude. "It's one small way to return the kindness you and Maeve have shown me." I punctuated the sentiment with an impulsive kiss on his ruddy cheek and he muttered something under his breath. "Beg your pardon?" I asked, cupping my ear.

"It'll be a fearful day should Maeve and ya ever join forces."

The crew arrived, raucous and good-humored. Guinness and whiskey flowed, and Maeve delivered a large shepherd's pie, ordering us to soak up our drink.

"Ah, Maeve." Paddy paused for a rapturous inhalation of the steam cloud rising from the casserole. "Why didn't I marry ya?"

"I wouldn't have ya!" She flounced back to her kitchen and the men roared with laughter.

Moira entered the pub and Liam waved her over. She greeted the table at large before saying, "The reno must be goin' well."

"Very." My smile verified the word.

Jamie, whose customary bashfulness eased after a few beers, said, "Have a pint; Clare and I will tell ya about it over a game a darts."

Even sober my attempts couldn't match Jamie and Moira's skill. Ciarán watched from the table and offered advice. "Widen your stance."

Adjusting my position, I threw again and sent the dart straight into the wall. "Dammit."

Ciarán came behind me, pushing my feet apart with a gentle, booted toe. "Hold steady from your center." My breath caught as he put a hand on my back, the other light on my hip. Satisfied with my alignment, he gave my shoulders a gentle tug backward. His warm breath stirred my hair, raising gooseflesh, as his mouth came closer. "I don't intend ta be over-familiar, darlin', but you're standin' wrong."

I stared at the dartboard, reddening. "It's OK."

"Good. Back straight, hips loose, and don't lock your knees. Dominant foot forward. Feel the difference?"

"Yes." I gave a slight turn of my head to acknowledge him without revealing my heated blush. "How tall are you?"

"Six three. Now, keep your eyes on the board and fix your target; nothin' exists but it and your center. Hold the dart light in your fingers. Don't clutch it. Imagine it's a bird ready ta fly. Keep your upper arm level, elbow bent. Don't thrust. All the action comes from here." He cupped my wrist and manipulated it with loose, tossing motions. "Feel it?"

I nodded, hoping he didn't detect the rapid shift in my pulse. "You're a good teacher."

"Your next toss will confirm, or not, the truth of it." He released me and stepped away. His scent of fresh air and sawdust still enveloped me, the tender sensation of his hand lingered, and I wondered what happened to my objective detachment.

"Hold your center," he said. "Straight and true. Breathe in and release on the exhale."

With a trembling hand, I threw wide. Embarrassed, I set my position again, emptying my mind of physical distractions and words loaded with double meaning. I eyed the target, breathing deep, and after a couple fluid movements of my wrist, let the dart go. Neat and steady, it hit well inside the board.

Liam cheered, "Fair play!" and Ciarán gave me a congratulatory clap on the back.

"It *is* all in the wrist, isn't it?" I stared at the complex joint between hand and arm, marveling at its ability.

With an arm draped across my shoulders, Ciarán gestured toward the wall, his hand like a blade. "Fix your target, aim true, and trust the physics."

"The Tao of darts."

Declan and his frown appeared alongside us. "This is cosy," he said, his tone peevish.

I hid flaming cheeks behind my hair as Ciarán released me and squeezed his brother's shoulder. "I'll fetch ya a pint."

Declan ignored him and riveted his attention on me. "I trust your project is on track."

"Of course. Paddy is a managerial genius." I tossed another successful dart.

Ciarán handed his brother a pint, disregarded his dour manner, and invited him to play. Declan shrugged off his jacket, and I noticed Nessa at a table with a book. "Would she want to join us?"

"Doubtful," Ciarán said, with a chortle. "She might enjoy herself."

"Be nice."

The doctor answered my greeting with predictable dispassion. I issued the invitation, then waited like a transfer student on the playground desperate for a new friend. Nessa sipped sherry, in seeming dismissal of me and the offer, then rose with her glass and replied with an offhand, "I suppose."

Declan teamed with me, and said, "Losers buy a round."

"How convenient," I replied. "My tab is still open."

Ciarán frowned with mock earnestness. "Don't give up yet. You've had superior trainin'."

"I concede nothing, sir."

Nessa and the O'Donnell brothers had the advantage of experience, but my competitive streak kicked in. Moira and Jamie shouted encouragement from the sidelines, and Ciarán's instructions focused my efforts. It took three games to determine the match. We lost, but I played better than ever.

After providing the winners with the whiskey they demanded, Ciarán raised his glass. "*Sláinte.* To a grand effort."

"Don't get cocky," I said, my head held high. "Let's have another match."

Declan loosened his tie, spirited. "We'll show them this time."

For the first time in our acquaintance, something bordering lighthearted banter replaced our usual tension. He cheered every point scored and offered encouragement after a miss. I returned the support and tucked away the positive memory against the next time he annoyed me.

Unfortunately, our *esprit de corps* did not affect my overall proficiency. While the victors celebrated another win, I thrust a warning finger in their direction. "Enjoy it while you can, O'Donnell. One day this Yankee is going to beat you."

"Ah," Ciarán moaned, his expression rapturous. "Nothin' inspires more than a woman with goals."

Chapter Eight

THE COTTAGE BECAME A pilgrimage site. Every day neighbors arrived, bearing welcome gifts which included bundles of peat briquettes and kindling, fresh bread, new milk, and blocks of creamy butter. Diane Delaney's two eldest shyly offered lettuce and bean starts, with hand-written instructions from their mother on indoor care and when to set them out in the garden.

A diminutive woman with brilliant copper hair, who introduced herself as Fiona, brought a dozen brown, speckled eggs. "And ya will not know this, comin' from America, but ya don't want ta keep 'em in the icebox."

Maeve had already explained how European countries processed eggs, leaving the cuticle of the shell intact, thus imparting a layer of protection from bacteria, and negating the need for refrigeration. But I thanked Fiona for her advice.

On Friday she returned with a live chicken. "Then you'll always have eggs when ya need 'em." An hour later she brought another hen and explained, "They lay better when they've company."

"Do you still have birds of your own?" Her generosity both delighted and alarmed me. At this rate, I'd have an entire flock by nightfall.

"I do," she clucked. "But there are more, if ya like."

"No! Thank you! Two is plenty."

Fiona swore they wouldn't fly over the garden wall, which alleviated but one concern of many. After an evening researching the care of poultry I spent a restless night worried they'd fall prey to a fox or other predatory horror.

Waking before dawn, but unable to find chickens in the dark, I distracted myself by phoning home. Mom answered, alarmed. "Is everything alright?"

"Why wouldn't it be?"

"You never call so late."

"Couldn't sleep. Did you get the photos of the garden?"

Plants could always distract Mom. "Yes. I'd forgotten Sean had such a variety of specimens."

"Nothing is identifiable to me beyond roses and lavender, but with your expert advice I can restore the grounds of the cottage, too." Perhaps the compliment would warm our frosty connection.

"Goodness, all this enthusiasm. Aren't you bored yet?"

I ignored her implication. "Impossible. The reno demands a lot of time and Maeve's giving me cooking lessons."

Mom went silent then sniffed. "How fascinating. Why do you suppose the domestic arts are more compelling in Ireland?" Her sarcasm rang with hurt, threatening our already strained civility.

"It's not personal, Mom."

"No, of course not."

After twenty-seven years, my record against Mom remained at zero; no sense in fighting a losing battle. "It's dawn; time to start my day. Give Daddy my love."

By the light of fresh-risen sun, the hens were easy to find. They roosted under a saggy, lichen covered bench, and I slid a slow, nervous hand under each imperturbable bird, coming came away with two warm eggs. "Good girls! But you can't live like this." Hunched on the thick, damp grass I watched them peck the ground.

A small brown rabbit peered out from a rangy bush, hopped one pace forward, and nibbled grass. I sat motionless, holding my breath. The rabbit breakfasted with an alert, riveted eye, before it hopped back to the safety of its silver-green leafed canopy.

"Oi!" called a familiar voice.

"Ah. You're a lark, not an owl."

"Both, as it happens. I like watchin' the sunrise at St. Dall's when I can," Ciarán said, hands propped on the gate. "You're awake early yourself."

"The first daily duty of a chatelaine is surveying the estate." Waving him in, I rose and gestured toward the chickens. "Meet my housewarming gift from Fiona."

He chuckled. "Didn't realize ya meant ta take up farmin'."

"Some are born farmers; some have farming thrust upon them. But the poor darlings slept under that rotten bench last night and it makes me sad."

Ciarán dialed his phone. "Paddy, if you're free, Clare has an emergency. The plumbin' is fine. She needs a coop." He pocketed his phone. "He'll finish his breakfast and be right over."

"Geez, Ciarán; you two deserve the weekend off."

"It won't feel like work."

His breezy smile didn't ease a nagging guilt. "Well, you need a meal, too."

"You're forgettin' I live at the pub. Now, where are ya wantin' the hen house?"

Paddy's truck rumbled up fifteen minutes later and while two voluble Irishmen hammered and joked in the garden, my attention turned to chores. Mom's caustic comments stung despite their truth. Housekeeping had never been a priority before now. The need to keep ahead of boot mud and lime dust factored in the shift, but caring for the cottage also signaled my commitment to her.

By late morning, the frame of a coop stood in the southeast corner. Fetching the rusty bike from the shed, I rode up The High, then followed the dirt track leading to O'Toole's feed store.

Set in a field behind the village, the warehouse resembled an oversized barn. Inside, burlap sacks of feed stacked against the plank walls. A clutter of tools, equipment, and other farm provisions filled the vast wooden floor. Chaff tickled my nose, inducing a sneeze.

The shopkeeper greeted me with frank surprise. "God bless ya, Miss Riordan. How may I help?"

"Fiona gifted me chickens, so any advice you could offer would be terrific." Mick O'Toole also functioned as the area's unofficial veterinarian.

"Fee keeps Golden Comets," he said, musing. "They're fine birds and lay year-round. Kitchen scraps and grubs will keep 'em happy, though they'll appreciate a small bit of feed. Even chickens like variety. They'll want a waterin' pan, too."

He assisted in the selection of the required items, offering other nuggets of wisdom as they occurred to him. After paying, I looped a small bucket for kitchen scraps and a beautiful willow basket for egg collection over the bike's handlebars, then adjusted a blue tin watering pan under one arm while Mr. O'Toole placed a feed sack the size of a healthy infant in the bike basket. Casting a dubious eye over the arrangement he said, "I make deliveries."

"Thanks, but I'll manage."

I kicked off and awkwardly pedaled home. Ciarán relieved me of the watering pan and swept an arm toward his and Paddy's handiwork. "A palace for your flock."

"It's beautiful!"

"It wants paint yet but we're startin' on the run."

My project had intruded on enough of their time; anything more struck as excessive. "Please don't bother. The girls can roam."

Paddy guffawed at the suggestion. "And here we thought ya were about havin' a kitchen garden."

Assuring me it would take next to no time, the men dug post holes and ran wire while I contributed by painting the roost a deep red with white trim. Ciarán constructed nesting boxes from scrap wood, and we filled them with swaths of sweet grass. Offering my thanks in the form of cider, we stood, glasses in hand, and admired the final product.

"This is off the payroll," Paddy said, with a smile which made clear he'd brook no protest. "It's a welcome gift."

"You've spent half a day on this. Let me make you supper tonight." The impulsive words spilled out before my mind considered the implications.

The men, ignorant of the diceyness of the proposition, accepted the invitation. From my thin repertoire of recipes, I settled on pasta with chicken and spent the late afternoon in careful, nervous preparation, hoping a beautifully set table would distract from the meal's inadequacies.

My nerves settled while fitting beeswax tapers in mismatched candlesticks and arranging forsythia branches, knobby with buds, in a cream white pitcher. Tea towels served for napkins. Edie had fortified my wardrobe by mailing a box of clothes, so I changed into a blue linen dress, elated with a sense of occasion.

My guests arrived together. Paddy traded his work clothes for a neat pair of decades-old trousers and braces over a badly pressed checked shirt. Ciarán, wearing a black wool vest and crisp white shirt, open at the collar to show off sun-kissed skin, offered a bottle of wine.

"Your hair!"

He dragged a hand over his head, grumbling. "Ma should hire out at shearin' time." Maeve had trimmed the sides short and close, but a profusion of curls still tumbled from the crown of his head. His beard, now reduced to a ginger scruff, made him appear surprisingly young.

"It looks good. You're less ethereal now."

"There's a relief, then. I'm indeed of this earth, with the clay feet ta prove it."

A knock sounded so Ciarán assumed sommelier duty, but my chipper mood dampened upon discovering Declan on the stoop.

"Howya, Dec," Ciarán said, with a cheerful brandish of the corkscrew.

The solicitor glowered. "Ya have company."

"Have a drink with us." I took his coat, making mental calculations. Anticipating Paddy's appetite, I'd quadrupled the recipe. The idea of Declan staying left me cold, but Denise taught me to welcome unexpected guests with grace and complain about them after.

Declan glanced around the table, squinting in confusion. "Appears ta be a celebration."

"Thanks to these gentlemen, the chickens Fiona gave me have a home. Their names are Daisy and May. The hens, I mean." He accepted a glass without comment on either the birds or the wine.

"Cottage on schedule, Paddy?"

"Yer conversation wants variety, lad. Everythin' is movin' right along. Ciarán is ahead of pace on the cabinetry and the icebox arrives next week."

"Along with a new mattress. And don't worry; Ciarán confirmed it's the correct size."

"He's a wondrous help." Declan's reply lacked sincerity.

Paddy answered with a pleased chortle and a friendly slap on Ciarán's shoulder. "He is and I'm glad of it. My nose is twitchin,' Clare. I could et the twelve apostles."

Despite my hopes, Declan made no move to go so I set another place, brought the platter to the table, and lifted my glass. "To the first cottage supper among friends."

Ciarán's eyes were warm on mine. "Ta your first supper."

"And ta many more!" Paddy examined his plate with a chuckle. "I trust ya didn't inform yer flock ya were dinin' on their kin tonight."

Not having made the ironic connection, my cheeks heated. "Daisy and May are safe."

"At least until they're old enough fer stew. Now, Clare, did I ever tell ya of the time Seamus and my Da stole the bishop's bicycle?" Thus began the first of many uproarious, embellished stories which carried us through the meal and neatly sidestepped the Cain and Abel dynamic of the brothers.

Three of us enjoyed the companionship, while Declan ate in impassive silence. He managed one brief but positive comment on the meal. "Thank you. My goal is to reach Maeve's standard."

"It's delicious and Ma would approve," Ciarán said. "She never complains, but pilgrim time tires her. A bit of kitchen help will be a blessin'."

Declan rounded on his brother. "Ya haven't been here; ya know nothing of what wears on Ma." Chastened, Ciarán dropped his head as Declan turned to me. "She once worked as head chef in Galway's finest restaurant."

"She's not a native?" Maeve seemed as much a fixture of Killarkin as the ruins.

"She brought her burdens to St. Dallán after Da died."

Da. Eamon wasn't his father. Ciarán met my surprised glance with a quiet twitch of his shoulder, as if to say, "It's his story."

"They were married three years, and me but two when he passed. Ma came here a year later." Sure nothing but excessive drink compelled the taciturn man to tell his family story, my glance stole to his glass, but it stood full.

"Fell in love with Eamon, she did," Paddy said. "Though I maintain she stayed outta charity, ta spare us the man's fair awful cookin'. She arrived with her wee lad and charmed the lot of us; Eamon most of all. Then this eejit came along." He clipped Ciarán with a jovial elbow.

Ciarán laughed, without irony. "We've been a lovin' family ever since."

"Stories with happy endings are the best. Speaking of which, who would like dessert?"

After cake from The Cosy and cups of tea, Paddy tilted back on his chair and patted his ample belly. "Sure, I've not had a finer meal since me blessed Cora departed."

I covered his rough hand with my own. "Oh, Paddy. Has she been gone long?"

"Twenty years now." He gave my fingers a grateful squeeze. "But then, if she preferred a thick Tullamore grocer ta the likes a me, well then, she had all the choice."

He cackled when I swatted his arm and said, "Wicked man!"

"True enough. And I should be ashamed takin' the piss off one who gave me such a grand meal and even better company. I apologize, darlin.' I'll away and atone."

Getting my revenge I asked, "Over a pint?"

Paddy grinned, unabashed. "Black stuff and darts aid the digestion." He kissed my cheek, shook hands with the brothers, and looped his fingers through his suspenders. "*Slán.*"

Ciarán began carrying plates to the sink. "Let me help with the dishes. Nothin' worse for a party mood than wakin' ta a filthy kitchen."

"Precisely why I never entertain."

"Ya should do. Ya have a gift." His musical laugh vibrated in my chest. The beard gone, his features were more precise. Though I'd downplayed the effect of his haircut, he still resembled an angel.

Grumpy, Declan vanished to the front room, muttering about tending the fire.

Mumbling an obscenity, I thumped left-over salad into the scrap bucket. "What's his problem?"

"Don't mind his growls. He's a good man underneath."

It amazed me how Ciarán could extend grace toward someone who seldom had a kind word for anyone, let alone his own brother. With any luck, Declan would grow bored and clear out before we finished the kitchen work, but we were too efficient.

"You've helped enough today, sir. Have a drink." We entered the front room, where a pleasant fire crackled, doing its best to warm the room. "Firelight is cozy, but it'll be nice when the radiators are installed."

Ciarán glanced at the tarped piles of building supplies ranged around the room. "I hope you'll find the end result worth the mayhem."

"It's controlled chaos and when we're done, the cottage will always be like this; comfortable and peaceful."

"There's the spirit," he said. "Focus on the lovely result, not the holey walls and floors."

"It will be beautiful and worth any price."

Declan loured like an impending storm; no doubt irritated by a reminder of the renovation's cost. Ciarán attempted to engage his brother in our conversation. "Are ya off ta Dublin this week?"

"No plans ta do." I could have screamed. With excruciating stubbornness, Declan refused to enter in but wouldn't leave. Though sympathetic about his father's early death, given his age at the time and the subsequent gift of a stepfather like Eamon, the tragedy didn't explain the man's hard edge.

"Will ya be returnin' ta Cara soon?" The question came out harsh, more accusation than inquiry.

Ciarán considered. "They're keen for me ta do policy work; but I don't fancy a desk job." His mouth quirked as he winked at me. "I'm still discernin'."

Desirous of turning conversation away from the bear in the corner I said, "Cara is an interesting name for an NGO."

"It means 'friend' in Gaeilge."

A shamed blush lit my cheeks. "Grand-da taught me a few words but..."

Ciaran grinned. "Which is about as much as most Irish know." He tipped his glass toward mine. "*Sláinte*."

"*Saol fada chugat*. Have you been with Cara long?"

"Ten years. Construction jobs paid my seminary fees. When I quit school, I took those skills ta Cara. Rebuildin' and helpin' folk get back on track after natural disasters is rewardin' work. Before the Middle East I'd not been near war."

He described the impoverished camps, the dignity of refugees amid fear and chaos, and the struggle to assist with inadequate resources. "When supplies got through, they were never enough. Despair hung relentless, like fog." He breathed out through his nose and pain etched his face. "Once I assisted at a birth; when the beautiful young mother first held her babby, she shone with pure love. Then she remembered. All her reasonable hopes drained from her smile, then from her cinnamon eyes. Of all the despairin' things I ever witnessed, her light dimmin' did me in. She couldn't give her child a future and I could do nothin' ta help."

Hushed by the weight of his experience and the subtext of guilt in his voice, I cradled one of his hands. "You did all you could."

He regarded me with mild surprise. "Did I? We never made any sort of dent in all the need." He pressed my hand and pulled away, his fingertips beating an angry tattoo on his knee. "If only politicians summoned a fraction of the will for a permanent peace as they expended gettin' our do-goodin' Western hides outta there."

He'd spent a decade risking his life in the service of others and witnessing his misery hurt my heart. "What's happening there is terrible, but it would be even worse if no one cared. Kindness makes a difference, even if you can't measure it."

"It's a fine philosophy." The haunted cast across his face suggested he hoped rather than believed it true.

Declan stirred; for a few blissful moments we had forgotten his existence. Ciarán noticed him, too, and recaptured his smile. "It's been a delightful evenin,' Clare, but we'd best give ya some quiet. Join me for a pint, Dec."

His brother rose, set his empty glass on the mantel, and with forced grace thanked me for a pleasant evening.

"Thank ya indeed." Ciarán gave my elbow a discrete squeeze. "What's next? The barn is roomy enough for a few sheep."

"Let's see how I manage poultry first."

After they left I sat cross-legged before the fire. Learning Ciarán attended seminary didn't startle—the priesthood suited his quiet spirituality and gentle humor—but what made him drop out? He'd given no evidence of being a quitter. I poked the blackened peat, also curious why of the two, he left Killarkin when Declan seemed more inclined to the anonymity of urban life.

A tiny flame licked up, then reconsidered. With accompanying prayers, older generations tamped the fire before bed, blowing the peat back to life the next morning. But those old ways weren't necessary now and my unskilled attempts might well set the cottage ablaze. With another prod of the dying fire, the peat smoked, sparked, and burned bright. I watched it for a long time.

Chapter Nine

A WEEK LATER I lay in bed, luxuriating in the joy of a firm mattress. When it arrived the crew had, with good humor and many curses, wrestled the four-poster upstairs and replaced the sagging mess which had outlived its purpose decades before. I had gone to bed early for the sheer pleasure of it.

Despite the gaping walls and other chaotic evidence of the renovation, my day began with an intense eagerness to create a semblance of home. The stained, faded quilt on the freshly made bed, however, struck a discordant note. Once the shops opened, it had to go.

My boots crunched on the rime as I went into the morning to feed Daisy and May. Vivid yellow flowers bloomed on the gray-brown branches of the forsythia and a brave cluster of velvety crocus peeped through frost dusted grass near the coop. Their purple heads brightened the dark garden like tiny lamps. I admired the ambition of those little flowers, pushing up slender white throats and making a bold declaration of spring when winter still fought to hold its chill grasp. The cupped blooms tokened hope, and we were kindred, incongruous yet planted firm in a muddy Irish garden.

Mrs. Fannin smiled when the bell announced my entrance. "Goodness, Clare! You're early this mornin'. How may I help ya?"

"Cathleen, every bit of linen in the cottage is threadbare, stained, or both and it's intolerable."

"We've a grand selection on those shelves beyond."

With painstaking care, I examined each item, choosing pairs of fine cotton sheets, pillow slips edged with tatted lace, and thick wool blankets. Then I swore.

Cathleen trotted from behind the counter to investigate the cause of my outburst. "I forgot about this! My sister-in-law is deadly with embroidery."

"No kidding!" In my hand lay the world's most beautiful coverlet, a white lawn confection worked all over with delicate flowers, knots, and vines, like Belleek rendered in cotton and satin.

"Coo!" Cathleen exclaimed as she read the price tag. "What Brigid thought I don't know. Two hundred euro! No one here would pay such a price. She'd do better sellin' it on Etsy."

The price seemed quite reasonable, if not too low, for such exquisite handiwork. Clutching it to my chest I said, "Sold!"

Compensating for what she believed an exorbitant amount, Cathleen offered a discount. "Thanks, but Brigid named her price." The coverlet joined the stack of linens on the counter and the shopkeeper ogled. "If you'd rather I paid now..."

She fluttered her fingers. "Not ta worry."

My voice thickened with inexplicable tears. "Whatever can be salvaged will but, but so much of what's in the cottage is worn beyond hope."

"Ya want the place filled with lovely objects and precious memories." Cathleen understood and I nodded, sure Grand-da wanted it, too. It wasn't enough to rehabilitate the cottage's bones; her beauty needed restoration, too. Lit with the realization, my purse strings unfurled. The pile on the counter grew with cutwork table linens, pottery bowls, and a set of creamy white dishware which closely matched the original remnants. I also ordered a proper urn for Grand-da's ashes.

Cathleen's eyes widened further as she tallied my purchases, and she announced the total with a note of apology. Despite her forbearance, she received payment on the spot. "Thank you, Cathleen. This will make such a difference. I'll have you and Gerry to supper after we finish the reno."

"What a treat. He can bring all this 'round later, if ya will be ta home."

"All day. Oh! I also need a shopping trolley."

A proper Killarkin always carried a basket or wheeled cart to the shops, and my new purchase marked me as a village member, not an interloper. Filled with an absurd sense of pride, I pulled it along the narrow sidewalk while visiting all the shops and buying more than one person could eat in a week.

Lugging it toward home, I noticed Paddy's old truck idling outside the pub and Ciarán called out its window. "Ah. Preparin' for the end of days."

"Christening my new cart, actually. Where are you headed?"

"Paddy gave me a mission in the Pale."

"Want some company?"

"I'd be glad of it."

"Give me seven minutes." After sticking my head back into Fannin's to inform Cathleen of my impulsive change of plan, I hurried home to stow the perishable groceries, and left a spare key in the drainpipe for Gerry. With a quick jog back toward the pub, I hopped into the truck and buckled the seat belt. "Would there be time for a little shopping?"

Ciarán pulled away from the curb with an assenting nod. "My errand won't take long. You're fair excited."

"My knowledge of Dublin is confined to the airport."

"Somethin' we'll rectify then, though there's no shoppin' in town ya can't get from Cathleen."

"When it comes to living room furniture, a photograph won't tell you if a couch is comfortable. Besides, the interior should say authentic Irish cottage, not Ikea catalog."

He chuckled at my vehemence. "You're eager ta be settled."

His comment provoked a weird nudge of sadness. "The house will be torn apart for months yet and then sold. It's silly, doing all this for someone else."

"Seamus would no doubt disagree."

Without question Grand-da intended a renovation; he'd funded it. But he wanted more from me, and I still hadn't figured out what. It pricked like a thorn. Ciarán's hands provided a distraction; his fingers beating out a restless rhythm on the steering wheel. "Do you play piano?"

"That's nothin' ta do with Dublin, furniture, or Seamus."

"You have such long fingers."

He laughed. "Ma always said I'd either be a concert pianist or a pickpocket. I took up carpentry instead. And guitar. Dec and I once had a punk band." I squeaked with glee, and he shoved the gear shift into third. "We played parties and tortured folk with fair repulsive tunes."

"Damn! I would give anything to have heard you! Does the tension between you two owe to some big Lennon-McCartney drama?" Ciarán rested an elbow on the back of the seat; the serious set of his mouth tamed my nosy enthusiasm. "Sorry. None of my business."

"It wasn't artistic differences. Around the time I went off with Cara, Ma fell ill with cancer. With me away and Da worried half ta death, Dec had ta manage the pub, along with his own work, then run ta Dublin for Ma's treatments. He grew resentful and had the right. I could have come home and did when we came close ta losin' her. But she rallied and I left again. There's the pride I confessed before; my noble purpose got ahead of the family. Dec can't forgive it."

"Ten years is a long time to nurse a grudge."

Unheeding, he continued. "He'd taken on the Malone practice and dreamt of openin' an office in the city. He fell in love. And he sacrificed it all because I couldn't be arsed ta help out."

Unable to imagine Declan loving anyone, I asked, "Someone in Dublin?"

"When they met. She's local now."

Examining my fingernails, I scanned mental images of women in the village. An absurd thought occurred then crystalized into perfect sense. "Nessa?"

Ciarán nodded. "She assisted on Ma's medical team. Ta hear Ma tell it, seein' them come together gave her another reason ta live." He gave me a sidelong grin. "She's dead keen for a passel of grandbabbies."

I laughed outright. "It's easy to picture her doting on a bunch of rug rats."

Ciarán chortled his agreement, then sobered again. "The short of the tale is Ma recovered and Nessa opened a practice in Killarkin. She and Dec planned ta marry. All turned right again, for a time. But Dec's worry and resentment didn't lift. He stopped speakin' ta me, and most other folk. He and Ness broke off the engagement, and both their hearts with it."

"But she stayed."

"She loved him and may still. But she also has a passion for her work. Have a care, darlin'; Ma and Ness are cautionary tales. Our wee town has a way of seducin' one and changin' her life."

I considered the emerald hills rolling by. "I wouldn't mind a life change, but it will take more than a sweet village to do it." We rode in silence a bit before I hazarded another question. "Why did you leave seminary?"

He drummed his fingers on the steering wheel. "I met a girl."

"Ah. Problematic." He nodded but didn't elaborate.

At his atypical reserve, questions popped up like jonquils in spring sunshine, but they remained unasked. It discomfited, knowing there existed a woman amazing enough to make a man like Ciarán leave the priesthood. Whoever she was, I envied her; an admission which sent me down an altogether different rabbit hole of wondering.

He slowed as we approached a twisting part of the road. "Now ya possess all the family secrets. Guard 'em with your life."

"Mum's the word."

"I hope we finish the cottage before your visa expires."

"Among his other puckish quirks, Grand-da gave us citizenship applications when we turned eighteen. None of us cared much, but we did it to please him. He always encouraged us to embrace our Irish; I'm convinced he left me the cottage to force my hand."

Ciarán's errand required a stop at a building supply warehouse outside of town. With his purchase loaded, we drove into Dublin proper and started my quest, informed by two fundamental criteria: sturdiness and comfort. Within a couple hours this translated into three wool rugs in traditional colors and patterns, and a leather couch the color of old whiskey, with rolled arms and wide cushions. I pictured it before the hearth, a vase of roses beside it, keeping company with Grand-da's chair.

"D'ya have a pain?" Ciarán asked. "You're clutchin' at your heart."

"It's clutching at me. This is perfect."

I placed my order, adding in some airy metal side tables and dusky rose throw pillows. When we gained the street Ciarán chortled. "I've never seen a happier salesclerk."

"She must work on commission." The extravagance of my purchases left me lightheaded, but Grand-da would approve.

Missions accomplished, Ciarán toured me around the center of the lovely old city, though he refused to take me to Temple Bar with an adamant, "No one need pay so much for a damn pint." Instead, we had a sushi lunch, then a drink at the Jameson Distillery, the only tourist activity on which I insisted. I bought a bottle of Black Label for Daddy's Christmas present.

As we drove home, I mewed with satisfaction. "It's always more fun learning about a place from a local. I hope you weren't bored."

"Your enthusiasm is catchin'."

"It's weird, all a sudden caring about stuff like this."

"By which ya mean—"

"Domestic stuff. But the cottage is more than a place; it represents family heritage, who Grand-da was, and who he thought I could be." With a self-conscious giggle I admitted my tendency to go along without a sense of purpose. "I've never had any direction, and still don't, but being here…it feels like the compass is nearby."

Ciarán slid into the loose-boned posture which accompanied his casual delivery of wisdom. "I reckon we're all born with a call on our life. Some, like Ness, know it sure. The best the rest of us can do is pay attention and amble the path we're set, trustin' we'll come ta recognize where it leads."

"Even if everyone along the way assumes we're aimless?"

He peered at me from the side of his eye. "Distractin' yourself with the opinion of others won't show ya where ya are or where you're goin'."

"It would help to have a goal."

He parked in front of the cottage, twisting toward me. "Shite, Clare; ya do. For now, it's the reno; ya needn't worry about what there is ahead. Appreciate the shape of each day given; this present moment is purpose enough."

A knot unkinked; one I hadn't realized even existed.

We unloaded the truck, then discovered the packages from Fannin's stacked on the table, tied in brown paper. "It's like Christmas morning!"

"If the holiday can wait, let's have a pint first."

He didn't need to persuade me. Already enamored of the pub's welcoming energy, I loved how it kicked into an even higher gear on weekends when spontaneous combos always took over a corner and played trad tunes. Sometimes Eamon even lent his gorgeous baritone.

The tables and snugs were full. Declan brooded over a pint at the bar. "Brother!" Ciarán greeted him with a clap on the back.

Declan glanced with an annoyed scowl. "Ya went missin', Clare."

My movements were none of his concern, but unwilling to spoil my cheerful mood I withheld a snarky reply. "We went to Dublin."

"I called by the cottage earlier."

For the sake of his charming family, if nothing else, I wanted to like Declan. But his bossing presumption and petulant tone irritated me like a case of hives. "I'm here now."

"Another time."

A table opened near the door. With reluctance, Declan accepted Ciarán's invitation to join us, and I ventured a last attempt at good will. If he didn't bite, my focus could return to his more entertaining brother. "Ciarán told me about your band. Did you write your own music?"

Declan squeezed his lips tight, so his brother answered. "We did covers, though Dec wrote our biggest hit: "Buggerin' the Sheep. A fine ballad, ta be sure."

"Disgusting!"

"In both content and execution. As ya know, we were rubbish."

"Ma did not approve," Declan said.

"Your shaved head gave her pause, there's the truth."

Trying to imagine it, I laughed with genuine delight. "Declan O'Donnell! Are there photos?"

"None you'll ever see." He scowled at Ciarán with a tiny, threatening spark lighting his eye.

"Ya were fierce." Ciarán put a hand on his brother's head. "Ya have a perfect skull."

Declan pushed him away. "Shut your gob, ya daft eejit."

Drinks turned into supper and through the magic of delicious food and good whiskey, Declan relaxed a bit. If only Nessa would come in. Despite my aversion to matchmaking, I couldn't help thinking they might be kinder, happier people if they found a way back to each other. The thought made me tender and when Eamon joined the session I listened, rapt and wistful.

Ciarán cupped my chin in a gentle hand and swiped a tear with his thumb. "Why are ya cryin'?"

"Your dad is such a beautiful singer."

He beamed with a heart-rending glow. "Oh, darlin'. Seamus got his wish; for an American, you're awful damn Irish. Darts?"

"One game; no more. There are presents at home."

The blissful day began with a captivating bedspread, ran its course through the success and illumination of my time with Ciarán, and topped off with the charm of trad music. Inspired, my hours of practice took root, allowing me to wield my darts with precision and win the match. Too thrilled by the progress of his pupil to rue defeat, Ciarán swung me off the floor in a jubilant embrace.

Smiling down, full of pride, my hands rested on his strong shoulders. A tiny flash of intimacy, too brief for definition, stuttered in my heart. "Thanks, O'Donnell."

"Ya always had it in ya." He set me on my feet, eyes sparkling. Collecting our darts, he said, "Now, give me a rematch before ya get too full of yourself."

Banter returned and the quirk I'd felt in his arms receded like an ocean wave from shore. "Another time. Tonight, allow me the triumph. Let's not prove it's a fluke, OK? Thanks again for the adventure. And the encouragement."

"Any time."

Declan offered to escort me home, provoking a giggle. "Afraid I'll be waylaid by sheep?"

"I want a word."

"Right. Come on then. I'll give you a drink. G'night, Coach."

Ciarán grinned and winked. "Rematch. Soon."

For a man in need of a word, Declan had a funny way of showing it. He lapsed into silence on the brief, sheep-free walk from the pub, then paced the front room, inspecting the walls without comment, while I poured drinks and gestured an invitation to the lumpy old couch. He perched on the edge of a cushion, shoulders rigid.

Taking Grand-da's chair and checking impatience I asked, "What's up?"

"Are ya happy here?"

"Yes. Please stop worrying."

Declan sipped his whiskey. "It's responsibility, not worry."

"You're obligated to your own happiness, not mine."

His familiar scowl returned. "Ciarán and ya get along."

"He's been very kind." Cradling my glass, I stretched my feet toward the hearth.

"Mind yourself there. He's not reliable."

"He told me all about it. Let it go; it's been a decade and people change."

"Ciarán is pleasant and friendly." He forced out the reluctant acknowledgement. "But he's naïve."

I snorted a laugh. "Hardly."

"You've known him a brief time. I'm a better judge of his character."

My defenses rose; it stunned to think Declan's resentment extended so far as turning me against his brother. "He's a decent man. I like him."

"Don't like him too much. He knows nothin' of women."

"What the hell?"

"He intended ta be a priest. The one woman he loved died and he ran off ta do aid work."

I turned toward the fire, repenting my earlier, frivolous thoughts. Ciarán's woman died. It hadn't been a one-sided temptation or other dismissible scenario. He loved her and the pain of her death, more permanent than any breakup, sent him into war zones. My heart ached for my friend.

Undeterred, Declan repeated his original premise. "He doesn't know women."

"You're warning me off because he might be a virgin?" His sober mouth stopped me from laughing out loud.

The couch springs squeaked when he left it to pace. "He won't know what ta do with the likes of ya. Sure, ya aren't what *I* anticipated."

Vexation soured my tongue. "Why? Because you expected a compliant little mouse who'd follow your every dictate?" I rose, indicating the end of the fruitless discussion. "It's late. If you have anything sensible to say, now's your chance."

Declan rested an elbow on the mantel and contemplated Grand-da's ashes. "When Seamus' lawyer contacted me, I assumed I'd be dealin' with an older, established woman—an efficient businessperson or a settled matron with children and a sense of expedience. I also considered ya might be an entitled brat. I could have dealt with any of those. But ya came here, all ginger curls and snappin' eyes, charmin' the shite out of everyone. You're maddenin'. You're lovely."

The unwanted compliment provoked a blush, but his sad eyes indicated it didn't make him happy either. "Declan—"

The moment turned surreal, as if Time drank too much and couldn't walk without tipping. He moved closer with a questioning look which, from another man in another moment, would have stirred me. Before the thought completed its articulation, he drew me to his chest and swept hair from my face. "I'd like ta kiss ya."

Time and sense righted themselves as he lowered his head, breathing whiskey and cigarettes. Before his lips met mine, I twisted away and darted across the room, attempting to control the furious tremble of my limbs. "I didn't say OK!"

Declan stood stoic by the fireplace. "Ya must have known."

"It's obvious I annoy the hell out of you." I put the back of my hand to my mouth, trying to comprehend his behavior.

"Ya don't like me much, do ya?" The pitiful expression which accompanied the question baffled me.

"You don't like me, either. How could you even think of kissing me when you've barely spoken a civil word to me?" Confused, I flattened against the wall, wondering at him. "And you were likeable enough earlier tonight when you took the stick out of your arse. But then you come in here, bad mouth your brother, and—" Staring, I tried to divine the workings of the mind behind his indecipherable expression. "If I've given you the wrong impression—"

Declan smoothed his tie, his face like stone. "Ya haven't." He sounded sincere but kept his attention riveted on the fire.

"Please tell me what's going on. This is all very confusing."

He stood another minute longer, staring at the hearth with an expression of abject humiliation. "I apologize for my behavior. Forget I said, or did, anythin'. If ya can." He left with wounded dignity, and I slammed the door bolt behind him.

Chapter Ten

I WAITED UNTIL THE music of church bells ended. With the villagers praying Sunday Mass, I could flee to St. Dallán's, sure to be alone. Ciarán always went to the ruins at dawn, and avoiding him seemed prudent, too. The brothers had a fraught enough relationship without him learning about Declan's almost-kiss. Once the final call to worship shimmered away on the air, I slipped out the back door, over the wall, and up the hill.

Bright sun showed through tatters of cloud. Rainwater filled the worn font and two small brown birds with rosy throats bathed there, the lone pilgrims. The plash of their tiny wings resonated in the still, tranquil ruins. My back against the stone wall, I watched them, envying their carefree existence.

My thoughts jumbled; messy as a kitchen after a group of unattended children tried their hands at baking. Hoping to find coherence and order, I hugged myself and wept instead, releasing a fusillade of tears which dripped on my bent knees, cleansing, but not naming, my confusion.

When the crying stopped, conflicting emotions queued in a straggling line. Frustration throbbed in my chest, torn between compassion for Declan's secret pain and a fierce urge to scratch out his eyes. I knew, before asking, none of my behavior toward him ever indicated a romantic interest. The attempted kiss came from nowhere; clueless about a lot, I still recognized sexual tension when it sparked and none glimmered between Declan and me. One fact, however, shone with perfect clarity; he sure wanted to drive a wedge between me and Ciarán.

The contented baa of nearby sheep pirouetted with a soapy whiff of lanolin. The peaceful gentleness of their presence calmed me enough to consider the next item on my perplexing agenda. Ciarán often inhabited a higher realm, and he might well be more broken than he appeared; but unless he took some self-flagellating vow after his woman died, I doubted he remained a virgin. A man possessed of so much innate caring would surely be open to love. Even if he were pure as washed wool, a girl could do worse than initiate him.

My hands pressed my aching ovaries. It had been a long time, but my life had enough uncertainty without entertaining a fling with a local. Ciarán's humor and kindness charmed me, and his beauty startled sometimes, like catching the wrong end of a lit match. It burned, brief and hot, then cooled without leaving a welt. But the sparks, however pleasant, didn't count against the wealth of having him as a friend.

If Declan were anyone but his brother, we could talk about what happened and he would soothe me with sage advice. But fueling their tensions for my own peace of mind would make matters worse. Declan asked me, with pitiful sincerity, to forget what happened. Telling anyone wouldn't be forgetting.

Another sob bubbled up. For the first time in weeks, I longed for Seattle and a brunch of eggs Benedict and mimosas with Edie and Aimee. They would counsel me, then process the incident into a hilarious, forgettable joke. Without them, I could only weep some more.

In time, the sobs slowed, and a deep, shuddering breath, full of the sweet scent of grass, cleansed me. Pushing away from the wall, I paced the perimeter of the ruins. Through thousands of years, women came here with an identical soup of emotions and wept the same tears. Once again, the ancient place granted perspective and left me feeling less alone.

The splashing birds lifted off and flew away. I trailed my fingers along the rough edge of the font. A tiny, buff colored feather floated on the water. I fished it out and stood small under the expansive bowl of sky, young amid centuries of bewildered, wounded hearts which crept here before me. My chest calmed and my pulse settled back into a steady rhythm.

Ciarán's darts instruction sounded clear, as if he stood beside me: *Here's your center.* Therein lay the problem. I had never controlled my own heart let alone possessed a single goal or aspiration tied to anything but the agenda of others. Even Grand-da, who loved me better than anyone, had an expectation and I resented it. I hadn't chosen Ireland or these complications.

Éire chose you, darlin'.

The words sounded like the lilting voice of my dead grandfather, and the statement rang hollow. Why would she want me? I had nothing to offer her; or anyone else.

So what?

This voice, recognizable as my own, came from a deep, defiant place. My life lacked any design, not so much as bullet points suggesting what the next year, let alone twenty, might bring. The puzzling encounter with Declan assured our next would be awkward, but none of this changed my plans. Mom's guilt trips, an absence of life goals, even protracted celibacy weren't the issue. Restoring my sweet little cottage and befriending whom I chose required no one's permission or approval. Anyone arguing otherwise could go to hell.

Shakey, but resolved, I held the gutsy notion tight and tucked the feather into my pocket. Like my Brigid's cross, I bestowed on it the totemic power to remind me. I'd chosen a path and would stay on it no matter how many turns it took or where it ended.

A new work week began, and after two months of apprenticeship, Paddy trusted my devotion. He no longer indulged me with busy work but assigned real, substantive projects. Each contribution from my hands inspired inordinate pride: a Riordan built the cottage; now another Riordan redeemed it.

On Tuesday and Thursday mornings Maeve continued my cooking lessons. She imparted many valuable recipes and culinary tricks, but they were nothing on her stories. She shared village histories, comical tales about her boys, and anecdotes about folks who moved to Killarkin seeking peace and quiet but found it didn't suit.

"But not ya, Clare. You've slotted in, like ya were born ta it. Make no mistake, I love Killarkin, but I swear ta ya, it took time. Most city folk find it dull after more'n a week."

"By urban standards, there's less to do here, but running around all the time at home didn't accomplish anything." I pulled a baking sheet of shortbread from the oven, burnt my thumb, and shoved it into my mouth. Tisking, Maeve fetched ice, wrapped it in a tea towel, and after placing the bundle in my hand, lit a candle to St. John. Nursing my thumb, I continued. "Truth is, I sought distractions to avoid soul-searching."

Maeve wagged her head with a knowing look. "Now ya know what ya want."

"Not entirely, but the reno keeps me focused. Better to have a short-term goal than none at all, right?"

"Sure. So long it's one ya care about."

"There's the trick." I removed the ice pack and shifted cooled cookies to a tin, careful not to break them.

Maeve held out her hand, demanding to inspect my thumb. She examined the small patch of taut pink skin, blew a gentle breath across it, and ended her ministrations with a tiny kiss. "You'll not have a blister. Take a few dozen of the shortbread home with ya."

"Thanks. For some reason, they don't turn out well in my kitchen and I won't foist them on the crew, not even Jamie, and he eats everything."

Our lessons took place in the quiet of late morning, when no one but Eamon, aul Tim, and the occasional delivery person were about. By limiting my pub time to those safe hours, I avoided my solicitor for two weeks. With luck, we wouldn't see one another until the reno ended. Then Paddy discovered water damage in a kitchen wall.

I gaped into the hole he'd opened in the plaster. "Did one of the leaks cause this?"

"It's older," he said, peering at the mottled, pocked lath. "A mercy Sorely didn't like this wobbly bit of the fireplace, or we'd not know. This section needs replacin' before he can shore up the brickwork."

"But it's not in the budget." The face I turned toward Ciarán must have been a special brand of pitiful because he offered to come along. "Declan doesn't worry me." The statement convinced no one, including me. "Yes, please."

Ciarán took dictation on a pad of notepaper while Paddy calculated the repair costs. "And sure, it won't require a penny more," he said, before giving me a bolstering squeeze around the shoulders.

Glum, I dragged my feet as we walked up The High. "Dec can't refuse," Ciarán said.

"He'll try."

"So what?"

As a mantra, those two words lacked elegance, but they had power. I halted in the middle of the street. "You're right. He doesn't matter." A current of boldness electrified my core and sparked my pace.

We arrived at the office, stepping over Orla, stretched and sleeping in a patch of sun on the front step. "Remind me to stop by Fannin's for cream when we're done."

We paused in the cool, narrow foyer before Ciarán disturbed the hush with two sharp raps and pushed open the office door. "Do ya have a minute, brother?"

Annoyed, Declan turned from his computer and without fanfare, I laid the itemized list on his desk and explained the problem. "Please transfer money from the contingency fund."

He shook his head, studying the page marked with Ciarán's crabbed block print, and muttered under his breath. but the words "drainin' the trust" were audible.

I braced clenched fists on my hips, an irksome gesture my mother made thousands of times, but which suited the moment. "I'll spend every damn cent of my money if necessary."

His lips tightened into a thin line, but he turned to the computer without eye contact. "I'll see ta it now." Thanking him with little grace, I strode out of the office.

Ciarán followed me across the street to Fannin's. "Bit tense there. He didn't regard ya once."

Declan's behavior struck me more as embarrassment than resistance but saying so would only draw unnecessary attention to the tension. "Unforeseen circumstances like this are the entire point of a contingency fund and he knows it."

Ciarán squinted into the sun. "It strikes me he's scared of ya."

"When it comes to the cottage, he should be."

A week later Maeve and I were finishing a lesson on ginger cake. The kitchen air swirled with the spicy perfume of our efforts. "Before ya go, Clare, would ya do me a favour?"

"Anything."

Loading one of the fresh cakes into a basket, she said, "Father Donovan is givin' the bishop tea. You'd oblige me if ya ran this ta him on your way."

Her face twisted as if she had asked for a kidney, and I smiled. "Consider it done."

The basket over my arm, I exited the pub and encountered Nessa, who paused, her brown eyes gleaming like agate. "Ya haven't been around much. Not of an evenin', anyway."

I tried not to register surprise at the doctor noticing, much less speaking to me. "It's noisy enough at the cottage during the day."

"The pub is the last place for quiet," she agreed. "It'll be worse soon enough."

"You'll be busier, too, won't you?"

"Turned ankles, mostly. It's amazin' how many people discover a shuck on their way ta St. Dall's. Come summer there will be bee stings, blisters, and at least one overweight Yank with palpitations."

"Ugh. Americans."

"The worst are the Irish Americans, givin' off like it makes them Irish." She stopped herself. "No offense."

"None taken." She managed a vague smile, and I gestured to the basket. "Gotta make a delivery for Maeve."

"He's sorry."

I slumped against the wall, mortified. "He told you?"

Nessa crossed her arms, her head wagging in the negative. "Details aren't in Dec's nature; he mentioned he'd been an arse and made ya fair angry. But as I'm the nearest thing ta a friend he allows, besides that wanker Garbhán, I reckoned bringin' it up at all meant he said somethin' regrettable."

A relieved breath blew out. "More like irritating, which is nothing new. Giving him a wide berth seems the best course."

A tiny wrinkle appeared on her brow as she considered. "I grant ya, his black mood is none too comfortable but avoidin' him makes it worse. Ya both live here; ya needn't stay clear of the pub or elsewhere on his account."

"Fair enough," I said, grinning. "Besides, the Riordans already have a recluse in the family tree."

My joke didn't land; Nessa wagged a serious head. "Folk need community. Call it an occupational hazard, but though I haven't a cure for what's ailin' him, I can't abandon Dec ta loneliness."

Her compassionate perspective altered my view of the situation. Declan's wounds pre-dated my arrival, but my attitude hadn't done anything to lessen them.

"Thanks, Nessa."

"Whatever for?"

"Talking to me. See you around."

"*Slán*, Clare."

I crossed The High, delivered Father Donovan's ginger cake, and, after a brief exchange about the marvels of Maeve's baking, started home. From the church yard the walled back gardens of The Low cottages caught my attention. Each had a gate which opened on a wide swath of grass so folks could access the back gate of the churchyard without hiking all the way around. Via a grassy alley between two of the houses, one could cross to The Low without trespassing. I decided on an alternate route home.

The cottage directly behind the church had quilts draped over the front garden wall. While admiring them, Moira emerged from the door. "Howya, Clare."

"Hey." I reddened, embarrassed she'd caught me nosing around the family wash. "You live here?"

"All my blessed life. She sells those, ya know."

"They're lovely." Puzzle pieces tumbled together. "Your mom is Brigid Fannin."

With a nod, she called over her shoulder, "Ma! Customer!" Then she leaned close. "Come here ta me. If ya fancy somethin', don't appear too eager. If she's willin' ta sell, she'll quote a firm price. Don't dare barter."

"Got it."

"Gran expects me at the shop. Will ya be 'round ta the pub tonight?"

Nessa's admonishment began its work. "Yeah."

"I'll see ya later then."

As her daughter ambled off, Brigid Fannin examined me from her doorway. "*Dia dhuit.*"

"*Dia is Muire dhuit.*" Saving myself further embarrassment, I added, "I don't have much Irish."

A tiny smile slipped onto her lips. "Are ya lost?"

"Headed home. To Sean's cottage. I'm Clare Riordan."

"Sure. Seamus' Clare. God rest him," she said, making the sign of the Cross. "My girl mentioned ya."

With a casual gesture toward the merchandise I said, "These are nice." Brigid left the safety of her door and approached as my vision snagged on a soft emerald-green blanket.

Embroidered with stylized rowan leaves and berries, the artisanship stunned. Each leaf had a bit of gold or bronze thread worked into, signaling the yellowing turn from summer to autumn; the base of every berry bore the distinctive five-pointed star, picked out in black. The accolades it deserved weren't in accord with Moira's advice, but I couldn't resist a casual, "This is pretty." Brigid studied me, wary of my motives. "Just right for a single bed."

"It is." She stepped closer; her attention sharp; like a lion one spring away from a kill. "The backin' is flannel." Peering at the stitching with faked disinterest, my fingers ran along the smooth, straight hem and performed whatever other examinations might suggest a reluctance to commit. The act must have passed the test because Brigid then quoted a price which again did not approach what her skill warranted.

"If you'll hold it for me, I'll come back with a check."

"Ack. I take all major debit and credit cards." With a blithe hand she pulled a smart phone from her apron pocket and fixed it with a card reader.

With my purchase folded in my arms, I walked back to the cottage, shaken to the core by my insular arrogance. I spoke with Moira every day and never bothered to learn about her family or where she lived. A country woman possessing more than a flip phone left me dumbstruck. Nessa brought nine or ten years of medical training from the city before settling in Killarkin. The galling truth rose clear: I considered my neighbors charming, but parochial. While most of the residents had been born, lived, and would die within the same five-mile radius, they were anything but backward or isolated. More to the point, they'd made far more of an effort with me than I had with them.

When I pushed into the kitchen, Ciarán stood at the table, reviewing cabinet sketches. He peered up, grinning. "You've been gone a while."

"I had to run an errand for Maeve, buy a blanket, and reckon with my narrow-mindedness." I set the quilt on a chair and switched on the kettle. "What did I miss?"

"Paddy wishes ta speak with ya about paint. He's upstairs."

The conversation with Nessa and my recent epiphany melded. "Are you going to the pub after work?"

"Thought I might, for a change."

"You want your rematch, wise guy?"

"I do, indeed. Loser buys supper."

❖

When Liam and Moira finished their game, Ciarán and I took the lane. After my close, but decisive defeat he scanned the pub. "Lady's choice: crowd the bar or force ourselves on Dec."

"Let's take him a pint."

Declan shook his newspaper with annoyance but laid it aside and accepted the beer. Before he could ask, I answered his inevitable question. "The unscheduled repairs are almost complete. Another couple of months and the cottage will again be a proper house without holes, rot, or plaster dust." I ignored the skeptical lift of his eyebrow.

"You've been fair patient," Ciarán said.

The compliment made me snort. "Patience is not one of my virtues, pal."

"Good news about the cottage," Declan said.

Ciarán cheered. "He can speak! I'll fetch a backup round ta forestall a relapse." With a conspiratorial wink he loped off.

Declan tucked his paper under an arm. "I'll leave ya ta your devices."

"Stay. Avoiding you played hell with my darts game."

"I'll not bother ya again; don't force yourself ta be friendly."

His obvious humiliation proved unbearable. "Don't overdramatize. You may be arrogant and patronizing, with a freakish need for control, but once upon a time you were a bass playing punk with a shaved head who loved his brother. I wouldn't have to force myself to like *him*."

Declan's head twitched in the direction of Ciarán. "Does he know?"

"Only if you said anything. You asked me to forget it."

His shamed face dispelled any doubts about his sincerity. "How can ya?"

"Don't wallow. You pissed me off, but I'm over it."

"I don't know what ta do with ya, Clare Riordan."

"Lighten up?"

His stony face turned pink. "I should apologize."

"You already did."

"Explain then."

I folded my hands under my chin. "Please do."

His gaze travelled toward the window and fixed on The High. "I don't reck why I compound my mistakes."

My chair faced the bar; Ciarán held a tray with our drinks while Liam and Jamie engaged him in conversation. We didn't have time for a full confession, but I wanted to leave the door open. "Given your line of work, you must know people screw up all the time. The problem isn't making errors so much as not learning from them." Ciarán took leave of the lads and moved toward us. "We can discuss this another time if you like; when there's more privacy." With a fleet touch on the back of Declan's elbow I said, "For now, you're forgiven. Please stop beating yourself up."

Ciarán set glasses before us. "Took you long enough," I said, grinning. "We were ready to call the garda."

"Jamie shared a *sceál* about his recent acquaintance with a German colleen on pilgrimage with her parents. They got on well enough and he needed no further encouragement. He attempted a kiss, and she clocked him upside the head. Jaysus, she gave him a shiner." Amused by Jamie's misfortune, Ciarán didn't notice his brother turning scarlet.

Fortunately, I spotted Nessa and waved her over. She lowered into a chair with an exhausted groan. "Jaysus, it's jammers and not even pilgrim time yet."

I took a sip of wine. "St. Dallán isn't the most popular of saints; it surprises me enough people visit his shrine to warrant a tourist season."

"You'll admit the ruins are worth the visit," Ciarán said.

"It's one of the most beautiful places on earth. I should have come here more often."

"Young ones can't be arsed with relics and ruins," Nessa said. "But you're an heiress now; ya can stop over whenever ya like." She smiled but her words rendered me self-conscious and silent until the conversation tripped over Nessa's stint with a medical NGO.

"You, too? Jaysus!"

Ciarán snorted into his beer and stared at me, his face mirthful. "What did ya say?"

I knit my eyebrows at the silly question. "You should have the good doctor check your ears."

He shook his head with another laugh. "I hear fine. Ya said Jaysus. You're startin' ta swear like an Irish."

I stuck out my tongue. "The point is you lot are amazing with all your selfless NGO work and pro bono lawyering."

"No one here will be canonized soon, unless you're thinkin' of Ciarán," Declan said, with a guffaw. "But bein' a carpenter doesn't make him the Christ."

Ciarán and Nessa laughed appreciatively, but despite my weak attempts to join in, the exchange still rankled the next morning. "I'm never going to understand banter," I admitted to Ciarán.

"Are ya bothered by what Dec said?"

"Nessa, too, and the heiress remark. The implication of privilege. It's not how I see myself."

He bent his head toward mine, his expression and voice soft as a misty day. "She'd have said three times worse if she thought ya did. It proves she's warmin' ta ya."

"Comforting," I said, still frowning. "But doesn't Declan's snark ever bother you?"

"He takes the piss outta me for bein' holy because I'm far from it. It would hurt if I aspired ta sainthood, but I don't."

"He called you a saint the first time he mentioned you."

Ciarán picked up a hammer, twirling it in agile fingers like a baton. "Dec is full of shite."

With a new understanding of how Irish teasing worked I chuckled. "That's the consensus."

Chapter Eleven

S PRINGTIME REVEALED A NEW aspect of Ireland's beauty. The rain turned mild and velvety. There were frequent sun breaks, with some downright balmy days. Wildflowers dazzled in hills and pastures. A profusion of bluebells and daffodils burst forth near the front step of the cottage door and in random clusters throughout the garden grass. Bright green leaves dressed the naked limbs of the rowans and hawthorns. Every leaf and bud nurtured a profound awe; my ancestral roots curled deep in the same spongey soil.

One morning Paddy and I had tea in the kitchen and held another round of healthy debate over paint colors while Sorely, covered with a fine dust of mortar, worked on the kitchen fireplace. "Will ya look at this!" he exclaimed.

Alarmed, Paddy shot his attention across the room. "More trouble, man?"

"Not ta worry but come here ta me." He had discovered a bread oven built into the fireplace. "Sure, it's an old one," he said. "Original ta the house, I reck."

Paddy blew out a long, admiring breath. "Why ever did they brick it over?"

"No respect." Sorely patted the oven, consoling it. "But I'll get her workin' again."

With a heart palpating at the thought of further delays I said, "Don't bother. It's extra work for you and the Stanley is plenty."

"But it'll come in useful for yer feasts and such." He turned his attention back to the rusted hinges of the oven door, muttering while he indexed the elements of disrepair.

My vision misted at the thought of family celebrations in the cottage, and through the blur came an image of Great-gran Mary as a young bride, her cheeks flushed with oven heat and pride, cradling a swaddled loaf of bread while Sean grinned beside her.

A clatter of tools brought me back and further argument died on my tongue. I would use the same oven from which my great-grandmother fed her family. The thought planted in my soul with a rightness which defied logic or facts.

The renovation had sparked an appreciation for the storytelling of artifacts and given me a fresh understanding of Mom's passion for home-keeping. With the cottage inching closer to its final shape and the family planning an August visit so we could inter Grand-da's ashes at Grace Church, my excitement manifested in more frequent calls home.

"Have you booked your return?" Mom asked.

"It's April."

"Fares will go up after Easter. There might still be room on our flight."

"Someone has to clean the cottage after the wake. Oh, and I've reserved rooms for you at the pub."

"I still don't understand why we can't stay with you."

I had it in me to be an excellent liar, save for the tell-tale flushes which accompanied the falsehood. But Mom couldn't see me. "The cottage is too tiny."

"Good lord, Clare. Sean raised six children there, not to mention our stay with you kids."

"Except there are only two bedrooms, Colin is married, and I have no intention of sharing a room with my brothers. Don't worry; we'll spend plenty of time here. Oh, Mom; wait until you all see the cottage! I bought a wonderful wool rug for the front room. You'll love it."

"You're investing too much on this project." Her disapproving tone rivaled Declan's. "Surely you realize a new owner will bring their own furniture."

"I'm not selling the cottage." The words flew out, like a bird startled from a tree.

"Oh, Clare!" The phone clattered to the table, and she shouted for Daddy. A moment later she spoke again, hissing like a snake. "You're on speaker. Repeat your ridiculous statement."

"Hi, Daddy. I'm not selling the cottage." The words sounded apologetic, like I'd smashed a window with an errant baseball. "We'll keep it in the family and take turns using it for vacations."

"Genius!"

The counterpoint of his enthusiasm did not sway Mom. "Before you two rhapsodize about Irish holidays, may I point out a few weeks of occupancy a year doesn't justify Clare disrupting her life or incurring all this expense."

"Grand-da rented the cottage to pilgrims, we can, too."

"Tourists." Mom huffed the word, implying there were no more nefarious class of humans. "What do you suppose they'll do to your nice furniture and fancy dishes?"

"Use them. Enjoy them. The trust can replace anything they break. Jaysus, Mom! It's just a house."

"Please don't swear!"

The phone clicked off from speaker and a pause indicated Daddy had sent Mom to her corner. "You OK, baby girl?"

I groaned, weary of the lifelong battle for Mom's approval. "Justifications exhaust me."

"She's scared, honey."

"Because a damn nun might pocket a soup spoon?"

"She's worried you're too attached to the cottage."

"I'm not going to marry it." Daddy chuckled, but I wanted to cry. "What's her issue?"

"She's afraid you won't come home at all."

My brow knit, with all the petulance of a three-year-old about to tantrum. "You'd think the prospect would thrill her."

"Enough, Clare." He had my attention; Daddy never took a stern tone with me. "Your defensiveness suggests she's on to something." I heard him breathe and pictured how he'd rub the bridge of his nose while he grappled for words. "It tells me you're wrestling with a decision."

"Daddy, the decision is made."

The call left me disappointed but resolved. The surprising words blurted straight from my soul; the thought nested long before its articulation. Grand-da wanted me to keep the cottage. I'd known it, one way or another, all my life. And whether the family joined me or not, I would return to Killarkin often. The people were dear to me, many were friends. Technology mitigates distance, but I couldn't Skype with St. Dallán's. Without the twinkle in the eye which confirmed the tease, Irish banter wouldn't translate well in an email. An invitation to Moira's wedding with one of the lads wouldn't be near as fun as watching the love affair unfold.

With the lion's portion of the building work complete, Paddy had more time for fussing about minor details, including our ongoing battle over my paint selections. A traditionalist, the idea of a kitchen wall painted sunflower yellow horrified him, and he did not appreciate my plans for the cabinets.

"The Irish painted furniture all the time." I pointed to the linen press, where vivid traces of blue hid in the wood grain.

Paddy's ruddy forehead folded into pleats of consternated woe. "But then ya mean ta put black—of all the colors ya could use—on the grand cupboards Ciarán slaved ta build!"

"Dark green." I pulled a paint chip from my pocket.

Paddy's look of triumph fell when he examined the card. "No difference."

"It will look amazing. And Ciarán helped me choose it."

Paddy shook his head, grabbed a consolatory fistful of scones, and muttered his defeat. "It's yer home."

I flounced toward the kitchen door. "And if you need me, I'll be in *my* barn."

I hadn't spent much time in the dilapidated outbuilding. With Ciarán and Liam engaged elsewhere in the cottage, their makeshift workshop stood silent. Silken afternoon light glowed through the pane-less window at the pitch of the roof. Tumbled stalls ran along one side, dirty straw and sawdust covered the floor. The air smelled of wood shavings, paste wax, and dust underscored by a faint hint of manure. But the space had potential.

Paddy chuckled from the doorway. "Are ya prayin'?"

I sneered over my shoulder. "Assume I am and don't disturb me with design critiques." His guffaw prompted an answering smile. "Paddy, what would it take to get the barn back to rights?"

He laughed with delighted glee. "I wondered when ya would get 'round ta realizin' its neglect." Without further discussion he paced the perimeter caressing stones, tapping posts, and testing windowsills with a penknife. "The roof repaired, a course. Most a them rafters want replacin'. She needs new windows, electrics, and a proper floor." He gestured to the weeds which swayed from cracked stones. "We can tear out the stalls, unless you're thinkin' of more creatures."

"Doubtful. It could be beautiful. And we could turn the loft into a guest space with a couple of bedrooms and a bath."

Paddy patted my head with affection. "It's not everyone who sees a wreck and pictures possibilities. Might take four months or so, but I've a might a work comin' in summer, so anythin' more than minor repairs must wait for autumn. Still, we've nothing but finish work in the cottage, which is Liam and Ciarán's lookout. Jamie and I can start on it, if ya like."

"Yes, please."

Paddy fixed me with a paternal mien. "Gird yerself for battle, darlin'."

"I'll manage Declan."

"And manage some shortbread, too. Jamie ate the last of 'em."

With a reassuring squeeze of his arm I said, "Next stop: The Cosy."

The aptly named tea shop delighted me. Small round tables, with chairs painted bright colors varied as the village doors, sat chummy in the front windows, and ran alongside the counter to a more spacious space behind. White tablecloths, doubtless embroidered by Brigid, and flowers in bud vases unified the décor. Every inch of wall space not consumed by a lace-hung window sported paintings and photographs, mostly of saints or sheep.

The official teatime crowd had not yet assembled, but Saoirse Delaney held court with her daughter-in-law and Diane's four children, who eviscerated scones with shrieks of delight. Nessa occupied a corner table, reading.

My order set Moira to chuckling over Jamie's shortbread addiction and she added the last of the day-old cookies to the box. "No charge. Ya can't run over here every few hours on the eejit's account." As the transaction ended, Nessa glanced my direction and nodded at the empty chair across from her.

The thaw between us had continued. We exchanged polite greetings when we met on the street or in the shops, and sometimes shared a darts game or supper with the O'Donnell brothers. But other than the time she advised me on Declan, we'd never had a private chat. When I joined her, she asked—as everyone did—about the cottage.

"Five or six weeks and it's done."

With a phlegmatic expression she said, "Then you'll be returnin' home."

"Not right away. Grand-da's funeral is in August." Two plausible statements, which struck my own ear as unrelated. They brushed the truth but didn't sum the whole.

Saoirse and Diane herded out the babies, apologizing for the crumbs, while Nessa fiddled with a teaspoon. "Ya should know, Seamus helped me ta open my practice. He outfitted the surgery." The admission gladdened me, and not because it provided any payback for her heiress remark. "We both lost little sisters. He understood my need ta help."

Had anyone else in the village said the same, I would have taken their hand; but Nessa wasn't like other Killarkins. "I'm so sorry; about your sister, I mean, not Grand-da's support."

"I specialized in cancer because of Annie, seein' how her doctors did their damnedest and her a wee thing of four." Nessa's face flickered with passion. "But my time with Doctors without Borders lit a spark and havin' a practice allowed for the whole of care. I could bring folk into the world, ease them out in their dyin', and tend all the necessary bits in-between. Seamus made my dream possible. The man had a gift for bringin' people home."

She hadn't revealed such personal information before. Glimpsing more of her heart and knowing her connection to Grand-da further shifted the emotional ground between us. "Thanks for telling me."

"It's no secret," she said, with a slight lift of her shoulder.

"You trusted me; it means a lot."

Stirring with affection, tears might have followed, but Jamie loomed in the doorway and cast a starved glance at the pasty box. "It's tea-time, Clare. Ya comin'?"

"Yep. Bye, Nessa."

She returned my smile. "*Slán*, Clare."

The gardens transformed in May. From a wealth of auburn leaves and new growth, rosebuds appeared. All the vegetable seedlings, tended with care since March, rooted into the kitchen garden and passed their days converting sunlight into vines and blossoms.

Similar signs of renewal abounded within me: a new-found certainty about what I knew and cared about and, more miraculous yet, a blissful lack of concern about all which remained a mystery. I also possessed new practical skills.

Under Maeve's tutelage my cooking improved, though replicating the fine crumb of her shortbread remained elusive. My gardening skills did not yet rival my mother's, but nothing had perished, either. And in addition to strong, if basic, carpentry skills, Liam taught me to refinish furniture.

I discovered the sensuous pleasure of applying paste wax to dry wood and buffing until it shone; mewing with euphoric satisfaction each time an old, dull piece of furniture transformed into something shimmering and alive with family history. A cradle with only one rocker, however, required more. I showed it to Ciarán. "What do you think?"

"I'm flattered, Miss Riordan, but we've known each other such a brief time."

I swung my hair forward over a rising tide of red. "Feck off. Can you repair it?"

Ciarán knelt beside the little bed and, with his attention diverted, I pressed cool palms to my burning face, envying the cradle as he ran his fingers over the peaked headboard, addressing the wood like a sentient being. He read its grain, stroked the surface, and pondered its construction. "Oak and pine. It's fine workmanship. I wonder if aul Sean built this."

I addressed the floor, my breath coming in shallow puffs. "No way of knowing but I'm romantic enough to hope so."

"Well, there's no sign of worm, so there's a blessin'. I can repair it easy enough." He stood and grinned, hands on his hips. "But it's time ya learned ta run a lathe."

I beamed from ear to ear. He could attribute any residual pink to excitement. "You trust me with power tools?"

"Ah, darlin'. If the mere promise lights ya so, it's worth the risk."

"Too eager?"

He cupped my cheek with a sweet smile, which did nothing to slow my breathing. "You're passionate. There's a difference."

Every salvageable item became precious; consecrated by work-worn hands, and in restoring them, I took my place alongside my forebearers. I became a student and gave a damn about practice. My lathe skills might never ascend to the level of table legs and chair spindles, but I managed bowls and cups. They were enough to leave my mark, alongside Sean's cradle and Mary's oven. One day my own granddaughter might stand in the cottage, point out a cherrywood salad bowl with a slight wobble and say, "My Nana Clare made this." The mythical granddaughter did not sound American. Her voice had all the tender, lilting music of Irish.

The thought exhilarated me, pulsing strong and steady with its rightness. It took more than twenty years to claim my legacy but upon doing so, I pledged to nurture it in the next generation. My children would know the cottage and Grand-da's stories. They would understand our love for this place. One of them might fall in love with one of Moira's kids and the familial roots would sink even deeper, bringing the family story full circle.

On a fair Sunday morning I phoned Edie from St. Dallán's. "Listen to this." I held the mobile above my head a moment before pressing it again to my ear. "Isn't it amazing?"

"I thought the call dropped."

"Hon, it's the literal sound of silence. My hamster wheel has gone quiet, too."

Edie chortled. "Stay there a while; make sure it takes."

"I've had similar thoughts, none of which came at three a.m. and kept me awake until dawn. Hon, I'm in love."

"Let me guess. You realized the lawyer isn't half bad." I snorted. "Then it must be the dishy brother with the ginger curls, gorgeous blue eyes, and cheekbones for days."

"Edie, I love Ireland."

"I know; the quiet, the pub, the bluebells. You talk about Ireland the way other women talk about sex." Then she drew a sharp breath. "How long?"

Despite the sun, a chill shiver ran through me. Crossing the threshold didn't frighten me, naming the intention did. "A while longer."

"Clare Maureen Riordan—"

I inhaled. "Indefinitely."

She chuckled. "I'd better ship the rest of your clothes."

"If you don't mind."

She stopped laughing. "You're serious." After a gulping pause she said, "I told Aimee this would happen."

"How could you know? It hit me like a bolt of lightning."

"Bolts illuminate what's already there. You *have* fallen in love. You didn't bail after the first rush of infatuation, but kept on to the real, inevitable thing."

Face lifted toward the sky, the peaceful accuracy of her words sank in. "I loved the cottage when I first saw her and ever since returning, there have been little signs, nudging me along."

"The cottage freed you." Edie dropped her voice. "Is it possible to be surprised and totally not at the same time?"

"It must be. I'm stunned but certain."

"What about Denise and Ewen?"

"Mom will lose it, but what's new? I'll tell them when they visit. Swear you won't spill the tea."

"On my honor."

"And for the record, I never called Ciarán a dish."

Edie sniggered; she knew me too well. "No, but you've drawn quite a picture. Do you still regard him with objective detachment?"

I slouched against the wall and a moan of longing joined the breeze. "No, but it's wonderful having him as a friend." My strategy for maintaining said friendship lay in ignoring the flutters sometimes provoked by our random moments of intimacy; my bud of self-assurance didn't yet extend to a confident ability to interpret those fleet exchanges with accuracy. "Let's not talk about him; it's confusing."

Her voice lost its snark. "You have time to figure it out, hon."

I arranged a time with Declan to discuss the barn and arrived to find Garbhán sprawled in one of the office chairs. He wore a smug grin whereas my solicitor appeared to have spent the morning sucking lemons.

"Is this an inconvenient time?"

"Ya have an appointment. We're done here." Declan gathered a stack of papers, giving his friend a dismissive nod.

Garbhán oozed past me, pressing closer than necessary. "Lookin' well, Clare." His deep voice made me shudder, as if I'd stepped barefoot on a slug. "Ya must show me 'round your castle one day soon."

I closed the door behind his unpleasant snicker.

"Not here with another crisis, are ya?" Declan said, his impatience obvious.

The corner of my mouth twitched with nerves. "No, but if you would please make another transfer to the reno account."

He squinted. "If there's no trouble with the house—"

"Paddy's going to fix the barn."

His eyes widened, staring like I'd blithely confessed being a serial killer. "Why bother?"

"To improve the property value."

"The trust is—"

"For 'any improvements or ventures Ms. Riordan deems appropriate'. I've read the will."

He shot a glance at the back of his door, long lashes shrouding his thoughts. "There's no time before ya return ta America."

"Paddy's schedule is the issue, not mine."

Declan chuckled, wagging his head. "Ya and your whims." Mustering calm I repeated the request. Giving his papers a smart whack, he filed them in a drawer and said, "I'll need a budget, then."

Stifling a groan, I set my jaw firm. "No delays this time. My attorney assures me this is within my rights."

He blanched and ceased his organizational fussing. "I'm your solicitor."

"You're my Irish representative. The lawyer who drew up Grand-da's will also advises me." I slid a piece of paper across the desk. "This is Paddy's estimate. Add an extra ten thousand, for good measure."

Declan conceded; his irises faded to a weary sage green. "I'll see ta it in the morning."

Chapter Twelve

I N ADDITION TO FLOWERS and revelations, springtime brought
weeds. Meadow grass, chickweed, and a dozen other varieties
ruled the garden plot for decades and would not cede land rights
without a fight. Every afternoon I battled nature and, in the process,
developed a taste for the bitter earthiness of dandelion greens;
nothing proved my upper hand like a well-dressed salad.

One afternoon, a week after the meeting with Declan, I toiled for
dominance—and supper—when a squat shadow loomed over me.
My stomach flopped. "Never thought ta see the likes of ya scrabblin'
like a field hand," Garbhán said.

"Back so soon?"

"Been in Tullamore these last few days and on my way back ta the
Pale now. But the road ta Killarkin pulls on a man. Can't drive past
without stoppin'."

"Don't let me keep you." I rose, dusting my hands.

"No way of knowin' when I'll next have time for a tour."

Unannounced guests were common place, but his presumption
irritated me. "It's a mess."

"I don't mind." He stood firm, showing no intention of leaving.

With reluctance I led him through the kitchen door, knowing
Ciarán and Liam were installing cabinets. Their presence lifted some
of my foreboding.

"I hope ya don't have a money pit here." Garbhán craned his thick neck, examining the chimney. Ciarán scowled.

"Being old doesn't make her a disaster," I replied, protective.

"Still, it's a lot for a young one ta be saddled with."

The sooner he got his tour, the sooner he'd leave and take his arrogance with him. Striding into the living room, I gestured toward open studs, paint cans, and stacks of lumber. "This is, well, what it is." The door to the back room stood open, revealing my furniture purchases. "The other room will be a guest room slash office, but right now it looks like a charity shop. Hardly worth turning off the highway."

"What's upstairs?" The question had an impertinent, lascivious tone.

"A fresh varnished floor. It's off limits."

Garbhán nodded. "Ya must find it enjoyable bein' surrounded by all these young bucks."

I sniffed at the offensive insinuation. "You've seen all there is to see. If you'll excuse me—"

"Now, Clare," he said, his voice dropping to a whispered purr. "You're settlin' in, makin' friends. I could be your friend, too. We're overdue for a chat. Go put on a fetchin' dress, and we'll go ta Dublin for a proper supper." He sidled close and pawed my arm with a sweaty hand.

I wrenched away, my stomach churning. "You should go."

"Now, ya liked me fine ta start. Give me a chance and you'll like me even better."

He reached toward me again, I sidestepped his outstretched hand, hissing. "Leave. Now."

Ciarán appeared in the doorway. A tiny narrowing of his eyes betrayed his otherwise insouciant posture. "Everything alright, Clare?"

"Dandy." I lifted my chin toward Garbhán like a sea captain giving orders. "He's leaving."

The man reddened with anger but retained his swagger. "Another time then; when you're less distracted." He winked and exited through the kitchen.

His departure didn't pacify me and I peeked through a front window until his stout form swashed beyond the garden gate and headed up The High. Ciarán made to speak but I shot past him and banged toward the back door. "We're heading ta the pub soon," he called after me.

"Not tonight."

Nothing happened, nor could it have with a house full of workers. But the incident left me sickened and angry. It took an hour of furious weeding to restore my calm.

"I brought ya cider."

Swinging around, I accepted the bottle with a grimy hand. "Why aren't you at the pub?"

"I reckoned ya needed a friend." Ciarán folded onto the ground, his back against a rowan trunk, and patted the grass beside him. "Come sit where it's cool."

Joining him in the leaf-dappled light, I heaved a freeing breath. "I love these trees."

"The Celts revered them."

Lapis bits of sky blinked through the breeze-blown leaves. "They're comforting; like sentinels on watch."

"Nothin' bad will happen here, darlin'. You've swept away any of the lingerin' unhappiness." He surveyed the garden. "Though I reckon Garbhán put ya out." His fingers curled into a fist. "Wise of him, leavin' when he did."

"What did you hear?"

"Unpleasant mutterin'. Did ya mind me steppin' in?"

"Not a bit."

Ciarán nudged my arm. "I'm well aware ya can manage yourself."

"But if I'd needed you—"

"He would have had his pan knocked in on your behalf and the other women he ever treated so."

Every tense muscle relaxed, leaving me feeling like an oven-fresh pudding. "Thank you. But it's difficult imagining you beating up anyone."

Ciarán glowered, as if Garbhán stood before him. "Sure, it would have been a first; but I'd have enjoyed it."

"You're a good friend. Do you wanna stay for supper?"

He stood, made a little bow, and offered a hand up. "Delighted."

We retrieved my basket of greens and went into the kitchen. While he made salad, I concerned myself with the entrée. Soon lamb chops sizzled in the skillet and when prodded with a fork, they gushed pink juice. The impulsive chicken coop dinner excepted, I'd never cooked for anyone. I glanced at Ciarán, whisking oil and vinegar with all the confidence of someone who grew up in a pub. He wouldn't get a five-star meal but, owing to Maeve, he didn't risk food poisoning, either.

We worked side-by-side, wearing tiny smiles. The only sounds were the brush of his whisk, the chop of my knife through young mint, and Ciarán sometimes humming a tune. The easy peace of it glowed in my heart.

"May I tell you a kooky story?"

He opened a bottle of wine and fetched two glasses. "We Irish love all sorts of stories."

"Splash a bit in the pan, please." He obliged and my belly quivered as his arm grazed mine. A fragrant cloud rose when the wine hit the hot iron. I diverted myself with deglazing, then enriching the pan juices with a knob of butter. While stirring, I shared the vision of my great-grandmother and Sean. "It reminded me love used to live here."

"Your connection ta the aul place would please Seamus."

"Hope so. It's all for him." I speared the finished chops onto a platter and bathed them with glossy sauce. "We're ready."

Ciarán brought the salad to the table and arranged himself on a chair. "Surely there's somethin' in it for ya as well."

Our wine glasses touched, emitting a tiny ping. "Must be. Selfishness is an art form with me."

"I've not noticed."

"Then you're not paying attention."

Ciarán assumed his knife and fork. "Yes, I am."

The 'yes' struck a beat straight into my core. Most Irish replied with a restatement rather than articles like 'yes' and 'no.' My breath grew shallow, and I rolled a pea across my plate. "I live in my head a lot."

"You're human." Ciarán sliced into his chop, chewed a bite, and nodded with approval.

"Being here has taught me so much, about myself most of all, but what if those lessons don't take?"

The knowing curve of his lips cued he would say something wise. "It's amazin' how thoughtful folk are never harder on anyone than themselves. Hold yourself gentle, darlin'. There's a fine line between contemplation and obsession. Cross it and ya defeat the purpose of the exercise."

"Damn, you should have been a priest."

The soft clucks of the hens provided dinner music; the lowering sun stood in for candlelight. We enjoyed our meal, accompanied by wide-ranging conversation and laughter. When our plates emptied, I suggested we go to the pub.

"Let's stay here, where it's quiet."

"Whiskey?"

"Please." He rose and gathered dirty dishes. "But after we clean up; ya know my views on the subject." As we worked, twilight crept over the garden, turning the sky a rich indigo. "Why did ya sigh?" he asked, draping the washcloth over the sink's rim.

"Did I?"

"Ya did."

I clasped a warm plate to my chest. "The Pacific Northwest is beautiful, but I took it for granted, seldom paying attention to the shift of light or all the shades of blue the sky can be. Now beauty slaps me upside the head every waking minute. It's hard to breathe." I dried the last plate, stacked the dishes on the dresser, and poured our drinks.

Ciarán braced his hands on either side of the sink, peering out the window. I nudged him with his glass. "What are you looking at?"

He drew his attention back to me. "Beauty." His everlasting grin lit his face as he stroked my cheek. "It is all around us."

The air in my lungs grew thick and I hugged myself, solar plexus throbbing. "Ciarán, may I ask a personal question?"

"Sure."

"Would you tell me about your woman?"

He hopped on the counter and rolled his neck but didn't hesitate, as if he'd decided to share the tale long before the prompt. "Siobhán taught at the parish school where I did my pastoral training. I took ta her straight off because she made me laugh. I like humor in a person." He gave his whiskey a contemplative swirl. "I came to want more than friendship, so ya can imagine the conflict. I nursed an exquisite torture, though I reckon the nobility of my sufferin' appealed most."

"Talk about being hard on yourself. Of course, you struggled. You had a calling to the priesthood."

Ciarán shook his head. "Love is the only callin' and I learned it too late."

I peered at him, sheepish. "Declan told me she died."

He exhaled, darkening with remembrance. "She had her class outside for playtime. A motorcyclist lost control and barreled into the yard. With mad instinct she threw herself in front of the children. I heard 'em, screamin' like the banshees they were, and ran outside. I held her while she died, pourin' out my heart, and her past hearin'. I wept out all my feeble love and couldn't even think ta pray."

"That's prayer enough." My whisper fell into the deeper hush of the room, my spirit flooding with a profound ache for the brave woman who died and the dear man who mourned her. My eyes welled and I struggled, then failed, to find words rich enough to offer. "I'm so sorry."

"Thank ya, darlin'." Ciarán stretched his long legs and stood. "There it is. I had too much pride for the priesthood and where there had been one woman, there'd no doubt be others." He quirked his head with an awkward smile. "Hubris and a disinclination for celibacy are wretched qualities in a priest." He crossed his arms and examined the scuffed toe of his work boot.

The sacred weight of his trust made me tender. "I'm honored you told me."

"Ah, Clare. I'd prefer givin' ya with a better impression, but it's impossible ta keep the truth from ya."

Crossing the room, I embraced him. We held one another light and wordless; when we pulled apart, we smiled; our friendship sealed.

Though I inherited my mother's round chin and narrow hips, her impeccable organizational skills appeared nowhere in my DNA. But pilgrim season neared, impacting the two people with key roles in Grand-da's funeral. Determined not to procrastinate, I began with Father Donovan.

His office had the aspect of a cloister. The stone walls were bare, save for a large crucifix behind the desk. Floor to ceiling bookshelves on one wall contained thick theological tomes and assorted prayer books.

A faint scent of incense perfumed the room, even though the sacristy lay on the other side of the church. Father gave me a cup of tea and a thin pamphlet on the funeral mass. "If ya would be so kind ta select the readings and Psalm. Take your time but have them ta me two weeks before the celebration."

Despite my familiarity with liturgical nomenclature, it seemed an odd word for the event. Grand-da hadn't suffered the slow decline which allowed time to prepare and accept, even welcome, the release from pain. We had no time for good-byes. His first service felt surreal; in part due to shock, but also because it didn't reflect the whole of him. I couldn't celebrate his passing, but this time he'd get the Mass and wake he would have wanted.

"Could we sing "Be Thou My Vision"?"

"Aul Seamus' favorite, eh? T'would be fittin', indeed. It's often attributed ta St. Dallán, ya know."

A wry smile twitched my lips. "He mentioned it one or two million times. Could we sing it in Irish?"

Father raised his dulcet tenor voice and sang the first words of the hymn. "*Bí Thusa 'mo shúile a Rí mhór na ndúil...*" He broke off with a self-conscious cough and impish wink. "Most folk know the first verse in Gaeilge. And those who don't will fake it."

After solving the liturgical piece of the puzzle, the focus turned to the main event and a discussion with Maeve. "We'll invite the whole village and have lots of music and food..."

"I'm familiar with wakes," she said, stirring one of her cauldrons.

"Sure. But it's important to do this right. Mom planned his memorial in Seattle. All quite nice, mind you, because everything she does is perfect. But Vivaldi, chardonnay, and chicken salad do not qualify as a wake."

Maeve smiled, beatific. "Don't fret, darlin'. I swear ta ya, we'll give Seamus a celebration worthy of his life."

"Including a keen."

She sprinkled a pinch of salt into the pot. "Oh, now, keenin's not done anymore."

Given my previous experience with the tradition, my crushed disappointment astonished me. "But Grand-da would have wanted it."

"It died out decades ago. How Seamus ever found someone ta keen over aul Sean I'll never know." Then she grew thoughtful. "Though I admit missin' it, myself. It's a fittin' thing, howlin' your grief ta God, and we lost somethin' in lettin' the tradition go, I do think. But ya know, darlin', keenin' isn't all mournin'; it allows the departed soul ta move on. Are ya ready ta loose Seamus?"

Tears sprang up, a profound response to a simple question, and I blew my nose on a tea towel before answering. "It's hard not to have someone top of mind when you're occupying their childhood home."

"Nor should ya not think on him. Lettin' go doesn't mean forgettin'." Maeve put her hands on my shoulders, her eyes soft as moss. "You've honored Seamus with every blessed thing you've done since ya arrived. Part a lettin' go is considerin' your own sweet self and the life you're breathin' now. You'll always hold the shape of him in your heart; ya honor his memory in how ya live your life without him." She bussed my cheek and turned back to her stove.

With the essentials in place, I phoned the folks to report in and asked Daddy to select the readings. Mom, of course, worried about the reception.

"It will be a proper wake, a lot like Sean's; except there won't be a keen."

"Good. It's a lot of pagan nonsense."

Her dismissal of the practice offended me. "It's a beautiful tradition and lost now. It's a privilege to have heard one."

"Even though it scared you to death?" Daddy asked, with a chuckle.

I harrumphed. "Everything is scary when you're five."

Mom had no patience for teasing and steered us back to our agenda. "Clare, you need to reserve a hall, hire a caterer…"

"We'll have it here, in the cottage, and there will be plenty to eat." Given her weird jealousy toward Maeve and general lack of faith in my abilities, I omitted the catering details. "Paddy will see to the live music and Colin is building a play list for the breaks."

"Goodness!" Mom said, with genuine surprise. "I expected you'd leave everything until the last minute."

I swam past her bait. "We'll give Grand-da a good old Irish send-off."

"Music, drink, and food," saidDaddy. "It's the way of our people."

"And everyone off with the fairies." Citing one of Grand-da's favorite phrases made me giggle.

With a pious sniff Mom said, "It's inappropriate to encourage drunkenness at a funeral."

A bus lumbered up the High, then disgorged a group of tourists. They clustered on the sidewalk outside the pub, snapping photos of Michael and his flock wandering toward the hills. Pilgrim season had commenced.

Nora Fannin, a pretty, blonde copy of her older sister, who boarded in Tullamore while she attended second level school, returned home. She and Moira, with the precision of synchronized swimmers, divided their time between the tea shop and the tiny visitors center in the post office, where pilgrims could learn about St. Dallán and take away a pamphlet on the venerable, quirky history of Killarkin. I dog-eared the page devoted to Seamus and mailed a copy to Daddy.

The village schedule changed. Shops opened an hour earlier so residents could tend to family business and leave the shank of the day, and longer lines, to pilgrims. The decibel level rose in the shops and the pub, even on the street, where cars and bicycles jostled for passage and limited parking space.

I offered to increase my kitchen hours with Maeve, a suggestion which engaged us in a variation of the tea ritual. "Now, darlin', there's no call—though I do appreciate the kindness of the offer and don't believe otherwise—but I've managed all these years, and ya have more than enough ta do."

"The cottage is almost finished; I'll have time."

"But I can't ask ya…"

"You didn't. I offered."

We went one more round before she relented, with gratitude.

Even with the reno ending, I had plenty of cottage projects. Upon the delivery of a large bale of Irish lace, Moira offered to help make curtains. She arrived one Sunday afternoon with a biscuit tin tucked under her arm. "You didn't need to bring treats," I said. "You're wasting a day off to help me."

She brandished the tin with a confused expression and said, "This is my sewin' kit. And it's no waste; more like a blessed relief. Now Nora's back, she and Ma go at it somethin' rotten."

With a sympathetic mutter I said, "My mom and I don't get on well, either."

Moira's eyes rounded with curiosity. "What does she find wrong with ya?"

"Everything. After two boys, she wanted a sweet, tiny replica of herself. Instead, she got a gangly limbed, ginger tomboy. She stresses because I haven't settled on a career or a man, even though she wouldn't approve of my choices anyway."

Moira's head bobbed with recognition. "Ma's the same, though Nora gets it worse, plannin' on uni and all. I reck some mams can't bear their children leavin' home." She ruminated on her statement then asked, "What does yours make of ya doin' over the cottage?"

"You get one guess."

Moira grinned and settled into Grand-da's chair. "I reckon your ma and mine would be fast friends. Now, let me show ya how ta hem a curtain." She demonstrated picking the delicate lace with the tip of the needle before whipping careful stitches. She scrutinized my tentative first attempt before taking up her own lace, then proceeded to hem two panels in the time it took me to finish one.

"You're as good as your mom with a needle," I said, a bit jealous.

Moira bit off a thread. "It's a necessary chore; I don't love it like she does."

I scowled at my handiwork. "It's wonky. Should I rip it out?"

"Give it here." She squinted, then held the lace high. "What do ya see?"

"A shite curtain."

Her mouth pulled straight in remonstrance. "It drapes well. Ya couldn't tell it from one of mine."

"Not from here, anyway."

Moira handed me another panel and returned to her chair. "If someone in your bedroom has no better business than inspectin' curtain hems, ya have bigger troubles."

Chapter Thirteen

Aⁿccording to the villagers, the first days of June were unseasonably warm, but partly sunny days with temperatures in the low sixties didn't strike me as unusual. Still, we kept the windows open for the comfort of the crew, and to clear the odors of varnish and paint.

The weather thrilled Paddy, as he deemed it ideal for the week's plastering agenda. I watched entranced while he and Ciarán finished the bedroom walls. Their strong hands wielded the trowels like paintbrushes, smoothing the plaster, then flicking their wrists to create a delicate texture.

"I believe ya have cabinets ta paint, miss," Ciarán said.

Shaking off my reverie I saluted. "Yes, sir."

"I'll come help soon."

I returned downstairs and applied a first coat of glossy paint, green as a forest pine, to the primed frames and short spindled legs of the cabinets, then started on the unattached doors ranged on sawhorses. Ciarán soon joined me, taking up a paintbrush of his own. "All done?"

"Paddy's finishin' up." He stood opposite me and started painting another door. "So, he's acquiesced ta your color scheme."

"It pains him, but he got his white everywhere else." Taking a break to stretch my back, I admired the freshly painted back wall. "Imagine this room, all bright with morning sun, glowing by candlelight in the evening."

"It'll be homely, indeed."

I bristled with defensiveness. "It will be beautiful!"

Ciarán laid a calm hand on my cheek, laughing. "I forgot Americans use the word another way. Here it means cosy and home-like, as ya intend."

"Oh, right. Sorry for the outrage."

"Your loyalty is appropriate, darlin'." He resumed his work. "Your cottage will be homely and a fair bit quieter, too."

A sad exhale acknowledged the impending change. "It will be weird not having you all here."

Ciarán snickered. "Odd you're waxin' nostalgic about havin' your house torn up."

My heart stirred with tiny pulses, like a hatchling nudging the inside of its shell. "It might be boring."

He made an amused snort. "No fear, darlin'. Pilgrim season is plenty lively. And about the time we grow weary of it, they disappear, we go back ta our ways and start planning the *céilí*. You've never seen such a thing. Dancin', drink, and carryin' on 'til dawn. There'll be many a hangover, one or two black eyes, and nine months later, several babbies."

"Sounds like the craic," I said, intent on my work.

Ciarán chuckled with the indulgence he granted whenever I used Irish slang or swears. "Thick in the winter, after months on our best behavior, we're ready ta misbehave. Shame you'll miss it."

"I might not." His brush ceased moving and he stared, one eyebrow arched.

"Do I have paint on my face?"

He smiled, brighter than usual. "Ya do. I'm also curious what ya mean."

Another heart-peck registered, then stilled as I glanced around the kitchen with pure affection. "Maeve hasn't finished my lessons, and neither have you; my bowls still wobble. My darts game isn't near good enough to beat Paddy when he's sober, and I have a sudden, overwhelming desire to dance at my first *céilí.*"

"A fine list of goals. Remember ta leave room for the unexpected."

The statement struck me funny; every bit of the last five months came as a surprise. "Like you and Dec getting the band back together?"

"The unexpected, darlin', not the impossible. I should never have mentioned it." Ciarán rocked back on his heels and scrutinized the paint job. "This will do for today. If ya don't have plans tomorrow, I'd like ta take ya on a picnic."

The morning came soft, and I met Ciarán in front of the cottage with my bike and a lunch basket. We whizzed away from Killarkin on narrow, winding roads. Potholes—or lack of any pavement at all—required dexterity and quick thinking, but we rode six kilometers in a light, refreshing drizzle which cleared by noon.

He slowed, pointing toward the hulking remains of a castle. "What do ya say ta restin' there?"

"Picnic worthy; without question."

We coasted off the road and up a grassy dirt lane. I stood on the pedals to gain traction, groaning as my thighs burned with the effort.

"We can walk in if you'd rather."

Dropping my feet to the ground, I straddling the bike while my chest pounded. "Yes, please."

When we gained the top of the hill I wheezed, and not from exertion. "Is this a thin place?"

"Ya tell me." We rested our bikes against a tree, ambled toward a fence, and viewed the ruined pile beyond. Dense ivy obscured most of the walls.

"How old is it?"

"Built somewhere in the fourteen-hundreds. I reckon the ivy and moss hold together what's left."

"It's beautiful." A herd of cows grazed in front of the castle, their lowing and the rustle of breeze-blown leaves made a toneless melody. "Let's go in."

Ciarán gestured toward a posted warning sign. "We're not supposed ta."

"Do you always follow rules?"

He laughed, and a huge black animal raised his head and regarded us with large, liquid eyes. "We'll have ta get past the bull, who appears none too inclined toward visitors. We'll eat first, safe on this side. If we appear disinterested, he may take a likin' ta us." We laid the blanket under the spreading branches of a huge alder. Ciarán threw himself down on one elbow, stretching one arm to the sky. "What an amazin' breeze."

I placed a sandwich in his upraised hand. "Please don't mock what you're about to hear."

"I'll behave."

I clasped gleeful hands over my cheeks. "We're picnicking in the shadow of a castle!" Ciarán couldn't resist a chuckle. "Of course it's silly to a European, surrounded as you are by so much ancient history."

"Ya have your Indigenous peoples."

"Sure, but the remaining evidence of them is scant and on protected land. You can't casually cycle around and stumble onto a cave dwelling or the like. You have to search it out. And even our more recent history doesn't compare to yours. Hell, the cottage is older than most of the buildings in the US."

"Well, I'm sincere in sayin' it's delightful ya appreciate it."

I reclined on the blanket with a groan. "It's so green here; Ireland has taught me the true meaning of verdant."

We lay in silence a bit, present to beauty, then, as if jerked by strings, sat up and tore into our sandwiches, ravenous from exercise. Ciarán paused his chewing and said, "Tell me what else you've learned."

"The magic of quiet. At first, I missed white noise. Here, stillness is the background with every sound unique, not mashed into a meaningless racket. It took adjustment."

"Your thoughts seem louder."

"Now you mention it."

Ciarán twiddled a bread crust between his fingers, pulling off bits and tossing them toward heard but unseen birds. "Ya said the other evening you're too much in your head. I reckon for the first time ya can hear yourself, is all." He dusted crumbs from his fingers and nodded toward the castle. "Bulls and official notices be damned. Let's dare it."

We climbed over the fence, stepping with care over loose rocks and around cow pats, then ducked through the open arch of the castle ruin. A shaft of sunlight, brilliant with a billion dancing motes, illuminated a wide, worn stone staircase. No roof remained but cerulean sky.

"Is the stair solid?"

"I reckon not much else is." Despite his assurances, a butterfly wing of nerves tickled my belly as Ciarán guided me by the hand. We climbed the stairs to a crumbled window which overlooked the countryside.

The phone remained in my pocket. No photograph could capture the full glory of the vista before us. Moss green pastures contrasted with the ruddy brown of plowed fields misted with the chartreuse of sprouted crops. In a crystal sky scattered with silver puffs of cloud, the sun lit the view with an alluring shimmer. My breath stopped and I turned from the window, a hand on my chest.

"A beauty ache?"

"Yep." The view overwhelmed, but I turned back to take in more.

Ciarán smiled, swathing an arm around me. "Where is heaven?"

"Right here." I leaned against him; the comfortable posture demonstrated all the ease of our friendship. Then his hand tightened on my shoulder and the world tilted. It felt like an earthquake except the seismic shift occurred within me. We surveyed the lush valley, and my pulse quickened with the work of my heart. The song of a greenfinch floated through the air and twined with Paddy and Nessa's words: *It's your home. Seamus had a gift for bringin' people home.*

I couched my decision to stay in careful language, evasive words like 'indefinitely' and 'a while'. My breath grew deeper as the absolute truth declared itself. Home beat here, in Ireland. Certainty spiraled in my belly and pooled in my heart with hallowed, sure calm.

"Thank you for bringing me here."

"Ya brought yourself, darlin'."

The truth of it hushed me. Saying 'yes' to the cottage set my foot upon a long-sought path. Enchantment wrapped around me and for long, silent minutes, I took in the blue and green of where I belonged.

Then, with a finger lighter than a bird wing, Ciarán lifted my chin and kissed my mouth.

The honeyed pleasure of it made me gasp and he stepped away; arms crossed over his chest like he held something from bursting out. "Did I do wrong?"

"You couldn't. We've known each other from the dawn of forever."

"*Anam cara.*" The words sounded like prayer. "Our souls recognized one another."

I leaned against the wall with caution; fearful my thudding pulse would collapse the archaic walls around us. "You're a beautiful man, Ciarán; and wiser than your years. Is it possible to have a thin place in yourself? Because my mind is still catching up, but my soul knows everything." I clasped his fingers and held his hand against my pounding chest. "Here's where they meet."

In a voice so deep and tender it vibrated through me, he posed a simple question. "Will ya be with me, Clare?"

I released his hand; he left it on my chest one lingering moment, then drew it away. In the space of a breath, I wrestled the temptation to gloss over the moment, but we were far beyond games now. "You've been honest with me; it's my turn. I'm shite at relationships. The idea of screwing up with you is unbearable."

He turned his attention out the window. "So, ya reckon friends can't be lovers." The last word jolted, an aftershock on the heart.

"How silly and counterintuitive. Trouble is, I've never managed before and am not sure it would be any different with you." I took his hand again, squeezing as if the pressure would communicate both my desire and fear. "Something always holds me back in relationships. Whether it's a case of having too many expectations or not enough isn't clear, but you deserve better. Let me sort it out so I have a chance to do right by you."

"Then you're not rejectin' me outright."

"I accepted you the day we met."

A triangle of birds sliced the azure sky with charcoal wings, and he drew me close. My ear lay on his heart, which beat rapid as my own. "I like ya too much not ta remain friends either way. Ya set the pace, darlin'." With a steady hand on my cheek, he kissed me again; a sweet, resolute pressure and nothing more. "Let's find a pint."

We pedaled away from the castle and toward Killarkin with Ciarán in the lead, singing snatches of trad tunes or pointing out landmarks and other objects of interest. I envied his ability to ride along as if we'd shared nothing but sandwiches because I could barely steer straight, near blind with craving and woe. My valid reasons for holding back notwithstanding, if my hesitation meant I'd already blown an opportunity with him... Unable to entertain the thought, I concentrated on keeping up with his bicycle.

We had traveled two kilometers when, with an abrupt "This way!" he gestured to his right, swerved onto a narrow, pocked road, and rode toward a small pub.

In a room not much larger than my kitchen, we settled at a corner table with pints of beer and cider, sharing a plate of chips. I peered around, unsettled. "This feels unfaithful."

"Da needn't know ya saw another pub on the side."

A barmaid hovered nearby, her pretty face frank with appreciation for my companion. Pressing my lower lip to the rim of my glass I said, "You have an admirer."

Ciarán rubbed his chin. "Don't be jealous."

"I'm the one having a drink with you. *I'm* the one, god help me, you kissed."

"If ya like, consider the kiss as a courtesy; ya can't make decisions without all the facts."

Laughing with a mouthful of cider rendered me incapable of an immediate reply. "Golly. No one has ever kissed me out of altruism. Dec's right: you are a saint, and I'll build you a shrine where despairing maidens can pray for true love."

He chuckled and raised one eyebrow. "Ya can visit it yourself."

"I'm neither despairing nor a maiden."

He sobered. "Clare, do ya regret the kiss?"

"Kisses. And no." Despite my sincerity, my cheeks flushed.

"Nor do I." Ciarán brushed my cheek with the back of his fingers. "It seemed natural as breathin'."

The barmaid appeared at his elbow, a hand on her hip. "Will ya be havin' another?"

He kept his eyes on mine, whispering low. "I hope so." Then louder he replied, "We'll be goin' on home."

The girl gave a saucy toss of her head when we rose to leave. "Yer welcome back anytime."

When we reached the cottage, late afternoon sun slanted over the garden. Ciarán straddled his bike as I parked mine against the wall and offered a glass of whiskey.

"I need a shower; come ta the pub later."

"Tempting, but I've got aching muscles to soak. Will I see you tomorrow?"

With a gentle pinch of my cheek he replied, "Darlin', ya see me every day."

"But especially tomorrow?" Everything pulsed around me, dreamlike. The kiss might have changed everything or nothing, but either way, I needed it tethered to reality.

"I promise."

Sun glared through partial clouds, the air uncomfortable and muggy, though a slight breeze came through the wide-open windows. Once we finished painting all the trims, the renovation would be complete, a fact both delightful and melancholy. Possessed by the latter mood, I flicked my paint brush with impatience.

"You'll make a bags of it if ya don't slow down." With a steady hand on mine, Ciarán guided a careful stroke along the windowsill. "Slow down."

"Yes, sir."

"Jaysus! It's like a sauna." He stripped off his t-shirt and tossed it on the bed.

"Not fair!"

"It's your house; do as ya like." Scowling, I tried to concentrate but couldn't resist envious glances at his naked torso. He applied paint to the new cornice. "I should sell tickets."

"Don't flatter yourself." Then my traitorous eyes sneaked another peek, and a strangled breath choked out.

"What's distractin' ya now? My perfect arse?"

"The scar on your shoulder."

"Got it in a bar fight."

"You're not the type."

"I wonder what sort I am," he said, his back quivering with evident amusement.

Our relationship had changed at the castle; not in essentials, but within me. It brought me more in tune with him, more aware of his layers. The man bore a scar, a long and frightening one, and I realized how many times he used levity to distract from the traumas of his life—those which marked his soul, not his body. He could be serious and unfold his truths to me in ways he didn't with anyone else then pass it off as of no account. I wouldn't allow him to tease past the moment.

I laid down my brush and may have stamped my foot. "You said you'd never been in a fight. Tell me what happened."

Ciarán climbed down the ladder and scrutinized me. "Iraq. Tensions sometimes run high in the camps, ya can imagine. A couple of lads had words, then more words until one of them got his hands on a knife. My shoulder intervened."

The past months spun out like a movie reel, but with every scene involving Ciarán left on the cutting room floor. He might have died before we ever had a chance to meet. His name squeaked past my lips and my heart ticked a thick, alarmed thud.

"It's nothin'. It more glanced than cut me."

He pivoted sideways. I moved close and with my forehead against his back, held his hip, tracing the pale thread which ran along his shoulder blade. Gooseflesh rose behind the touch, and the heat of his skin registered on my fingertips. "It's seven inches long. You're not telling the truth." He stood silent, his breathing heavy. I released him, my own breath ragged. "Tell me what happened."

He turned to me, bearing an expression of unmistakable desire and, more critical in the moment, trust. "I spent a day or so in hospital, but it would be a kindness if ya didn't mention it ta Ma. She'd never let me out of her sight."

Protective ferocity surged within me. "Who'd blame her? You should avoid dangerous places."

He climbed the ladder while his baritone laugh rang through the room. "Can't seem ta help it. I'm in a rare spot of peril here."

"Sure. The lathe might take a finger, or you could fall off a ladder."

He glanced over his shoulder with a smirk. "Ah, well, I'm tumblin' all right. Ladders are the least of my worries."

After work, I went to Fannin's and bumped into Nessa, knocking her shopping basket to the ground. "Jaysus! I'm so sorry!" I knelt to retrieve spilled vegetables. "Thank goodness you didn't have eggs."

"Those were next."

I handed her the basket, still apologizing. "I don't watch where I'm going."

"I'm short and easy ta overlook."

"Not to cut into Cathleen's trade, but my chickens lay more eggs than one person can use. Take some as a peace offering."

"We're not warrin'," she said, with a half-smile.

"Then take them as a gift."

As we walked to the cottage, I mentioned my idea for a housewarming party. "It's more a way to honor the crew than anything. You're welcome to come."

"I didn't help, and I don't like parties."

"It will be like a night at the pub, without darts."

"That's different then."

During my tour of the house, Nessa's head bobbed with approval. "I'd have not known the place."

"We have more painting down here, but we're finished upstairs. Would you like to see?" In my estimation, the two most beautiful places in Killarkin were St. Dallán's and my bedroom. The fresh, open space delighted me. The gorgeous four poster—its oak frame waxed to a high shine—boasted pillowcases trimmed with thick lace and Brigid's beautiful spread. Sunlight through the new curtains cast a delicate filagree of vining patterns against the pure white walls.

Nessa did not gush but her appreciative grunts sufficed. "This is grand." Her finger ran over the dancing row of triskeles which scrolled across the edge of the mantel.

"Ciarán did all the casework. Sorely found these old tiles." I traced the rune with my thumb. "He put one over every fireplace. They're a blessing." I blushed; positive Nessa thought me silly. "I've loved watching such gifted craftspeople work."

"It's been a labor of love. Yours and theirs."

We returned to the kitchen where I wrapped a half dozen eggs, laid them in her basket, and offered tea.

"Don't trouble, I should get on."

Acknowledging her refusal with a nod I said, "I always have a cup around this time."

She stood immobile, the basket on her arm. "I can't stay."

I switched on the kettle. "One cup, then off you go."

Nessa laughed and set down her groceries. "I'll have a scald, then."

Proud of my performance I asked, "How do you take it?"

"*Bainne agus siúcre.*"

"Excuse me?"

"Milk and sugar."

The afternoon sun winked through the windows while I prepared the tray, taking care in arranging the biscuits on their plate; Nessa choosing to stay counted as a particular honor.

Her nose made a dubious twitch. "I'm not terrible fond of Aideen's shortbread. Too dry."

I shook out my napkin, grinning. "These are homemade. I've mastered Maeve's recipe at last."

Her expression didn't change, save for a brief uptick of eyebrow. "You're mates with all the O'Donnell's now."

"Most of them."

She stirred her tea, intent on the swirls in her cup. "I reckon Declan still gives ya trouble."

"He's less of a shite, but I would have liked knowing the once-upon-a-time punk."

Nessa's eyes were soft with distant memory. "*Fadó.* It means long ago. I'd have liked it, too."

Her words hung in the air and every impulse—from American curiosity to deep-seated sisterhood—urged questions. But Nessa held herself in a fortress and my respect for her discretion wouldn't allow a breach.

She nibbled a cookie and gave a brief nod, the Nessa Cassidy sign of approval. "They called themselves the Blatherin' Shites and made a terrible racket. One night, while ossified, Dec played a tape for me."

I clasped my hands in supplication. "Ness, please find it! I'll give you my first-born child."

A wry smile lifted the corner of her mouth. "I've no use for a babby and the music, if ya dare call it so, is pure foul. But since you're keen, I'll check around."

Chapter Fourteen

C IARÁN AND I SAT on the floor, our backs against the couch. Paddy lounged splay-legged in Grand-da's chair. Ciarán nudged him alert when he snuffled a snore. After a massive yawn, he grinned. "Mission accomplished, Clare."

"And a month earlier than planned. I adore every inch of this cottage, except this piece of shite." My smack on the old sofa released a cloud of dust which provoked a succession of sneezes. "It can't go soon enough."

"We'll help ya with it," Ciarán said.

"And I risk rootin' ta this chair if I don't rouse myself." Paddy rose with an emphatic groan. "Down your beer, lad, and we'll finish the job."

After we installed the new living room furniture, I gave Paddy's sweat-glazed cheek a grateful kiss. "Go on with ya," he said. "I can't go about blushin' like a bride."

He ambled toward the gate, and we followed without attempting to imitate his jig. The remarkable lightness of the large man's bearing awed me. "I'll need dance lessons before the *céili.*"

"Oh, most of the trad steps are easy ta follow," Ciarán replied.

"Says the guy whose been doing them all his life."

He paused, his hand on the open gate. "Are ya comin' ta the pub?"

"Not tonight."

"Ya want ta commune with your house." A stream of pure understanding flowed between our locked eyes. He lifted my hand, gave it a graceful turn, and pressed a gentle mouth to my wrist. At the pressure of his lips, a flutter winged up my arm and into my heart.

"Thank you, Ciarán. It wouldn't be half so beautiful without your handiwork."

"I'm the one whose grateful," he said, giving my hand a soft squeeze. "Workin' on it gave me purpose." Our fingers slid apart and Ciarán smiled. "*Slán abhaile*, Clare."

Safe home. Tears budded at the corner of my eyes. He couldn't have said anything more perfect.

Still thrilling from his touch, I re-entered the restored cottage; thrilled by knowing it belonged to me, and I never had to leave it. Like a dew-kissed rose unfurling in the morning sun, I stood open to whatever adventure lay ahead. Every decision and experience from now on laid another block in the life I would build in Ireland.

The house grew close and quiet, as if the walls expanded for the work crew and now contracted to a collection of rooms small enough to again hear the whisper of long-gone voices. I stood a moment in silence, hands crossed over my chest, brimming with gratitude.

With The Cranberries playing in the background, I mixed a batch of brown bread. Then, with the homey fragrance of baking on the air, I pulled tarps from furniture and tidied, eager to arrange my home. The breeze stirred and blew through like a blessing.

My local hero glamor had faded, proven by everyone calling me Clare rather than Miss, and a marked increase in teasing. In a small village which kept few secrets, my friendship with Ciarán had not gone unnoticed and my ability to turn scarlet with little provocation didn't improve matters. Chaff from Moira and the lads didn't bother me much, but other manifestations of interest were less comfortable. Aideen

Fannin took keen note of each purchase of honey cakes. Diane Delaney, who had never spoken more than twelve words to me, designated herself my tutor in Irish housewifery, taking every opportunity to chat about babies. Maeve never outright quizzed me but based on her pleased countenance whenever she spotted me with her son, she'd drawn her own conclusions.

"It's disconcerting," I confessed to Edie.

Her voice shifted into the singsong of an adolescent girl. "Because you like him."

"Of course, I do! But here we are, being circumspect and not rushing, while everyone else assumes we're sleeping together."

"You'd tell me if you were, right?"

"I tell you everything."

"*Are* you going to sleep with him?"

"I don't know!" My cheeks reddened.

Edie snickered without remorse. "Don't blush."

"You are awful annoying sometimes."

"Why? Because, after sixteen years I'm aware you go beet red when you like a guy?"

I had a particular liking for the guy in question and the challenge had little to do with all the attention and more with the risk. I valued our friendship beyond words but my track record with men wasn't any more impressive than my resume. Both histories were magpie nests, filled with bright attempts and sparkling ideals. Once the shine wore off, I flew away, searching out the next brilliant opportunity.

"I don't want to cock it up, Edie."

"Fascinating choice of words. You won't. You're not bringing the same bundle of insecurity and people pleasing into the equation this time. Look at what you've accomplished with the cottage."

"I almost didn't do anything."

"A temporary lapse. You proved you have what it takes to see something through."

"True, but assuming the same will apply in another context might be a stretch."

"Not at all. The reno happened because you gave a shit. If you want to make a relationship with O'Dish work, you will."

Edie made perfect sense, but she'd also assumed an outcome more serious than the circumstances indicated. In the three weeks since the picnic, banter with Ciarán seemed more flirtatious, and my breath sometimes snagged against certain glimpses from the glittering velvet of his eyes. But other than the wrist kiss at the gate, we never touched, never anything romantic, anyway. Ciarán didn't presume based on a couple of kisses, so neither would I.

One evening Paddy sidled into our snug with his dinner plate and announced, "Miz Fallon is right pleased with yer and Liam's work."

"Good ta hear. We'll finish next week."

"Grand; we've the rectory the week followin', and I don't fancy startin' without ya. I trust the cottage is holdin' up, Clare."

"She's so perfect it's hard leaving her."

Paddy chortled, shoveled a scoop of mash into his mouth, and elbowed Ciarán's ribs. "Ya found one or two reasons fer steppin' out."

Ciarán covered for me. "She's determined ta beat ya at darts."

Paddy attempted a frightened shiver, then loosed his lion's roar of a laugh. "Ah, well. Then after supper she'll have an opportunity."

But by the time we finished our meal, Paddy and his fiddle had joined the session, so we played against Moira and Liam instead. "Where's Jamie?" Ciarán asked.

"Moonin' after Nora," Liam replied with a snigger.

Moira made the sort of shudder reserved for disgusting creatures like rats or maggots. "Follows her three paces behind everywhere she goes and how she stands it I don't know."

Liam glanced toward the band where Nora danced with a group of young women while Jamie lurked nearby. "But then, he's not choosy; any lass who speaks ta him will do." He slapped Ciarán's shoulder. "Other men are more discriminatin'."

After the match, Ciarán and I strolled around the village. A soft mist fell, imperceptible until tiny droplets accumulated on our hair and lashes. Our shadows were long in the mauve-hued light. "I've had it with nosy neighbors. Let's have supper at the cottage tomorrow night. If they don't see us together, they won't talk."

My naivete made him snicker. "Oh, they're talkin' either way."

"And nudging ribs with relentless teasing."

"Not ta mention Ma all expectant and cheerful, like her apron pocket holds the banns."

I groaned, all too familiar with the expression. "Since we can't win, you may as well come for supper."

Distant thunder rumbled while a chicken and leek pie baked. I set the table, then showered. My current social life didn't warrant fancy clothes; a uniform of jeans or overalls suited quotidian activities. Though I'd given Ciarán supper before, this first post-renovation meal struck like the oil of confirmation. Donning one of my nicer dresses and troubling to accessorize suited the occasion.

I went outside for flowers and discovered Orla on the garden wall, her tail in an elegant drape over her front paws. "You're a classy cat, miss. They should have called you Audrey Hepburn." She hopped to the ground and strolled toward the stoop, her lithe poise implying she both understood and endorsed the assessment. After fetching her a saucer of cream, my attention turned to cutting roses.

My head swiveled when the gate creaked open, and I beamed with delight as Ciarán whistled up the walk. He wore the white shirt and black vest from the chicken coop supper, obviously best categorized as his "special occasion" ensemble. "Ya and Orla make a homely sight," he said.

"Appropriate, since we couldn't be more at home. Come on in." The first fat drops of rain plashed on the fresh-laid cobble walk and Ciarán helped latch windows before I gave him a glass of wine and pulled the pie from the oven, golden brown and bubbling.

With a broad grin he said, "You're an astonishment. Despite workin' hard all day, there ya are, presentin' a pie, fresh and lovely like ya never lifted a finger. It's a joy ta witness."

"I've sure been in the throes of well-being, lately. But joy is a better word." Over the length of three heart beats, I reflected on the gossamer of happiness, the fleet pleasures which endure no longer than a moment or an hour. The new sensation within felt more like a taproot pushing its way deep, anchored but ever growing. It would take more than a puff of wind to shake it. "Whatever this is, it's a quieter, less giddy state than happiness."

Ciarán gave me one of his comprehending winks and tucked into his meal. "This is delicious. Ma couldn't do better."

"High praise. She taught me everything."

"Ya had the ability; she showed ya the pleasure of it."

Rain pattered against the windows, and the open back door allowed fragrant petrichor to wash through the room. Ciarán gave a contented groan and served himself another helping of pie. "There's little lovelier than rain on dry summer grass."

Conversation came easy, dancing and wending over subjects both personal and general. But before placing another confidence in his keeping I asked, "How are you with secrets?"

"Sad to say, not much better than Ma."

"Edie is the sole other person who knows this one."

He straightened his back and laid aside his fork. "Then I'll hold your sacred trust dear."

"I'm staying in Ireland."

He continued eating. "Ya said so weeks ago."

"To live."

He laid aside his fork and the ocean depths of his eyes were tides of contented gaiety. "Full stop?"

"Yep."

"I warned ya," he said, with a wink.

"Maeve and Ness are decent company."

He pressed my hand. "This is delightful news, though your secret will be in peril once folk 'round here notice ya haven't left."

"Golly, you're astute. This isn't over-the-phone news; I'll tell the family when they're here in August. Everyone in the village knows I'm staying for the funeral, so they won't suspect anything."

Ciarán's expression shone with something unspoken, but he swore to keep quiet. "I'll be curious ta see how your folks take it."

"Daddy will be supportive. Once Mom sees the cottage and has some context, she might understand." My shoulder twitched with acceptance. "Or she won't." While reaching for my wine glass, Ciarán caught my hand, turning it in the candlelight.

"I've not noticed this pretty bauble before."

"It's Grand-nan's wedding diamond. Grand-da had it reset for my twenty-first birthday." I stretched my fingers, admiring the little winks of fire. "He proposed to her in the pub. It's been kept safe since we started the reno, but tonight it seemed appropriate."

"It's come full circle."

"It's home."

Ciarán grew quiet, his attention on my hand. The skin between my shoulder blades warmed and I moved away so he wouldn't be sensible of my heart smacking against my breastbone. His loveliness filled my vision; his easy, gentle grace, the crinkles around his smiling eyes. I covered my mouth, chewing away the maddening impulse to kiss him.

"It's a gift, knowin' where ya belong and holdin' it certain with profound love. The Irish word is *bhaile*. It can mean any place ya live—a town or a cottage—but the poetic sense of it is 'where we come home'."

The perfection of the word swelled within me, and I whispered his name. He turned and without a word we moved closer and my mouth grazed his. His lips played over mine, then he put his hands in my hair and pulled me into a slow, deep kiss.

Time stopped, then his mouth. With my hair still twisted in his fingers he said, "Ya were fair clear about not startin' anythin'."

Ciarán's breath against my cheek turned me to water, but like a child caught mid-mischief, I sat straight. "I'm not."

Cupping my face, his thumbs played a delicate dance over my mouth. "Then explain why ya kissed me so."

"Sorry."

"Altogether the wrong response." He released my head. I concentrated on the cluster of ginger hair below his neck. "Please look at me."

"Better not." Our breath, his rapid but steady and mine uneven, filled the room.

"I'm happy with friendship, Clare. I don't *have* ta kiss ya." He tilted my head, assessing the statement with a gentle exploration of my mouth before pulling away. "There's the trouble. I want more than kissin'. But ya aren't sure."

"I doubt myself, not you. You give my soul a beauty ache." Weightless, I floated toward him, mind blank of anything but the desire to hold him. He came in for another kiss as a powerful knock hammered the front door.

We both cursed as I hopped off his lap and scuttled into the front room, arranging my tumbled hair. "Howya, Liam," I said, with a modicum of dignity. "What brings you by?"

Boisterous and teasing in a group, the young man who waited outside modeled timidity. His cap swung in his hand and his feet tapped with nervous energy. "Sorry ta trouble ya."

"You're not. Ciarán's here for supper. Are you hungry?"

"I could take a bite."

"Then get in here, man, or fight me for the last of it," Ciarán called.

Over pie and a beer Liam explained his errand. "The woman we're workin' for has furniture she needs fixed up, but she don't want the mess of it on site. If it's no bother, I wonder if I might have use of the workshop."

"Of course. Would you like some help?"

Liam's posture softened with relief. "I wouldn't mind it. There's a beast of a kitchen dresser wot will take a week of work on its own."

"I can strip it, unless you'd rather wait until you can supervise."

Liam pushed away his empty plate, emitting a soft belch. "Nothin' like. Ya did a grand job with your own stuff. I'd appreciate the help, so long as I'm not imposin'."

"Not a bit. It will be fun."

Ciarán gave Liam a grin. "I reckon your hopes are comin' ta life."

Liam hunched over the table, borne down under the weight of the idea. "There's a thought too heavy for thinkin' on."

"Ya'd best start. A connection like Miz Fallon can open any number of doors for ya."

The conversation pricked my curiosity. "Will you tell me about it, Liam?"

Shy, but with a glow which signaled the depth of his aspirations, he said. "It's ta do with The Folly; the pile at the other end a town."

"The building across the road?"

Liam nodded. "I always fancied livin' there, with a furniture shop down. I save what I can, but it would take a heap ta make the place serve. It's been empty my whole life." He scraped his fork across his plate. "Doesn't hurt ta dream, I suppose."

"Trust me, not doing anything about it hurts more."

"Then I'll bring the furniture around tomorrow after work." His ebullient spirit regained, he stood with a broad smile. "Thanks for the supper, Clare, and the use of your barn. I'll let ya two get back at yer shiftin'."

After closing the door behind him, I rejoined Ciarán. "Two questions."

"Shiftin' means makin' out." Ciarán laid his hand on one burning cheek. "Darlin', he couldn't have known. What's the other question?"

"Why do they call it The Folly?"

"It's proper name is Finnin's Folly. He built it to rival the Lamb and Thistle."

"The bastard!"

Ciarán chuckled. "There's the general consensus. But aul Finnin didn't have Ma and Da's knack for hospitality. His enterprise failed and the buildin' has sat idle since."

"Until Liam. It's sweet, how he's always dreamed of living there."

Ciarán, incapable of skirting more intimate topics, returned to the real subject of the evening. "Ya said somethin' lovely ta me before he interrupted. Clare, I care for ya, too." He gave my nose a playful tap and poured himself more wine. "Are ya relieved Liam arrived when he did?"

"Maybe?"

"I'm grateful he saved us from ourselves. I'd bed ya with delight this moment but I'm not certain ya wouldn't turn from me with regret come morning." In the candlelight his eyes were prismatic chips of lapis. "Take your time decidin', darlin'. Whatever ya choose, ya have to want all of it."

Chapter Fifteen

M s. Fallon's beautiful old kitchen dresser loomed in the barn, and I started stripping away years of paint. The piece had simple lines, without much ornamentation. I finished the straightforward job before the week ended and Liam's pleased approval thrilled me.

When not required at the rectory, he joined me in refinishing Ms. Fallon's dining table and the eight maddening chairs which were all spindles, curves, and flutes. The job furthered my education in both furniture and Liam. He'd already demonstrated himself as a hard worker, but in our pleasant hours together he revealed a deep, thoughtful nature.

One evening, a week after we finished our project, I arrived at the pub door at the same time as Aideen. "Why, Clare! I didn't recognize ya without a man on yer arm. You're always accompanied by someone or the other. Ya even have Paddy in your thrall. Young folk these days, I swear. Our Moira can't arse herself ta choose between the O'Rourke or the Forsyth lad, although saints know if Liam will be available much longer." She tisked and cocked her head. "I notice he's been callin' around the cottage of late."

Her insinuation horrified me. "I'm helping him with a project!"

"Are ya, now. There's news as will come as a blessed relief ta more than one party." I gaped after her while she minced in ahead of me.

A happy racket always filled the pub on Friday nights; the addition of pilgrims added to the pitch. Moira and the lads conducted a raucous darts match and Paddy played fiddle in the corner with Dan and Padraic. Dozens of conversations littered the air. The mayhem forced intimacy; to hear one another, Ciarán and I bent our heads close. We didn't touch, but his nearness vibrated against my skin. "I don't mind this," he said.

"Not even Aideen Fannin's nosy nose?"

Ciarán followed my pouting gaze to the bar where Aideen, perched like a hawk, watched us with raptor eyes. Waggling cheery fingers her direction he said, "She's harmless."

"Gossip about other people's affairs is mean."

"Are ya after havin' an affair?"

Banter didn't often make my chest tight. "Not one; three."

"And who would the lucky fellas be?" Ciarán's evident amusement demonstrated the silliness of harboring annoyance over tittle-tattle.

"You, obviously. But Liam and Paddy are contenders."

"Ho! Paddy, eh? Give her some fresh meat and flirt with aul Tim."

"Brilliant! Then she'd see how ridiculous her speculations are."

Ciarán's smile held, but it dimmed. "Are all your prospects absurd?"

I dipped my head, and a tinge of bloom ran to my face. "My adoration of Paddy is no secret."

"Ya have grand taste." He chuckled but seemed relieved.

Liam approached and handed me a folded paper. Given the context, I stared at the envelope, terrified it contained a love letter. "Your wages," he said. "Miz Fallon paid me this mornin'." He flashed a conspiratorial smile. "It's cash. The Revenue don't have ta know."

I pushed the money toward him. "This is yours. I did it for the craic."

"Ya earned it. Miz Fallon has told all her friends about our work; one of them is phonin' tonight. Seems ya were right, Ciarán."

Liam's happiness strengthened my conviction. "You have to take back the money now. I appreciate the thought, but you can invest it in your future."

The rims of his eyes grew pink, then he pocketed the envelope, lifted a chip off Ciarán's plate, and winked again. "Join us for darts, if ya can bear ta be apart."

Ciarán chortled, then returned his attention to me. "Now, tell me more about your affairs."

Nervousness dissolved in a laugh. "Gawd, sometimes you remind me so much of Edie. She'd make the same joke."

"Ya miss her." He watched me with tender empathy.

"Not when you're around. It's pretty magical finding one soul mate, two is beyond all expectation."

"We don't find soul mates. We recognize them."

The words tickled my belly, but Declan stopped by our table, grim as a storm, and interrupted my reply. "Is your barn alright, then?"

"Still a work in progress; see for yourself next Sunday at my housewarming party. Your folks and Nessa will be there."

"I'll come." Whether the invitation itself or the specificity of the guest list were inducement didn't matter. His acceptance proved a thaw, and I hid a smile as he addressed his brother. "Paddy keepin' ya busy?"

Ciarán huffed with an amused laugh. "Haven't had any encounters with the garda for weeks. I'm stayin' out of trouble."

Declan shot a glance toward me, whether affectionate or teasing I couldn't divine. "I hope so."

After supper, Ciarán and Paddy challenged Liam and Jamie to a match; Moira and I opted to watch. "Those two," she said, as the lads shoved each other. "Always actin' the maggot; I doubt they'll ever grow up."

I gulped before risking an awkward conversation. "Moira, your grandma thinks there's something going on between me and Liam, but you should know—"

She stopped my mouth with her hand. "Gran is a fair cat, and gossip is her cream. She gave me no end a grief over Liam long before ya got here. I don't mind her, and neither should ya."

"So, you and he—"

Moira set her head back in a laugh. "Mind your business, darlin'. I can start on ya about lads easy enough myself. At least ya had the sense ta start up with a man, not a babby like those two eejits."

Liam appeared at our elbows with a smirk and exaggerated bow. "If ya ladies would be so kind, my friend and I would like ya ta lend your services in our game."

Moira sneered. "I'll service your arse with me boot, Liam Forsyth."

"So, you're agreed. Ya comin', Clare?"

"Maybe later."

He cast a knowing glance toward Ciarán, who had headed toward the bar. "And Miz Fallon's friend rang; we have another commission. I'll come by tomorrow ta discuss it."

Moira drained her pint with one hand on her hip. "Right. Buy me another beer, man, and I'll take on both ya cabbages."

When they cleared off, I joined Ciarán. "You're not after squarin' the triangle?"

"The lads aren't my type. I'm into Celtic gods."

His piercing expression stirred butterflies. "Careful, darlin'. Such sweet remarks put me in mind of kissin' ya."

The next morning, I rested against the ruined wall at St. Dallán's, head bent skyward, feeling freckles pop out in response to the sun. In the blissful silence, my mind shuffled ideas like tarot cards.

"Thought I'd find ya here. What are ya meditatin' on?"

A smile answered the deep, lovely voice. "The power of dreams." Opening my eyes, I turned to Ciarán, legs crisscrossed. He aped my posture; our knees touched, and desire vibrated through me. I settled it with a breath. "Grand-da's gift showed me the possibilities of my life. I want to do the same for others."

"This is about Liam."

"How did you know?"

He stroked the furrow of surprise on my brow. "If it's worryin' ya, I can't read your mind. But ya sparked like flint on steel when he told ya about The Folly."

"Who owns it?"

"Finnin Malone gifted it to the village."

An unpleasant thought occurred. "Does Declan have anything to do with it?"

"Dan Delaney has its keepin'." Proving he could, in fact, read my mind he added, "If one were interested in buyin' it, they'd discuss it with him."

I almost shouted with a rush of relieved joy. "Fantastic. And while Declan squabbles with me over money, Liam will have time to get licenses and whatever else he needs." I frowned. "This isn't going to come off as some sort of patronage, is it?"

He again drew a hand across my forehead, ironing wrinkles. "Clare, ya needn't apologize for Seamus settin' ya up."

I bunched my shoulders. "Having so much handed to me makes me feel guilty."

"But ya don't presume entitlement or put on airs like we should be kissin' your feet. Although, I reckon ya have adorable toes."

"You're easily distracted."

His finger strayed over my cheek. "Your blushes are like summer roses; they make ya even lovelier ta me."

"Are you flirtin' with me, Mr. O'Donnell?"

All the teasing and soft looks melted into a straight-set mouth. "Flirtin' implies a lack of serious intent."

My flush turned crimson. But if it made me attractive to Ciarán, it leveled the field. The man often left me speechless, breathless, or both. It wasn't always his words, but the intimate timbre of his voice and magic variance of light playing within him and sparkling out like a multi-faceted jewel. Everything about him sounded in me like a bell.

The admission dried my mouth and tightened my chest, but I affected nonchalance. "I want to help people, like Seamus did."

In an instant the smile returned. "Jaysus. Your eyes are afire. You're warmin' ta this idea more every second."

"This isn't like me."

"I've never known ya any way but strong and determined."

His words jolted. My mind carried two versions of myself: screw-up Clare and maybe-someday Clare. The first disappointed her mother, never asserted herself, and couldn't see anything through to its conclusion. Gaping at Ciarán, the awed realization struck. The latter, aspirational version had already manifested. Someday Clare had arrived, possessed of long-yearned-for strength and resolve. Ciarán saw it, and others shined the same light of belief: Edie, Daddy, Grand-da. No one in Killarkin, except Declan, considered me a push-over or a failure. All those loving eyes and encouraging words spoke louder than any "Oh, Clare" ever uttered.

"Thanks for believing in me. I'm going to find Dan."

Even to my untrained eye, The Folly needed a lot of work, but the cracked plaster, water stains, and bowed floor didn't distract from the potential. A cavernous fireplace dominated one end of the open room. The boarded windows were tall; unhindered they would allow a magnificent amount of light into a workshop and retail space. Creaky stairs led to a warren of odd-sized rooms on the second level. The right hands could transform it into a beautiful apartment, large enough for a family.

Dan shook a mournful head. "It's been vacant thirty years or more, repairs mountin' all the while. I can't say which it requires more: money or courage."

I scanned the high-above rafters, counting bird nests. "Both, I reckon. Why didn't Grand-da ever take it on?"

Dan yanked at a weed pushing up through the floor. "No one had a use. The land is worth more than the buildin'. You'd have a better investment if ya razed the beast."

"She deserves another chance first." Paying earnest money out of the barn renovation funds, I promised the remainder of the down payment the following week. "Until then, though, let's keep this between ourselves." There had likely never been a heavier ask in the history of Killarkin.

"Ya have my word, Clare." He clasped my hand, pumping it with enthusiasm. "It's a pleasure doin' business with another Riordan."

My American attorney assured me there were no legal impediments to the project and even anticipating Declan's inevitable disagreement couldn't mute my excitement. I went to the pub to celebrate and found Ciarán at the bar, chatting with his dad. Eamon gave me a smiling nod and moved a prudent distance away. "Howya," Ciarán said, with the briefest touch on the small of my back.

"Hi. Do you want to come over?"

"I would, but as your party is tomorrow, Ma insists on a family supper tonight."

With eyebrows knit, I glanced around the busy room. "Saturday night at the pub does scream intimacy."

Ciarán chuckled and gestured to the empty spot beside him. "Dec's on his way. We'll chat ta Da when able, and Ma will pester us when she can."

"Well, bless her dedication to tradition." He curled a discrete pinky around mine and I traced his palm with my thumb before pocketing my hand. "We can celebrate another time."

"Ah. It went all right with Dan." My grin answered the question. "Aul Seamus judged right when he left ya his legacy. I wish I could join ya."

"Me, too. But family supper is sacrosanct. If you like, you could stay for a while tomorrow night, after the party."

The words came out huskier than intended, like a lusty frog lurked in my throat. I made a clearing little cough, but before making matters worse—or better—Nessa appeared. Eamon placed a glass of sherry before her, and she gave him a tired, grateful smile. "I'll sit with ya two, if ya don't mind."

"Join me," I said. "The O'Donnell's are having Sunday supper."

Nessa cast a disbelieving eye over Eamon pulling taps and Maeve bustling about with loaded plates. "Far be it from us ta intrude on a private family moment."

We found a table and Nessa lowered into her chair with an exhausted exhale. "I should know better than expectin' any peace here on a Saturday night."

"Long day?"

"I'm dead on my feet and starvin' but couldn't be arsed ta cook. Not sure I'm fit for conversation, either, but we'll start with ya explainin' why you're lookin' so keen."

Owing to Nessa's taciturn nature, gossip didn't interest her so there were no qualms about confiding my plans. "But it has to stay secret until I've won the inevitable argument with Declan and finalized the deal. It wouldn't do for Liam to get his hopes up. Then there's the matter of Paddy."

"What has he done?"

"Nothing. Obviously, he's the man for the job if it happens, but he'll be doing it without one of his crew, which is my fault."

Nessa made a dismissive sniff. "Don't give it a thought. He'll be chuffed for Liam. This is an astonishin' bit of news, Clare."

"At last I'll become a contributing member of the community."

"What are ya on about? No one would argue otherwise."

I sank into the corner of the snug, limp with gratification. "It's all so unexpected; finding a unique, Clare-shaped place. The most amazing part is how natural it feels."

"*Bhaile.*"

"Where we come home."

Nessa grinned. "Killarkin is my *bhaile*, too."

"Even though—" I stopped myself, embarrassed. We never discussed our relationships with the O'Donnell brothers and insensitive prying now might risk our budding friendship.

A fleet grimace screwed up her features, then resolved to her usual composure. "I expected Ciarán, Maeve, or both would have said somethin' by now."

"It's none of my business."

She wore a tiny half-smile, one which indicated objective patience more than subjective amusement. "I never thought ta be sharin' confidences with ya."

"Me either. But friendship with me means you can say anything or nothing at all."

"Fair terms." Nessa's fingers stroked the stem of the glass while, I assumed, she weighed the pros and cons of an alliance. She smiled, having decided. "At our best, I knew Dec fair happy; thankful for Maeve's health, inclined toward forgivin' Ciarán, pleased with me. But he went missin' in his soul. His happiness faded; he withheld himself from me, from everyone." Nessa clenched and unclenched her hand. "I encouraged him ta share what burdened him so, but he wouldn't do. Whatever ate him kept chewin' until he stopped bein' whole."

"I'm sorry, Nessa." To my shock, my pain for her extended to Declan in equal measure.

"I am, too, but I deserved better. Rather than tell me his heart, he broke our engagement."

"Did you ever consider returning to Dublin?"

"I fit here, too."

Her trust and admirable strength almost made me cry. Instead, I fetched her another glass of sherry and watched Ciarán from the other end of the bar, unable to imagine seeing him every day of my life without being with him. I couldn't do it and told Nessa so when I returned with our drinks.

"Sure, ya could. Ya came here for Seamus but stayed for yourself. If you're planted here, setbacks or heartache won't be enough ta uproot ya. There's another Gaeilge word: *dúchas*. It means havin' a birthright *and* the drive to fulfill it."

I gasped. "Such a small word to hold so much meaning."

"Irish is like that."

Chapter Sixteen

A KEG WAITED BESIDE the table heaped with platters of cheese, sausages, and cakes. The mouth-watering fragrance of shepherd's pie wafted from the bread oven. Roses, rounded and full as teacups, bloused in a large white pitcher. Lit candles adorned the mantel.

Every spare minute of the past two weeks I scrubbed, baked, and cooked; driven by the desire to honor everyone who contributed toward the cottage's restoration and to celebrate their friendship.

Eamon and Maeve arrived early, the latter bearing a large casserole of stew. Frowning, I admonished her. "The food is covered. I told you."

"And sweet ya were about it; but it didn't feel right not helpin'."

Eamon chuckled and busied himself with the keg. "Ya know how she is, Clare."

"No different than you, Mr. O'Donnell. My university education included how to tap a keg."

"Sure, darlin'. Still, ya have your hostin' obligations. Leave the beer ta me."

Maeve bustled about the kitchen—her native environment—approving of every detail. "It's lovely, Clare. I never thought of yellow for a kitchen. Makes me think I'm a bee inside a sunflower, and I'm sure I don't know why Paddy went on about them stunnin' cupboards. I don't say I'd ever think ta use dark green, but true, with the white and gold, why it's the spittin' image of a sunflower." She made toward an apron on a hook. "Now, how can I help?"

I thwarted her grasp and kissed her cheek. "You're incorrigible, Maeve. You're my guest tonight."

Moira arrived with Liam, Jamie, and Nora. Behind them came Sorely who, to my surprise, had Chicken Fiona on his arm. "Ma! Let me show ya the jacks I helped build!" Jamie ushered her toward the upstairs bathroom.

During rare Fiona sightings in the shops we only ever discussed poultry; I never realized she and Sorely were married. Once Jamie finished touring her around, I took her to visit Daisy and May.

"They are thrivin'. I trust they're layin' well."

"I haven't bought eggs since you gave them to me."

She cocked her coppery head in my direction. "Seems you're thrivin', too."

"Fair assessment."

She pulled her shawl around her shoulders, like a hen about to roost. "Grand."

As we returned to the house, Nessa blew through the front door like a harried breeze. "Pilgrim with a sprained ankle," she said, explaining her tardiness.

"There's sherry."

With deliberate composure she replied, "I'll take it in the tallest glass ya own, if ya please."

As I poured a healthy dose and filled a plate for her, Declan appeared. He tossed around a cursory glance and pronounced the final product acceptable.

"Jaysus, Dec," Nessa said. "Layin' it on so thick will swell everyone's head."

He ignored her sarcasm and helped himself to a lamb sausage. "Done ta a turn, Ma."

With a guilty swish of her arm Maeve turned from the oven which held her stew and whirled on him, hands on hips. "Clare did all her own cookin', I'll have ya know."

"The sorcerer's apprentice." Declan made a neat turn and exited to the front room.

Nessa shot daggers after him. "If he's determined ta be foul, he needn't have bothered comin'."

"Now, now," Maeve said. "He's been workin' hard in Dublin all this week, the poor darlin'. Come ta the parlor and chat with me."

Paddy arrived, setting his ubiquitous fiddle on the mantel before entering the kitchen. He pulled himself a beer then encircled my waist with a paternal arm. "This is a fittin' party fer yer grand little house, darlin'."

I cuddled against him. "This wouldn't have happened without you."

He returned the embrace and bussed my head. "We saw it through together. Aul Seamus would be proud of ya. Yer a credit ta the Riordan name."

Ciarán loomed in the doorway, arms crossed over his chest. "When will ya post the banns?"

With slow deliberation Paddy disengaged his arm. "Were I thirty years younger, I'd give ya a run for yer money, ya daft eegit." He piled a mound of pie on a plate, gave my cheek a loud, smacking kiss, and knocked a playful shoulder against Ciarán before settling into Grand-da's chair.

Ciarán chuckled and moved closer. "Ah, darlin'. You'll not be content until every man in Killarkin is in love with ya."

I arched my eyebrows with a menacing squint. "You have deduced my evil plot. Now I shall have to kill you."

"Do your worst." He poured two glasses of whiskey, lifting his in a toast. "Ta all the poor bastards."

I tipped my glass toward his. "Long life to them."

Ciarán inclined his head, his breath tickling my cheek. "Did ya bathe in pears?" My pulse throbbed, my heart yearning with everything yet unspoken. Then Gerry and Cathleen arrived, and the opportunity evaporated.

Cooing over the improvements, Cathleen thrust a small package into my hands. "A token," she said. "Beeswax candles give out such a homely scent." Her eyes swept the room. "Oh, but it's lovely, Clare. I would never have recognized the place; would ya have, Gerry?"

Loading his plate, her husband agreed. "It's like new."

When they joined the party, I stood on tiptoe and whispered, "Dan has the paperwork ready."

"When will ya speak ta Dec?"

"Next week, if he's around. Meantime, I'll go to St. Dall's every day and will it into being."

Ciarán pushed a curl from my cheek, his face thoughtful. "Do ya pray, darlin'?"

"Not the 'Dear God, sincerely, Clare' business. But whatever mystery is behind all this, I'm connected to it, especially at St. Dall's. Do you?"

"All the time."

The answer shouldn't have stunned, but it did. "For what?"

"Those I love and the many I've failed; the courage ta be a better man."

I shoved against him, gentle and teasing. "Cut it out. Improve much more and you'll be insufferable."

He rested against the counter, hands in his pockets. My lips itched to kiss him, but not in public. Someone had found my iPod in its dock and conversation levels rose to match the music's volume. In minutes, the gathering shifted from polite conviviality to full on shindig. At any second someone would come in for more beer or another helping of food. "Time to play hostess."

"Always a grasp of essentials."

"The requisite one is catching Declan in a moment when he has an open mind."

"He can't stop ya."

"No, he can't," I said, with vehemence. "Joel is coming in October to look The Folly over and start on a design. He'll do wonders with it."

"Who's doin' wonders now?" Declan asked as he forked sausages onto his plate.

I swung around, drawing a deep breath. "An architect friend. I have another project."

A scoop of mash hung midair as he regarded me. "Ya finished the cottage; the barn isn't far behind. You're sellin' and goin' back ta the States."

"I'm not. This isn't the time for details, but I'd like a meeting with you to discuss an investment."

He dropped the spoon into the dish, ghost white and staring. "Of course, you're leavin'."

"I've decided to stay."

"How long?"

The question tripped the hair trigger wired long ago, which fired off with the interference of a smug older brother. "My personal life is none of your concern."

He shot a wicked glare at Ciarán. "Ah. Then not so long."

Since February Declan had provoked me to annoyance, frustration, or anger. Now, his attitude tipped me into outrage. "There's no need to insult me *or* your brother."

"Ya came here ta restore the cottage. Job done. Now sell it and get on with your life."

Declan towered over me with level shoulders and a jutted chin. Filling with uncommon poise, I squared up, stepped forward, and, mindful of the guests in the other room, calmly replied, "What, where, and with whom I do anything is none of your fecking business."

Declan took no heed, instead wheeling on his brother with a rumbling growl. "You're a self-servin' bastard, but even ya can't be encouragin' this lunacy."

Ciarán didn't flinch. He modulated his tone, but his eyes were hot blue fire. "Nothin' mad about benefittin' the community. Hear Clare out and you'll agree." He placed a conciliatory hand on his brother's shoulder. "Dec, she's followin' Seamus' footsteps. Ya loved the man; give his granddaughter the same credit."

Declan shook off his brother as Nessa entered with a round-eyed, worried mien. "What's the row?"

My voice dropped to a whisper. "Jaysus. Did everyone hear?"

"They're all near ta bein' off their tits. I, however, have practiced moderation." She lifted her full glass as proof.

My eyes shot daggers toward the fuming solicitor. "Prepare for a shock, Ness; someone here doesn't approve of my plans."

"Dec," she said, gentle as a mother with a child. "Clare has every right ta—"

Declan whirled on her like she'd stuck a hot poker in his back. "Jaysus! You're conspirin' with them?"

"Hush, man; you're actin' a maggot and I'll be damned if ya ruin Clare's party." She lifted a chicken fillet roll from the near empty platter and clutched Declan's forearm. This time he didn't resist the hand. "A walk will settle ya." She steered him toward the back door with more mildness than he deserved, and over her shoulder said, "Come 'round for tea tomorrow, Clare. Bring biscuits; I've got feck all in the house. Thank ya for havin' us."

Appreciation for Nessa's intervention did little to moderate my anger. "So much for an open mind."

"I wish I knew his trouble," Ciarán said, his voice strained with concern. "But ya have a house full of guests who are, by the sounds of it, rearrangin' your furniture ta dance. Let's join 'em." He clipped my chin between his thumb and forefinger, pressed his lips to mine, and led me out of the kitchen.

We danced and drank, Declan's extreme behavior forgotten in the embrace of everyone's merriment. Paddy, ever the raconteur, enthralled us with an origin story of the cottage, a tale short on substantive facts and long on fantasy. Then the guests, young and old, rendered their own narratives of Seamus' kindness. The tales were less about his charitable works than the good man behind them. "He went ta America, but never truly left us," Eamon said, summing everyone's sentiments.

The waxing quarter moon peeped through the window, then capered in an arc above the house. When the bottles emptied and the full platters diminished to crumbs and smears, my happy guests began making their way home.

Paddy left second to last, and when the door closed after him I rested against it, facing Ciarán. "Would you like another drink?"

"I'd like ta help ya clean."

"We can think of better things to do."

"Ya can't wake ta all this chaos."

I shook my head with amusement. "Fine. But I'm ordering a dishwasher tomorrow morning and you're going to install it."

He washed while I collected the scant leftovers. When we finished, he wiped his hands on a towel and smiled. "Ya threw a fine party, despite my brother. I'm sorry he went off."

"What's worse is you and Ness got dragged into it."

"We can't help it; we're with ya on this."

"Thanks, but it's not my intention to contribute any more trouble between the three of you."

"Nessa and I make our own choices. Darlin', I love my stubborn arsed mule of a brother, but it's no problem takin' your part, especially when you're in the right. Don't fret about me and Ness. We know our way around Dec."

He followed me into the front room, but halted on the kitchen threshold, regarding me with a blush-inducing grin. "You're too far away."

"It's safer over here."

"A man who's survived war zones can't be scared of me. Unless you're afraid I'll steal your virtue."

Ciarán chuckled, tender and low, as he crossed the room. "There's none ta take."

"Thank heaven," I said, scribing a circle in the air. "It's awful to think of all this going to waste."

He caught my hand between both of his and held it one precious moment before releasing it. "Ya don't frighten me, darlin'; except when ya make me forget ta breathe."

I hooked a finger on his belt. Words hovered on my tongue; ones squelched too long out of fear. "Stay with me."

Ciarán placed his hands on my shoulders. "I must check on Declan."

"Not tonight; let him cool down." A pleasant sensation tickled my scalp as he idled with one of my curls. My chest rose and fell with shallow breaths. "Don't toy with me."

He bent closer and my heart thumped. "I swear, I want ya more than words can say." He gritted his teeth. "But I must talk sense ta the man. He sees this as betrayal, and I've already failed him once."

With a grunt of frustration, I gave his cheek a soft kiss. "He doesn't deserve you."

Ciarán embraced me, leaving no doubt about his level of desire. "I don't want ta leave ya."

"But you're distracted."

He pulled back and stroked my cheek. "And I would be attentive the first time we—"

I stopped him with a kiss, my chest tight. "Go on then. Good luck."

He hesitated to release me. "Please understand, Clare. This isn't for me alone. I'm not sure Dec and I can ever be close again, but his unhappiness is past bearin'."

"You might be the best human ever."

The corner of his lips quirked. "Fair sure I'm not."

"When it comes to you, my judgement is sound." Resisting the urge to pout, I kissed him and closed the door on him and the dark night. A dying ember winked against a stray glass under Grand-da's chair, and I carried it to the sink.

Disinclined for bed given how close I'd come to sharing it, I poured a tiny tot of whiskey and stood at the kitchen window, watching the shifting light as clouds blew over and away from the moon's face.

A gust of wind moaned through the rowans and the front gate clattered, swinging loose on its hinges. Stepping outside to close it, I stopped cold, staring at the crumpled, motionless form of Ciarán lying in the street.

Chapter Seventeen

After a wild scan of the inky garden, I sank on my knees and, sick with dread, placed two cold fingers on Ciarán's neck. He had a pulse, but my hand came away slick with blood.

It seemed impossible something could have happened in the mere minutes since he'd left. Everything in me stormed; blood rushed like wind and my heart thundered so hard my limbs shook. Breath wouldn't catch and nothing made sense.

Pulling the mobile from his pocket left a dark smear on his hip. My fingers trembled so bad I scrolled past Nessa's contact number twice. Managing an inhale sufficient to steady myself, I made an accurate jab on the phone, but she didn't answer. Fear clawing my gut, I tried to scream, but as if in the throes of a nightmare, nothing came out. A second attempt manifested only a weak bleat. Unwilling to leave Ciarán alone, I dialed Nessa again, fighting back soundless, ragged sobs.

"Jaysus, man. I'm sleepin'!"

Incoherent words tumbled out. "Please come—it's Ciarán—there's blood—"

"Don't move him!"

She clicked off and I knelt beside Ciarán, chuffing his hand, and entreating him to wake or move or, Jaysus, anything but lie there. He had too much vibrance, a life left to live with me—with someone, anyone—so long as he lived and breathed and shared his light in a tattered world.

I pressed my forehead to his; my tears laving his cheeks. Random but apt fragments of my favorite Pogues song drifted through my panic, listing all the simple magics of loving someone. But he couldn't take me where I'd never gone before if he left me now. "Darling, please."

My fingers stroked his still face. Lost in a rigid state of shock, I didn't hear the doctor's feet on the pavement of The High nor register her arrival until she squatted beside me and felt for a pulse. "What happened, Clare?"

Hearing my name roused me. "Damned if I know!"

She examined Ciarán's head and neck with delicate, skilled fingers. "We need ta move him inside. I can't see a damn thing out here. Ring Paddy ta help, then fetch a towel."

I made the call while running inside for the towel and a flashlight, which I then held as Nessa dabbed at Ciaran's head. My hands trembled so bad it required both of them to hold the beam of light steady but doing something blunted my nerviness.

Paddy scurried around the bend from The Low, barefoot, wearing pajamas, and clutching an ancient shotgun. "Jaysus, man. Put your wretched *gunna* away!" Obedient to Nessa's order, he leaned it against the garden wall while she cradled Ciarán's head. "Take him under the shoulders, Paddy. Clare, manage his feet. Go slow."

When we got Ciarán onto the couch Nessa asked for water, more towels, and an empty basin while Paddy fetched his gun. Upon his return he swore. "What the hell happened? He's all over blood."

"We don't know," Nessa said, positioning the empty bowl on the coffee table. "Ring the family. And I'll not say it again; put away your feckin' gun!" While she cleansed the wound behind Ciarán's ear, he moaned. The weak mewl eased the taut set of her mouth. "When did he leave the party?"

"Around eleven-thirty."

He made another small noise as Nessa checked her watch. "We're alright, then."

There wasn't time to ask what she meant; Maeve and Eamon ran through the open door, wrapped in bathrobes and spewing frantic questions which Nessa answered with a terse, "All we know is he's been clocked good."

"Declan didn't answer," Paddy said.

"He doesn't sleep with his phone," she replied. "And he'd be no help anyway." She mumbled curses and bent over her patient. "The gash is bleedin' like fury, and he'll have an impressive knot. Clare, hold the towel on him, firm but gentle."

Kneeling beside Ciarán, I followed the doctor's instructions while she performed a more thorough examination. She commanded Ciarán to speak, and he made an inarticulate attempt. "Open your eyes, man."

He bleated my name. "Right here, sweetheart." He tried to sit up, his arms limp as dead fish.

Nessa held him down. "Not yet. Follow my finger." She ran tests then raised him. "What's your name?"

"Ya know my name, Ness. Jaysus, I ache." He lifted a pale hand to the back of his head.

"Ya had an accident. Where are ya?"

"At Clare's." he said, first annoyed, then confused. His eyes darted around the room. "I left."

My fingers tightened over his. "You tried, but didn't get far."

Ciarán paled and groaned. "Hold his head, Clare," Nessa said, grabbing the basin and cradling it under him as he vomited. "Good and concussed ya are. But your neck is fine and there are no discernible skull fractures."

Wiping his mouth with the back of his hand he replied, "Hard head."

Maeve, practiced in managing the more disgusting elements of parenthood, dealt with the bowl, doubtless relieved to contribute toward her son's care.

Nessa clutched Ciarán's shoulder, peering into his eyes. "Listen, ya need sutures. I'll numb ya first, all right?" In no position to argue, he nodded, then winced as the needle pricked him. With expert gentleness Nessa shifted him onto his side. While waiting for the anesthetic to take effect, she shaved a field around the gash and cleaned it again.

"A few quick stitches, now." She murmured soothing words while employing the needle with swift, expert strokes, then tied off the threads, and covered the wound with gauze. "OK?" Ciarán nodded. "Answer me. Use words."

"Been better."

Nessa blew a relieved breath. "Eamon, see him ta the jacks, will ya?" All the tenderness between the two men manifested in the way Eamon lifted his son and how Ciarán leaned against his father.

Nessa studied their progress toward the bathroom before giving me instructions. "We'll not move him tonight, if ya don't mind. Don't let him alone. Keep ice on the wound until he can't stand it; it will help with the swellin'. He must rest but wake him every two hours and pace him around the room. Ask simple questions, like I did. If he won't wake, seems disoriented, or can't walk straight, call me." She pressed a bottle of pills in my hand. "Dose him with this; but if his headache worsens or he keeps pukin', call me. If he loses consciousness or starts seizin'—"

"Call you." My robotic answer belied a growing terror at the accumulating list of potential threats.

"How he passes the night will tell me more." My heart chilled. Grand-da's doctor used the same sickening words. Reading my fear Nessa said, "Don't fret, Clare. I'll have the phone beside me all night." She took my hands. "Ya did well. I'll be back first thing. And lock your doors."

Alarm shot through me, different from the panic of the last hour. "Who would do this?"

"I don't know, darlin'."

"I'll stay with ya," Paddy pledged, his weapon shouldered.

I nodded agreement. Despite my deep loathing of guns, the idea of a large, armed man in the house overnight brought tremendous comfort.

Maeve and Eamon offered to stay, too, but Nessa insisted they go home. "The man needs rest, and ya do, too. You'll have the nursin' of him the next couple of days." Maeve sobbed once and I hugged her, trying hard not to snuffle myself. "Jaysus," Nessa said, more like her old self. "He'll live. Everyone out."

I locked the doors behind them and sent Paddy to the guest room, vowing to summon him if needed. Blood matted Ciarán's beautiful curls, so I filled a bowl with fresh water and rubbed his head until most of it came away.

"Shoulda stayed."

I kissed his wan brow. "Let it be a lesson to you. Do you want pills?"

"Please." After swallowing them, he laid back. "Sorry ta be such trouble."

"You're a real menace, O'Donnell and your shirt is a mess. Let me make you comfortable." I removed his shoes, then unbuttoned his shirt and pulled it from his arms. "Hold the ice pack and I'll clean you up." After wiping tacky blood from his neck and shoulder, I covered him with Brigid's green quilt, and dimmed all the lights save one low lamp.

"Off ta bed, darlin'. I'm grand."

"You're less than OK." I pulled a chair close and passed a hand over his forehead. "Besides, the doctor ordered me to stay with you. Close your eyes."

The eerie night mirrored the awful one a year before, when my family sat a silent vigil around Grand-da's hospital bed. I'd held his hand, too; awaiting a pressure of fingers, a flicker of eyelids, but no sign came.

Grand-da's ice-cold hand lay motionless while my thumb traced the veins and bones. My whispered "I love you" went unanswered; he died the next morning. My head dipped to Ciarán's shoulder. "Please. Not again."

I set a timer but couldn't rest, afraid of sleeping through it. The long hours oozed past, a disorienting swing between fretful dozing and boiling nerves. Ciarán responded each time I woke him and during the few minutes he paced the living room and answered questions, I experienced grateful relief. But once he slept again, worry crept back in.

Sun peeked through the windows when I nudged my patient for his six o'clock wakeup.

"Let me sleep."

"Darling, please. Who am I?"

His lids fluttered open, revealing pools of cerulean. "My Clare."

An hour later, a hesitant rap on the door woke me. Maeve waited outside, pallid, and anxious; Declan lurked behind her. With a finger on my lips I said, "He still has an hour to sleep." Maeve bustled toward the kitchen, but Declan hovered over the couch and chewed a thumbnail. I pulled him away. "Let him rest."

My hands fumbled with the kettle and Maeve intervened, pressed the switch, and collected the red box of Barry's. "Did ya get any sleep, darlin'?"

"Did you?"

"I prayed rosaries til dawn."

"It must have worked. He had an uneventful night."

"Thank the Virgin and all the saints! And a curse on the foul creature who hurt my boy."

Paddy joined us; we drank tea. But behind the familiar comfort lay sick-making knowledge: someone attacked Ciarán. I excused myself to wash my face and the memory of his bloodied head made me retch.

Nessa arrived on the dot of seven and ran her battery of tests. "Maeve, fetch the man a clean shirt, please. Dec, get your car and drive him ta my office; I'd rather he didn't walk. I'll meet ya there."

Ciarán and I waited on the couch while everyone ran off on their errands. "Thanks for tendin' me."

"Pure selfishness on my part. Someone had to make sure you stuck around." Grinning, he kissed the corner of my mouth.

Declan returned, bearing a clean shirt and with a surprising degree of gentleness, helped his brother into it before escorting him out the door. Craving the oblivion of sleep I went to bed, but despite heavy eyelids, my mind wouldn't shut off. Substituting a cold shower and coffee for rest, I shoved a piece of toast in my teeth and went to feed the chickens. Someone called my name, startling me. Declan stood at the gate with two police officers, a tall, young man with close-cropped hair: the other stocky and middle-aged.

The older man addressed me. "Miss Riordan, we're sorry ta disturb your breakfast. I'm Sargent Corcoran. A word, please."

"Of course." Chucking the toast toward the chickens, I joined the men.

"Mr. O'Donnell tells me ya found the victim." The extreme, if accurate, word jolted.

"Ciarán, yes. He lay right there."

The Sargent scanned the spot. An abstract rose of dried blood stained the gray pavement. "And the victim attended a party ya hosted last evenin'."

"Yes."

"What time did it end?"

"Around eleven. He stayed to help clean and left around half past."

"Had he been drinkin'?"

"We all had. He wasn't drunk."

Corcoran scribbled in a blue notebook. "And the mood of the victim?"

The objectifying word set me off; distress and weariness overwhelmed good sense. "Could you please not refer to him as if..." Declan's warning eye halted me from barking at the police officer. "Forgive me, Sargent. It was a long, horrible night."

Corcoran acknowledged the apology with a "Quite so, miss" and resumed his questioning. "Mr. O'Donnell's mood."

"Fine."

"You'd not quarreled?"

I answered the ridiculous question with admirable patience. "No, sir. He left and I went to the kitchen. The wind rose and there were storm noises, branches on the roof and the like. The gate banged and I looked out the window."

"Show me, please."

He followed me into the kitchen and examined my vantage point. "I assumed Ciarán forgot the latch so went out to secure the gate."

"Is your gate always closed?"

"It's to keep out the sheep." The absurd but true statement provoked a nervous giggle, but memory sobered me quick enough. "He lay in the street and wouldn't wake up. Not wanting to leave him alone, I used his phone and called the doctor."

"And ya didn't observe any movement on the street? Anythin' untoward?"

"Except Ciarán unconscious? No. There wasn't anyone around."

"Do ya remember anythin' else?" Corcoran asked with unperturbed patience.

"Honestly, everything else is a blur."

The Sargent examined his notebook and gave a curt nod in Declan's direction. "Accordin' ta Mr. O'Donnell, ya have been in Ireland since February. Are ya here legally?"

I understood the question; a tourist visa would have expired by now. "I'm an Irish citizen, sir."

"If ya would fetch proof, please. It's a formality, miss."

I collected my EU passport, hands shaking. The entire situation had taken on the surreal aspect of a dream.

After a careful inspection of the document, Corcoran wrote the passport number in his little notebook. "With your permission, Officer Waite and I will search the gardens."

"Of course."

"Thank ya for your cooperation, Miss Riordan." He handed me a card. "Ring should anythin' else occur ta ya. Often, after the excitement wears off, bits come back. Any little detail helps. We'll ask ya not ta leave the area until the investigation concludes."

"I'm not going anywhere."

Declan's phone rang and his anguished features softened as he answered. "Be right there," he said, hanging up. The smile he managed hovered between cloud and sunshine. "Time ta take the man home." The statement alleviated some tension; Ciarán didn't require hospitalization. "Come along, if ya like."

The officers already stooped and crawled over the garden like overgrown children on an egg hunt. "Am I allowed to leave?"

"Sargent," Declan called. "My brother will be ready for questioning soon. We'll be in the pub when you're ready. Miss Riordan will be there as well."

Corcoran held a hasty conversation with his partner, then sought my permission for the latter to take photographic evidence. Declan left for the pub in the company of the Sargent while I accommodated Officer Waite. The ten minutes it took him to gather his photographic evidence seemed like thirty. When he resumed his search outside, I locked the door and jogged to the pub.

Eamon pulled clean glasses from the dishwasher, his cheeks ashy over a clenched jaw. But he gave me a sad smile and said, "Ciarán's in bed. No fractures, thank God. Nessa says he'll recover." His face crumpled and he sobbed, bent and awkward against my shoulder. Then, blowing his nose on a bar towel he said, "Thank the good Lord ya were with him."

I placed a hand on his ruddy cheek. "Let me make you tea."

"I'm grand, darlin'. It's the shock and relief of it all. Go in ta him." He patted my shoulder and returned to his glassware.

Maeve sat in the kitchen; hands folded under her chin; the swinging crucifix at the end of her rosary clicked against the arm of the chair as she worked the beads. "Clare, darlin'! The detective is with Ciarán, though why he won't let the poor lamb rest I don't know. I can't fathom this wretchedness, can ya? We have our troubles here, like everywhere else in this broken world, but no one I know is capable of such violence."

"The mystery is the worst part." I chewed a nail as an awful thought crossed my mind. "Dec got upset with Ciarán last night. I didn't tell the police, but he wouldn't—"

"Of course, he'd not! He's never raised a hand ta a soul!"

We hushed when Nessa emerged with Sargent Corcoran. "Ciarán's thick skull is undamaged, Clare. He'll mend with a few days of rest." The blissful words sent me across the room and though she'd hate it, I embraced her, weeping my thanks. "Jaysus," she said. "It's my job." But her all-business manner didn't prevent a sympathetic squeeze of my hand.

Sargent Corcoran requested a list of my party guests. "Dr. Cassidy's report indicates the blow came from below. I warrant the assailant is of shorter stature than Mr. O'Donnell."

I jotted names and handed it to Corcoran. Height eliminated anyone six feet or more from the list, but I agreed with Maeve; none of Killarkin's gentle souls would harm anyone, least of all Ciarán. "Everyone left a good thirty minutes before he did."

"Someone may have lingered or returned. Miz O'Donnell, ya have guests stayin' here?"

Exhausted, and fragile with worry, Maeve took umbrage. "And all of 'em God-fearin' pilgrims. I don't reckon them the violent sort."

"Perhaps not, ma'am, but someone may have seen or heard somethin'. And if ya could indicate those who occupy the rooms facin' the street."

Maeve offered no further argument. "I'll fetch the register. Clare, ya go in ta the lad."

Ciarán lay in his bed, wearing a clean bandage. The scrapes on his forehead were pink and taut. He slept, unperturbed, his face boyish and peaceful. Kicking off my shoes, I laid beside him. He didn't wake, but when my hand rested on his chest, he stirred and curled around me, his nose buried in my hair. He smelled of sleep and iodine. I kissed the inside of his wrist. "How do you feel?"

He answered first with a kiss on my neck. "Like shite." He pulled closer, his drowsy warmth and the steady beat of his heart a comfort. "Never better."

I took his face in my hands. "I love you, Ciarán O'Donnell."

He stroked my forehead, pushing hair from my eyes. "I know it, darlin'." Everything in him shone as he kissed me and said, "And I love ya."

His arms wrapped around me; I nestled close and dropped into a tender sleep.

The late afternoon sun hung golden and mellow. We rested our backs against the headboard, me on top of the blankets, Ciarán tucked under them. We held hands, still as statues, except for the play of our laced fingers. Maeve pushed open the door with her shoulder, her smile an encompassing beacon of love and gratitude.

"I brought ya a bite, son." She placed a tray of soup, strips of toast, and a glass of water on the nightstand. "And there's tablets for your poor head."

"The headache has eased ta a dull roar, Ma."

"Praise Jaysus! Clare, are ya wantin' for anythin'?"

"Thanks, Maeve. But no. I should go home. The girls will be hungry."

"Visit whenever ya like." She bent to kiss her son.

"I love ya, Ma." Maeve glowed and with an apron-swipe of her cheeks, closed the door behind her.

"May I have a sip of your water?"

"Sure, if I had any." He gestured to the glass with a thumb. "That'll be flat 7-up; it and toast soldiers are the beloved cure-all of Irish mammies. Though I don't reckon either will much help a concussion."

A sniff of the glass confirmed his claim. "Eew. No disrespect, but I'll pass on this particular custom. Do you need help?"

"I can manage a soup spoon, darlin'."

After pressing my lips against his fingers, I faced him, arms tight around my knees. "What do you remember?"

"Leavin' ya in the lamplight like a feckin' eejit. I remember the moon, the fragrance of night flowers, and needin' ya. Then nothin' but wakin' ta your stricken, beautiful face."

"Do you have any enemies?"

Ciarán chuckled. "American curiosity or are ya a detective now?"

"It's all so scary."

"The shades will figure it out. What matters is ya found me, and I've lived ta see another day. Nessa says I can't do anything strenuous for a week." He gave me a sly wink, inducing a blush which almost hurt. "If I behave, she'll allow the resumption of normal activities."

I kissed him, relishing the freedom to do so. "Then be good. Normal activities are my favorite."

The police officers greeted my return to the cottage. Sargent Corcoran held a plastic evidence bag containing a chunk of rock, its jagged side marked with blood and said, "We may have found our weapon. The assailant would have smashed it up like this." He pantomimed the action and bile burned my throat. "Once Mr. O'Donnell went down, he or she chucked it over the wall. It suggests the act of a mad moment; someone who planned an attack would have brought a proper weapon. The surface is too rough for prints, but if the blood matches Mr. O'Donnell's, it's somethin'." He handed the bag to Waite, who locked it in the trunk of the police car. "We'll be off now. We appreciate your cooperation, miss."

"Sargent, Ciarán's shirt is still in the house. It's a literal bloody mess but if you want it..."

"Evidence is evidence." Corcoran followed me into the cottage and claimed the garment, the shoulder of it stiff with dried blood. "Mercy," he said. "Head wounds are terrible gory."

After the officers left, I huddled on the couch, my gaze riveted on the cold hearth. Less than twenty-four hours had passed. Blood stained the pillow where Ciarán's head had first lain. I roused myself to deal with it, but futile dabs with a damp cloth made it worse. My arms and legs went leaden with unbearable weariness. I tossed the pillow in the bin, locked the doors, and fell into bed.

Chapter Eighteen

T HE ATTACK DOMINATED VILLAGE conversation. Father
Donovan convened his pilgrims to pray for Ciarán's recovery
and villagers called at the pub, though Maeve allowed few visitors. She
wouldn't hear of me working until I'd visited the patient. "He's already
bored out of his head. You're tonic for him."

Ciarán sat beside the window, tapping agitated fingers on the pages of
an open book. "Still working on your spies?"

"Le Carre is too close for comfort." He displayed a collection of Oscar
Wilde's fairy stories. "I'm allowed the pictures, provided I don't think
on them. I'm ta rest my brain."

I touched his lips with mine, then knelt beside him. "Is kissing too
strenuous."

"Ya set my pulse racin', so Ness would not approve." The sweetness of
his grin seeded the storm cloud within; raining tears, I sobbed against his
knee. He locked his fingers in my hair. "Ah, darlin'. Don't take on so. I
swear she'll never know."

I lifted my head, managing a smile. "Shite. Sorry. Chalk it up to a
combination of relief, terror, and gratitude."

"Why are ya scared?"

"It's not obvious?"

"Ya could be referrin' ta my injury or our declarations."

The intensity of his gaze caused me to squirm. "Both?"

"As ta the latter, anythin' worth doin' is a gamble."

"You have more experience with risk than me."

"In one way." He plucked the wool blanket over his knees. "But I've never hazarded anythin' for a woman before."

"You're the first man I ever considered worth the bother."

"Then, as it's mutual, I reckon we're neither of us in too much peril." His bloodshot eyes still sparkled like afternoon sunlight on a lake.

Wiping my face, I gave him another watery smile. "My words were true, though. It wasn't an overwrought reaction. I love you."

"I believe ya, darlin'. But ya can change your mind."

My head bobbled as if it rested on a spring. "Mind, sure. Not my heart. I've known a while; at least since the castle."

Ciarán attempted a disapproving scowl but couldn't help laughing. "So, ya were playin' hard ta get."

"No games, no doubts; not about you, anyway." I hugged my knees to my chest. "I had to believe myself up to the task and embrace the wonder of the universe granting me more than I ever imagined."

He bowed his head over mine. "Jaysus. I hope ta warrant such a beautiful sentiment."

"Who you are is the gift. It's enough. But these last couple of days have left me feeling delicate as spun glass."

Ciarán stroked my hair. "Love and lives are fragile. And there's nothin' like a bash on the head ta remind ya of it. Life is a breath and over in a blink." His voice grew husky. "But we have now and thank God for it."

The sober truth did not settle me. Clasping my hands around his ankles, I changed the subject. "What will you do today?"

"Rest my brain and try not ta excite myself with thoughts of ya, though I'm already failin' on the last point."

"Come hang out with me and Maeve."

He pulled me up for another kiss, his mouth tender and lingering. "I may do."

"I swear, the mornin' flies when you're here." Maeve tasted my fish stew with an approving nod. "Good as my own."

"It should be. You taught me to make it."

"Ya have been so keen ta learn. Ya may take this amiss, and I dearly hope you'll not, but sometimes when we're about our business here I imagine havin' a daughter would have been like this: gossipin' over the soup pot, handin' down recipes and traditions."

"It doesn't bother me a bit." The corner of my eye grew damp.

"And I'm grateful ta ya beyond words for savin' my boy."

"The wind saved him." But for the mercy of a rattling gate, the outcome might have been quite different. The thought made me shudder.

A candle on Maeve's altar guttered and smoked black soot against the side of the tall votive glass. She jumped to place a fresh candle in the jar. As she lit it she said, "St. John Licci, pray for us."

"Patron saint of head injuries?"

She nodded. "Nessa assures me Ciarán will be back ta devilin' me in no time, and God knows I trust her skill for doctorin' but I never found extra prayers ta do any harm."

"His intercessions would have come in handy last October."

She rushed from the stove and embraced me. "Oh, my gracious, I never thought how the other night must have haunted ya. Ya sweet darlin', worryin' about my boy and recallin' poor Seamus' last hours. I should ha' stayed with ya."

Returning the hug, I rested my chin on her shoulder. "It's OK, Maeve. If anything, it made me hope all the harder Ciarán would be all right."

"Well, I regret not bein' with ya even so." She grew tearful and we held each other a moment before she patted her top knot, smoothed her apron, and gave a determined huff. "Now, the bread won't make itself.

If you start it, darlin', I'll see ta the cakes. I thought lemon sponge and ginger, although we served the ginger three nights ago, so perhaps apple cake with custard sauce. What do ya reckon?"

"Folk will eat whatever you serve them, but no one has ever complained about your ginger cake."

Maeve smiled. "True, now ya mention it, and I'm glad ya did; Ciarán loves it and ta my mind nothin' heals ya faster than your favorite dishes."

"Mornin', Ma. Is he awake?" I hadn't seen Declan since the morning after the party. Shadows the shade of a ripe aubergine lay under his eyes and pronounced creases around his mouth made clear he hadn't slept. He answered my offer of tea with a negative wag of his head.

Maeve bestowed a kiss on her son's cheek. "Go on in ta your brother. If ya find him anywhere but in a chair or bed ya let me know straight away. And don't chat long."

"I'll not break the rules." He shuffled away toward Ciarán's room.

I turned to Maeve, puzzled. "You have rules about the length of visits?"

"I don't, and if ya tell Dec otherwise I'll deny it. The poor man is worried sick and if allowed, he'd stay beside Ciarán day and night. His frettin' doesn't benefit either of them though I don't mind tellin' ya, it gladdens me seein' the boy carin' about his brother again."

"He's remembered what's important."

"I dare say you're correct and it's kind a ya ta be so generous. I know he hasn't been any too easy on ya." Maeve wagged her head, mournful. "Oh, his dominatin' ways; though I can't say much about it; he gets it from me."

I snickered, the closest thing to a proper laugh in two days. "It's even distracted him from bossing me around. Hey! If I'm like a daughter to you, it makes him my big brother. It explains everything."

Maeve snorted with glee. "I would have dearly loved ta give him a little sister or three."

"Liar. You would have loved it on your own account."

"Fair play. And failin' ta have more children, I must content myself with waitin' on those boys for the joy." She began cracking eggs into a large mixing bowl, her expression innocent. "Are ya after havin' babbies yourself?"

"Not any time soon. I'm up to my elbows in bread dough."

Ciarán joined us an hour later, lured by the sweet spiciness of baking ginger cake. As we'd finished preparing lunch, Maeve had license to hover over him, plying him with soup and bread, then sweets and tea until he begged her to stop. "Bless ya carin', Ma, but you'll see me bigger than Paddy if ya don't leave off."

We jumped when the pub door banged open. Seconds later Garbhán burst into the kitchen, making a bee line for the table. Cringing, I moved closer to Ciarán, who held my hand under the table.

"Good God, man! I heard the news! How are ya farin'?"

"Aside from havin' ta answer the same question forty times a day I'm well, thanks."

"Have a scald," Maeve said.

Too distracted for the ritual he took a teacup. "Thank ya, Maeve. And you're truly all right, boyo?"

"Forty-one. Stickin' out."

Ciarán's grin did nothing to mitigate Garbhán's agitation. "Killarkin is the quietest place on earth; makes no sense havin' someone turn on the likes of ya. Do ya reck who did it?"

"Someone short, capable of wielding the proverbial blunt object with sufficient force," I replied.

Ciarán smirked. "My money's on Fiona."

"Hell hath no fury, and all."

"Ya might be next, darlin'. We should double your security."

Maeve batted her son's shoulder with exasperation. "Leave off, ya two. Not a bit about this is amusin'."

"Sorry, Ma, but laughter keeps the darkness at bay."

Never switching his attention from Ciarán, Garbhán asked, "Do ya remember anythin'?"

"Not a bit."

Garbhán spun toward me, desperate with concern. "And ya didn't see anythin', Clare?"

"No one did. We're clueless."

"It beats all," he said, shaking his head in consternation.

Maeve slapped both hands on the table, pushing herself up. "I've had enough of this talk." Pooling tears belied her brisk words. "Go on with ya, man. I'll be servin' lunch soon. And ya get ta bed, son."

The men complied, and after pulling the finished cakes from the oven, I took myself off, too, pausing outside the pub to scratch Orla's head.

"Clare." Garbhán sauntered over from the stoop of Declan's building and for once did not crowd close with his smug sneer and waxy hair. "Might we talk? In the cottage, where it's private."

Refusing to be alone with the man, I lied. "It's a crime scene. No one allowed."

"Sure. I wasn't thinkin'." Then in a quiet, uncharacteristic register he added, "Dec doesn't seem himself."

"Someone assaulted his brother." Garbhán grimaced, unconvinced. "Why? Do you know something?"

"Not about Ciarán, I'm afraid. But somethin's not right with Declan."

"We're none of us ourselves these days."

"Sure. And no reason ya would be. I'll be pushin' on, but watch yourself, Clare. Ya and the lad meant ta make light of your troubles, but I wouldn't want harm comin' ta anyone else."

His concern raised my anxiety. The self-centered Garbhán McAllister giving a shite about Ciarán made the attack feel more ominous.

I carried the worry to St. Dallán's but neither ruins nor clean Irish air brought comfort. The dense grass rolled like waves on the ocean but couldn't soothe an incoming tide of jitters. I loved Killarkin, had staked my future on her, and she betrayed me.

Restless, I wandered back toward the village. A note on Nessa's door announced her out on a call. There would be company at the pub, but my mood didn't suit the muttered speculations and sympathetic questions of well-meaning folk. Before turning back toward the cottage Father Donovan exited the pub, waving as he jogged across the street.

"Calling on the patient?"

Father folded his hands over his plump belly. "Indeed. Praise God he's doin' well. This is a terrible business."

"It is. Have you calmed your pilgrims?"

"Ya can't blame their alarm, but I've done my best ta assure them, though none are inclined toward roamin' on their own for now. And how are ya farin', my child?"

"Pretty well." I plucked a leaf from the ivy growing along the wall, blunting the ends of the pointed lobes with my thumbnail. "I'm grateful Ciarán is alright."

"I'd like ta show ya somethin'." Father led me into the church yard, his cassock billowing like a sail in the breeze. He docked before a cluster of headstones; a tall granite spire stood amid them, my family name carved on the surface. "Seamus had this installed a few years back. Most of the older markers are nothin' but slabs, the names worn away by weather and no way of tellin' who's here. Seamus wanted folk ta know where his people lived and died."

I traced the letters with my finger. "It rained all day when we buried Sean."

"I expect the weather will be fine for Seamus as we're havin' such a dry summer. Climate change, ya know."

The unexpected remark provoked a giggle. "I expect more conservative platitudes from a priest."

"Platitudes, whatever their stripe, don't hold against facts." Then, with mild, clerical perspicacity, he said, "I reckon you're findin' the facts a challenge."

When the sacraments still meant something to me, I always opted for the anonymity of the confessional booth. Now, in the open air, I faced my confessor. "Nothing feels safe anymore."

"There's the trouble with evil. It unsettles us, challenges what we believe, even what we know, about the goodness of others."

I bowed my head against the granite marker; the stone cooling my forehead. "Everyone in Killarkin is decent and kind. But *someone* hurt Ciarán. The shadow it's thrown on us makes me angry."

"And there's not a person here who couldn't say the same, includin' me. Ta tell ya true, each day I pray for justice on Ciarán's behalf and when it comes, for God ta give me the grace ta forgive." He peered through his wire rim glasses. "And the sweet Christ already knows I'm not yet inclined toward mercy. But we mustn't any of us yield ta the anger and fear of it; there's the lastin' harm ta our spirits. The evil doer will give an account one day: ta God, if not the authorities. Ya can still trust the friendship and goodwill you've known here." He bent and pulled a weed from Sean's plot. "Not too platitudinous, I hope."

A genuine grin lifted my cheeks. "No, Father. Thank you."

"Go in peace, child," he said, his face dimpled and kind. "I mean it."

For a week I spent most of my waking hours either in the pub kitchen or near Ciarán, with trips home only for chores or sleep, reluctant to stay longer than necessary. The cottage and her protection trees had broken faith. But Father's counsel worked on me; my trust needed restoration.

A good-hearted villager had already scrubbed the blood from the street, and with hot soapy water and a wire brush I removed the tiny spatters on the walk and front stoop. I swept the front room, pushing out the pain and fear of the awful night. With pillows plumped, towels laundered, and basins washed, I flung open all the windows, allowing the breeze to carry away whatever menace still lingered.

The villagers themselves completed the work. As they had in March, they came again bearing casseroles and cakes, posies of flowers, or baskets heaped with garden vegetables. No one pried, confining any mention of Ciarán to offers of concern and assurances of their prayers. It did me a world of healing good.

The draining week nearly ended, I met Nessa and the O'Donnell brothers for supper at the pub. Nessa greeted me with a conspiratorial grin. "I've a rare treat, Clare," she said, reaching into the pocket of her denim jacket. Handing over a scratched cassette box, she added, "Have a care; it's a relic."

I squealed, snatching it from her hand. "It's a miracle!"

Declan groaned like she'd thrust him with a broad sword. "Nessa Cassidy! What have ya gone and done? Give it, Clare."

Ignoring his outstretched hand I clutched the cassette safe to my chest, scooted out of the snug, and rushed toward the bar. "Eamon, please play this. And crank it."

I faced the snug triumphant, elbows braced on the bar, as the first gritty chords assaulted our ears. Mortified, Declan and Ciarán prostrated themselves on the table, heads buried under their arms. A group of nuns sat petrified with alarm. Two minutes later, the song screeched to an end, and with a forceful jab of his thumb, Eamon ejected the tape and proffered it like a dead rodent. "We've had quite enough noise!"

Reclaiming my prize, I pogoed back to the table.

Ciarán glared, the tips of his ears red as his hair. "Jaysus! Be merciful, woman. I have a head injury."

"Now we all do," Nessa replied.

My delight knew no bounds. "It's epically awful! A glorious, delightful mess of dreadful. I have never been happier! Ness, may I keep this? I want to listen to every terrible bit."

Even awful music has charms to soothe. The specter of the assault lifted away from our conversation and even our thoughts. Heavy, fearful spirits lightened in the normalcy of a regular pub night.

As we finished our meal Ciarán stifled a yawn and confessed, "I'm shattered."

With a clinical squint Nessa asked, "Headache?"

"None, doctor," he said, with a look of absolute distain. "It's on account of endurin' a week of excruciatin' boredom."

"You'll survive two days more. Come 'round first thing Monday."

"Wouldn't miss it." I stood so he could slide off the bench, then he bent close. "Visit me tomorrow."

"Of course. And Monday, after Nessa gives you a clean bill of health, we can celebrate with supper at the cottage if you want."

Ciarán tilted my chin with a finger. "Ya know I do. G'night, darlin'." Then he gave me a tiny kiss.

Nessa prepared to leave, too, and my repeated thanks for the cassette provoked another groan from Declan. Nessa ruffled his hair, a tease which jolted with its intimacy. "You'll survive a small dose of public humiliation, Dec. It builds character. *Slán*, Clare."

"*Slán abhaile*, Ness." Declan rose but I stopped him with an invitation for another round. "It's too early to go home."

He agreed, on the condition we didn't discuss music. "I enjoyed behavin' normal tonight."

"Maybe we'll get past this nightmare, after all."

The furrows returned to his brow. "Findin' the bastard who did this would help."

"Agreed. Oh, shite." Garbhán seated himself beside me, much too close. I pushed him off. "Do you mind? There's plenty of room."

He snickered but moved away and asked after Ciarán with respectful concern.

"He's much better."

"Glad ta hear it. And what of you? Word is you're after makin' an investment."

I scowled at Declan, who had the grace to redden with shame. "It's not public knowledge."

Garbhán took a long pull on his pint. "Save yourself the trouble and come in with me."

"Enough of your schemes, man," Declan growled. "Let's play darts, Clare." For once, I didn't mind following his orders.

Chapter Nineteen

MONDAY DAWNED WITH A kaleidoscope of butterflies fluttering in my belly. Barring interruptions or attacks, Ciarán would end the day in my bed. Feathery tickles of joy and anticipation danced against my ribs, sending my breath shallow.

After morning chores, I cut a fresh bouquet of roses, and with a heated blush, changed the bed linens. Supper would come from the veritable smorgasbord in the fridge, but I trotted out to the shops for wine and honey cakes before meeting Maeve.

She tasked me with the day's soda bread; a fortuitous choice given my lack of concentration. The mantel clock received more attention than the dough and my scant patience evaporated as the clock ticked closer to ten. "What's taking him so long?"

"Saints alive I don't know but the wait is showin' itself in the soup." Maeve dumped a kettle of broth into the sink, disgusted. "I used twice the salt I know ta do. Where is the man?"

"You don't think...Ness would phone if..."

"She'd phone if what?" Ciarán lounged against the door jamb, a cheerful, if self-satisfied, smile on his lips.

Maeve snapped his thigh with a tea towel. "If ya stroked out on her examination table, ya eegit. What do ya mean makin' us wait and fret all this time?"

"Apologies, Ma. But I had to find these." He pulled two posies of flowers from behind his back. "Tributes for the prettiest women in

Killarkin." He kissed his mother's cheek and pressed a bouquet into her hands. My face went hot when he addressed me with a wink and proffered flowers with a brief brush of a kiss. Then, without ceremony, he grabbed a fresh scone and plopped his feet on the table, ankles crossed.

Maeve pushed his boots to the floor with a disapproving noise. "Ya may be fair pleased with yourself but there's no call for your filthy shoes on my clean table and me tryin' ta get lunch ready, no thanks ta the distraction of wonderin' what in Christ's name kept ya. I raised ya better. Now, stop smirkin' like a cat in a dairy and tell us what Nessa said."

"Dr. Cassidy pronounced me fit."

Immediate tears softened Maeve's scolding expression. "You'd best be tellin' the truth. Ya have no permanent damage?"

"Save a tiny scar no one will ever see. Now, Ma, don't carry on."

She sobbed, clutching her flowers hard enough to bend the stems. "I can't help broodin', son. We don't know who hurt ya or the why of it."

Ciarán stood and folded her in a tender embrace. "We might never know. The mystery is nothin' ta everyone's lovin' care of me this last week. Quit frettin', Ma. I love ya for it, but I wish ya wouldn't."

Maeve's generous bosom heaved with her sobs. "You'll understand when ya have babbies of your own. A parent can't help it, not from the moment ya learn your child is comin' til the day ya die."

Ciarán raised both eyebrows. "There's a ringin' endorsement; I'll rush out and get a score of 'em."

Maeve sniffed back her tears. "Oh, go on with ya." She pushed him away and dabbed her cheeks. "You've been a pitiful layabout. Make yourself useful; there's a heap of wash and Clare volunteered her help."

Laundry has never ranked high on my list of favorite chores; but Ciarán insisted on giving me a kiss for every sheet run through the mangle, rendering the task much more enjoyable.

"Take a break, darlin'. I wouldn't have ya worn out." He held my waist, pinning me against the huge laundry table.

"Bold move, kissing me in front of your mother. Bet she's already planning the wedding."

"And namin' the babbies."

"Will she be upset when we name the twins Moe and Larry?"

"Even ya can agree those are terrible names for *cailíní*."

I stoked his collarbone with my lips. "This is really happening?"

"I'm ready if ya are willin', Clare. A blow ta the head gives a man perspective."

The enormity of the moment raised roses to my cheeks, and I buried my face against his shirt, hiding it from the relentless sparkle of his eyes. Time stopped for the length of a breath. From this fixed point, from our next words, we could not go back. "I don't want you hurt or disappointed."

Ciarán kissed me with such passion it felt like my bones would melt. He yearned against me, and my hands dropped to his hips. "And how could ya ever do so?"

"Loving is a messy business."

He settled against me, his face luminous. "The day we met, ya appeared out of the mist, hair burnished like flame, and I recognized your soul. It delighted and terrified me. But darlin', I'm familiar with an easy exchange a flesh. What I want is your love if you'll offer it."

"Not saying it sooner made that awful night even worse. If something had happened..." With a thumb on his lips, I drank in his beautiful features. "No more missed opportunities or close calls. We're finished here; please come home with me."

We returned to the kitchen where Maeve evaluated a mouthful of soup, added a pinch of salt, and gave the pot another stir. "It's rainin' again; amuse yourselves with darts until supper."

"It's only spittin' and I'm eatin' at Clare's."

"Have a cuppa before ya go."

Ciarán retrieved my flowers, then placed a hand on his mother's shoulder. Maeve noted him with an innocent, questioning stare. "Ma, I'm goin' with Clare. I'll see ya tomorrow." He waited until comprehension dawned on her face.

"Oh!" A hand fluttered to her chest. "Alright. Well, then, ya two have a pleasant—rather, enjoy your—Jaysus! Go on with ya." Ciarán kissed Maeve's scarlet cheek and led me away. We exited the pub with dignity, containing our laughter until we were outside.

"Not at all awkward," I said, wiping my eyes.

"She'd have worried if I didn't come home." He took my hand, and we ran through the rain to the cottage. Orla perched on the front step, still and watchful as Bast.

"You have lousy timing, cat." I poured a saucer of cream and invited Ciarán to investigate the buffet of sympathy meals in the fridge. After dealing with Orla, I found him leaning against the counter. "Make a selection?"

"It's far too early for supper."

In the petal-pink light of dawn I watched Ciarán sleep, his curls arranged in mad whorls and cowlicks. Now I knew the impossible downiness of those curls on my breasts and belly, his hands in my hair while he moaned and kissed me. One hand rested on my pillow and his long, muscled legs twined around mine. I groaned with the memory of the generosity with which he filled and released me, and the complete surrender of his own release. Sunrise fell across his shoulders and the ruin of our clothes on the floor. He breathed beside me, my perfume on his skin. I kissed his hand. Eyes still closed, he reached for me and took me again.

We woke two hours later, and he laughed, full and from his belly. I perched on an elbow. "Someone woke on the right side of the bed."

"I woke in yours. Gawd! You've spoiled me for any other woman."

"OK." I sat over him, wrapping in the quilt.

"That won't do."

"It's chilly."

"But you're interferin' with my view." Ciarán lowered the blanket from my shoulders. "There's a fair compromise."

"Enjoy it while you can, mister. It's time to get to work."

He buried a cold nose between my sleep-warmed breasts, eliciting a squeal. "Stay."

I lifted his head with a giggle. "Maeve expects me."

"Bunk off."

"Shagging you all day sounds like heaven but I never throw over my girls for a guy." Ciarán caressed my thighs but with a quick, determined kiss, I hopped off him. "I am going to the pub!" He followed me to the bathroom. "Ciarán O'Donnell..."

"I'll help. You'll be ready in no time."

Maeve hurried into the kitchen, cradling a sack of sugar, and stopped short, flustered. "I didn't reckon I'd see ya this mornin'."

My traitorous cheeks lit like a struck match, and I wanted to shrink to the size of an ant. "This is my regular time."

"Well, since you're here, it's best we talk. Have a sit." My body chilled. Maeve took a chair across from me, stout arms crossed over her bosom.

"Oh, Clare." Dammit; the clarion refrain of disapproving mothers the world over. "I can't remember when last I knew this much happiness."

My mouth fell open. "Pardon me?"

Her features lit with mirth. "Oh, I hoped, of course, and there's no more than the truth. I watched how ya were with each other and all the feelin' neither of ya realized or, if ya did, were too stubborn ta admit. I didn't know whether ta pray ta St. Jude or St. Joseph, so I put 'em both on the case." She surveyed her altar. "And I thank ya blessed saints. Now, Clare, darlin'; Ciarán is the dearest, the best man, though I'm his mother, but anyone who's met him will say the same."

"The fact is well known, Maeve."

"I'll not be pesterin' ya about intentions or babbies and the like, although nothin' would make me happier, which you'll consider old news, still, it can't help but delight me, the joy of the two of ya together, and if..."

"Maeve."

Her breathless ramble ceased. "Oh, I'm so pleased."

I peered up, sheepish. She beamed like a sun, and I didn't want to cloud her elation. But her happiness notwithstanding, she had a strong faith, and my mind struggled to find an inoffensive way of expressing my intention to sleep with her son, with or without the sacrament of marriage. "This is brand new, Maeve. It's not like we're ready to...you may not approve, but..."

"Pft; you're both grown, aren't ya?" Then her manner grew impassive, and it had nothing to do with her views on fornication. "I love ya, Clare; believe me, and have from the start like ya were my own, but I loved him first."

"And if I hurt him, you'll have me drawn and quartered."

"Tarred, feathered, and run from town."

"Understood."

Maeve dropped her stern mask and chortled. "And he'll be getting' the self-same warnin'."

My laughter harmonized with hers, even as a tear fell. "I'll love him as perfectly as my imperfect heart can manage."

She patted my hand, and her eyes welled, too. "Make all the promises ya want ta Ciarán. But be sure, ya have my blessin', and Eamon's, too. Oh, ya have our blessin'. And from today, consider yourself welcome ta join us for Sunday supper."

Before heading home, I stopped by The Cosy, where Moira's cheeky grin dispelled any hope of keeping secrets. "Cakes for your fella?"

"Please."

She smirked as she filled my order. "Any comments on your curtain hems of late?" She pretended not to notice my flush. "We missed ya last evenin'. Are ya comin' 'round tonight?"

"Sure."

She handed over my package with a wink. "Have a kip meantime; ya look as if ya had a restless night."

I fled to the sanctuary of the cottage before another neighbor weighed in. But the embarrassment of Moira's good-natured gibes couldn't compete with the delicious flutters in my solar plexus with each memory of Ciarán's ministrations. The approval or censure of Killarkin's citizenry could not touch the joy.

Conviction quailed later, however, as I wavered before the solidity of the pub door, alternately steeling myself for an evening of teasing or contemplating a bolt back home. Then a pilgrim opened the door, framing me on the threshold. The warmth and chatter of the room rushed around me as Ciarán handed his darts to Liam and strode forward to take my hand. There were plenty of snickers, but when he whispered my name nothing mattered except him.

Tucked away in a corner table he said, "I did feck all today. Couldn't be arsed with anythin' save thoughts of ya. I endured no end of slaggin'."

"Who spilled the tea?"

"Darlin'," he said, grinning. "We kissed in the pub on Friday and neither of us were here last night; I reckon we did."

"Right." My cheekbones lifted over a broad smile. "Truth is, I'm too happy to care." Clasping his hand I asked, "By the way, what is the Irish position on public displays of affection?"

"This one doesn't mind it at all." His kissed my fingers as proof. "Did ya have a good day?"

"Your darling mother almost gave me a medal for shagging you."

"Did she, now?"

"She warned me against hurting you, on pain of morbid humiliation, then claimed my time on Sunday evenings. Subtlety isn't Maeve's forte, and she may consider my attendance at family supper equivalent to posting banns, but she's pleased about us."

"Ma and Da have considered ya one of us a long time now. If ya will believe it, she would have invited ya before but feared it would seem ta be throwin' us together."

Behind him I noted the subject of our conversation, busy with customers, and smiled. "I take it back; she's very subtle and sweet."

Aside from the delightful presence of a man in my bed each evening and occasional bad dreams while my subconscious processed the attack, life returned to its peaceful rhythm, which meant the time had come to meet with Declan. After a conversation with my American attorney, I discussed my plans with Ciarán. "Given his reaction at the party, everything he said, it's impossible to believe he's only operating out of fiduciary responsibility. It makes me sick, to be honest. It might insult him and it for sure risks fecking up the thaw between the two of you, but nothing will heal all the way if he remains involved with the trust."

"I understand. Dec will, too."

"As my lover you're obligated to be supportive. It's the right choice, but will it make matters worse?"

"Bein' honest is one way of supportin' ya and confrontin' him is brave. If Dec takes offense, it's on him." With an impish smile he added, "Besides, now ya have a man ta watch after ya; his perceived obligation is discharged."

The next morning, Declan and I met at his office. He greeted me, offering coffee with the sobriety of a judge. Once served, he occupied his desk, fussed with pens, and said, "Before we begin, I'll apologize for my behavior the night of your party." He appeared pained, his skin full of deep etched lines. He held himself both tense and loose boned, like a man making amends ahead of an impending and gruesome death.

"Apology accepted. This constant battle between us has to end."

He heaved a weary breath. "Agreed. And as to Garbhán, don't be thinkin' I tell him all your business."

"Yet he's aware of my latest venture. Ness and Ciarán wouldn't have told him."

"Seamus' trust and the reno were not secrets," he said, with a wisp of defensiveness.

"But my investment plans are not common knowledge." I couldn't flinch now, despite Declan's obvious discomfort.

He gripped a pen and hovered it over a pad of paper. "How much do ya need?"

I provided him with the paperwork for The Folly. "The Council approved the sale. Please review the contract and transfer the balance of the deposit."

"The moment we finish here."

I expected more vehemence or even bewilderment, but if he had further thoughts on the matter, he kept them close. Though it relieved me to have avoided an argument, we hadn't reached the hardest part. "I also request your resignation as trustee."

Declan's eyes turned flinty with surprise, but he retained a semblance of professionalism. "That's not necessary."

"Would you prefer we go to Probate Court?"

He stared, too stunned for offense. "My behavior has resulted in a loss of your confidence, but I assure ya—"

"The issue is your lack of objectivity, which may worsen going forward."

"Because of Ciarán."

I made a brief nod. The clock ticked, abnormally loud. "This is the first project, but when other opportunities arise, I intend to meet them. My US attorney will function as the successor trustee until I'm thirty."

Declan's hand twitched and he grasped it with the other. "There's no express statement in the terms, but Seamus preferred havin' someone local overseein' things; someone who understood the ways of the village."

"I'm local and aware of Grand-da's intent. He gave me the cottage hoping I'd fall in love with Killarkin and continue his charitable legacy. I did and I will."

Thankfully, Declan registered my firm words and not the manic twitching of my legs. He nodded, weary. "Such unprofessional behavior is gallin'. Ya should have sacked me months ago."

What happened next astonished me. We proceeded to conduct a mature, civilized discussion while he explained each of the accounts, stock holdings, and rates of return. "One or two of these are under-performin'. I can suggest alternatives if ya like."

"I welcome your recommendations."

He lowered his head. "I am sorry, Clare."

Stretching an arm across the desk, I clasped the tips of his fingers. "I appreciate all you've done, Declan. This isn't personal; but it's best."

His face softened and the tense set of his shoulders eased, as he slid his hand out from under mine. "I agree. If askin' isn't presumptuous, what do ya intend ta do with The Folly?"

"Rent it to a young entrepreneur."

A tiny current of a smile flickered, erasing the last harsh line of his mouth. "It's the sort of thing Seamus would have done."

Chapter Twenty

D ADDY'S BALD HEAD EMERGED from the terminal, and he waved. Holding Mom's elbow, he loped toward me with a glowing smile. "Baby girl! Man, I've missed you!" He swung me up and into his arms.

When he set me down, I pecked Mom's cheek. "Your hair has grown so long, Clare. And what a pretty dress."

After introductions and the requisite pleasantries, I said, "Mom and Daddy, you're with us. Declan will drive the sibs. We'll have supper at the cottage at six, but feel free to come over after you've settled at the pub."

"Is there whiskey?" Colin asked.

"On tap."

"You shouldn't have gone to all this fuss," Mom said. "We could have rented cars."

Ciarán flashed a disarming smile. "It's no trouble, Mrs. Riordan. We're all terrible fond of Clare."

As anticipated, Mom used the car ride to quiz me for the millionth time about the arrangements. "Food and wine are set. Eamon will bring the kegs tomorrow morning, along with extra chairs for the garden. We've also set up party space in the barn. The weather should be fine, and Father Donovan has arranged a beautiful church service. You'll like him." I hoped the rapid flood of information would swamp a thousand other questions.

"And the headstone?"

"Ciarán and Paddy installed it yesterday. It's lovely."

"Seems you've thought of everything."

Her tone of grudging astonishment, designed to tempt me into a defensive reaction, went ignored. "You taught me well." If there were any hiccups or deficiencies with the to-do list, we had time to fix them. The real challenge lay in my ability to hold on to my new-found confidence in the face of entrenched family dynamics.

Golden sunshine showered the countryside. "It is pretty here, when it doesn't rain," Mom said, prompting me and Ciarán to share a sidelong smile. Some variety of rain fell most days, bestowing the very lushness she admired.

We beat Declan back to Killarkin, but once the folks checked into the pub, Daddy didn't want to linger. "You have to show us the cottage within the next ten minutes, or I'll explode."

We walked up the street and the snow-white trim of the cottage winked a welcome. Mr. Bunbun nibbled grass beneath a rose bush, and the dulcet music of the clucking hens serenaded us. The pastoral moment seemed a good omen.

Daddy worked the gate back and forth, marveling at its smooth action and solid, well-oiled hinges. "You repaired the gate!"

"We fixed all of it, Daddy."

Once inside, Mom assessed the front room with a squint. "I'd forgotten how small it is. But it's cozy, I suppose."

Daddy's hug lifted my feet from the floor. "Who would have believed the place could become this nice. You did a wonderful job, honey."

"Besides all the unsexy, behind-the-walls stuff, there's fresh plaster, paint, and refinished floors. Ciarán made all the new casework."

Daddy admired the bookshelves flanking the fireplace. "You're a talented craftsman, son."

Mom's effort to refrain from anything which smacked of overt approval failed when she entered my bedroom. She could not repress her delight. "It's an aerie! The coverlet is exquisite."

"A local woman embroidered it."

Mom's eyes gleamed with her lust for bed linens. "Does she sell other things?"

"She does. We'll go 'round before you leave."

Daddy glanced out a back window and snuffled. "Da would have loved all of this."

"Are those tears, old man?"

He drew the back of his hand across his face. "Allergies."

When the siblings arrived, a large pot of stew simmered on the stove and fresh loaves of bread waited on the counter. We gathered around the table and Daddy emitted a satisfied groan. "The Riordans are together again, in the place where it all started." He covered another sniffle with a long draught of whiskey.

Throughout the meal we caught up on family news and my brothers goaded each other about the respective standings of the Mariners and Cubs. Then my sister-in-law grew impatient. "If you two don't mind, I'd like to know how Clare keeps busy."

"With a lot: tending the house and garden, cooking at the pub, refinishing furniture with my friend Liam, and working on my darts game." Virginia's mystified face didn't surprise me; a list of homey activities couldn't begin to convey the richness of my simple life.

"But you must be eager to come home," Mom said.

The pivotal moment arrived and Ciarán answered my 'uh oh' glance with an encouraging smile. "I'm going to live here." Forks and knives clattered to plates, Stephen choked on his beer, and five pairs of eyeballs gawked without blinking.

Mom's brow twitched. Ignoring the decisiveness of my statement she said, "You came to restore the cottage and bury Seamus. After tomorrow there's no reason to stay."

A hint of panic hid behind her words, but my conviction held. "This is home, Mom. I didn't anticipate how much I'd love it here." Then, because no one had yet found their voice, I shared my plans for The Folly.

Mom clutched the gold locket at her throat. "You're going to be a landlord?"

"Until Liam can buy me out. The main goal is to help; like Grand-da did."

At my request, Declan had digitized the old ledger and the original now sat on the hutch. I retrieved it and presented the record of Grand-da's legacy to Daddy. "He did so much here. It's an honor to carry it on."

His hand convulsed as he turned the first pages, reading the entries. "When you told me what Da did, it didn't much surprise me. But I never dreamt it went this deep."

"How long have you known?" Mom's voice came muffled, her head downcast toward the clasped hands on her lap.

"About staying? A while."

"How long exactly?" She turned up her head, more grieved than blind-sided.

"April."

"All this time without a word."

Daddy wrapped an arm around her shoulder. "But you suspected, Denise. Be honest; it's not a shock." He laid his free hand over mine. "I'm proud of you, baby girl. Seamus would be, too." With a squeeze, he removed his hand from mine and flicked moisture from his cheek. "Damn allergies."

After supper we walked to the pub, where the family received the full local hero treatment, complete with hearty handshakes, and rounds of beer. Ciarán and Declan played darts with my brothers while Virginia and I watched from a nearby table. "You'll have to meet my friend Nessa tomorrow; she's out on a call."

Virginia refilled my wine glass. "Knowing you have friends here makes me less inclined to worry about you. Besides, it's good to have a few minutes alone. Clare, your news is incredibly exciting but why didn't you tip me off?"

"Sorry about the bombshell, Gin, but you're horrible with secrets."

She nodded in rueful agreement. "The pressure to please is the curse of the first in-law. But, for the record, I support your decision. If I lived in your adorable little cottage, I wouldn't leave either."

I glanced at Mom, who seemed comfortable chatting with Cathleen and Saoirse. "Denise managed the news better than expected."

"She's changing in your absence. You're different, too."

"More than either of us could have imagined."

Virginia smiled. "You've always reminded me of a loose ping pong ball, restless energy, adorable and entertaining, but undirected. You've settled, and not in a horrible, boring way; your vibrancy is more focused."

Her approval made me tender. "All my life I've struggled to get one damn thing right, the ideal career, a Denise Riordan level dinner party. But the answer, as it happens, wasn't in doing but in being. Once I started getting myself right, everything else started sorting out."

My sister-in-law nodded toward the darts lane. "Including a fling with tall, ginger, and Irish over there?"

I tossed my head in a silent laugh. "Oh, gawd! I aged out of falling into bed for no good reason a long time ago."

"He's gorgeous."

"And he's every bit as beautiful on the inside."

Gin made a teasing pout. "I'm so out of the loop I didn't even know you were dating anyone."

Until she used the word, I hadn't realized our relationship manifested without the trappings of American courtship. The picnic might have qualified as a date, but neither of us regarded it so at the time. "We've never dated, not the way you mean. We became friends working on the cottage and hung out here most evenings. Then one day the same instinct which kept me here woke me to him." My lover caught my eye and winked; the gloss spreading across my cheekbones didn't spring from embarrassment.

Virginia let out a tiny joyful yelp. "My god, a Clare Riordan first. You're in love! I'm thrilled, sister o' mine."

As a dart thunked and cheers went up, Mom lowered beside me, nodding like a drowsy cat.

"You're a tired mama."

"It's been a long day, and though he won't admit it, your father is dead on his feet."

The men crowded around us with their pints of beer. "Who won?" Virginia asked.

Stephen groused with a glare toward the O'Donnell brothers. "Bunch of ringers."

I consoled him with a glass of whiskey. "This will ease the pain."

Mom grasped Daddy's hand. "Let's take a stroll before bed, Ewen."

"Of course, honey."

I gave the siblings a rundown of the next day's schedule and Colin, a little tipsy, answered with a bleary salute.

Ciarán shook hands all around. "Pleasure meetin' ya all."

Stephen growled. "I want a rematch, O'Donnell."

"Anytime ya like."

Ciarán and I accompanied my parents to the door and watched them walk away, with Orla trailing behind them, her tail ramrod straight. When the trio turned toward The Low, he circled my waist with an arm. "It went well."

"One day down, two to go."

"Are ya tired?"

"Racked."

"I can stay here tonight." The lamplight threw a blue shadow over his face.

"May I never know such a level of exhaustion. Come home with me. Our bed is waiting."

I pulled my hair into a sober twist befitting my black dress and pearls, watching Ciarán knot his tie. "Clothes don't make the man and all, but you're positively edible in a suit."

"You're quite a ride, yourself."

"Do you mean what I think you do?"

"It's a noun, a compliment." He tweaked my ear. "It's a verb, too."

We were downstairs by the time the family arrived and after a solemn whiskey toast to Grand-da, we walked to the service. The closed shops bore black ribbons on their doors. Orla sat on the wide stone steps of the church and licked her paw.

Father Donovan greeted Mom and Daddy at the door, expressing sincere admiration for Grand-da, and kind words about me. "It's a blessin' ta meet the intervenin' generation."

Then, with his gentle authority, he sorted the procession; Daddy and the boys, with the urn and pall, took their places among the acolytes and servers. I whispered to Ciarán, "Sit with me."

"If ya wish." We took a side aisle to the front pew and joined Mom and Virginia. I folded my hands, devoid of emotion in the anti-climactic moment. Seamus left us ten months ago; we'd already done this.

The pews filled. Babies cried and feet shuffled. I fixed on the crucifix above the altar as the first notes of "*Bi Thusa 'mo Shúile*" rolled out of the small pipe organ and bittersweet incense wafted through the nave. The congregation rustled to their feet and sang with the full-throated luster of Celtic voices. Mute, I mentally recited the English lyrics. Knowing

Gaeilge wouldn't have mattered; the song couldn't push past the fiery knot searing my throat.

After the opening rites we settled into our pew, Ciarán's arm solid against mine. A keen longing manifested; a desire to lean close and breathe his calming, clean scent of bay and fresh grass. Instead, remembering the handkerchief dolls Grand-da made to keep me still during Mass, I knotted and unknotted a square of embroidered linen.

Father Donovan officiated with solemn dignity and intoned the prayers with a gravity and elegance worthy of the Vatican. His homily extolled Grand-da's virtues with a sweet combination of appropriate seriousness and charming wit. After communion Colin delivered a loving, poetic eulogy on behalf of the family. I held off a prick of tears.

Clouds floated like feathers in a sapphire sky as we exited the church and walked toward the family plot where a fresh-dug grave waited. The stately tombstone, bearing Grand-da's dates and the simple inscription: 'Seamus Riordan, son of Killarkin', stood over it, incongruous among the other weathered markers. Father read the final rites, Paddy lowered the ashes into the sod, and Daddy spilled a shovelful of dirt into the grave; the earth pattering onto the urn like fallen coins. He drew a hand across his brow and passed the shovel to Stephen.

Tears spilled as we filled the grave. We *hadn't* done this before and what seemed a formality now shook us with its finality: Grand-da rested beneath his beloved Irish sod. The silent shudder of Daddy's shoulders undid me. I reached a blind hand and Ciarán grasped it. Father gave the dismissal, and the church bells tolled the nine tailors which signaled the passing of a man, followed by ninety-five single peals for each year of Seamus' life.

As congregants swarmed my parents with condolences I begged Ciarán to take me home then wept like a child the whole way, supported by his strong arm. Leaving him in charge of the door, I fled to the sanctuary of my room, wanting nothing more than to crawl into bed and free however many sobs needed out. But footsteps clattered below. Splashing my blotchy face with chilly water and drawing a deep breath, I returned downstairs to greet guests.

In lieu of a keen, Dan and Padraic played a funeral dirge on pipes and flute. Five-year-old Clare clenched, but a stronger woman had replaced the overwhelmed child. The tune resonated, with the same eerie beauty and mournful impact of a keen. Standing near the front door, hands braced behind me on the cool plaster wall, the sorrow in the tune met my pain, lifted it away, and sent it off like breath on a dandelion clock. Grand-da hadn't left me; he pulsed through all of us. When the music ended, Daddy embraced me and after drying one another's tears, I recommended Guinness for his allergies.

Eamon tapped the first keg and there were toasts. Older folks gathered in groups throughout the downstairs. Covers clattered off dishes and laughter sang over the clink of plates and cutlery. Younger guests made their way outside to enjoy the mellow afternoon. Daisy and May clucked contentedly; Orla dozed on a chair. People sought me out, each with a story about Seamus. My ears rang with their music.

The afternoon slipped off its spool into evening. Resisting a perverse desire to slip the Blatherin' Shites into Colin's playlist of trad tunes and modern Irish music, I watched the dancers. Declan approached and handed me a whiskey. "It's a grand party. Seamus would have loved it."

"Agreed. Why aren't you dancing?"

The pleasant curve of his smile reverted into the familiar straight line. "I'm out of practice."

"Shite, man. Leave your damn burdens at home once in a while."

Frowning, he shifted his shoulders. "Ya can't don happiness like a shirt."

"Why not?"

He shrugged off his jacket, folding it over his arm. "I don't know what makes me happy."

I peered over the rim of my glass and across the garden where Virginia and Nessa chatted. "Ness is even more fetching than usual, don't you think?"

Declan shook his head. "She doesn't deserve bein' dragged into this."

"Into what? Jaysus! I wouldn't fancy a man with such a dour puss, but Ness doesn't mind it. She's a glutton for punishment."

He attempted a scowl, but a hint of grin fought back. "Clare Riordan, bein' at it with my brother doesn't give ya license ta interfere in my affairs."

With an innocent bat of my lashes, I affected a poor brogue and lilted, "Why, Declan O'Donnell! If ya had any, there'd be no need ta interfere."

A tiny chuckle softened his attempted growl. "Shut yer gob."

Night folded over the valley and the guests lingered on. The fourth keg tapped out, the waxing moon lit the garden, and boozy couples danced to a single fiddle. I studied them, drowsily weaving to the tune's beat. Ciarán found me and placed a hand on my head. "You're knackered, my love; let me take ya ta bed."

"Yes, please." He enlisted Paddy to nudge the last guests out the door. Maeve supervised the kitchen clean-up, and I kissed her cheek for thanks. Then, with the house left to the family, we joined Mom on the couch; Daddy sprawled in Grand-da's chair.

I smiled. "Seeing you there is so perfect. It's appropriate."

"I can't believe you kept this piece of crap."

"It's a charming, battered relic," I said, with mock umbrage. "And it's comfy as hell." I reached to stroke the cracked leather. "Bury me with it."

Daddy snorted and pulled himself into a close approximation of an upright position. "We'll put it on pontoons and set it on fire, like the Vikings."

"Those bastards did know how to give someone a fitting send-off. Speaking of which, how'd we do?"

"Oh, baby girl; Da couldn't have asked for better." Content, I rested my sleepy head on Ciarán's shoulder. Daddy started recounting a story from Sean's wake, but I didn't hear the end. I fell asleep to the airy melody of a fiddle and the deep voice of my father.

Chapter Twenty-One

T HE FOLKS ARRIVED FOR breakfast the next morning; Mom barged into the kitchen, wild-eyed and frantic. "We have to check into our hotel by three."

"Any time *after* three, honey." Daddy said with his standard calm.

She ignored his patient correction. "And our cruise leaves first thing tomorrow."

"Have a cup of coffee, Mom. We'll have you to the hotel in plenty of time."

"I don't know why your father thinks this is a clever idea." An accusatory glare in Daddy's direction accompanied the remark.

Inured to his wife's tizzies, he answered with measured calm. "Because we need a vacation, Denise. Whenever one of those river cruise ads comes on, you rave about how much fun it would be. We've come all the way here; let's have an adventure."

Mom huffed her disagreement and squared her shoulders under her impeccable sweater set. "It's an awful lot under the circumstances, Ewen."

"Oh, please. You're pissed off because I surprised you and you didn't have time for any damn planning." He chuckled and blew her a kiss. "Lighten up, honey." I turned to the stove, hiding my glee at his teasing confrontation.

Undaunted, Mom continued. "I said they *seemed* fun, but after our horrible cruise to Puerto Vallarta I vowed never again. Did you forget my five days in a stateroom, sick to death with food poisoning?"

Daddy groaned. "You won't let me! You weren't dying, and no one will poison you. Don't fret."

Mom rested her hands on her belly, already bilious. "This is a simple recounting of my sum experience with cruises. Well!" Her tone switched from complaint to avid interest. "Good *morning*, Ciarán."

"Mornin', Denise. Ewen." With a gallant dip of his head toward my parents, he sauntered barefoot to the stove. "Can I help, darlin'?"

I handed him the wooden spoon. "If you'll serve, I'll finish the toast."

"Do you have another major announcement, Clare?" Mom's eyes glittered like a gimlet.

Snorting a laugh Daddy said, "You have eyes in your head, Denise. Leave her alone."

Ciarán laid a platter of eggs and rashers on the table and said, "I hope ya approve, sir."

"Of you or the breakfast? I win either way. Serving me bacon is sufficient, but if you're responsible in some measure for my daughter's happiness, we're friends for life."

Aside from commenting on her inability to comprehend fried tomatoes as a breakfast item, Mom spoke little during the meal. Instead, she made a rabid study of Ciarán, at last inquiring if he held a degree.

"I received a bachelor's in world religions and theology from Trinners."

"Trinity College. How nice. Did *you* know, Clare?"

"Sure."

The kitchen clock chimed the hour, providing a diversion. "We're meeting Gerry and Stephen soon," Daddy said.

Ciarán drained the last of his coffee. "Then I'd best fetch my clubs."

"And your shoes," Mom said, with excessive sweetness.

"Thanks for the reminder, Denise."

Stifling a guffaw I said, "Let me show you the garden, Mom."

After inspecting the grounds with the solemnity of a judge at a horticulture fair, Mom pronounced the overall effect "pleasant" and the roses "very healthy."

"They get doses of Epsom salts and frequent cutting, per your advice. And you were right about the garlic. Mr. Bunbun and his friends stay away from the veg." Mom chuckled as I stooped to pulled a weed. "What's so funny?"

"You. Like this."

"Proof a good example always comes home to roost." I stood back, admiring my little plot. "Next spring we'll install raised beds."

"Next year. I can't believe you're staying."

"Kids are supposed to leave home."

Mom harrumphed. "But not so far away."

"Stephen never came back from university."

Mom plucked a lavender stem and rubbed the spike between her fingers, releasing the soapy, herbal scent. "Chicago is still in America; visiting him doesn't involve three airports and several time zones."

"I'll fly over, Mom. And you're always welcome here. Come see the barn. We're building guest suites over the stables. You'll have a room next time you visit."

Mom's imagination proved sufficient for her to visualize the finished work. "But it's a lot of expense for something you'll use infrequently."

"You're forgetting pilgrim season. But family and friends will always have priority."

Paddy's truck rumbled outside, and I left her to prowl. While we loaded the borrowed chairs he said, "It must be a fair treat havin' yer family here. Lovely folk."

"They'll do."

With the last of the party cleanup complete I went to fetch Mom and found her examining the shelves behind the lathe. "These are beautiful," she said, her fingers grazing the evidence of my woodworking lessons.

"Ciarán is teaching me. He made the candlesticks, but most of the dishes are mine. Take one if you like."

She selected a cherrywood bowl, stroking the rim with sincere appreciation. "It's so pretty. You should keep it."

"I can make more. The men will be gone for hours. Before we go 'round to Brigid's, would you like to visit St. Dall's?"

Mom roamed the ruins, her hands folded as if in prayer. The gentle wind ruffled her flaxen hair, and the sun highlighted beautiful silver streaks. She hadn't had those when I left. She circled back and joined me on the wall, her view trained on the distant hills. "Tell me about Ciarán."

"About him or about him and me?" She glowered. "He grew up here. After university he attended seminary but didn't finish. He did aid work for ten years, out of the country; now he does carpentry for Paddy." I pressed my hands into the wall, gathering strength from the stones. "But he's more than his biography. He has a lyrical, expansive soul and is kind, decent man. We're best friends." I pet the wall. "We met right here. We're happy."

"As Daddy said, your connection is obvious. Him waltzing downstairs like he owned the place wasn't required for proof."

"Hate to break it to you, Mom, but my virginity disappeared a while ago."

"Don't be crass." She scrunched her shoulders. "It all happened so fast. My goodness, Clare, you can't sacrifice everything for a man you've known less than a year."

The other shoe dropped, with a same tone and delivery of every reprimand uttered over twenty-seven years. We couldn't break the cycle yet, but it would be a while before we could try again.

"Any good parent would care enough to ask the question. But try and understand: Grand-da's gift transformed my life. Every loose piece of me clicked together here. It may seem hasty or frivolous to you, but if you'd lived it, you'd believe it."

Mom rubbed her nose and gazed out over the valley. "Edie often mentioned you had changed. Now I realize she meant to prepare me. I suppose she knows?"

"She figured it out before me."

"And she knew about Ciarán, too."

"Sure. So did you."

"He factored in a lot of your stories, as did other people. You never hinted at anything more."

"It wasn't sneakiness, Mom. Each inevitable decision, from restoring the cottage to choosing to stay, answered an inarticulate something in my soul. I found myself here; it became home, then so did he."

The corners of her lips puckered. "Hardly a comfort."

My poor mom struggled against the arc of parenthood, the unsettling moment when you recognize the infant you once cradled has become a full-fledged adult. She deserved the time needed to come around.

She cinched her shoulders back, head erect. "Well, you're young. Anything could happen. And I suppose it's nice having a—companion—while you're here."

A breeze blew over us, cool with mist. "He's much more." I told her about the attack. "Watching over him throughout the wretched night, I vowed to love him while I could."

Mom's head pivoted toward me. "Love? You've never used such a word about a guy."

"This is different. Before, relationships were something to worry about, countless silly questions threaded together with a ridiculous number of 'what ifs.' But the ground under me and Ciarán is solid."

I paced to the altar stone, savoring the moment. My ability to—for once—remain steady in the truth of my life rather than revert to the defensive form of a child, allowed us to have a better conversation than our usual standard.

Mom joined me a few minutes later. "I do like him, Clare. He's polite and charming; his parents are nice."

"The best."

"His brother is a little—"

"Off-putting? He grows on you."

Quick as Irish weather, Mom's mood clouded, and surprising as a rain on the heels of sunshine, she started crying. "I don't want my grandchildren in Ireland. They'll never know me."

I threw up my hands, as if she were an unbridled horse. "Whoa! Slow down, please. Don't worry about kids who might never be born."

"Oh, Clare, you'll have Ciarán's babies. If you stay here, you'll marry him and have his wild Irish babies, and they'll grow up without me!" Mom wept over her unborn grandchildren with genuine grief. Nonplussed, I patted her shoulder until something within me veered.

We hadn't exchanged a genuine embrace in years. Now I held her tight. "Mom, I love you. If there are children, a million years from now, you will know them. But please let me make a life with the man first."

She snuffled like a piglet, her cheek damp against my shoulder. "I want what's best for you."

"Of course, you do. But you and Daddy did your job. My choices, and my mistakes, are all on me now."

"You're my baby."

"I'm your daughter and proud of it."

We left the ruins and walked to Brigid's, arms encircling waists, and with a spot of retail therapy, Mom regained her equilibrium. On our way back to the cottage, we encountered the men returning sun-pink and jovial from their golf. After a late lunch at the pub, Daddy and Eamon played a last game of darts. Mom perched on a stool and watched, hyper animated and cheerful, but the tight set of her mouth indicated her brain seethed with the implications of my decision and our conversation.

Daddy called out from the darts lane. "Ciarán says you're pretty good."

I flounced a shoulder. "Good enough."

"Wanna prove it? A little two on two; youth versus experience."

"Naw. Riordan versus O'Donnell."

The competition ended with Ciarán grinning. "It is customary ta buy a round for the winners."

"You can pay up later," I said, with a consolatory kiss on his nose. "Let's get these people to Dublin."

When we arrived at the hotel, well ahead of check-in time, Ciarán paid his debt. Mom admired the appointments of the bar and tittered at Ciarán and Daddy's banter, but often stared into her wine glass, a finger tapping its foot. After one such episode, with a wavering voice, she said, "Clare, would you—the two of you—consider coming to Seattle for Christmas?"

"Kind of ya, Denise," Ciarán said. He seemed amenable but with a glance left the commitment to me.

"We'll try to work it out." The manner of the invitation moved me for two reasons: she made a request, not a demand, and her inclusion of Ciarán signaled acceptance of his presence in my life.

She grew tearful when we said our goodbyes, but then, so did Daddy. "Here's hoping those allergies don't interfere with your cruise," I said, wiping my own eyes.

"Maybe the breezes off the Shannon will clear them up," Daddy said, kissing my forehead. "But I doubt it."

As we drove home the clear blue sky filled with clouds dark as heather. There hadn't been a serious rain in several days and I'd missed it. I held my hand out the window as fat drops pounded down. Five minutes later, the ever-mercurial weather changed its mind, and the clouds billowed past, taking their burden toward Tullamore.

Ciarán shifted gears, peering at the damp pavement. "I like your folks."

"They like you."

"Denise seemed subdued."

"We had a grown-up talk this morning. The unaccustomed effort did her in." Stretching an arm across the bench, I massaged his neck. "It's great they came over but I am so ready to get back to my normal."

"Which is?"

"Waking with you, feeding Daisy and May, embracing whatever jumbled miracle the day brings, feeding the chickens again, and sleeping in your arms."

Ciarán chortled. "Your constants are me and chickens?"

"Yep. Well, and St. Dallán's, too. Then there's the pub, dear Paddy with his candy apple cheeks, and Nessa, though my need for her far exceeds hers for me." My gaze wandered to the far away rain blowing aslant over distant hills. "The list also includes green grass, whiskey, Maeve's stew, Eamon's songs, Moira's smart mouth, and darts."

"And if ya have all those, along with me and chickens, you're content?"

"I'm a woman of simple needs."

We bumped off the highway and along the dirt road toward Killarkin. When we arrived, Ciarán parked before Declan's office and pecked my cheek. "I'll leave the keys and meet ya at your place."

On entering the cottage my eyes turned, from habit, toward the mantel. A stirring, like the scudding of autumn leaves, fluttered. I dialed Mom's cell phone, and she answered on the first ring. "Is everything alright?"

"Of course. We got home a few minutes ago. Mom, do you have a photo of Grand-da and Grand-nan?"

"Daddy has one in his study. Why?"

"Are there any of Sean and Mary?"

"There may be, in all the boxes from Seamus' house."

"No rush. But if you find one, I'd like a copy. And one of you and Daddy, too."

"Why the sudden interest?"

My breath sounded loud in the stillness. "The mantel is naked now; I'd like to fill it with photos. Records are important."

"Oh, Clare." For the first time the phrase sounded sweet. "Seems to me you've already secured the most important family record."

My eyes misted. "Thanks, Mom."

"I'm glad we talked today," she said, her voice hushed.

"Me, too."

"I miss you already."

"Go figure, Mommy; I miss you, too."

After the call, I wandered into the garden, softhearted and thoughtful. The gate clattered open, announcing Ciarán's return, and I welcomed him with a kiss. "I love ya, Clare."

"You've made it quite clear."

He answered my wanton grin with one of his own. "All the same, be sure of it."

"I'm certain enough to ask if you'd like to live here."

"Ya *are* after a scandal, then."

"Consider it a treat for Aileen." My head rested on his chest. "All we have is right now. Siobhán and the Great Head Bashin' of '14 are proof." With every word my conviction grew stronger. "It doesn't matter how we do this. Whatever you want is fine, but please let's make the most of the time we have."

Ciarán pulled me closer. Over his shoulder my gaze took in the fields waving with summer grasses, the flit of beribboned gray-white clouds through the crystalline dome of blue. The timing of his answer didn't matter, and we didn't need to fill the air with promises. We were here now, we loved each other; the question wanted asking, so I asked. Pulling away, I extended my hand. "Will you stay to supper?"

"Thank ya, but it's Sunday; Ma's expectin' us." He glanced toward St. Dallán's, and his mouth worked like he pondered a matter weightier than social engagements. "There's the chief trouble of livin' together. When I move in, you'll have no need of askin' me ta supper."

My laughter didn't dismiss his point. Familiarity and proximity can breed inattention, if not contempt. Placing a solemn hand on my heart, I made him a promise. "My heart will never take you for granted and you will always be invited to supper." We started toward the house, then his words registered. "You said when."

His eyes glowed like summer stars. "I'm in your bed every night and won't occupy anyone else's. And it'd be convenient keepin' my socks in one place." In answer to my delighted squeal, he kissed my forehead. "Where did ya come from, Clare Riordan? How did I get so lucky?"

"You're Irish, sweetheart."

"We can bring my things over after supper." I clapped my hands to my mouth to suppress the continued squeaks of joy and he chortled. "Darlin', I've already been underfoot for the last two months."

"You've been under me occasionally, but never underfoot."

"Now you're givin' me ideas."

"Tell me what they are. Maeve won't serve for at least two hours."

The sun dipped low and shimmered gold in the corners. I roused from a love-doused nap; my hair spilled over Ciarán's chest. He chuckled as he wound it over his fingers. "I am looped in the loops of her hair."

"Mm. Beautiful image."

"It's Yeats. I never reckoned what it meant 'til now."

I rested my head on folded arms, admiring him. "You are so lovely."

He huffed. "Men are not lovely."

"You are. Every part of you, from the curls on your head to the crooked toe on your right foot and every beautiful inch between. I love the tense of your muscles, the glow of your incredible blue eyes, and your ridiculously perfect thighs. I love your heart and the way you love me. You're here, and when you leave, this is where you'll come home."

"Ah, darlin'. Ya make me wish I were a poet."

Chapter Twenty-Two

With the family now privy to my intentions and the sale of The Folly in the works, I offered Liam a rent-to-own deal. His response came in the form of tearful, repeated thanks and ended in a bear hug which bruised a rib. It also set off a chain of events. Liam hired Moira to keep his books and I asked her to do the same for the trust. She, it turned out, had long dreamed of taking her basic accounting accreditation to the next level and work toward becoming a Certified Chartered Accountant. Meanwhile, they discovered my past life included website design and I found myself involved in their enterprises beyond the role of mere investor. My home office morphed into the temporary headquarters for their businesses and the trust.

Two weeks after Grand-da's funeral, while Ciarán lunched in Dublin with mates from Cara, Liam called a meeting to update Moira and me on his progress. With a gleam of nervous excitement, he informed us he had the paperwork for his business license ready to submit.

"What name did you settle on?" I asked.

"Forsyth Furniture," he said, his chest puffed with pride.

"Great. I'll register the domain and start setting up social media accounts. And you need a logo. Two f's intertwined would be cool, maybe with the knot pattern you burn into the pieces you build. A good graphic designer could create something lovely with it. I've got some friends who owe me a favor, unless you know someone."

"Shite, Clare. Thanks," Liam said. In a half-whisper he added. "It's truly happenin'."

"It is," Moira said. "And I had a thought, man. Ya might consider carryin' a line a smaller goods, too; at least until you're a mogul."

"Go on with ya." Liam chortled and a beguiling flush darkened his cheeks. "And what else would I sell?"

"The other bits folk need for a home, like the bowls Clare makes." My throat knotted, but Moira didn't give me time to protest; she pivoted toward Liam, bright with ideas. "There's any number a folk hereabout who make pottery or wot not."

"Like your ma," Liam said.

"There ya are. Sell the bed *and* the quilt."

"I never considered." The wooden office chair creaked as he gave it a spin, his pinched forehead indicating he thought about it now.

Moira set her mouth in a straight line, more serious than I'd ever seen, and leaned forward to grip his shoulder. "What ya make is beautiful, Liam. Your heart and soul are in 'em. Right now, I reck ya feel like a train's rushin' in on ya, but ya have us ta help. Forsyth Furniture will be a success."

I closed the oven door on a casserole of stew when Ciarán arrived home. "Hello, you. Supper will be ready in a couple of hours. Shower or cocktail?"

He sniffed at the fresh bread cooling on the table and let out an 'ahh' of satisfaction. "Cocktail, please. Tell me about your day."

"Moira's website is done, Liam named his business, and I practiced candlesticks." I gestured toward the firebox. "My mistakes will keep us comfy come autumn."

He chuckled and embraced me. "I'm proud of ya."

"You should be. Not everyone burns designer firewood." My nose wrinkled, in the way of a child announcing something she knows is silly. "Liam wants to sell our stuff on his website."

"Fine by me."

"Seriously?"

"Sure. We can't use it all. And this should set ta rest any worries Denise harbors about whether you'll stay busy or not. Don't look like ya have a pain, darlin'. Ya do fine work."

"Arguable, but yours is great. And we'll approach other artisans for home goods. It's a great idea; the furniture will move more slowly, and this will give Liam another revenue stream."

A smile quirked his mouth. "Ya seem pleased."

"The responsibility weighs heavy sometimes, but it's satisfying—like the last piece of a puzzle snapping into place."

"I'm happy for ya, darlin'."

Late afternoon light filled the kitchen, winking in the amber of our whiskey and glowing on the yellow wall. "Tell me about your lunch."

"I enjoyed seein' my mates. I miss collaboratin' with them."

My heart missed a beat; the word implied more than meeting up for the occasional meal. "What are you saying?"

Ciarán's fingers fretted at the embroidery of the tablecloth, his smile dimmed. "I'll be spendin' more time in Dublin. They offered me a job weeks ago; I've decided ta accept it."

My body tensed and went cold. "Oh." The idea of him going back to Cara terrified me. How many more scars would his flesh bear? The thought sent my hands trembling and despite a keen desire to be supportive, I could only manage an indelicate, "Why didn't you mention it?"

"Ya were busy with the funeral and such."

A flush of embarrassment swamped other concerns. "My stuff isn't more important than yours."

His gaze moved from me to his hands. "I wouldn't waste your time with my ditherin'." He clasped my fingers with a gentle squeeze, his eyes back on mine. "Clare, I don't take my commitments here light, and the organization will accommodate me. I'll run ta town a couple days a week but work mostly from home."

Immense relief heated me, like a wool blanket on a winter night, and my tightly held breath released. He wouldn't be in harm's way. "What will you do?"

"Analysis and program recommendations; trainin' folk headin' into the field."

"There's no one better suited. They must be thrilled to have you back."

"You're not angry?"

"You could have told me from the off. You're patient when I dither, and supportive when I land. Let me do the same for you."

He gave me a chastened grin. "I need ta practice sharin' a life."

"It takes more than a couple weeks to become an expert. When do you start?"

"Monday."

"Wow. You need a car."

"I'll borrow Dec's or take the bus. I'll stay with friends if Dec won't let me use his flat."

"You know he will." Ciarán grew pensive and I laid a hand on his knee. "Are you excited?"

"Sure, but it's now I'm realizin' the change it will be for us and Paddy."

"You're an amazing carpenter, but this means more. He'll understand."

He set aside his glass. "It's not about degrees of importance. My work with Cara isn't more valuable than what Paddy or ya do."

"The dream is what matters. If this is what you want, do it." I grinned and stroked his cheek, but his attention turned back on the table, where his finger wandered the maze of an embroidered Dara knot on the cloth. "Anything else?"

He shook his head and laid his palm flat, fingers outstretched and still. "I'll miss ya when I'm away."

"Yeah but imagine the reunions."

He gave me a thoughtful smile. "It's no doubt best ta have spaces in our life together. If we're too enmeshed, we might come ta resent it."

My hand withdrew from his hand. "You feel trapped."

"Ah, darlin', not at all, I assure ya." The eyes which searched my face, however, were less emphatic. "What were ya doin' this time last year?"

"Well, being unaware Grand-da would die in two months and change my life, odds are, barbecuing hamburgers and ordering Joel to bring me another gin and tonic."

"A great deal has happened since. Your life has been a whirl from Seamus' passing til now. Though it seems impossible, life *will* settle down."

My blood cooled. "Life always changes. You're wondering if one of these days I'll decide it's a mistake and don't want to be here anymore."

Numb, I carried our glasses to the sink and stared at the garden shadows. A flash of white tail feathers provoked an irritated swear. "Daisy's escaped again." He reached for me, but I eluded him. "The damn chicken is out!" The kitchen door slammed behind me.

I stalked the hen across the garden until she paused, scratching under a rosebush. At my soft, coaxing clucks, she cocked her head, an insolent mock in her beady eye. "Come here you stupid bleedin' gobshite of a bird!" Catching her, further Irish insults spilled out as my arm scraped against thorns. Ruby beads of blood dotted the stinging skin. "Awesome, Daisy. You'll be delicious with dumplings." Carrying her like a football back to the run, I set her inside the fence with more gentleness than she deserved. "Now stay there!"

A curling flap of wire had come away from the bottom of a post and I secured it with a stone, then watched the birds for a few moments. When Ciarán wrapped his arms around me from behind, I stiffened. "I'll mend the fence tomorrow," he said.

"I can manage."

"Sure, but I'm offerin' ta help."

I twisted out of his embrace. "Simple repairs are within my capabilities and if necessary, so is being without you. You said I had to want all of it." My arms flung wide, as if embracing the countryside. "This is me, all in. Last-summer-Clare is nowhere near who I am now. I didn't come to Ireland, or stay here, because of you. I love you, but if you want out, fine. I'll cry; but don't expect me to run home to Mommy. I'll still live here, chasing after stupid damn chickens and drinking at the pub. Maybe I'll marry Paddy."

My hand-waving, vehement declaration left Ciarán halfway between laughter and tears. "Paddy would be lucky ta have ya, but I don't fancy givin' him or any other man the chance."

He kissed me, considering the matter resolved, but while he showered, I turned down the oven and took my confusion for a walk. Clouds blew overhead, layered like street pavers. Sheep baas punctuated the hum of farm machinery. The beauty soothed, but Ciarán's announcement shook loose old insecurities, and their return frustrated me. My resolve to not give way didn't diminish the sucker punch in my solar plexus. After passing the pub on my second lap, I turned back, deciding a round of darts might help.

Nessa nursed a sherry at the bar, and it took little effort to coax her into the darts lane. Twenty minutes into our match she said, "I'm afraid of ya."

"I may go pro."

"Ciarán back from the Pale?"

"For now." I threw another dart, dead center.

"Jaysus! I'm glad there's no money on this game. What do ya mean?"

"He's rejoining Cara." Her groan of genuine distress brought me to my senses. "It's an office job. He'll be in Dublin a few days a week." Saying it out loud made my overreaction obvious, but a question still niggled. "Am I a flake, Ness?"

"I thought so once," she answered, emphasizing her matter-of-fact statement with the thunk of a dart. "I made ya for a little rich girl playin' house."

"My first impressions aren't great. I have to grow on you."

"Ya did do." Her next dart hit the rim and fell to the floor. "Bollocks, ya win. I assume ya want whiskey?"

I did, as well as a change of subject. When we tucked into opposite corners of a snug, I asked about her day. Despite the occasional carp about a patient, she took evident joy in her work. "I used to envy people like you." I said. "Before this, jobs funded my lifestyle, with no other attachment beyond the paycheck."

"Yet everythin' ya did prior fit ya for the work you're doin' now."

My perspective returned. "It's amazing, having all those disparate bits turning into something whole. It's wonderful Ciarán has work he loves, too."

Nessa nodded, sage and composed, then smirked. "Sure, but a less mournful face would make your statement more convincin'."

Studying the photo of Michael Collins above us, ashamed of my foolishness, I apologized. "Sorry to be a pill. The manner of the announcement bothers me, not the job. His decision impacts me, too, but we never discussed it. He never even mentioned the possibility of it."

Nessa positioned her elbows on the table; everything in her face soft and firm at once. "I've known the man a good long while and reckon he believed it considerate ta not trouble you with it."

"But it's part of the deal when you're in a relationship."

"It is. But he has ta learn as much. Clare, before ya arrived, he never committed ta anythin' but Cara. He may still be workin' out the surprise of findin' ya, but he's sure." She claimed her glass and peered over it. "Unless you're havin' doubts." A fervent shake of my head answered her. "My medical advice is better than the other sort but trust your fella and what ya are together. Don't borrow trouble where there is none."

"Your non-medical advice is excellent, too. Baseless worry profits nothing, but here I am, learning the same damn lesson all over again."

Nessa poised a cheek on her hand. "Imagine your life like a spiral, ever reachin' up. You're bound ta encounter the same turns of your story along the way, but ya meet it different each time, because ya know more. It's not a failure, but an opportunity ta take the learnin' deeper."

I knew better than to embrace her but did hazard a thank you.

"You're welcome. Now stop actin' the maggot."

We drank a toast, and my spirit once again turned peaceful. The delicious aromas of roasting lamb and fresh bread wafted from Maeve's kitchen, a promise of comfort and satisfaction. "I love when the pub is sleepy and quiet like this."

"It'll be jammers again soon enough."

"I love it then, too."

A genuine smile breached her serious face. "I'm glad you're stayin', Clare. It's good havin' a friend."

"Nessa Cassidy, you almost sound sentimental."

After a lusty swig of sherry, she smiled and said, "Feck off."

Chapter Twenty-Three

CIARÁN AND I RIGHTED ourselves from our hiccup. He enjoyed his new work, my days were full, and our reunions *were* wonderful. Sometimes, in his absence, a vague ill ease would surface, a hangover from a previous life of never feeling enough for myself, let alone someone else. Then I'd breathe, hug his pillow to my chest, and exhale the concern.

Mom's search for ancestral photos had not yet borne fruit, but she did ship a large box of other memorabilia. Having no time to go through it, I stowed it in the closet under the stairs, then plopped on the dusty floor, back against the wall. Ciarán found me there and squatted outside the open door with a grin. An inadvertent blush warmed my face. "This is my secret chamber."

"Is it now? You're like a *cailín* sittin' there."

"Once, yes. A little, terrified girl." My throat thickened with remembrance. "I hid here during great Grand-da's wake. The keening freaked me out. Being out in the light with all the noise scared me more than the idea of hiding with spiders."

"Were there any?"

I smiled. "No. But a boy found me. He had beautiful eyes, a voice like a lullaby, and his kindness made me feel safe. He promised not to rat me out and brought me a blanket and a cake."

"A honey cake."

"Did I tell you this story already?" I blew out a breath and surveyed the space. The cutout crosses on the open door threw distorted silhouettes on the hallway wall.

"I love ya, Clare."

His voice vibrated through my soul; its frequency tuned like a perfect chord. I gazed into the rich cornflower pools of his eyes and sucked an audible breath. "Oh, Jaysus. I never told you this story."

"No need; it's my story, too."

"You always remembered?" My words faded on the catch in my throat.

Ciarán moved to sit beside me. "The wee, terrified one under the stairs."

"You took care of me."

"And ya don't need takin' care of now, all grown and amazin' and not afraid of spiders, keeners, or anythin' else."

Knowing the reality, I snorted. "Remind me at three a.m. when my head starts nattering."

He kissed my hand, a tender pressure. "Ah. The hamster wheel started again."

"It creaks sometimes, when you're away."

He cuddled close. "Share your concerns, darlin'."

"Ambient worries don't even hold in daylight let alone merit discussion."

My evasion relied on his empathy and sure enough, he wrapped comforting arms around me, his expression sweet and sad. "My goin' back ta Cara hasn't anythin' ta do with us. I never anticipated the way lovin' ya would change me, but I won't fear it."

Easing onto his lap, I smoothed the grim set of his mouth with my thumb. "I don't want to be afraid, either."

"You're all I want."

"All is too much pressure." With my hands on his strong shoulders, I touched my nose to his. "But Ciarán, while we're here in the secret chamber, please promise we'll try our best. Promise the second you can't or don't want this anymore you'll tell me straight out, even though your tender soul won't want to say it and my broken heart won't want to hear it."

"If ya make the same vow."

"I swear."

"Me too." He traced my cheekbone, watching me in wonderment. "Do ya have time now for lovin' me?"

I peered at my wrist, reading freckles as if they were a watch face. "My next appointment can wait."

We had no trouble with words. There were plenty of stories, old and new, to share. We used words to learn about each other, tease, encourage, and challenge. But we spoke a different language in bed; the communication of skin and muscle, passion translated with tender expressions and hands, mouths, and heat. We had a new conversation every time.

When we finished, I lay beside him, spent. "Oh, how lovely."

"Did it ease the last of your cares?"

"The real struggle is against a desperate need to get this right."

He answered with a huffing laugh. "You've given me no cause for complaint, and I'll endeavor not ta give ya any."

"You don't. Besides, worry is a waste of time."

Ciarán kissed my shoulder. "Your boundless energy can be put ta far more interestin' uses."

The phone rang on August twenty-eighth at five-eleven a.m.—the exact moment of my birth—in a ritual Mom established when I started university. "Happy birthday, Clare. What are your plans?"

"Ciarán's plotting something, and Edie sent champagne. Otherwise, no one knows about it."

"What? No party?" Daddy said, in mock horror. I had a legendary fondness for celebrations.

"In a village where everything about everyone is common knowledge, it's nice having a secret."

"Well, we had a party for you this evening. I baked coconut cake."

"Of course, you did." Mom always whipped up her cloudlike confection for my birthday.

"We miss you." Mom's voice faltered. "Have a wonderful secret birthday."

"I'm counting on it." My day would, in fact, be no more than a compilation of fulfilling chores and a quiet evening with my lover, but I couldn't imagine anything better.

Still, some drama awaited me; I arrived at work to find a distracted Maeve, grumbling before the door of an open refrigerator. "Trouble?"

"Ya won't fathom it, nor can I, but I miscalculated my grocery order. Be a darlin' and run over ta Delaney's for three more chickens."

"Sure. And I'll take Daisy along. She got out again this morning. She's committed to being free-range."

The errand took longer than necessary, as Saoirse's gift for expounding on nothing particular exacerbated the straightforward purchase of poultry. But after freeing myself—and returning to the pub to receive profuse thanks for my trouble—Maeve set me to grating potatoes while she dressed and trussed the chickens. We were back on schedule.

In the afternoon, while working like fury on Liam's website, Declan interrupted with a request to meet for a conversation about the trust. "Can it wait? Ciarán will be home soon, and I smell like garlic."

"I'll leave ya time ta bathe, but we should finalize matters before I leave again for Dublin."

We'd made our peace, but the inconvenient demand raised vestiges of my old grudge. Still, for the sake of family peace and the formal end of our business relationship, I agreed. Despite his promise, the meeting ran longer than desired because, true to his nature, he larded the agenda with a healthy dose of well-intentioned admonition and advice.

When he released me, I ran home to shower and emerged from the steamy bathroom, wrapped in a towel, to discover Edie reclining on the bed, reading a magazine. "Hi, hon," she said.

"What the actual hell?"

My friend tossed aside her *Vogue*. "Sorry I didn't call earlier; I've been traveling." Unable to process her presence, I could only gape. She lifted my chin, closing my mouth. "Don't swallow your tongue. We've always celebrated your birthday together, why the hell should this year be different?"

"How did you get here?"

"An airplane; a big metal tube which, by some inexplicable magic, flies through the air."

I knit my brow, hands on hips. "Edie King—"

"I rendezvoused with O'Dish in Dublin. Nice guy." Then she winked and added, "I approve."

Sobbing, I threw myself into her arms. "This is unbelievable."

She hugged me, petting my hair. "Don't start; boo hooing makes you blotchy. I've missed you, hon." She pulled away and dabbed her eye, careful not to disturb her makeup. "I am not crying."

"Yeah. Daddy gets those allergies, too."

The surprise of her appearing in my bedroom made me realize how much I'd missed her. But there she stood—her always perfect manicure on point, her long ebony braids silky and flawless against brown skin—wearing an ensemble fit for the pages of the fashion magazine beside her.

She urged me to dress adding, "And your birthday is an occasion. No jeans." I succeeded in choosing an outfit which nudged my appearance nearer to her impeccable standard but drew the line at heels. "Even you can't navigate The High wearing stilettos."

"Really?" She made a casual examination of her nails. "Are you assuming Ciarán carried me here?"

"You're amazing."

"Never forget it. Now get a move on. Don't keep a hot Irishman waiting."

When we came downstairs Ciarán appeared more than pleased with himself. After a brief kiss I said, "You're pretty cute when you're smug."

"I came close ta spillin' the tea any number of times."

He'd laid the table with a cheese plate and we started on our aperitif while Ciarán poured wine and listened with unfeigned interest as Edie and I chattered through the first layer of our catch up. Then I clasped both their hands. "This still doesn't feel real. How did you pull it off?"

"Edie got my number from your da and proposed a birthday treat."

"The trick lay in getting you out of the house. You know I love theatrical entrances. So O'Dish here worked it out with the lawyer."

"You had Declan in on it, too? Damn. You lot are amazing."

Ciarán grew sheepish. "Ya don't mind surprises, then?"

Around a mouthful of brie I said, "Not nice ones like this."

"There's a relief. I've warned ya I'm shite with secrets." Pulling me onto my feet he answered my quizzical expression. "We'd best get ta the pub."

The clamorous Lamb and Thistle didn't appear to have a spare seat anywhere, let alone three together. Then Maeve, wreathed in smiles, emerged from the kitchen with a huge platter of chicken and nodded toward the back of the room, where friends gathered around a large table, decorated with late summer flowers.

The entire day had passed without the need or desire for a party, but there now seemed nothing better than celebrating with new friends and old. We ate a monstrous amount of food. There were toasts; hilarious, sweet, and, in Nessa's case, wittily dry. Then Maeve presented the cake, an airy marvel of ginger and lemon cream. "Please do forgive me sending ya off this morning," she said. "But I couldn't ice it with ya in the room."

For hours we drank and danced, and when Eamon called time, it felt like waking in the real world after inhabiting an ageless fairy land.

The last lingering villagers made their way home and pilgrims shuffled toward their rooms. The band packed their instruments, and a frowning Paddy laid aside his fiddle. Eamon pulled the blinds, dimmed the lights, and with a nod toward our table, disappeared.

"It's only 12:30," Edie said, grumbling.

"But we have your champagne back at the house."

Ciarán rested an arm across the back of my chair, his hand on my shoulder in gentle restraint. "There's no hurry, darlin'."

Maeve cleared glasses from an adjoining table, but everyone in our party sat still, save for sly nudges and winks. Eamon returned, cast a shrewd glance around the otherwise empty pub, and slammed home the front door bolt.

"What the hell is going on?" Edie wore the stricken aspect of a horror film ingenue.

"Your first lock-in," Ciarán said, with a hearty laugh. "Who's got the next round?"

Eamon brought me a large glass of whiskey and bussed my cheek. "Jamie wishes ya a happy birthday." Paddy plucked his fiddle and started a singsong. The party didn't end until three a.m. and might have gone longer had our conductor not gone hoarse.

As we returned home Edie marveled. "Shit. I thought the whole bursting into song schtick only happened in musicals. You Irish sure know how to party." She weaved precariously and Ciarán caught her arm. "OK, No champagne." Her words slurred. "I'll die if we start it now. Thanks for the lift, O'Dish."

"Delighted, darlin'. Thanks for aidin' and abettin'."

I saw Edie to bed, setting her up with a pitcher of water before joining Ciarán. The open bedroom windows let in a cool breeze and brief laughter filtered up from the street, then faded. "If you're not too knackered, you've one more present."

"I hope so," I said, drawing a hand down his chest.

Grinning, he placed a silver cuff of spiral knots on my wrist, a bracelet delicate enough to have been smithed by the fae. He turned my wrist in the lamplight, appreciating the glimmering sheen. "It's grand, but it might be better appreciated without this distractin' frock." He unbuttoned my bodice and lowered it off my shoulders. The dress fell, he kissed my throat and lifted me onto the bed.

Lying hip to hip, I admired the bracelet. "It's beautiful. Thank you. You gave me an amazing birthday."

"You're welcome, darlin'. Though I should be thankin' Denise and Ewen for havin' the good sense ta make ya." He traced a spiral with a finger then encircled my wrist with his hand. "May I ask ya somethin'?"

The intent glow in his eyes made my heart thump. "Anything."

"Why does Edie call me O'Dish?"

The guest room door banged open, and a rumpled Edie barged into the kitchen, demanding to know where we kept the hairy dogs. I administered tiny tots of whiskey and strong cups of coffee, while Ciarán made a fry.

With an inarticulate mumble, Edie jammed the knuckles of her right hand into her temple. "Ireland is treacherous."

"You usually drink everyone under the table."

"They train 'em different here." She glared at Ciarán as he served breakfast.

He raised his palms, as if warding off an imminent attack. "In my defense, I never poured whiskey down your throat."

"What the hell didja expect, man? Your father locked me in a pub! You're responsible by proxy." She stabbed a sausage and groaned. "There's a carsick baby in my brain."

She spent the morning fit for nothing, but by afternoon, Edie's strong constitution rendered her capable of a walk to St. Dallán's. A light drizzle provided the last of her restoration. "This isn't bad."

"The Irish call it a spittin' rain."

"In other words, a typical Seattle day." She perched on the plinth of a pillar. "And this is the famous sacred ground. I get why you like it." She appraised the hills around us. "There are a hella lot of sheep around here."

"They outnumber the citizenry; thankfully, they aren't smart enough to organize." The breeze blew hair spangled with tiny raindrops across my face. "Gawd, I love it here."

"I know."

"These last seven months have provided quite an education."

"You were always more capable than you believed, Clare." She grew pensive. "I didn't count on you not coming back, though."

I admired her profile; sharp, clear, and near enough to touch. "Love your face, Edie."

"Love yours, hon."

We surveyed the village below in silence and I smiled at the far off sight of Ciarán in the garden with the roller mower. "Grand-da knew I'd find myself here."

"Seamus always made Killarkin sound like a magic realm." She squeezed my fingers. "He wasn't wrong."

The weekend concluded with birthday champagne and Edie's delicious home-made pizza. Then, quick as she'd arrived, she left. The crying started when we dropped her at the airport and Ciarán tucked an arm around me. "Did I make it worse, bringin' her over?"

"Not a bit!"

"But you're sad now."

I shook my head, my arm tight around him. "Far from it. Edie's always been strong enough to own herself with boldness, never caring how others perceived her while I, the tremulous second-guesser, spent most of our friendship wishing to be more like her and failing miserably. This time we met on an equal plane. She's always encouraged me to trust myself and damn the consequences; now she's seen me do it." I nudged his arm. "And she likes my boyfriend."

Ciarán woofed with relief. "I wouldn't have taken it ta heart if your parents didn't approve, but Edie's opinion counts for somethin'."

My strong, self-assured man could not possibly have worried in earnest. "You weren't truly nervous about meeting her, were you?"

"Chronic."

I chuckled. "Breathe easy; you passed the test."

We stayed in Dublin for a week. While Ciarán worked, I occupied myself with the website. When he returned in the evening we commenced the holiday portion of our time. After supper, whether we went out or cooked in the tiny kitchen of Declan's flat, we walked through Stephen's Green for a dose of nature, or Merrion Square Park, to admire the Georgian architecture of the surrounding buildings and indulge my affection for the statue of Oscar Wilde.

On our last evening Ciarán said, "I wonder if a week here made ya miss city livin'."

"A dose of urbanity has been great; Dublin is wonderful. But home is home."

Chapter Twenty-Four

S UMMER BEGAN CEDING TO autumn. The rowans filled with berries, orange as flame. Mornings were cool and dewy, and evenings often required a small fire. Pilgrim season trickled toward its end in the early days of September and Killarkin regained its gentle pace.

One morning I visited the post office on my way home from St. Dallán's, collecting a sweet postcard from Mom and an envelope bearing a Dublin postmark. Stock prospectuses and unfathomable financial documents arrived often; piling up until someone could translate. This envelope contained a single account statement, but not recognizing the name of the firm, I added it to the collection of papers to show Declan later.

After work, I changed my shirt, grabbed the mystery file, and hustled to the pub. The straw-colored light of an early September evening suffused the quiet street, slowing my steps and deepening my breath.

Declan folded his newspaper with a crinkle when I joined him. "Where's Ness?"

"You'll have ta make do with me. Diane's babby has croup."

"Sinéad had a bad cold last week. I can't fathom how my mom managed three so close together, let alone how Di copes with four."

"And another on the way."

"Geez! It's like the Donnellys have a moral obligation to assure the next generation of Killarkins."

"Job security for Padraic," Declan said, chuckling. "Ciarán due home in the mornin'?" I nodded, my mouth full of wine. "And it's goin' alright with the two of ya?"

"Yes, big brother."

"I'm glad of it. Ya make him happy."

"It's mutual."

We enjoyed a companionable meal, talking with ease and laughing at each other's jokes. "Ya should have taken your money out of my hands sooner," he said. "Bein' friends is preferable."

"Agreed, but you aren't free yet." I pushed forward the folder. "Translate, please. The one on the top arrived this morning. Is it one of the stocks you suggested?"

As Declan examined the document the blood drained from his face. With a dull rasp he asked, "Where'd ya get this?"

"It came in the mail. Are you OK? Want a whiskey?" Declan's eyes darted around the pub before he leaned forward, loosening his tie. Alarmed, I started up for a restorative, but he clutched my wrist with a hand like a block of ice. "Dec, what the hell? You're scaring me. Are you choking?"

He stared at the paper one long, leaden minute, his mouth grim. Then with a resigned exhale, he tucked the letter into the folder with its companions and said, "I want a smoke. Come along out back, wouldja?" Gaping and disconcerted, I followed him and the folder out. He waited at the end of the garden, restive. "Come along ta the office, this way."

Rather than taking The High, we crossed back gardens and climbed over low stone walls to reach his building. After securing the outer doors and inspecting the downstairs, he unlocked the office. He pulled the drapes closed, switched on the lamp, and tossed the folder on his desk, glaring at it with crossed arms. "I'm quite a storyteller, Clare."

With shaky hands I poured two glasses of whiskey, but Declan didn't touch his; he stood like a marble statue, the twitch in his bloodless cheek the only proof he still breathed. He'd displayed any number of moods before, but the desperation he manifested now shocked me and anxiety tweaked my belly. "Are we having a Quaker meeting, or are you gonna tell me why a piece of paper has you so spooked?"

He lowered into his chair and loosed a breath heavy with despair. "It's proof of fraud."

"Hysterical, Dec. What is it really?"

He rubbed his forehead. "Durin' our first conversation about the trust, I withheld information."

I had a sudden urge to vomit. He sat, elbows on the desk, his chin resting on stacked hands. The posture had a gravity of its own. He didn't speak until several minutes passed. The tick of the mantel clock, loud in the silence, made me beat with eerie nerves, but whatever he had to say, I'd scream if he didn't say it soon. Curling into one of the leather chairs I said, "I've got all night."

After another deep exhale Declan unfolded a markedly different tale from the first. "I made out Fergus Malone, the first trustee, as an honest, altruistic sort," he said. "Instead, he exploited the advantage of an absentee landlord." He removed the offending document from its manila cover and waved it like a flag of surrender. "He skimmed the money Seamus remitted and opened a separate account."

My body went cold. "But Grand-da knew how much he sent. He would have noticed a shortfall."

"It's customary, when committin' a fraud, ta keep two sets of books. Everythin' Seamus saw showed each penny safe, with no deficits save the ones he authorized. Before Fergus died, he put the account under his son's name so as not to risk inquiries." Declan folded his hands atop the desk and spoke with clipped, precise tones, like he offered legal counsel. "Those who commit foul deeds prefer keepin 'em in the shadows." He pulled off his tie and flung it across the room.

"The son proved greedy as his father, but more cautious. When Seamus started givin' away money, Finnin suggested chargin' interest." Declan's voice dripped sarcasm. "A nominal fee, of course, ta lend gravity ta the transactions and spare pride. Seamus, bein' bighearted, endorsed the plan and never knew Finnin charged a higher rate, not enough ta be usurious, mind—he wouldn't risk complaints gettin' back ta Seamus. But he pocketed a pleasant bit of change. He used a similar scheme with the cottage rentals." Declan shot back his whiskey and poured another.

I held out my glass. He obliged, set the bottle in its caddy, and continued. "Finnin had a knack with investments and persuaded Seamus into other ventures. With the trust robust, he had no reason ta question the man's advice. If a speculation went bad, he credited it ta market risk and didn't fuss so long as losses didn't impact the principle."

I studied the dignified room, tarnished by malfeasance, with a sickening picture of my darling, unsuspecting Grand-da occupying this exact chair while Finnin simpered lies into his face. Pressing the heel of my hand against my breastbone, I rubbed the tightness in my chest. "Declan, please tell me you weren't involved."

He stared at the curtained window, hollow-eyed and still. "Finnin grew ill, same feckin' blight as took his da. He made me a full partner and before he passed, had my name on all the accounts and necessary documents, notarized and legitimate. And frankly, I'd nothin' but gratitude for his kindness toward me." Declan turned embarrassed and regretful. "It's the way of chancers ta stroke egos and I needed appreciation."

Puzzle pieces snapped together. "This all happened when Maeve—"

"I convinced myself no one understood my burden."

Unable to endure seeing Declan in such despair, something maternal loosed in me. "You know it's not true," I said, soft and soothing.

"'Course, I feckin' know it!" He apologized for the outburst, but anger still pinked his cheeks. "I knew it then; but martyrdom is a sickness like drink or drugs." A pen rolled to the floor as he smashed a vexed fist on the desk. Then he buried his head between his hands, humiliated. "Oh, Finnin saw me ripe for the pickin'."

"Dec, let's do this later." I feared he'd rupture a blood vessel if we continued.

"Sorry, Clare." He drew his hand across his mouth, composing himself. "After Finnin died, I had the one set of books, none the wiser, and managed the trust per Seamus' instructions without either of us knowin' what went before. Do ya mind if I smoke?"

I shook my head and his hand trembled as he lit the cigarette. His distress hurt my heart. "Your name is on some documents. Big deal."

"It's not so simple, darlin'. Everyone believed Finnin ta be a good husband and friend, a pillar of the community, but the man had an entire other life. He fathered a child with one of his mistresses and provided for his secret family without ever compromisin' the fiction he created here."

I exhaled, enough to ease the squeeze in my chest. "The plot thickens."

"When the woman died, Finnin had the decency ta provide the boy an education. Then he offered ta fund a business venture of the lad's choosin', hopin' ta discharge his duty. But the young man decided it sounded too much like work and offered his silence in exchange for a regular allowance. Finnin paid him from the secret account and the son kept away from Killarkin." Declan eyes scoured my face. "Might ya put a name ta the man?"

"Shit." My stomach turned and even a straight shot of Jameson failed to cleanse the taste of bile. "Garbhán. And you know all this because you're friends."

"We're not," Declan said bitterly. "Nor are we business partners." He paced to the window, flicked open the drapes, and scrutinized the street before letting them fall again. The smoke of his cigarette curled blue in the dim light.

Of all his faults, Declan never struck me as dishonest. Fighting back nausea, I said, "You *were* involved."

"I swear not, Clare. While Finnin lived he negotiated the village loans and received the payments, knowin' I'd have noted the discrepancies. In his last illness he reissued the existin' loans at the true interest rate, which folk interpreted as more of Seamus' generosity. Before he died, Finnin closed his personal accounts, tellin' me he'd donated it all ta charity. Given I believed him a model of kindness, it seemed a plausible tale." Declan huffed. "He covered his tracks, and I might never have learned any of it."

My relief rushed out on an exhale. "Then why the hell are you so morbid about it?"

"No one here knew Garbhán existed, so no one informed him when Finnin died. About six months later, with no further funds coming his way, he came prowlin' for his money and was none too pleased on discoverin' his father had died and left the family business ta a clueless gobshite. Not wishin' ta lose his source of income, he filled me in, expectin' I'd go along with the scheme. When I refused, he threatened ta tell Seamus."

I snorted a harsh laugh. "Grand-da would have sent him to hell and sued for his money into the bargain."

Declan smiled. "I said as much, swearing I'd inform Seamus myself. He backed off then and I thought we'd ended it. Garbhán lurked around Killarkin for a day or two, affable and friendly; ya know how he is, the ingratiatin' bastard. Then he came ta me, sayin' my name on the accounts suggested a connection ta it all. I argued it proved nothin' and he asked how I'd convince a judge I *hadn't* colluded with Finnin. Havin' come into possession of the second set of books, he had ample evidence of his da's evil doin'."

"You said Finnin covered his tracks."

Declan's mood didn't lighten, but with each bit of the story his forehead smoothed, his shoulders grew less rigid. "He did, where it concerned me, but he showed less caution with his spawn. Finnin kept a Dublin flat for his philanderin' and mailed the payments there; Garbhán had a key. Without shame he admitted often snoopin' about for loose cash and the like; he found the ledger on one of his raids. He made me a straightforward proposition: find a way ta pay him or have a care about the well-bein' of my fiancé." Declan halted his tale, tears hovering on his bottom lids.

The revolting intimidation choked me. "He threatened Nessa?"

"And the folks."

"Jaysus!" I jumped up and paced the room. "He's a gangster. 'Nice little place they have there, shame if anything happened to it.' This is the worst story any Irishman ever told."

"Can ya bear anymore?"

It all made me sick; but something in Declan tilted. He'd carried secrets over ten years, the heft of them creating the distant, controlling man I first met. Telling the whole of it lanced the boil of pain. Out of the love I bore his family and Nessa, I accepted the trust he placed in me. "You must have been terrified, Dec."

"And frightened people act desperate and foolish. Ah, Clare, fearin' for Ness and the folks, I couldn't risk tellin' Seamus."

"You had to protect your family."

His gaze drifted across the room, staring into a void only he could see. When he spoke again his voice cracked. "I had money set aside for a house for me and Ness. Somethin' bigger than my flat here. Room enough..." He grimaced. "It went ta Garbhán instead and when those funds ran out, I paid him from my income. He threatened the family and my professional standin', but he couldn't corrupt me."

My pent emotion vented in a torrent of weeping. Declan moved to the chair beside me, offered a handkerchief, and placed a hand over mine.

"Clare, I wish I'd told Seamus the truth and risked the consequences. He deserved better and so did ya. Fecked up thinkin' is no excuse."

I blotted my face, tensed with sympathy. "You had no options, Dec."

He slunk back, then pushed out of the chair, and crossed again to the window. I followed with open arms. He clung to me, desperate. "You broke off the engagement to keep her safe." He shuddered, his head on my shoulder, before releasing me. "He must have freaked when Grand-da died."

Declan crossed his arms and shook his head. "Not at first. The entitled bugger meant ta manipulate ya. I warned him ya might well take the inheritance and there it would end. When ya decided ta make over the cottage I feared what he'd do."

I now saw his earlier behavior through a different lens. "You *did* try to stall the renovation, not because you didn't like me, but because you wanted me to give up, take the money, and leave." He stood hunched and humiliated. "Oh, god. And when you made a pass at me...you were trying to scare me back to America."

Cherry red patches bloomed on his cheeks. "I wasn't thinkin', Clare, and behaved wild and desperate as a consequence." He attempted a grin and failed. "I couldn't dissuade ya from the reno and should ha' known unwanted attentions wouldn't sway ya, either."

Compassion flowed over the last shallow holes in our tentative friendship. All along he meant to protect, not interfere. "Sorry I'm so stubborn."

He managed a genuine smile. "I wouldn't have ya any other way. Once I recked you'd see the reno through, the job turned ta holding off Garbhán the best I could. When ya decided against sellin', he read the writin' on the wall."

"All those investment ideas."

He nodded. "Schemes he surely intended ta fail, if they existed at all."

My leg muscles went squishy as marshmallows, and I slithered down the wall. He sank to the floor beside me. "Everything Garbhán ever said makes so much sense now." Memory induced a shiver of revulsion. "He came on to me once."

A furious breath blew from between Declan's clenched teeth. "Damn his eyes. There's more than one way ta scam an heir. Did he hurt ya?"

"I ordered him out. Plus, Ciarán and Liam were in the cottage at the time."

"Good." He blew out a breath. "He phoned the night of your party, out of patience and sayin' there'd be consequences if ya weren't brought ta heel."

"Charming. No wonder you lost it when you found out about The Folly."

"Nessa told me off good after; said whatever my feckin' problems were, the time had come ta deal with them."

I managed a smile, hearing her words as if she'd said them in my presence. "Dr. Cassidy is a wise woman."

Declan smiled, too, rueful. "She is. I phoned McAllister and told him I meant ta report myself ta the Law Society."

Of all he might have said, this gave me extreme pause. "For what?"

"Withholding information from a client, ta start. I'd had enough, Clare, and confession proved the best way ta protect any of ya. He believed me then."

The impact of his words crashed like a boulder down a hillside. I grabbed his hand, he chuffed it and answered my unspoken question. "He would have had time ta get here from Dublin."

The air stilled and the mantel clock snicked once for every three rapid beats of my heart. "He's a smarmy bully but would he truly hurt someone?"

"I reckon he intended puttin' a scare into ya enough ta coerce a deal. Meantime, he encountered Ciarán."

"One blow to hurt us all." I pressed my head against the windowsill and squeezed Declan's hand, willing the dizzying spin of the room to stop. "You have to call Sargent Corcoran." In answer, he pulled his phone from his pocket. "How much trouble will you be in, Dec?"

"A fair amount, I reckon.

Chapter Twenty-Five

S LEEP AMOUNTED TO NO more than a shallow nap haunted by ghoulish men, bank registers, and Declan's exhausted face. When Ciarán lay beside me, he received a groggy moan in greeting. "Why are ya still abed, darlin'?"

"Bad night." Pressing against him, my skin clammy with the fog of nightmares, I wished to crawl under his flesh and tether to his bones.

His phone bleated and he chuckled. "Dec has rotten timin'."

I bolted upright. "Answer it."

Ciarán grimaced but complied. "Brother, I've only now got home. Let me..." He paused to listen. "We'll be right along." He clicked off, puzzled. "We've been summoned."

We gathered in the O'Donnell's dining room, around the family table. Nessa, bristling with impatience, arrived not long after we did. "I got in at dawn," she said. "What's so feckin' urgent?"

We listened in silence as Declan told the essence of his tale again. When he shared his speculations about the attack, shock vented in whispered oaths. Declan seemed tired but peaceful. "The garda will be here soon. I wanted ya prepared."

Maeve's chest quaked with a forceful exhalation and I half-expected her to spit fire. "I never liked the stinkin' bugger with his greasy hair and face like a self-satisfied hawk."

"Ma, you're missin' the point," Declan said.

Before he could explain, Sargent Corcoran entered and asked, "What's all this, then?"

After another recitation of the story, Sargent Corcoran reviewed the bank statement, his forehead creased with thought and his stubby fingers drumming the table. "You're suggestin' McAllister sent this ta raise Miss Riordan's suspicions."

"He knew she'd ask questions. Whatever he intended, he's not done attemptin' ta lay his hands on her money."

"If he had this statement, he may have them all. You're sure his name isn't on any of the other accounts?"

"If it were, Clare would have no inheritance."

"Do ya possess the second set of books?"

"I made a copy one night when he got well lashed."

Corcoran nodded. "Officer Waite, notify the Dublin garda. Have 'em invite Mr. McAllister in for questionin' concernin' the assault of Mr. Ciarán O'Donnell." He considered his notebook. "Havin' a suspect opens lines of inquiry, ta be sure." He turned doleful eyes on Declan. "Is Ms. Riordan aware of her rights concernin' your behavior?"

"She may sue if she wishes, but I'll be reportin' myself regardless."

I squeaked like a panicked mouse, half-rising from my chair before Ciarán's quick hand restrained me. "McAllister's the one who deserves punishment!"

Declan answered, his voice low and tired. "Clare, he benefited from his father's fraud; he didn't instigate it."

"Isn't extortion against the law in Ireland?"

"It is, darlin', but it's a matter of my word against his, thus near impossible ta prove."

Sargent Corcoran resumed control of the meeting. "Mr. O'Donnell, on the other hand, violated his duty by withholdin' information from ya and your grand-da."

I thumped a clenched fist on the table; teacups jangled like sleighbells. "McAllister threatened his family!"

With unbelievable tenderness Declan said, "It's alright, Clare."

"In what universe? The original perpetrators are dead, as is their victim. You didn't have a clue about any of it until McAllister forced your hand and you paid off the arse with your own money. I'm glad you didn't tell Grand-da, Dec. You protected my family and yours!" I didn't intend to shout, or for tears to spill on my frustration-reddened cheeks but couldn't contain myself.

"Miss Riordan, I realize this is upsettin'."

Hiccupping, I swiped my face. "With all due respect, Sargent, focus on finding McAllister. The rest is between me and Declan. He's a victim, too. Hell, he's suffered more than anyone. Please leave him alone."

The officer examined me, steady and professional, and I stared back, watery but resolute. Corcoran clicked closed his notebook. "We're done for now. We'll need a formal statement once he's brought in."

"Assumin' ya find him," Declan said. "I've not heard from him since July."

Corcoran swaggered with absolute confidence in the Irish garda. "We'll find him. After all this time, I reck he doesn't fancy himself a suspect. If he's run, it strengthens our case." Corcoran finished his cold tea with a slurp and rose. "Still, your information moves us along. Thank ya all for your time."

When the door closed behind him, Maeve's hand fluttered to her heaving bosom. "I swear on the blessed Mother, never did I hear such a tale of evil dealin'! And my poor Declan, carryin' all the burden and worryin' so." She wagged her head. "Eamon, we're closed for the day. Folk can cook their own damn suppers tonight."

A few stunned minutes passed before anyone else moved. Then Nessa pushed away from the table and with deliberate, careful grace crossed to Declan, held his face, and kissed his mouth.

Ciarán and I walked to the cottage arm in arm, more to steady ourselves than touch. "Jaysus! My head is spinnin'." I halted, analyzing his condition. "From the revelations," he said, with a reassuring pat.

We resumed our walk. Despite the lake-blue sky the air grew thicker. "It'll storm soon."

"Funny timin'. The real tempest has passed. Sweet of ya, invitin' everyone ta supper."

"We should be together. At least now we understand what happened to Dec and maybe even who hurt you."

Ciarán agreed we had cause for a party but proposed a more intimate method of celebration in the meantime. Emotions drained and energy exhausted, I had doubts, but my weariness trembled away under his touch. I wept a little; he did, too, our kisses salty with tears of painful remembrance and relief. Then he sank deeper within me, and the tremors of our lovemaking released into a healing, grateful peace.

"How did I ever find such perfection?"

He yawned and tickled my hip. "I'm not perfect."

"Pretty damn close. Except the toilet seat thing. Seriously, the hinge swings both directions." Ciarán gave one of his huffing laughs, an endearing exhalation.

He embraced me, his eyes tender with admiration. "It's a gift, Clare; experiencin' both the hard and soft of life with someone. I should have been more convincin' at the castle. We wouldn't have wasted so much time."

"We had to be ready for each other."

"I will never be ready for ya, Ms. Riordan."

I smiled, sleepy and love drunk. "The fact of you mystifies me daily. If either of us had made different choices, we wouldn't have met. Well, met again."

"Were we destined?"

"Destiny suggests a lack of agency. God, or whatever, must have better things to do than plan out the minutiae of every life ever lived on the planet. We make choices and, if we care enough, redeem the bad ones." I wrapped my legs around his and pulled closed. "We might have lived all our lives never knowing the other existed."

"There's a thought too awful ta contemplate."

A vase of cosmos adorned the kitchen table, and the mouth-watering fragrance of butter and herbs kissed the kitchen air. I turned the roasting chicken, pleased with its golden color. "If only we had champagne."

Ciarán nosed about the icebox. "There's prosecco."

"Close enough."

"It's a miracle, finally understandin' all Declan's woe. I wish he'd told us sooner."

"At least he's done it. And what about Nessa? Have you ever witnessed a sweeter, more poignant moment than when she kissed him?"

Ciarán pulled plates from the cupboard and started setting the table. "If gettin' my head bashed brought them ta their senses I'd have arranged for it earlier."

My fingers touched the spot on the back of his head where his curls hid the scar. "Hardly seems a fair exchange. Back to Dublin on Tuesday?"

"Monday, I'll be spendin' more time there over the next few weeks."

I returned to the stove and poured thick, yellow cream into a skillet. "Why? Or is it classified?"

"I'm an aid worker, darlin', not a spy. We're preparin' a team for deployment ta South Sudan. They've a horrible famine there." His light darkened. "I hope you'll join me when ya can."

"Of course. Hand me the timer, please." I covered the pan and pulled bread from the oven.

"Come ta me." I obliged and Ciarán settled me on his lap. "Thank ya for bein' so accommodatin'."

"You show me the same consideration. It's how this love stuff works." With a kiss, we returned to the dinner preparations.

Eamon and Maeve arrived with four bottles of champagne and if anyone harbored residual tension from the morning, it evaporated with the belch of the first cork. Maeve alternated between volubility and grateful tears. Eamon sang and his resonant voice wove joy through the room. Nessa joked with minimal sarcasm and Declan possessed a beautiful, easy smile.

After opening the second bottle Eamon rose from the table, lifting his glass high. "My heart is too full for proper words, but there's much ta be thankful for. Ta all of it!"

"Ta all of it!" we chorused.

Eamon sat and Nessa took his place. "Before we're all too lashed, I've a toast as well." She held her glass toward Declan with an expression of remarkable tenderness. "Darlin', ya bore a terrible burden for the sake of those ya love. From today, live deep in the freedom of havin' laid it down."

Declan drained his glass, then grinned at her. "I will."

She resumed her seat with a nod of satisfaction. "Prove it, ya eegit, and marry me."

A brief, stunned hush fell on the room before Maeve crossed herself and said, "Praise the saints!"

Laughing, Eamon took his wife's hand. "Let the man accept first, darlin'."

Declan's smile transformed him. "I'll marry ya, Ness."

"There!" Maeve sniffed, justified. "It's come right, and none too soon, I dare say. September is a fine month for a weddin'; it'll take some doin', though Father could manage the service in his sleep, but there's a dress ta get and food ta plan—still, if we all work together, I'm sure—"

Declan chuckled, his hand on his breathless mother's shoulder. "Ma, it'll take three months for the license. But I'll petition the Family Court. I'd like this settled."

"Tell them you've waited ten years," I said. "You might get credit for time served."

Connections and determination bent bureaucracy to Declan's will, and he and Nessa set October third as their wedding date. Nessa gave a dismissive sniff at my offer of help with the arrangements. "If ya imagine me the sort ta fuss about dresses and bridesmaids, ya haven't met me." Nessa became fascinated with her glass of golden-brown sherry. "But I'll need a witness, if ya don't mind."

"Sure." I made the bland answer in deference to my phlegmatic friend but could have danced with joy.

Maeve, however, fussed. She bemoaned Declan and Nessa's insistence on sufficing with the civil ceremony and negotiated for a week before accepting their decision. "But ya must have a reception."

Nessa shook a vehement head. "Not if it means all of Killarkin jammed in the pub with gifts we don't need and fruitcake. It's bleedin' nonsense."

Save for a lack of feathers, Maeve bore a perfect resemblance to a ruffled hen. She pivoted on her future daughter-in-law, emphatic fists embedded on her hips and raised her voice a full octave. "Nessa Cassidy! Celebratin' a marriage, even a civil one—God love ya—isn't nonsense. Ya don't hold with the sacraments, which is one matter and bad enough if ya ask me, though ya didn't so I'll keep my counsel. But ya must celebrate."

Nessa turned to Declan, defeated. "Ma, be reasonable," he pleaded.

These dear people had endured enough over the last decade and the thought of them suffering further misunderstandings or disagreements made me miserable. "What if Ciarán and I host a nice, no-fuss family supper at the cottage?"

Ciarán draped his arms about Maeve and Nessa's shoulders. "Will it do?" Maeve gave a grudging nod. Nessa inclined her head. "Done then." He winked at me. "Once again an American negotiates an Irish accord."

Maeve batted his arm, affronted. "Jaysus, Joseph, and Mary; don't ya dare suggest this is anythin' like bringin' an end ta The Troubles. I swear, the temerity of my own flesh suggestin' Nessa and I were at it hammer and tongs. Know us better, man. We don't bear a mite of ill will toward the other."

Tension dissolved as Ciarán and Declan convulsed with laughter and the rest of us followed close behind.

Maeve pushed aside the curls which had escaped their pins, retied her apron, and gave her belly a dignified pat. "If ya like, Clare, I'll help ya plan the menu."

Before dawn on the autumnal equinox Ciarán and I hiked to St. Dall's through a clinging mist. "*Uisce breatha,*" he said.

"Translation, please."

He kissed my hand. "It means water of life, how it's all around us here; below, above, within." Then he chuckled. "It also means whiskey."

"How Irish," I said, joining his laugh. "I want to learn the language. It's poetry."

"We're taught it in school but many stop speakin' it after."

"All the more reason to learn. It shouldn't disappear."

Villagers filled the ruins, their ranks swollen with folks from other towns. It almost resembled a church again but felt nicer. Thin places accommodated both pagans and Christians.

We found a spot near the altar and faced east. The sky cleared and shone silver. Light peeked over the horizon, red as hawthorn berries. Bright rays of honey and marigold shimmered on the ruins and turned the hills black, then the sun bounded up through petal pink clouds and cast shadows from the circle of stones. Requiring no words or rituals, nature danced, and a new season dawned. A contented ache welled within. "Autumn is my favorite. Rain, crisp mornings, and cozy, fire-lit nights. Grand-da loved autumn, too."

"You're grievin' still."

"Celebrating. He's here." I rested my head on Ciarán's shoulder, and a lark sang a joyous ode to the morning.

The first Thursday of October we drove into Dublin. Ciarán and Eamon gave Declan a stag night, and I bought Maeve and Ness supper in our hotel. Maeve grew tipsy on champagne and waxed sentimental with stories of Declan's father, Ronan. "Oh, what a fella, tall with wild, dark hair. I thought ta die when I lost him, but I had my cherub cheeked boy, always smilin' so sweet. It's hard believin' now, but babby Dec were all rolls and puffs and gave the dearest hugs. I vowed he'd never want for anythin', hopin' ta soften the loss of his da."

Nessa laid on hand on Maeve's. "Then ya gave him Eamon."

"Found my man without hope or expectation. I tell ya true; me a ship comin' through fog and him my calm, sunlit harbor." Maeve drank more champagne and emitted a tiny, embarrassed burp. "And Nessa, oh,

Declan put ya through your paces, and it's a shame, but ya loved him all the way through, while he couldn't be arsed ta pay attention."

"I thought myself half mad yearnin' after the man, but still loved him true and though he couldn't show it, he loved me. Now we know how much."

The statement, however true, discomfited me. "They say love demands sacrifice."

"Compromise ta be sure, sacrifice sometimes," Nessa replied, her expression warm. "But never martyrdom. Dec got in the weeds there, but he'll not again. I won't have it."

Maeve beamed, proud and tearful at once. "Keep lovin' my boy, Ness; saints know ya can't help doin' so."

Near midnight, we settled Nessa into her room then took to ours. Even with the blinds closed, the diffuse city light made the hotel room too bright. Traffic hissed from the street below. I tossed, now accustomed to sleeping best when embraced by inky dark and country silence. "You're my hero, Maeve."

"Kind of ya ta say, darlin', but I'm sure I don't know why."

"The way you love your family; how you support your sons, even when you don't agree with them."

"Pft. I despaired of either of my boys findin' love, so I'd be a right eejit ta fuss about details now. I love the Church, ya know I do. But here's somethin' about the sacraments, though Father D would no doubt argue, but the priests don't know it all, ta be sure." She grew so quiet I rolled over to check if she'd fallen asleep. But her eyes were on the ceiling, hands folded on her pillowy bosom. "Ronan and I eloped, and it broke Ma's heart. She claimed it no true marriage in the eyes of God. Then he died and me bein' young and foolish, I reckoned sure the Lord took him ta punish me. But Eamon and I had a church weddin' and it didn't spare us troubles nor bind us any tighter than Ronan and me. The sacrament isn't the vows or where ya make 'em. Ya create it with your love; there's what does the bindin'. Still, Ciarán and ya might well marry in church."

Her eternal theme provoked a chuckle. "I can't promise anything right now."

She reached toward me, her hand waving soft in the gap between our beds. "Take your time; I'm content. Oh, it's a blessin' havin' my sons happy and two beautiful daughters ta love because of it, although I confess, I do hope those boys are about givin' me grandbabbies before I leave this world."

"Ness and I have a say, you know." I curled on my side. "But we love you, too."

❁

My expectations for a civil ceremony were low; sure it wouldn't be more than transactional and bureaucratic, comprised of a few brusque words from a detached magistrate and the bang of an official stamp followed by a terse "next, please." Nothing prepared me for the ancient elegance of the registrar's office or the gentle, earnest way she urged the rights and obligations of marriage. Nor did I anticipate Nessa's tears, Declan's assured kiss, or the registrar insisting she be first to drink health to the happy couple.

The newlyweds celebrated their wedding night in Dublin; the rest of us drove home in Nessa's car. Along the way Maeve and I discussed a suitable supper menu. "And I'll be over early tomorrow ta help ya," she said.

"You will not. You're the mother of the groom and you're on holiday. Enjoy it."

She protested and I turned around with the same warning expression Mom used when her rowdy kids fought in the backseat. "Maeve

O'Donnell, not another word. We'll manage this once without your help."

Eamon hooted and held his wife's hand. "Leave it, darlin'. You've met your match."

We reconciled the divide between fuss and celebration with a simple menu and plenty of champagne. Then one tiny mistake of timing sent everything sideways, and I tumbled into the gap.

"I'm full of shit!" Ciarán rushed into the kitchen where a loaf of bread smoldered on the counter while tears of furious disappointment cascaded down my cheeks.

"Oh, darlin'." He observed the charred mass and chuckled.

"Don't you dare laugh! I made a bollocks of it!"

His laughing visage transformed into a scowl. "Those are Denise's words."

"Mom never said bollocks in her life."

Ciarán surveyed the bubbling pots and freshly laid tablecloth. "Clare, you're doin' a beautiful job. I'll help."

Infuriated by the smoking bread I refused comfort or assurance. "There's no time! The family will be here in—dammit! An hour! The cake needs icing, the sauce isn't ready, and the table's not set." Ciarán repeated his offer of assistance with maddening calm, and I grabbed the blackened loaf and flung it into the scrap bucket. "There's no fecking bread!"

"Jaysus, Clare! Ma can bring it along."

"I said I'd do it! I wanted everything perfect!" My tearful shouting gave me a case of hiccups.

"Ya have nothin' ta prove; not ta your ma, mine, or any other living soul. Perfection is a myth: the flaws let in life." I sobbed noisily into a tea towel, sensible of my childish behavior. After sniffling my way to the end of the hysterics, Ciarán kissed my forehead with tender indulgence. "I'll take the burnt offering ta the chickens and await your orders."

We worked together and he jollied me back into humor. Within half an hour everything fell into place. Sauce warmed in its boat and the cake, adorned with blue borage flowers and the last dusky rose petals, couldn't have been prettier. Ciarán sent me upstairs to change and upon my return to the kitchen, he pulled a beautiful golden-brown loaf of soda bread from the oven. He crowed, triumphant. "It's perfect."

"A wise man told me perfection is a myth."

"He's not so wise; you're perfect."

"You have ample evidence to the contrary."

"I'll amend. You're perfect for me."

The compliment, and regret for my earlier behavior, made me flush. "Sorry about the tantrum. The perfectionism gene never manifested so bad before."

"Clare, if ya suffer from anythin', it's an abundance of love. Besides, it's a gift when ya lose your shite every now and again. It reminds me you're human."

Perfection *is* an illusion and its quest a thorny lie we tell ourselves. But we celebrated Declan and Nessa well, knit together with food, wine, and laughter. It lit my soul: Ciarán's limpid, joyful eyes, Declan's free laugh, and the glow Nessa manifested as her usual dismissive mien surrendered to genuine delight. Eamon serenaded the new couple, and I rested in the circle of Ciarán's arms, overwhelmed by the magic light of love.

Chapter Twenty-Six

C IARÁN HAD BEEN IN Dublin a full week, longer than usual. I'd planned a special dinner and started preparing early, but as the time of his arrival drew closer excitement interfered with concentration. Giving up, I splashed whiskey into a glass and sat on the front step to wait.

The late afternoon air—mild, but crisp as a fresh-picked apple—smelled of fallen leaves and drying grass. Orla appeared and settled beside me. "You missed him, too, huh?" The cat nudged my arm with her head, begging for a scratch between her ears, a ministration abandoned as soon as Ciarán arrived at the gate. Racing to embrace and kiss him, hard, I cried, "Welcome home! Will ya have supper with me?"

Grinning, he bent for a second kiss. "Delighted."

Hand-in-hand we went inside, where he dropped his bag by the door and offered his help. "There's not much left to do. Relax and catch me up."

He poured himself a beer and settled at the table. "Ya go first."

I dipped a spoon into the mash and checked the seasoning. "The trust is purchasing laptops for the school, Liam's website is finished, Nessa taught me to say please, thank you, and 'I like wine' in Irish, and Paddy starts on The Folly in next week." I pulled a casserole of lamb stew from the oven and placed it before him.

"Recite your lessons, please."

"Le do thoil, go raibh maith agat, is maith liom fíon."

"Excellent!"

I dropped a shallow curtsey. "And you?"

"Nothin' near so excitin'. Long days; longer, lonelier nights." He inhaled the aroma of the stew as he served. "Ah, this is lovely, darlin'."

"How did training go?"

"Grand. The team is ready."

We enjoyed our meal in sweet joy, sharing news of all we'd done and seen while apart, grateful to have the other across the table again. After a second helping of stew, Ciarán pushed his plate aside and held a hand against my cheek. "If ya don't mind, I'd like ta stay in tonight and keep ya ta myself."

"I'll make tea."

He loaded the dishwasher, I switched on the kettle, and by the time he finished his chore the tea had steeped. He carried the tray into the front room, then poked the turve and said, "Curious ya don't find peat reek an abomination."

"Why the hell should sweet smoke bother me?"

He dropped a kiss on my cheek before settling on the couch, then opened his battered satchel with an apologetic grimace. "I've one report to read, then you'll have my undivided attention all weekend." I filled our cups, grabbed a biscuit, and plopped on the opposite end with a book. Ciarán winked and concentrated on his file.

The room filled with homey music: the pop of the fire, the soft rustle of turning pages, the occasional scratch of Ciarán's pen. Cozy, fed, and tucked secure in our snug home, contentment and gratitude eddied through me. He stretched, making a sound somewhere between a groan and a yawn, set aside his work, and opened his arms.

I moved into his embrace, and my body quivered with recognition, molding against him with a vibrant remembrance of his flesh, bone, and thrumming pulse. "I'm glad you're home."

He tightened his sinewy arms around me. "When does Joel arrive?"

"Tuesday. I'm eager for you two to meet."

Ciarán kissed my head. "Afraid I'll have ta miss him this time."

I sat up, puzzled. "He's here for ten days."

"The team leader contracted measles," he replied. "We exercise extreme caution in such situations, given the vulnerability of the folk we serve. I'll be takin' his place."

The breath left my body; his blithe tone shaking me more than his words. My hands chilled, as if the blood emptied from capillaries and veins for the sole purpose of rushing to protect my bruising heart. "You're going to the Sudan? Next week?"

"I'll return come February." He made it sound like a simple run out to the shops.

Unable to speak and not trusting any words which might come, I rose and returned the tea tray to the kitchen. We hadn't snuffed the dinner candles; one guttered in its stick. I blew out the other and dipped my finger in the melted wax. Mom's scolding voice sounded in memory. *Stop playing around, Clare! You'll ruin the tablecloth.* It didn't matter now; these were my damn candles and my tablecloth to risk.

I registered Ciarán's appearance in the doorway but didn't acknowledge him. "Whaddaya doin'?"

"Playin' with wax."

"Interestin' choice." He sounded amused.

A waxy thimble peeled from my finger. "It's at least sensation."

His tone sobered. "I'm sorry ta spring it on ya, but trust ya understand."

It wasn't hard to comprehend: one minute we were cozy and safe, then he dropped his bomb, ripping a crater in the floor of my sheltered happiness. "The urgency around a case of measles makes sense, but my idiot brain doesn't reckon much else."

"You're not an eegit, Clare."

I couldn't look at him. His tone made clear he watched me with bemused affection, but the actual sight of him would send me over the edge. "Idiots make assumptions. When we first met, you spoke about Cara a handful of times, then not at all. I never, not even once, considered asking if you missed it. You seemed content with your new role; I assumed it took field work out of the equation."

"Don't worry, darlin'. I won't take assignments longer than six months."

My heart bent in on itself; he had cut in half any future we had, and the notion didn't even bother him. Tears threatened but I refused to reveal my pitiful feelings. "I assumed you were happy."

With genuine surprise he knelt beside me. "This is nothin' ta do with us. In a perfect world, I'd be with ya always."

I tapped my nose, the way Daddy used to do when one of us kids worked out the correct answer to a math problem. "This is not a perfect world. Ergo, you can't be with me all the time."

With a voice full of tenderness he said, "I don't want ta leave ya."

"But in a couple days you will." The truth landed like a stone in my belly. "Ciarán, you always go dark when contemplating the suffering of others. Doing good is your calling and I respect your altruism. It's my mistake for never considering the implications of it." Pacing to the other side of the kitchen, I stared at the burnished yellow wall and struggled to accept dawning facts. "How do we share a life while living apart?"

"I have plenty of colleagues with families." Impatience tinged his words.

I hugged myself, rubbing my arms. "There are people everywhere with loved ones in the military, or who are first responders, who say goodbye to their darling with no assurance they'll come home. But most of them likely had a conversation about it."

Ciarán's defensiveness rose like a wall between us, and I predicted what came next. "Would ya have not had me if I never left Cara?"

"Impossible to say. I never knew that guy. It might have made me more hesitant; but it wouldn't have tipped the scales against you." Tears slipped down my cheeks. "But this is a troubling pattern. You delivered the news about returning to Cara as a *fait accompli* and we never discussed this trip."

Ciarán's jaw tensed, and a measure of cold frosted his words. "It's an emergency, Clare. The team heads out next week: they need a trained leader."

"Yes. And you might have found two minutes to call and talk about it." I screwed up the courage to meet his face. "But you didn't need a discussion. Your decision is supposed to be good enough for everyone else."

"Darlin'."

"I'm shattered." Ciarán would believe I succumbed to extreme weariness, but the slang word rang true. Everything within me tumbled to the bottom of my soul, dragging all energy with it. "I'm going to bed."

"We need ta talk."

"Now you want to talk? I love you, but right now I'm sad and pissed; American pissed." I stormed upstairs and curled tight in the bed. He would follow, blanket me with his beautiful body, and urge me to respond. But any words would be regrettable. When he did join me, I feigned sleep.

Waking before dawn, I slid out of bed, and wept during my shower, heaving sobs muffled by running water. We couldn't slough off this impasse with gentle words, teases, or sex. I occupied myself with the morning chores and started transforming the office into a guest room. Ciarán's tread sounded on the stairs and I exhaled with relief as his steps turned toward the kitchen. New Clare had gone missing-in-action, and the insecure coward left behind wanted to avoid him for as long as possible.

A moment later he appeared in the doorway. "I brought ya coffee. It's astonishin' ya started the day without it."

"Welcome to the new order." I shook out the green quilt, ignoring the proffered cup.

"Don't be angry, darlin'." The plea in his voice made me ache, but not enough.

"I *am* angry. I'll get over it; but until then, you'll have to deal with it."

"I can't leave ya like this."

The iron bedstead creaked when I dropped upon it, sinking under the ballast of frustrated impatience. "Ciarán, you're leaving me whether or not we resolve anything."

He set the coffee on the desk and moved toward me, but I warded him off with an emphatic shake of my head. His arms fell limp at his side. "Ya act like I've betrayed ya."

His hurt made me furious. "You kinda did. I wouldn't be thrilled even if you'd told me about it, but the courtesy of a discussion would demonstrate we were in this together."

"Darlin', please don't over-react."

I snarled and forced a pillow into its slip. "Why is that the last refuge of a man who's wrong? Hurt is *not* an overreaction. You claim you love me, then exclude me from huge decisions. Be clear: you don't need my permission; conduct your life any way you god-damn please. But Jaysus, don't expect me to celebrate being an afterthought." I fluffed the pillow with indignant vigor.

The knuckles of Ciarán's clenched fists ridged the denim of his jeans. "I acknowledge ya see it so, but please know ya are—"

I shot up, slamming the pillow on the bed. "I swear to God, spare me the bullshit about my importance to you. I'll scream."

"You're worried, darlin', but—"

"Of course, I am! Gawd! I've seen your scar; proof of how quick good intentions turn ugly. Not long ago I sat vigil beside you, praying you'd live." I waited until the flutter in my throat subsided. "This is worse. If something happens to you over there, we'll get a damn call telling us you're hurt or missing or feckin' dead. I'll worry about your safety every second you're away and I'm even more concerned about what happens *if* you come home."

"Clare, I'll return ta ya and we'll go on like we've done these last months."

The sentence, more outrageous by virtue of its innocence, drained my rage, and I laid a gentle hand on his sweet, clueless face. "That is precisely what we can't do."

I resumed tidying; he disappeared to make breakfast, but I had no appetite. I drank my coffee and left for the shops. Upon returning, I found him upstairs with his backpack. "Did you say goodbye to your folks?"

"I'll speak ta them later." He pushed the bag aside with his foot. "With this done, we'll have no other distractions."

"I've gotta get ready for our, my guest."

His hand darted for my arm, halting my progress toward the stairs. "Please don't be angry with me, Clare."

"The needle is now ticking between confusion and abject terror."

The admission made me limp, and I didn't resist when he lifted me in his strong arms and laid me across the bed. He kissed me, his mouth hungry. His vital heart, the one I cherished and wanted safe, beat against mine. I did not trust words or my mare's nest of emotions. I needed him like this, his arms around me, his precious breath tickling my ear. It would not fix anything, but we didn't have much time. We'd hold one another while we could.

His whisper breezed a caress on my neck. "Be with me. Let me love ya." He drew my arms over my head, hands dove-like on my wrists. "Six months is a long time."

"No kidding."

He released my arms, and we undressed each other. Our bodies yielded together, and I clutched his hips, holding him still. Tears pooled, blurring the angles of his face. "Don't move. I want to memorize the poetry of you inside me."

"Don't cry, darlin'." He kissed away the tears and found my mouth. "You're so far away."

"It's not possible ta be closer."

I closed my eyes, hiding from his penetrating gaze, terrified we held one another for the last time.

From my first Sunday supper, I loved the O'Donnell dining room. The sturdy old table, covered with Irish lace and resting on a forest green wool rug, occupied the center. Beside the stone fireplace, a large, painted dresser served as a sideboard and bar. The room had a comfortable intimacy, scented by beeswax candles and a rich base note of smoky peat.

But the family around the old table provided the room's signature loveliness, the bonds of family and friendship strengthened over amazing meals sauced with laughter. But the night before Ciarán left, the mood differed from previous Sundays. Maeve erupted with fretful tears every seven minutes. Declan ate in cold silence, like a man auditioning for the role of a dolman. Eamon listened with patience when Ciarán spoke about his mission, but his clenched jawbone threatened to rip the skin on his face.

By dint of Nessa's and my efforts at a jolliness neither of us felt, we made it through the meal, though Declan brought an abrupt end to the evening when he took his wife away before Maeve served the pudding.

Ciarán and I went home and made love with a starving desperation which left me sore and empty. The next morning, before he left me, he coiled my hair in his hands. "I love ya, Clare. More than—"

I pressed a hand against his mouth, my fingers white as the bone beneath the skin. "I know."

"You'll hear from the Family Coordinator before ya hear from me; but I'll phone soon as possible."

"OK. Go. The bus won't wait."

Backpack slung across his shoulder, he started toward the gate. Orla appeared on the walk, flicked her tail, and rubbed against his calf, communicating a goodbye. The ordinary feline gesture did me in. I lifted a hand to wave, hoping the dawn light didn't show my tears.

The day passed in a painful blur, my attention squirrely and scattered. I spent most of the time in garden mud, except for one numbed, chilled hour surrounded by the fog swirling at the base of the ruins.

In the late afternoon I met Nessa for a game of darts. A party of day-trippers enjoyed tea and the venerable aul Tim sat sentry on his usual stool. Eamon and Maeve went through their paces with hospitable smiles despite their decided lack of spirit.

Nessa took a diminutive sip of sherry and gestured toward a large glass of whiskey. I had a nip, then pushed it aside. "Don't let me finish it."

"In my professional opinion, ya need it."

I took another dose, on doctor's orders. "OK, but don't let me order another one."

"He's off then?"

"At first light."

"Ya were fair brave last evenin'."

"Maeve is upset enough for the lot of us." I tossed my first dart.

"It all came about a mite fast. Tell me what ya will, but ya needn't pretend. Dec is none too pleased with him, either."

"He made it clear enough last night. But why is *he* upset?"

"Like all of us, he's hurt. Ciarán never indicated a thing; we all assumed he'd stopped riskin' life and limb."

I threw my second dart too hard. "Feck it! I'm useless tonight." I pulled the dart from the wall with a long, frustrated mewl. "How is it possible to have a relationship with someone who makes important decisions without you?"

Nessa snorted. "Havin' spent ten years apart from such a man, I'm the last person ya should ask."

"But Declan intended to protect you. Ciarán didn't factor me into the equation at all."

"Dec learned from his mistake; Ciarán will, too."

She intended encouragement, but the idea depressed me. If you deny you've done anything wrong, there's no incentive to change.

Nessa noted my silence, threw her dart wide, and said, "We're both shite this evenin'. Let's finish our drinks."

"It would be a better use of our time." The darts clattered as they dropped from my hands into their bin.

"Dec is joinin' me soon. Have supper with us."

"Thanks, but there are sulks to banish before Joel shows up."

Nessa squinted with concern. "Ya shouldn't be alone."

"I *am* alone." Crossing my arms over my head, I twisted into a stretch. "I've wasted all day being pathetic and have come to the end of myself. I'll go home and throw something against a wall; only a pillow so there's no mess to clean. Then I'll bake scones and not drink. And if I cry, I'll wash my blotchy face and get on with life. I've done it before, not the baking scones part, but the rest of it. Don't worry about me."

"I'll prescribe your medicine ta Dec. I may even allow him ta throw somethin' breakable."

"Make him wear safety goggles." I caught Maeve scrutinizing us and blew her a kiss.

Nessa grasped my hand, peering straight into my eyes. "Whatever happens, you're not alone. Ya have us, darlin'."

"Oh, Jaysus, Ness. I'm pitiful, but not enough to justify you using endearments." For the first time since knowing her, I kissed her cheek. "Rematch tomorrow?"

Chapter Twenty-Seven

J OEL CLAPPED HIS HANDS, squealing like an excited child. "It's a damn jewel box! Your photos didn't do it justice. I want to put this house in my pocket and keep it forever!"

His enthusiasm coaxed a pleased smile. "Glad you approve."

"William Morris would have loved this place."

"The gross wallpaper guy?"

Joel groaned. "I concede his designs are busy, and if he were here, he'd plaster his birds and leaves all over. But he said, 'Have nothing in your home which you do not know to be useful or believe to be beautiful.' Your cottage embodies his philosophy and I'm gonna write about it."

"Please be discrete. Paparazzi are such a bother."

"I'm serious. *Architectural Digest* or someone would love this story." His zeal gave me a fresh perspective. The cottage had been a problem to solve, then a project to complete. It had since become a home full of friendship, industry, and love. But I'd given little objective consideration to her concise lines, the comfort inherent in the simple mix of objects and the space around them.

The timing of Joel's visit could not have been better; he buoyed my mood with his enthusiasm for tea towels, stone walls, and lush green grass. He photographed every painted door in the village, incapable of choosing a favorite, and wept when he first saw The Folly.

"It's a challenge, alright."

"It's stunning." He roamed the vast room with the air of a tourist in a cathedral.

"Sweetie, the word you want is wreck."

He bristled with defensiveness, like I'd insulted his new lover. "It is *not*! The potential is incredible."

"Agreed, but she needs a lot of sorting out."

"Stick to charity work, Pumpkin. I'll worry about architecture." He paced the large main floor with a sketch book open and ready. "This will be such fun! It's my first live-work project. Before starting, I'll need to interview all the principals."

"Already arranged; Liam and Paddy will meet you here within the hour."

"Excellent." Assessing the beams overhead, he patted my shoulder in an absent-minded way, already distracted by ideas.

"You two get acquainted. See you later."

Joel returned at lunchtime, his sketchbook full of notes, drawings, and measurements. After discussing the particulars of the structure with Paddy, he quizzed Liam about his requirements. "And your friend Moira showed up. She had definite opinions about the retail and office space."

"Yeah, she's dedicated to the business."

"And Liam, too?"

"The proof isn't solid, but my inkling is they're pretty sweet on each other."

Joel sat at the table and put his feet up on another chair. "She's a fan of yours, too. She said you should have an office."

"I'm helping with the social media stuff."

"And making bowls."

I twitched a dismissive shoulder. "A little bit of product, to get him started. It's not my life work or anything."

He smirked. "Life work is where you focus your passion. Based on the evidence, you're doing your life's work twenty-four seven." He opened his laptop and said, "Now get out of here; time to make magic. You may disturb me in the event of catastrophe or beer."

His words resonated as I hiked to St. Dallán's. After a lifetime chasing after purpose, envying those with one and feeling the paucity of my own ambition like a thorn, I found myself awash in job titles, though none ranked higher than the others. Words like craftsperson or philanthropist described my actions but summing them into a singular vocation made no more sense than choosing a single bone or organ to describe the human body. They were all part of me and engaged me with entire satisfaction.

Joel's arrival also provided a balm to soothe the rawness of Ciarán's departure. We rose early every morning, had breakfast together, then set to our work. Most evenings, I dragged him to the pub where he, Paddy, and Liam held animated discussions about loadbearing walls and construction techniques.

One evening Nessa observed them as Paddy gesticulated like he conducted a band and Joel's eyeglasses bobbled from forceful nods as he sketched. "Your friend is grinnin' so broad I'm fearin' he'll dislocate his jaw."

"He's enraptured. It's wonderful having him here. It's a kind of confirmation; staying in Ireland didn't cost me friends." I cut the musing short, keenly aware of the one friend I might yet lose. Nessa watched me; full of questions she would not ask. "Please don't watch me like a forbearing doe."

She harrumphed. "I haven't doe eyes. These are the steely, cold twins of my unfeelin' heart."

Despite the wet and cold of autumn, I visited St. Dallán's every day, much in need of the invigorating walk and the thundering quiet of the hilltop ruins. Sometimes haze blurred the edges of the remnants, swathing the place in deeper mystery, shrouding it from what lay beyond. But seen or unseen, the entire world spread around me, from valley to sky and toward the invisible ocean shores. I played a diminutive role in the incomprehensible vastness, but the notion anchored me, pinning my attention on the present rather than whatever nonsense tomorrow might bring.

Heading back from the ruins one afternoon, I encountered Michael and his flock. "Howya, Clare."

"Howya." No twelve-year-old worked harder than Michael O'Toole. Each morning he herded his father's sheep to pasture, leaving them and his border collie with Neal Fannin and his flock, then collected them after school, never considering his American counterparts spent their free time with soccer practice and game consoles.

"Hi! Niamh!" he chirruped. She sprang from her spot at his side and nipped the heels of an ewe who had straggled off to investigate a tussock. The sheep leapt back among the flock with an annoyed bleat. "Good girl." Michael rewarded the dog with a head pat when she returned to her place beside him.

"You're so good with her. It's amazing watching her work."

"She's a smart one. Don't know how she whelped an eejit." He gestured toward a puppy capering alongside its mother.

"He's adorable."

"He won't learn." Michael's tone bore all the scorn of a disappointed professor. "He acts more like a setter, always playin' and runnin' about. Nine months old and he won't be useful. Da despairs of him." The boy couldn't conceive of anyone—creature or human—not being of service.

"I should get a dog."

"Ya haven't any sheep."

His earnestness prompted a smile. "For a pet. Someone to hang out with."

Michael regarded me from the corner of his eye and with a lift of his shoulder said, "Ya can have him."

"Honey, I'm home." I hung my sodden coat, grateful for the snug warmth of the cottage. Joel stuck his head through the kitchen doorway, wearing one of my aprons and drying his hands on a tea towel. "Where are Wally and the Beav?"

He pulled a face, unimpressed with my joke. "Dinner's almost ready. Where have you been?" Then a spray of water hit him as my puppy shook his soaking fur. "Who's this?"

"Joel, meet Whiskey."

"Well, hey, there little fella!" Joel went on his knees when the dog bounded over. "Where'd you come from?"

We sat on the floor, playing with the puppy. "He's the runt of the litter. Mr. O'Toole says he's none too bright but he's wrong. You're a smart boy, aren't you?" Whiskey lifted his head and licked my face. "You have loftier aspirations than chasing sheep."

Joel's mouth tightened in a censorious line. "He *is* a working dog, Clare. He needs a job. Otherwise, he'll get bored and tear apart your house."

"Mr. O'Toole told me." I ruffled the pup's head. "You'll stay busy, won't you? We'll take walks and you'll herd the chickens and learn all sorts of tricks. He's a purebred border collie; I could enter him in agility trials."

Joel howled a laugh. "Right; you have *so* much time for dog training. And he's more likely to eat your chickens."

"No, he won't! Daisy gets out of the run all the damn time and it's annoying chasing after the ridiculous bird. You'll help me, won't you, boy?"

"Well, he's too cute for words and given the amount of baby talk, it's obvious you're smitten. What will Ciarán think?"

I kissed the dog's head. "It doesn't matter, does it, Whiskey? You're not negotiable."

Before returning to Seattle, Joel presented a draft of the blueprints. They represented a large, adaptable workshop and showroom downstairs, with commodious offices and an ample apartment on the second floor. "Warehouse is here, with a loading dock, and there's still plenty of space upstairs. We'll leave it open for now; then if Liam needs a bigger place or you want to add another apartment you can."

"It's perfect, Joel. I love you for doing this."

"You're paying me."

"Which takes nothing away from appreciating your effort. Although, you should know, Paddy doesn't work from drawings."

Joel pushed up his glasses, unconcerned. "Doesn't have to; the man's brain is composed of mechanical pencils and T squares. He knows what he's doing; he's a good head."

"He is. Man, he's gonna miss having Ciarán on this project. Who will he find to do the cabinets?"

Joel put his arm around me and squeezed. "You miss him."

"Of course, I do! But it's part of the package; sometimes he'll be here, sometimes he won't."

"You make it sound simple."

I hadn't spoken any of my thoughts aloud, not even to Edie. They fumbled in my mouth before they flowed. "Our relationship—it happening at all—defied any of my expectations or hopes. It's worth fighting for. Obviously, he needs to do a better job of communicating what's most important to him, but given my lack of perfection, I can extend him some grace while he learns. Everything between us happened with so little drama; it seduced me into assuming it would always be easy. Surprise! We're just like every other couple."

"The curse of fairy tales."

"Maybe. But I've never worked at much of anything."

"Until you got here."

I blew out a breath, unburdened but a little depressed. "The worst part is the constant fear of him being hurt." I paused, facing my terror about bombs and bullets. "But hell, he could have died outside my gate this summer. As Ciarán once said, quite accurately, any place is dangerous and safe at once. It's a matter of timing." Oddly, the uncomfortable insight quieted my internal noise.

"It'll be OK, Clare. He'll come home and you two will figure it out." Joel slapped my knee and pulled me off the couch. "Let's get to the pub so I can say goodbye for now."

"You're coming back?"

He tweaked my nose. "I can't miss the grand opening."

"I miss ya, darlin'." The satellite phone crackled and Ciarán's voice transmitted tinny. "Can ya make me out?"

"Pretty well. How are you?"

"Tired and lonely. And ya?"

"My boyfriend keeps me company."

Ciarán chortled. "Ya wasted no time. Tell me about this fella of yours."

"He's shorter than you, but he's handsome, with beautiful, silky hair and gorgeous brown eyes. He'd sit on my lap and kiss me all day if he could."

"How did ya meet?"

"On a walk; same way I meet all my boyfriends."

After a sharp exhale he replied, "I'm still in the runnin' then. Ya were none too pleased with me when I left."

I couldn't expect honest communication without offering it myself. "I regret behaving like an infant. Why didn't you tell me the truth from the get?"

Another exhale met my words, this one full of weary frustration, conjuring a picture of him drumming his fingers on the nearest surface. "I explained, Clare; it all happened so quick."

"The part about how you missed field work."

"I hadn't realized it myself."

"Until the opportunity arose."

"Don't make out like I couldn't wait ta leave ya. Ya know it's not the case. Would ya be happier if I were followin' ya around every moment?"

"No. Whiskey gets away with it because he's a dog and obligated to single minded devotion."

Ciarán huffed a relieved chuckle. "I reckon I can compete with a dog."

Whiskey lifted his head and tongued my chin. "You already have him beat; your kisses are a lot less slobbery."

"There's a comfort. Hold on a minute." After some inarticulate muttering, he breathed over the line, sounding fatigued. "I've got ta ring off, darlin'."

"Dammit! Sorry for wasting all our time trying to make you envious of my imaginary boyfriend."

"There were pangs of jealousy. I don't fancy anyone on your lap but me."

We exchanged sweet words which meant "I love you" but the phrase itself felt too loaded and best avoided.

Our brief, infrequent phone calls left me feeling unfinished; we never had time to get beyond the surface and Ciarán's disembodied voice made his physical absence more palpable. But as the time passed, I realized everyone in Killarkin struggled; everyone missed him, especially his family.

Maeve still expected me for Sunday supper, but in the early weeks we dined in a fraught atmosphere. We started out cheerful enough, but once Ciarán's name came up, as it always did, either Maeve or Declan would turn angry or petulant. I kept my issues private, with a tenuous grasp on cheer and no wish to compound their concern or make them choose nonexistent sides. But the effort exhausted me.

Over tea one afternoon Nessa confessed she too had reached her limit. "The way those two go on. I allow they have cause; most days I'd dearly love ta skin the man alive. But he's made his choice and Maeve and Dec must make their peace with it." Her eyes glimmered. "They don't reckon how their carryin' on hurts ya, either. I'll have a word and if they won't stop, I'll eat here on Sundays, providin' ya cook. I'm shite in the kitchen."

The gauntlet flung, the next Sunday proceeded without drama. The comfortable O'Donnell hearth, and the pleasant conversation assured under Nessa's hawkish vigilance, made me reluctant to return to the stillness of the cottage. After kissing Eamon and Maeve goodnight, Whiskey and I took a slow ramble around the village. Lamplight showed with a muted glow on the wet pavement of the empty street. Passing the shuttered houses, I imagined families gathered around dining tables in cozy rooms full of laughter. The perfume of peat smoke, rain-washed earth, and damp stone hung on the air. My boot heels clicked on the sidewalk.

My pace slowed as the merest sliver of the waxing crescent moon peeked between shifting clouds. Did Ciarán watch the same moon, imagining it showering its wan radiance on his home?

My soul clenched with a tender ache. There were people who didn't confine their notion of home to a building or town; it instead encompassed the whole wide world. And I loved one of them. For both our sakes, I either had to share Ciarán, or let him go. He had needs and desires I could never fill and clinging to any thought otherwise would choke the life out of what we had.

Every moment I missed him, worried about him, or both. But I couldn't expect him to sacrifice his passions on my account and still hold any claim on his love.

Rain started falling, and Whiskey and I cut through the pitch-black church yard to gain The High. "Come on, boy. Let's race."

Chapter Twenty-Eight

W HEN CIARÁN FIRST LEFT, I donned a plastic smile, a mask of casual indifference, mostly as a ward against the well-meaning attempts of others to take my emotional temperature. As the weeks passed, full of chores, work, and any number of activities requiring power tools, my mood changed, becoming more-cheerful-than-not. As a result, the villagers stopped tiptoeing around me and opened their own hearts. It most often took the form of a fond reminiscence, followed by a chest heave and casual, "I do miss the man." But it sometimes went deeper.

One afternoon, while helping Paddy at The Folly, he said, "Not ta suggest I don't appreciate havin' ya about, darlin, but I could do with Ciarán's help."

"He'll be back before we know it."

"There's a consolation." The rims of his eyes reddened, and he blew into a large red kerchief with a great deal of noise before laughing at himself. "Don't know why I'm blubberin'."

"Because you love him."

He nodded. "He's like a son ta me. Grandson more like." His mouth twitched in concentration; brows knit together. "I never married, ya know. Never had any children I know of."

I frowned. "You said your wife left you for a Tullamore grocer."

"I mentioned Cora, but nothin' about bein' married."

I pushed against his shoulder. "You're a scoundrel, Padraig Flannery."

"In the day, darlin', back in the day." He ceased his self-amused chuckling and laid a hand on my shoulder, fixing me with a concerned, loving expression. "My carin' for yer fella and ya goes deep. I'd do anythin' fer either of ya."

I laid a cheek on his hand. "You're a good friend."

"And friends watch out for each other. I'm not slaggin' Ciarán; he's a grand fella." His head wagged. "I reckoned this time were different but called it wrong. He's run off again." He straightened his shoulders and admitted, "I'm steppin' where I've no business, but I won't have ya hurt."

"I'm fine."

"Sure, ya are. Ya know what yer about and are ferocious as Gráinne Mhaol into the bargain. Ciarán's right ta fear ya!"

I bent and retrieved a fallen nail, hiding a scowl of confusion. "He's in a damned war zone right now. He's not afraid of anything."

"Nothin' but his heart."

Ciarán said as much himself when we met, but personal experience and loyalty dictated protest. "You're not making sense."

"Jaysus knows he loves ya, but he fears losin' it somethin' terrible. It's easier ta bolt."

"His passion for helping others pre-dates me. I don't expect to be the only thing he loves."

"Such a young one ta be so wise! Had I met the likes a ya I might ha' married after all!"

Paddy's concern came from a place of profound love and a history with Ciarán which far outpaced mine, but his perspective struck at the core of my own doubt. Some questions couldn't wait until February.

I rehearsed what to say, but when he phoned on the weekend, confidence flagged in the decisive moment, and I whispered past a knotted throat. "Did we rush into living together?"

"Nothin' of the kind!"

"It seemed reasonable at the time but—"

"Clare, I moved in because ya wisely pointed out life's fragility." He paused while an airplane roared overhead. I clutched the phone, panicked by the notion of his vulnerability. When the plane rumbled away, he continued. "And it is convenient keepin' my socks in one place." I managed an unconvincing laugh. "What's troublin' ya, darlin'?"

"If aid work is your calling, I accept the terms. But if it is easier or better for you to stay unattached, I understand."

His breath came over the wire. "I love ya, darlin'."

"Not the issue." My heart thumped in the following silence. "Remember the secret chamber promise."

"Clare, I've no time ta think about promises right now."

A sudden rise of nausea halted my words. Struggling past it I said, "This isn't about eternal declarations or anything. But understanding what I'm waiting for would make it easier to count the days."

A tiny laugh came over the phone. "My poor impatient darlin'."

"I'm working on it. What do *you* want?"

"I've been discernin'."

At his admission, a chunk of my heart dislodged. "Fair enough. Let me know when you arrive, well, anywhere."

"I do love ya, Clare."

"The funny part is, I'm certain you do."

Whiskey laid his head on my knee, and I stroked the satin fur under his neck. Unable to discern heat or cold, it seemed pointless to lay a turve. Ciarán couldn't provide the concrete answer my heart craved, but no anxiety appeared, the hamster wheel made nary a squeak; for now, my fitful head had to wait.

"The universe is determined to teach me patience." Whiskey lifted his head, regarding me. "No. It pisses me off. But thanks for asking." He lashed my cheek with his wet tongue and lay down again.

Halloween arrived and Moira insisted I celebrate with her and the lads. "Ya must have your first barmbrack."

I scrunched my face, as if she'd offered me gizzards. "What is it with the Irish and weird fruitcake?"

Moira muttered something about the gaps in my Celtic education. "It's a Samhain tradition. Ya bake charms in the cake and what ya get tells your fortune."

"Sounds like an effective way to break a tooth but I'll come along for the craic."

Villagers filled the pub, feasting on colcannon and cake. After a dubious examination of the dense, speckled loaf of barmbrack, I squinted at Moira. "Now what?"

"Here's my trick for it." She served our slices, assumed her fork like someone disarming a bomb, and reduced the cake to bites before she excavated a small bit of parchment, its ends twisted tight.

Jamie crowed when she unwrapped the charm. "Ho! Moira! Ya got the coin! There's double good luck: if ya get rich, it means Liam will, too. Go on, then, Clare."

I unearthed and opened my packet. "A pea?"

Moira made a mournful tisk. "A shame, but you'll not marry this year."

"Not surprising, given the sole man with a chance is out of the country until February."

Liam pulled apart his slice with his fingers. He received a ring and Moira's laugh rang through the pub. "What's so funny?" I asked.

She wiped her eye with a sleeve. "He'll wed next year."

Liam's face reddened with umbrage. "I might do, Moira Fannin. I might marry ya."

The suggestion induced fresh gales of laughter. "You're talkin' nonsense."

Liam's face fell, but he replied with a huff. "Ya should take me more serious."

Moira tossed her hair, tinged pumpkin orange for the season. "Give me a reason ta do."

With a woeful expression, Jamie examined the button on his plate and Liam managed a chuckle. "Well, there's no more than the truth!"

"Never wanted ta marry anyway." Jamie snorted with disgust and bashed Liam's ribs with his elbow. "Let's have a game." As the young men took their bruised egos to the darts lane, Jamie threw the offending button at the wall; it ricocheted and plinked against Liam's pint.

"He took his fortune a bit hard."

Moira watched him with a gentle countenance. "Poor eejit. If he stopped moonin' after Nora and did somethin' about it, he'd change his fate."

The lads jostled and teased, masking truer feelings under pints and jolly smiles. "If he fancies Nora, why does he spend all his time with you?"

"He hopes I'll fix it for him, but if he won't give it a lash and chat ta her, he hasn't got the stones for more."

"Excellent point." With a sly smile I added, "Liam doesn't suffer the same affliction; he pretty much proposed to you just now."

Her guffaws were loud enough to swivel heads our direction. "Ask Eamon ta hold a comedy night. You're hilarious." But after a sip of whiskey her tone sobered. "I fancy him. He's hard workin', serious when he needs ta be. But I want someone who delights in me for who I am, like ya and Ciarán do."

"Jaysus, we're no kind of model. We have a hell of a lot to figure out."

"'Course ya do; you're human, ain't ya? But ya leave each other free to do what ya need; and when you're together the satisfaction of it is like singin'."

"I can't carry a tune."

"Ya can with Ciarán. It's a pretty song ya make."

"We have talked way too much about men." I winked back a tear and checked my watch. "Two more hours until we launch the website."

"We'll let the lads finish their game and head back to the cottage, then. It's all so excitin'."

Her enthusiasm both delighted and scared me. The potential for disappointing my friends loomed large. "The social media accounts are growing, but it could be months before we see significant traffic."

"Sure, and he knows it. But I'll tell ya true, I've never known him ta fail at anythin'."

The clock pulled closer to midnight and our collective nerves heightened. We attempted to work them out with darts, but by eleven-thirty abandoned the pretense and hurried to the cottage. We gathered around the computer and my hand trembled while clicking the 'publish' button. No one breathed as we watched the meter crawl toward one hundred percent.

Moira cheered and Liam chuckled like a child on his birthday. "Let's check the sales page."

"Even if people sat ready with credit cards, they have to shop the site and place orders." I refreshed the screen and pointed at the site meter. "But you've had five visitors so far."

"Seems a good start."

"It is, but let's do ourselves a favor and leave it until morning. Come have a drink."

Hopeful confidence didn't translate into a restful night. I rose early and Liam knocked on the door minutes later. "You couldn't sleep either?"

"Not a wink. Do ya mind?"

I booted the computer and opened the sales page. There were over a dozen orders and one consultation request. We startled when another order pinged.

Liam glowed like a summer star. "Have ya ever known the rightness of somethin' so gut-deep ya can't deny it? I reck it takes time ta build a business; but Jaysus, all my life I've wanted this. I'm so grateful ta ya, Clare."

A constricted throat prevented any attempts at pretty speeches. Instead, I clapped a hand on his shoulder and swallowed hard. "Right. When Moira gets here we'll pack these orders."

After a busy, gratifying morning I emailed the Family Coordinator, utterly sensible of the absurdity of reporting housewares sales to a man saving lives in the Sudan. But if our relationship survived, this would be our normal. There could someday be a message announcing the birth of his child. The painful truth pricked. For months at a time, he would miss the big occasions and tiny triumphs which compose a shared life. He already had.

Moira's words from the night before whispered again. We were human, Ciarán and me, which meant neither of us were paragons. With self-aware honesty, he named his failings early on and, impressed by his maturity and grounding, I errantly glossed over the confessions. His effortless declaration in a ruined castle, his preternatural patience with my dithering, further seduced me into believing he had all the answers. He didn't, nor could I demand them of him. A soft warmth snuggled around my heart. I loved a flawed person and so did he. We were equals.

Whiskey had two distinct reactions when someone came to the door. A perky series of yips signaled a friend's arrival. He greeted strangers with a low, wolfish growl which gave over to a sharp, short bark. The dog roused himself from his pillow and barked his friendly greeting. I opened the door to Declan, his hand poised to knock.

"Are ya psychic?"

"Whiskey is. Want a cuppa?"

Declan offered a bottle of champagne. "I've somethin' better."

"What's the occasion?"

"Ciarán asked me ta bring this along and tell ya he's fair proud."

"We had a decent first day but it hardly warrants bubbles."

Declan tisked like I'd gotten a sum wrong, "Continuin' Seamus' legacy is well worth celebratin'."

My head bobbed like an astonished cockatoo. "This is quite a turnaround, Mr. O'Donnell! It almost sounds like you're supportive."

"Feck off. I'll need somethin' ta pour into."

I fetched glasses and returned, only to balk. Declan's new-found ease around me still startled. In this case, he slumped comfortably in a corner of the couch, his legs stretched out on the coffee table. "Sometimes you're unrecognizable."

"Ta myself as well." He sat up, served the drinks and, after the requisite toast added, "It won't shock ya ta hear it, but I underestimated ya. You're made of strong cloth. I hope my wayfarin' brother knows it."

I perched beside him. "He figured it out before either of us."

"His greatest virtue is seein' ya true. Ness does the same for me." He tapped his glass against mine. "I can take myself off if you're knackered."

"Stick around. It's too quiet here of an evening. Whiskey is attentive but he's not much of a conversationalist."

Ignoring the joke, Declan scowled. "It's Ciarán who should be here. He cheesed me off today with his chirpy 'take my darlin' a bottle of champagne' business. If he cared so damn much, he might consider not leavin' his woman when she needs him, and I told him so."

I clapped a hand to my forehead, groaning. "Oh, Dec; you didn't."

"No fear, darlin'. I made clear I spoke for myself."

"What exactly did you say?"

"There are better ways of showin' his love than runnin' off ta Africa."

"Why does everyone keep using that damn verb?"

"It's what Ciarán does."

"Did you ever consider he actually cares about me?"

Declan's held his chin firm, but everything else in his face grew pliant. "Of course, he does and the depth of it frightens him."

Worn down from pacing the same ground for weeks, my small store of patience vanished. "Healing the brokenness of the world instead of holding my hand doesn't make him a selfish bastard, Dec. Shite, if he's running, it's not from me but toward a mission. Stop warning me off!"

Declan squeezed my hand. "I didn't intend ta upset ya. But someone had ta call him ta account. He should be here for those he says he loves."

"Cara gives him purpose. Every relationship has a cost, and I've weighed the price of ours. Don't speculate on his motives; it's not fair and brings me no comfort."

Declan bent forward, hands clasped. "Ten long years I hated him; despised him valuin' his work ahead of the family." His head dipped lower. "I resented him bein' gone when I needed him. I only got him back and now he's left us again."

I leaned against Declan's arm. "His work doesn't take away from anything. Being of service helps him love us more."

"How is it ya don't worry about him?"

"Don't be thick. Every moment is under the shadow. Thoughts sometimes brood with an unspeakable *if*. But I'd rather lose him in the cause than watch the slow death of our relationship; he needs more, and I won't stand in the way."

Declan shook his head, disbelieving. "Ya can't mean it."

Conviction gripped, tight as it did when I decided about the cottage. "We all want him safe and home." I gulped, determined not to undercut the truth by crying. "But it's his choice."

When Declan left, I went out into the November drizzle to feed Daisy and May. Shoving my hand into the feed bucket I rolled the tiny grains in my palm. The dusty chaff tickled my nose with a sneeze. I tossed a handful, watching it arc across the yard, exciting the chickens. Their tiny heads bobbed with precise pecks of the ground. Placing the bucket on its shelf, I whistled for Whiskey. "Come on, boy. Mommy needs a walk."

Chapter Twenty-Nine

ONE FRIGID AFTERNOON, MOIRA worked on the books while I sprawled on the guest bed and added product photos to the website. We both startled when Whiskey barked his stranger alert. "Ridiculous pup, "I said, patting his head. "You can't freak out every damn time someone visits." Upon opening the door I regretted my words.

"Howya, Clare! Didja miss me?" Garbhán forced himself past without an invitation.

The stink of his pomade turned my stomach, and my panicked mind raced. "Declan is at his office."

"Oh, we'll catch up, no mistake about it." He affected an off-hand manner, but his ominous tone read clear. "Thought I'd first stop by ta see the finished cottage and hear about your little enterprise." He glared at the dog. "Not a biter, is he?"

"Whiskey, sit." The collie complied, but remained wary and vigilant, never shifting his interest from Garbhán. "Good boy. He tolerates strangers, in time."

"With luck he'll know me well soon enough." His hand hovered over Whiskey's head, but the dog growled low and pressed his body against my leg.

"He's protective." I'd never been so grateful for the animal's unique take on shepherding.

Garbhán stood bandy-legged, hands on hips, and surveyed the front room as if he owned it. "It's finer than I expected and damn well should be after all the money ya threw after it." He nodded toward the kitchen. "Ya might offer a fella a glass of somethin' now."

My belly churned, eager to get him off to Declan so I could call the garda. "This isn't a convenient time. I have a lot of work."

He sprawled on the couch. "No doubt, though why ya bother I don't know."

"Following Grand-da's footsteps." I tried to joke past another heave of alarm. "If you'll excuse me..."

"Now, don't be showin' me out when we've so much ta discuss." He patted the seat beside him; I remained near the door. He leered, demon foul, and laid one stubby hand on the back of the couch.

Bile rose as I imagined the short, thick fingers wrapped tight around a rock. "Where have you been?"

"Ah, ya did missed me. Germany. A bit of business turned into a holiday." His deep-set eyes glinted. How had I ever mistaken the hard glitter for anything but menace? "Where's your fella?"

"Out. He'll be home soon." Glancing toward the office, my mind worked on excuses to get in there alone. "Go find Declan and we'll have a drink later."

"Why not here and now? We don't need holy Joe and his dry shite brother for the craic."

Blessedly, Moira chose the moment to leave the office. She started at Garbhán's presence. "Sorry for interruptin'. I thought I heard Liam."

"It's all right. Do you know Garbhán McAllister?"

"Sure. I've seen ya 'round the pub with Declan. I can finish later, if ya like."

"You will not!" I answered with such sharpness she gasped. "Those reports must be finished today. Excuse me a minute, Garbhán. Let me deal with this and then you can tell me about your trip."

With an assertive toss of my head, I marched out of the room, a cowed Moira behind me. She closed the door, near tears. "What'd I do wrong?"

My voice dropped. "Gawd, nothing. It's all a show. When I go back out there, ring Declan. Tell him Garbhán is here and ask him to phone Sargent Corcoran. Tell him—oh, Jaysus, Moira—tell him to come here quick."

Her features collapsed with confusion. "What can ya want with the garda?"

Clutching her hand I nodded toward the door. "It's possible the man out there attacked Ciarán. After you call Dec, stay here. Whatever you do, please don't leave me alone."

"I'll not." She braced her shoulders, ready for battle. "I'll ring the lads, too. They can put a watch on the doors."

"Excellent idea. But have them stay outside unless I scream or something."

Moira blanched and gulped. "You're afraid of him. I'll make the calls and join ya."

I squeezed her fingers, buttressed by her stalwart friendship. "Wait until Dec arrives, OK? I owe you, Moira."

"I'll be here." She stood firm, like a fierce and graceful swan.

Forcing my lips into a bright smile, I returned to my visitor. "Sorry. She's a new employee."

"Ya gotta give the help the boss eyes or they'll run all over ya," Garbhán replied.

"I'm a rotten host. Give me one minute." Fleeing to the kitchen, I collected glasses on a tray, poured a finger of whiskey with trembling hands, and shot it back. Acting wasn't one of my talents; all my emotions remain clear on the surface, obvious in quick blushes and readable expressions. But if the tremors ceased and I refrained from smashing the Jameson bottle across Garbhán's malicious face, I might manage.

Chilled with nerves, I set the tray on the coffee table then tended the fire. "This is cosy. Too bad we're not alone." Garbhán flicked his head toward the office door.

I affected a casual laugh and replaced the poker with reluctance; it would be more useful jabbed into the disgusting creature's gut. "There's not much privacy here these days."

"Who is this Liam fella the bitta fluff mentioned? You're not steppin' out on Ciarán, are ya?"

"A friend of Moira's."

"I'll bet he is," he said, with an unpleasant snigger.

"Damn. I forgot water. One minute." Scuttling like a crab into the kitchen, I propped against the counter. Agitation, Garbhán's cheap view of relationships, and the cloying stench of his waxed hair made me woozy. I opened the window over the sink and inhaled as the cold evening raced in, waiting until the invigorating air lifted my brain fog.

I remember the moon, the fragrance of night flowers, and desirin' ya. Ciarán's words sounded in memory, clear as if he were beside me. I drew another deep breath and filled a carafe with water, desperate for Declan's arrival.

"What's keepin' ya?" Garbhán's greasy voice made me jump.

I composed my guise into a mask of hospitality and turned. "It's been a long day." He stepped closer, but I danced away from him to the relative safety of the front room.

He simpered, winked, and helped himself to the whiskey. "What had ya so enthralled ya forgot about a guest?"

"Remembering the night of Ciarán's attack. It still haunts me. We never found out who did it."

Leather creaked as he readjusted his haunches on the couch. "It's fearful, ta be sure." He swallowed the unconvincing statement along with a stiff pull of his drink. "The shades should do their bleedin' job. What do we pay taxes for, I wonder?"

The dog barked again and Garbhán jumped; but my knots of anxiety eased. I allowed time for the knock before answering. "Declan!" I hoped the enthusiastic greeting didn't betray my sheer relief. "Guess who's here!"

"Well, Garbhán McAllister," Declan said. "This is a surprise. We thought ya were dead." He settled into Grand-da's chair, the model of composure, and poured a drink.

"We're catching up," I said.

"Sure," Declan said, as if we had cozy gossips with would-be murderers every day. "Such a lot has happened since we saw ya last, man. You've been gone a fair while."

"He's been on holiday."

Declan pouted. "Shame on ya, never sendin' your old friend a postcard."

The solicitor's intrusion and uncharacteristically jovial demeanor disconcerted Garbhán but had the opposite effect upon me. I passed a bowl of walnuts to Declan and asked, "How's Ness?"

"Never better." He beamed with unfeigned delight, selected a nut, and cracked it open between his palms.

"Nessa?" Garbhán's countenance shed more of its smirk.

Declan leaned back, the pleased smile on his face genuine. "We married last month. If ya answered your phone, we'd have invited ya ta the weddin'. Class, it was."

Having already stacked an impressive pile of lies I clasped hands in pretend rapture. "Beyond lovely. The church brimmed with flowers and Nessa made *such* a beautiful bride."

A chuckle burbled from Declan, no doubt in appreciation for the convincing performance. "Ta say nothin' of your shenanigans at the reception."

"Don't you dare, Dec," I said, with a coquettish laugh. "What happens in the pub stays there."

Garbhán's teeth clenched. "Shame I missed it; though it's hard believin' you two reconciled after all this time." Witnessing Garbhán McAllister unmanned gave me wicked joy.

Declan stretched his hands toward the fire. "Fear and stupidity kept us apart too long. It's a fool who lets anythin' or anyone thwart his heart's desire."

The office door creaked open and Moira peeked out, blanched with concern. "I've finished, miss."

"Oh, Moira. I forgot you were here." The imperious ruse felt unnatural, but atonement had to wait until after the show. "You may go now, but please don't be late again tomorrow."

She played her part well. "I'll not, miss, and I'm so sorry about this mornin'." Sidling behind Garbhán she flashed a quick OK sign. Whiskey barked again and she opened the door. "Ya have more company, miss."

I rose to greet the visitor. "Sargent Corcoran! Please come in. You know Declan, of course. And this is our good friend, Garbhán McAllister. Let me get you tea; or whiskey, if you're off duty."

A man on a mission, Corcoran didn't bother with rituals. "Tea would be grand if it's no trouble. Thank ya." He reclined in the chair nearest the door, blocking egress. I struggled against laughter when he and Declan began a casual chat about hurling.

While the kettle boiled, I locked the back door, glimpsing the darkened, comforting forms of Jamie and Liam milling outside. After he received his tea, Corcoran asked, "Is the younger Mr. O'Donnell about?"

"He's in the Sudan." Garbhán couldn't hurt me now; I told the truth and ignored his angry gape.

"Is he now? Can ya get word ta him?"

"Sure. Have you learned something?"

Corcoran nodded as he consulted his notebook. "As a matter of fact. We traced the suspect ta the Dublin airport, then the trail went dead cold. But he hired a car around nine the evenin' of Mr. O'Donnell's attack and returned it near one the next mornin'. The mileage is consistent with a drive ta Killarkin and back."

I gave Garbhán a huge, perverse smile. "What good news!"

"Sure." He coughed and glowered at his drink.

Ever judicious, Corcoran said, "He might have driven elsewhere, of course, but with the other evidence we've uncovered, this gives our theory weight."

"Clare, ya told me there were no witnesses." Twenty minutes earlier Garbhán's menacing stare would have distressed me. Now a mere flick of my hand answered him.

Corcoran had formidable acting chops and addressed Garbhán with bland innocence. "Witnesses corroborate information, Mr. McAllister. No one saw the wicked attack, true enough." His head wagged from side to side. "One wonders what sort of coward hides in darkness and bashes a man from behind." Then he abandoned philosophical musings and returned to business. "We uncovered a motive and worked back from there ta solid proof. Police work is painstakin' business. Facts serve better than theories."

I topped off Declan's drink. "Sargent, you told me sometimes bits come back after the first excitement. You were right. Tonight, I remembered Ciarán telling me he smelled night flowers right before the attack."

Corcoran's head tilted. "And why do ya reckon it's significant?"

"The garden hasn't any night flowers."

The detective's posture straightened. "None ya say? Are ya suggestin' the perpetrator wore perfume?" He scribbled in his notebook with a studious expression.

"Or anything with a strong, floral scent."

Declan lifted the whiskey bottle. "Have another tot, Garbhán. You've gone pale."

"Temptin' offer, but I'm intrudin' on official business. I'll find ya later, Clare."

He rose and wiped sweaty palms on his trousers, but with a forceful tone Sargent Corcoran said, "Before ya go, what were ya doin' on the night in question?"

Garbhán slouched back onto the couch, his hunted eyes disabusing any doubts about his involvement. "The attack happened months ago."

The Sargent tapped his pen against the notebook. "I wish for a specific account of your time from late evenin' on the sixth of July into the mornin' after."

"In bed, I reck."

"And could ya provide corroboration for your alibi?"

"What are ya implyin'? It's the God's truth. My home is in the Pale, and I come here now and again on business."

Corcoran nodded, his attention on his notes. "But you're acquainted with Mr. O'Donnell and in such matters it's necessary ta question friends and associates of the victim. The Dublin garda attempted contactin' ya earlier but found ya had disappeared."

"He's been in Germany," I said with helpful sweetness.

"Right ya are." Garbhán's eyes darted like starlings while he worked out his next gambit. "I would help if I could, Sargent, but didn't learn of the trouble until days after."

"And he rushed here the second he heard," I said. "He couldn't have been more concerned."

His relief genuine, Garbhán dared a winking nod, as if we were allies. "Came over as soon as Declan gave the word. Terrible business."

With the grace of a stalking tiger, Declan set aside his glass. "It's a heartwarmin', but flawed tale. We haven't spoken since ya demanded I bring Clare in hand."

"I never," Garbhán hissed, with a furious, warning squint.

Declan placed a finger on his temple. "Ya added somethin' about your methods bein' more effective."

The room grew silent as dawn at St. Dallán's. Garbhán stared, incredulous his power over Declan had vanished. Then he glared, baleful as a thunder cloud. "Ya bastard."

Corcoran thumbed through his notebook as if he hadn't regarded the exchange. "Mr. McAllister, why did ya hire a car the night of the attack?"

"Why, I...it had ta be..." Garbhán sputtered, a literal last gasp.

"I'll ask ya again where ya were and what ya were doin' the night in question."

He mustered enough of his draining energy to reply, "I'll not say another bleedin' word without counsel present!"

"Suit yourself." Corcoran rose, placid and steady, and placed Garbhán under arrest.

"Jaysus!" Ciarán's voice fizzed over the wire. "It's resolved."

Declan and I huddled around his office phone, but he allowed me to deliver the good news. "Done and dusted."

"It's hard imaginin' him goin' down without a fight."

"Like all bullies, his bluster hasn't any substance," Declan said. "Corcoran is an excellent detective; he discovered other victims. McAllister had a habit of extortion, and the preponderance of evidence turned his bantam of an attorney green. He'll be in gaol a long time. Ma is fair beside herself with joy. We all are."

"Are ya in the clear, Dec?" Ciarán asked, with unmistakable love.

"It's bein' decided." He gave me a brotherly smile. "Clare entered a statement on my behalf. Time will tell, but I'll not worry ahead of it."

"Good. I'm grateful ta ya, man. If it's not a trouble, may I speak with her alone?"

"I'll talk ta ya later, brother."

"Give Ness my love."

The door clicked shut behind Declan and I lifted the receiver. "We forgot to mention the court ordered restitution. Cara will receive a sizable donation in memory of Seamus Riordan."

"Under the circumstances, I'd think you'd prefer another charity."

"McAllister hurt you and benefited from money Grand-da would have used for a worthy cause. It's poetic."

"You're an amazin' woman, Clare Riordan."

"Why did you want privacy?"

"I've felt shite since our last conversation."

His words gave me no pleasure. Hoping he would make out my earnestness I said, "Please don't, Ciarán. You were right; you aren't in a position to deal with those questions right now; I should have waited until we could talk in person. Don't worry about me; I'm making peace with the unknown. And, please, believe me; whatever happens, I will never regret loving you."

Chapter Thirty

T HE QUIET SEASON OF Advent arrived. Garland and holly wreaths swagged village buildings; the front windows of every home glowed with candlelight, lighting the way for Mary and Joseph. I didn't recall the Holy Family passing through Ireland in their quest for succor, but the notion charmed. Each evening my taper burned along with the rest of the community; our tiny flames affirming hope against the ebony winter night.

One day Cathleen and Gerry arrived at the cottage, wearing festive sweaters, and bearing a large box. "We've brought your Christmas hamper," she said, with a tinkling laugh. I stared, uncomprehending.

"It's tradition for shop keepers ta thank ya for your custom with a little somethin' at Christmas," Gerry explained. "You'll find Aideen's gifts included."

Bemused by the size of the box and the wealth of foodstuffs and other tidbits within, I later asked Maeve, "How do they stay in business giving a month's worth of groceries to every family in town?"

"Oh, each hamper is different," she said, rolling out pastry dough. "The size owes ta how much ya spent with them over the year."

I blanched with guilt. Thanks to the reno, thousands of Riordan euros had poured into the Fannin's coffers, but never with an expectation of dividends. Maeve glanced at me and laughed. "Oh, darlin', it's not as if ya stole from them. It's the custom, though I can't say the shopkeepers in Dublin or Cork and the like trouble with it now days. More like they hand out tokens or such, but don't fuss. It's what we do, ya see, and ya live here now so..." She faded off with a toss of her shoulder and I pocketed another unique feature of Irish life.

In a last-minute decision, I planned a trip to Seattle for the holiday. Mom considered the itinerary too brief, but between work and dog ownership, I couldn't spare more than a week. Moira agreed to housesit, I delivered early gifts to friends and girded my loins for a last call from Ciarán. "I'll be with my family over Christmas." It came out cheerier than my jangled nerves warranted.

"I can still ring ya."

"You get so little opportunity anyway; call your folks, instead. It will mean a lot to Maeve. It might be good for you, too."

"How do ya reck?"

If I'd had an old-fashioned land line, I would have nervously wound the cord around my cold fingers. "I won't be an obligation. Take all the time and space you need to work out your problems."

"You're not a problem, darlin'." His quiet voice made me sensible of the miles, continents, and seas between us.

"Your questions, then. Point is, you need a clear field to do it."

"Is it what ya want?"

"I want happiness, but never at your expense. What we offer one another must be without conditions; anything less would be pathetic and wouldn't have a hope of lasting. I've claimed my joy, sweetheart. Be courageous enough to claim yours and I'll be brave enough to be happy for you."

It wrenched to leave all I'd gained in Ireland, but returning to the US allowed me to step away from daily reminders of the bit I might yet lose. Still, as the plane lowered through the clouds, revealing the familiar landmarks of Mt. Rainier glistening with snow, and the sweep of downtown nestling Elliot Bay, I felt like a tourist returning to a well-loved vacation spot; I knew my way around, but it wasn't home.

On Christmas Eve I met Edie downtown for our ritual shenanigans. Taking in the holiday lights I said, "This is worth the entire trip." I inhaled a deep breath and coughed. Seattle never struck me as polluted but compared to fresh, clean Irish air it stank.

"It made me so happy when you said you'd be home." Edie said. "Not doing all our traditional shit would have ruined Christmas for everyone."

We jostled our way through Nordstrom, the floors thronged with last-minute shoppers. "Remind me again why this is part of our tradition. It's so loud!"

Edie groaned with a disgusted frown. "Oh, god, I'll lose my damn mind if you've turned into a bumpkin."

My chin lifted in an impersonation of a haughty queen. "Don't be a snob; I've merely forgotten how to bustle."

"You're back in civilization, girlfriend; bustle, dammit. Do you have any shopping? I gotta get Denise's caramels and pick up Aimee's present. What are you giving Ciarán?"

"Nothing." My fingers fondled a pair of beautiful, useless red silk stilettos.

Edie batted her lashes toward the heavens. "Of course. He needs nothing more than you."

"It's not like refugee camps require a shirt and tie."

"Give him a quintessential token from your hometown."

"Like a Seahawks jersey? He's not a sports guy." I considered. "He likes all kinds of music, although he's a bit mired in the 'nineties."

"Get him an mp3 player and load it with music from this century."

"Not a terrible idea. But how would he charge it out in the field?"

"How the hell should I know? It's his problem." Edie checked the time. "Alright; you take care of O'Dish, I'll get my shit, and we'll meet at the park in thirty."

From the time we were thirteen and our moms trusted us to go downtown alone, we observed the same routine: shopping, riding the

Westlake Park carousel, then admiring the gingerbread houses displayed in the Sheraton lobby. Once we were legal, we couldn't leave the hotel without cocktails.

"I'll be perverse and have an Irish coffee," Edie said. "Is it actually Irish?"

"It is. I'll have the same." A table opened by the time the bartender mixed our drinks and as we settled I asked. "What's Aimee's gift?" Edie, the queen of composure, grew bashful. Perching on the edge of my chair, I said. "Edie King! Show me right now!" She handed over a small burgundy box. Cradling it, I squinted in warning. "This better not be a boring pair of earrings."

"Open it."

Both feather-light and staid, I flipped open the lid and clasped a hand to my mouth. "Oh, gawd, Edie."

My composed friend quailed a tiny bit. "Will she like it?"

"She'll love it! It's so sparkly."

Edie's equanimity returned. "Aimee loves fairy tale shit, so I'll indulge her."

"Cuz she's your princess."

"Yeah, she is."

I handed back the engagement ring and wiped my eye. "You don't like ooey gooey, so I'll behave; but I am so happy."

"Me, too. I blame the terrible influence of your romantic Celtic adventure."

My smile slipped. "Best not pin this on me." I'd given Edie a broad stroke narrative about Ciarán's leaving; now I filled in the details, fretting the damp paper napkin under my drink, while her expression grew more alarmed by the minute.

"Why didn't you tell me before?"

"Too busy working it out on my own. Don't panic yet. I'm hopeful, most of the time." I scrunched my nose. "It's his decision."

Edie signaled the waiter. "This is so unlike you. First, you struggle with all these questions without a discussion, then when you fess up you're calm and matter of fact. Where's the drama?"

I grinned, sheepish. "Breaking news: I'm not the center of the universe."

Edie reached a hand for mine. "He loves you, Clare."

"This isn't about feelings."

"I hate being sad on Christmas Eve." Few people modeled self-command better than Edie; the downward slump of her mouth hurt.

"Nothing is definitive enough for sadness, hon."

"I wish you didn't live half a world away."

"Move to Killarkin. You and Aimee can live in my barn until you find a place."

"We'll take it under advisement." Edie smiled but remained gloomy. "Clare, if things don't work out with O'Dish, will you come back home?"

"It'll crack my heart wide open if this doesn't take, but I'll stay in Ireland, with or without him."

"We're quoting Bono now?"

I glared. "Plus, I have Whiskey."

Edie tapped my half-empty mug. "You always have whiskey, hon. Oh, you mean the dog. Gawd, you have a house, a pet—"

"Chickens and matching sheets. It's appalling. I've committed to grownup shite left and right."

"Completely out of character." The waiter hovered near Edie's elbow. "Do we have time for another round?"

I checked my phone with a pout. "Damn! No. Traditional fondue extravaganza in an hour, then Midnight Mass."

Edie cupped her cheeks, the model of innocence. "Tell Denise the holiday traffic is horrible and spend the night with us."

"Tempting, but Mom must have all her kids under the roof Christmas morning."

"Her grown-ass children?"

"'Fraid so. Besides, you need privacy for the deed. Will you accomplish it before Christmas dinner?"

Edie hid a mincing smile in her shoulder. "I'm proposing tonight. I'll text when it's official."

"Best Christmas ever!"

Religious cynicism aside, Midnight Mass reduced me to sentimental mush. I sat with my family in the candlelit nave and thought of my Irish friends. They would have listened to the same readings, made the same responses and prayers. I pictured Ciarán surrounded by desert and hoped he and his comrades celebrated. I cherished my far-flung loves while singing carols with my family, sensible this could be our last Christmas together for a while. Daddy put his arm around me, and I laid my head on his shoulder. Wistful tears pricked as a noiseless peace swelled my soul.

In Denise Riordan's household, a strict timeline and choreographed liturgy directed Christmas day, including careful preservation of wrapping paper, forced good cheer, and an afternoon of frenzied cooking. Around three, Mom's polite requests for help would crescendo into frantic, barked orders. Then, in a ritual important as the tree and stockings, Daddy would deliver a glass of wine and remind her we celebrated Christ's birth, not a re-enactment of the Normandy invasion. Sniffling into her Chardonnay, she'd summon her will, and hours later welcome guests into a pristine, festive house with her hospitable smile giving nary a hint of the fraught irritations which preceded.

Resigned to the drama, but lured by the fragrance of cinnamon and coffee, I shuffled into the kitchen where Mom greeted me with a chirpy, "Good morning, Clare! Merry Christmas!"

"Merry Christmas, Mom. Can I help?"

"Grab the orange juice and champagne while I finish these."

After admiring the intricate, lacy patterns on her pastries, I opened a fridge filled with lidded casseroles and foil wrapped baking pans. "What's all this?"

"I prepped dinner while you were with Edie. All I have left is roasting the turkey." Mom arranged rolls on a tiered stand. "Your father suggested I not waste your visit in the kitchen."

"Yay, Daddy!" Mom mixed mimosas and asked about the renovation of The Folly. "It's going well. Paddy hopes to finish by summer."

"And then what will you do?"

I smiled. "Find other projects."

Mom served me a steaming roll, oozing molten, spicy sugar. She brimmed with obvious curiosity but took pains to refrain from pushing. "Will there be more renovations?"

"Who knows? This won't settle your mommy worries, but Killarkin is my job. Grand-da didn't map it out, either; he responded to needs as they arose. I'll do the same."

"This mommy's heart is overflowing; whatever you do will be spectacular." Trying hard not to gawk, I thanked her and bit into my roll. She adjusted herself on her stool. "I'm proud of you, honey. I don't say it often enough."

The rare, precious words were a treasure. "Thanks for saying it now."

Mom grew tentative. "How is Ciarán?"

"Safe, as of three days ago."

She mewed with empathy, not disapproval. "This must be so difficult for you."

She refilled our glasses with champagne and topped them with orange juice. Cherishing our camaraderie, I tread light. "I'd worry about him no matter how he made a living." This answer would no doubt send her into questions about our plans or ravings about wild Irish babies, but to my utter shock, she praised my maturity and inquired after Eamon and Maeve.

The rest of the clan straggled in. Colin made a second pot of coffee, then a third. Mom finally gathered us around the tree, a good two hours later than usual, and Daddy, with a battered Santa hat on his head, handed Stephen's new girlfriend a gift. Alice slipped a careful finger under the tape, obviously schooled on the family protocol.

Mom waved her hand. "Oh, tear into it, honey. It ends up in the recycling anyway."

My brothers, Virginia, and I exchanged glances of amused astonishment. Colin laughed and said, "You're not our mother!"

"I have the C-section scars to prove it," she replied, with a sniff.

She surprised us again later when she announced her intention to nap. Bewildered by the gift of a lazy Christmas afternoon sans hysteria, I followed Daddy into his study. "Wanna hang out?" He grinned, pulling two glasses and a bottle of Jameson from the bar. I propped my feet on an ottoman and burrowed into the couch. I loved Daddy's den. The masculine aroma of leather, whiskey, and the occasional cigar he sneaked out the window juxtaposed with its womb-like embrace. "What's with Mom?"

"She's mellowed."

"Jaysus, come spring, you can compost the garden with her. She hasn't uttered a single, 'Oh, Clare'."

"She misses you, baby girl. She's always ridden you pretty hard, but she wants a real relationship with you."

Black branches of bare maple trees traced the turquoise sky, framed by the tall window behind the desk. "I got a glimpse of what that looks like this morning. It's nice." Daddy sipped his whiskey, the chink of ice cubes musical against the glass. "Thank you again for the wonderful photographs."

"We could have sent them earlier, but Denise wanted custom frames." Then, with a guilty expression, he abruptly changed the subject. "Ciarán and I email."

"Cool. It's cool, right?"

"Very. I like the guy. I've never known most of your boyfriends, let alone considered any of them friends. He's different."

"In many ways. But in case you hadn't figured it out, most of my nonsense with boys owed to me and not them."

"Genetic predisposition on the maternal side," he said with a chuckle. He tilted back, one leg crossed over the other knee, relaxed and open: the classic Daddy pose.

"Well, you and Grand-da set a high bar, too."

He threw back his head with a laugh. "You can't find better than the likes of us."

"True. End of the day, though, my abysmal dating record owed to waiting for the equivalent of little cartoon birds singing over my head. When no sign came, I cut my losses and kept looking."

"We should never have let you watch Disney movies."

I swirled my glass, sniffing malted sweetness. "Every generation screws up their kids."

Daddy's eyes grew red rimmed. "You're not screwed up, Clare. Your mom and I are crazy proud of you. We show it different, but all either of us want is you kids happy in yourselves and knowing your place in the world."

I dabbed the air with an invisible fairy wand. "Wish granted. My life and the people who share it make me more than happy."

His foot thumped to the floor as he slapped a knee. "It's obvious I can't call you 'baby girl' anymore. Recognizing your blessings, even when everything isn't perfect, is a true mark of maturity." Then his brow wrinkled. "Ciarán has chosen an interesting profession."

Daddy's concern notwithstanding, the full story could wait until it had an ending. Instead, my answer came from the truth of the present moment. "I never expected someone like him. He struck me as not of this earth, sitting on a ruined wall, serene and beautiful, like the stones had birthed him. We started talking and became friends from the off."

"He tells a similar story, although in his version you were an 'alabaster angel with wild ginger curls comin' over the ridge like a gift' or some such Irish nonsense." I blushed, though Ciarán had said as much to me. Daddy smiled, tender and kind. "Believe me, nothing makes a dad happier than knowing the man who loves his daughter sees her true."

Emotion manifested in foggy eyes and husky throat. "The irony is, while searching for perfection, I didn't consider myself worthy of it. With Ciarán. I'm my whole self. It's freeing."

"Even when he pulled out the rug?"

"Circumstances challenge truth; they can't change it." I huffed, like Ciarán did, increasing my degree of tenderness. "The Sudan business proved he isn't perfect. Better to know it up front."

Daddy nodded. "Something similar happened with your mom. Not so dramatic, but a moment came when my idealized image of her cracked." He stared ahead until reflection morphed into grinning. "After the shock of it, when the dust settled, I realized my life would be a hell of a lot more interesting with the more complicated version. Thirty-six years and three great kids proved me right."

I cleared my throat. "Two. The jury is still out on Stephen."

Daddy chortled. "How do you like Alice?"

"She's too good for him. The bastard got lucky."

"Clare, I've repeatedly told you he's legitimate." He gave me a mischievous wink. "So, you'll stick with the imperfect guy who's perfect for you?"

My mouth twisted in a thoughtful smile. "If I can."

He poured himself a tot more whiskey and toasted. "Here's to it."

My fingers combed the fringe of a crocheted throw slung over the arm of the couch. "Daddy, the night of great Grand-da's wake, how did I get to bed?"

His face clouded with confusion, then cleared. "The party ended, a few families stayed to help clean. We couldn't find you, but before your frantic mother called the garda, a kid showed me where you were hiding. You were sound asleep under the stairs, with cake crumbs in your hair."

"We found each other by a ruined wall, but we met under a stair."

Daddy grinned with delight. "He's the kid? Ya don't say."

"Excellent meal, Denise. You never disappoint."

"Thank you, Edie. Did everyone leave room for dessert?"

Stephen groaned in answer and Daddy suggested we take a walk. "It's not too cold. We'll check out the Christmas lights and digest." The novelty of the suggestion and the frosty December night enlivened us. Mom and Daddy led the way; Edie, Aimee, and I tailed behind, arms linked, giggling over their wedding plans.

Christmas celebrates incarnation—a mystery made manifest—and I regarded it not as a calendar date so much as a fleet and sublime instance, unplanned and elicited by anything. The Christmas of 2014 the moment sparkled as our laughter rose toward the wintery night sky.

A light rain began falling, and we turned back. As we arrived at the house my phone rang, displaying Ciarán's number. If his personal phone had service, his team must have moved near a larger town. Remaining outside to minimize interference with the signal, I answered with a chirpy, "Howya."

"Merry Christmas, darlin'."

He sounded peaceful; I'd missed the gentle, laughing tone of his voice. "Christmas is over where you are."

"There are twelve days of it. How's the family?"

"We've had the best, least fraught holiday in our history. How did you celebrate?"

"We roasted a lamb, and I phoned the folks. And the evenin' stars were a wonder, shinin' so bright I wept."

"How appropriate. Did you feel like a Wise Man?"

"I did fancy myself a traveler under 'em."

"Keep your eye on them, and they'll lead you right."

"I thought of ya under the same stars, imaginin' ya beside me." His voice landed like a caress, and I shivered. "I love ya, darlin'."

"I love you, too."

When I came inside, pink cheeked with cold and joy, Stephen nudged my arm. "Secret admirer?"

"A Christmas miracle. Ciarán called."

"Aww." Stephen followed his teasing purr with pantomimed kissing.

I swatted him on the shoulder. "Jaysus, you're such a twelve-year-old."

Chapter Thirty-One

"Dec!" I sprinted from the terminal door and threw myself into his arms. "What are you doing here?"

"We couldn't have ya ridin' the bus home at this hour." He embraced me, took my bag, and we made our way to the garage. "Didja have a happy Christmas?"

"Yes; except for missing you all. Where's Ness?"

"She would have come along, but she's been tired of late." He attempted a serious set to his mouth but failed. "She'll be fine in about five months' time."

A delighted thrill ran through me and my hand clutched his arm. "Are you serious?"

"Don't make a scene, Clare," he muttered, embarrassed but pleased. "Contain yourself until we're in the car."

Once on the road my squeals of joyous excitement burst out. "Oh, Dec! A baby! You do mean a baby?" He nodded with a smile which met his ears. "It's the most incredible news." I held the bliss of it, arms wrapped around my belly. "After all you two have been through...wait." I made a quick calculation and chortled. "You dog."

He blushed over his grin. "We confirmed it after the weddin'."

"Damn. Why didn't Ness tell me?"

"She wanted ta clear the first trimester before announcin' anythin'. Then, since she wasn't showin' much, we decided it would make a grand Christmas present for the folks."

His understatement made me laugh. "Maeve must be ecstatic."

"Da should have her pried from the ceilin' by New Year."

"First Edie gets engaged and now this." I squeezed his bicep in lieu of jumping up and down. "Congratulations. Dec!"

"Thank ya." He wiped an eye and sniffed. "It's a little overwhelmin', ta be honest. I never imagined this happiness."

"You and Ness deserve every bit of it. But fair warning, this auntie intends to spoil the little shite rotten." The affirming rightness of Declan and Nessa becoming parents validated my notions of redemption in the most fulfilling way.

The trip home sped by, consumed by village gossip interspersed with giddy squeaks every time I thought of the baby. In what seemed no time, Declan parked in front of his office. "Ness is eager ta see ya. Are ya too shattered, or will ya come ta the pub? Ma's made a little supper."

"Of course, she has. Let me settle and reunite with my boy first."

Declan flashed an indulgent grin. "Bring him along. Ma likes him."

A fire burned on the hearth and the perfume of home—peat, black tea, and wet dog— welcomed me. Whiskey galloped from the kitchen, and I sank on my knees to greet him. "Oh, my little buddy. I missed you! Where's Auntie Moira?"

"She's gone."

I collapsed on the floor. "What are you doing here?"

"This is my home." Ciarán knelt beside me, his eyes bright as fine cut sapphires.

"But it's December."

"Ah, you've not heard of Christmas miracles. Are ya too bewildered ta kiss me?"

Climbing onto his lap, I clasped his head to my chest. My throat burned with tears, but weeping could wait. He'd come home safe. I breathed him in, and when he kissed my throat, the dog barked. "Shut your gob, pup," Ciarán said. "I have prior claim."

"Whiskey, lie down." The obedient animal plopped beside me. "Good boy. Has he been out?"

"He has. We've been makin' friends but I reck he didn't realize we'd be sharin' ya."

I held Ciarán's head and examined him. "Shite, you're gorgeous. Are you truly here?"

"Kiss me again." Complying, my arms engulfed his solidness and the sense of dreaming vanished. "Do ya need other proofs?"

"Mm, no doubt. But Maeve expects me, well, us, for supper."

He protested with another kiss. "They'll still be there tomorrow, and I've missed ya somethin' chronic."

I caught his caressing hands and bussed his nose. "I promised Declan. Shite: he knew you were here."

"Sure. I arrived yesterday."

"You and your secrets. Why didn't you tell me when you phoned?"

"Delays with my replacement. No sense in getting anyone's hopes up, includin' my own."

My fingers traced over his cheekbones; gratitude overwhelming me to the point of feeling slightly drunk. Then I squinted at him. "Any wounds to disclose?"

"One bruise, on my right thigh. Got it whackin' into a railin' at the airport."

"Could happen to anyone." I rose, a hand extended. "The family is waiting."

Whiskey ran ahead of us and disappeared around the back of the pub. "The dog knows where we're goin'?"

"He always comes to Sunday supper." We walked around the back and through the family door, Whiskey's tail wagging franticly. Maeve scampered into the hall and crushed me to her bosom. "Come sit, ya two. Supper's ready."

After a playful cuff of Declan's head, I took the chair beside Nessa, positioned my napkin, and gave her a blasé nod. "Heard your news. Congratulations."

A tiny puff of laughter escaped her throat. "Go on then and have done with it. You're dyin' ta."

Addressing my friend's midsection I said, "Howya, baby. I'm your Auntie Clare and I'm your favorite." After patting Nessa's belly, I pledged to refrain from such intemperate fuss in future.

"Welcome home, darlin'." She grinned; contentment enhanced her beauty.

Maeve served a platter of spiced beef, sat beside Eamon, and took his hand. With an expression of encompassing love, she offered thanksgiving for all the family together again.

Eamon passed a dish, chortling. "Did ya expect such a homecomin', Clare?"

"No, but you'll not hear me complain." Ciarán squeezed my hand, pine boughs and beeswax perfumed the familiar room, and the moment froze in joy. My heart surged, suffused with astonished gratitude and love. "It's good being home."

Supper conversation centered on holiday celebrations and the baby. Maeve, replete with happiness, couldn't even describe her spiced beef recipe without joyful tears; a vulnerability her sons exploited with relentless teasing.

"Enough," she said, drawing her stout frame into imperial rigidity. "I'll not apologize for bein' sensible of my many blessings and if the two a ya expect any puddin' you'll mind your manners. Mockin' your poor aul ma for her depth a feelin', I swear." In high dudgeon she made for the sideboard but dropped a kiss on Ciarán's shoulder as she passed. "Eamon, darlin', fetch the whiskey, please."

"When do ya go out again, Ciarán?" Declan asked.

"Oh, merciful saints!" Maeve thumped the cake plate on the table, rattling the teacups. "Don't ya dare start. The poor darlin's been home a day, and it's Christmas, though sure ya forgot, and ya should be ashamed. Be peaceable for the sake of the season, for Chrissake!"

"I'm not startin' anythin', Ma," Declan protested, earnest and abashed. "I thought we might be prepared next time."

"I'm not leavin' again," Ciarán said.

Stating a fact without reproach Nessa replied, "Ya didn't plan on the last trip."

"True enough, for which you're all owed an apology."

"Now, son, no need for regret." Maeve rushed on, in her inimitable way. "It's never been easy havin' ya away and I won't say otherwise; we worry about ya, of course, and why wouldn't we? But ya have a lovin' soul and if it takes ya far from us now and again, well, better ya care about the state of the world than not at all. We understand, darlin'."

Ciarán waited through the breathless delivery before he answered. "It's generous of ya ta say, but it's pure selfishness placin' all the burden of understandin' on my loved ones. You'll not need do again. I'm leavin' Cara for good and all now."

Maeve cried out with an impulsive, sincere one-eighty. "Praise Jaysus! I'm sorry, son. I know ya love it, but if you're inclined such a way I, for one, am glad of the news, though I'm sure I'm not alone and won't lie by sayin' otherwise."

Ciarán smiled but his lips bent downward when he met my perplexed expression. "Are ya not pleased?"

I rose and began collecting empty plates. "Let me help clear, Maeve."

Ciarán and I stood outside the pub, shivering in the abrupt transition from warmth to chill. "Whiskey needs a walk. Do you want to come along or meet back home?"

"I'll join ya."

Lambent light from windows lengthened our shadows on the sidewalk of the silent High. Whiskey trotted ahead, his expectant nose twitching in the wintry air. We were home, a truth vast as the dark sky above. Whatever happened, I'd found my center; not in the dog, the man, or the looped street of Killarkin, but in discovering the hearth and home of my own damn heart. I reached for Ciarán's hand.

"I feared you'd never touch me again." His voice called me out of my reverie.

"You're a ridiculously touchable man. Whiskey, come." The dog scampered away from a trash bin and trotted beside me.

"I'm leavin' Cara."

"So you said. Why?"

"Because of ya."

"Altogether the wrong reason." We reached the end of The High. "Leave it if *you* want, but don't you dare do it for me."

"Ya confound me, Clare Riordan."

"Do I now?" I moved close to kiss him. "Your lips are cold." We walked the village circuit, then made our way to the cottage, our coat collars turned up against light sleet. "You have a terrible habit of making unilateral decisions."

"Declan said I owed it ta ya."

"We've established most of what he says is shite." He unlocked the door, and we entered the welcoming house. Whiskey cantered toward the fireplace, and after spattering rain drops with an enthusiastic shake, stretched onto the floor. I stirred the peat and laid another turve with an involuntary shiver, whether from cold or anticipation of the inevitable conversation ahead, I didn't know. Sitting cross-legged beside my dog I buried a hand in his satiny coat.

Grand-da's chair creaked as Ciarán sat in it, stretching his legs toward the fire. "Dec told me ta stop runnin'."

"I'm not convinced you do."

"I run from my heart."

Placing a hand on my chest I said, "But then you gave it to me. I've held it all this time and it hasn't gone anywhere. But if you'll be away half the time, it's crucial we make important decisions together."

Deep, bruised shadows of weariness lay under his eyes, but he smiled, soft. "I don't want ta be away, sleepin' alone in a tent and yearnin' for home. I left this time considerin' what I wanted and nothin' more. It won't do." The fire sputtered and he rose to tend it.

"Being together doesn't preclude personal fulfillment. Don't sacrifice your work and call it love."

Ciarán lowered himself on the floor beside me, and I stoked his head, tracing the scar behind his ear. All the dread of the night he got it shuddered back; it ebbed when I cupped the base of his skull, felt the bones beneath his skin, and the pulse beating in his neck.

"I won't lose ya."

"Someday you will. Or I'll lose you. We're not promised a single moment beyond this one." I punctuated the words with a kiss which he answered with hungry urgency.

"I would do anything for ya." He embraced me, moaning into my neck.

"Dance with me at the *céilí*."

"You're a bold one." Ciarán grinned and splayed his fingers across my bosom. "I'll dance with ya, darlin'; whenever ya ask."

❁

Whiskey snored at the foot of the bed. Ciarán slept on his back, one hand on his chest. The radiator clicked, emanating heat, but the seeping chill of December lay on the room. I pulled the hem of my robe from under the dog's dead weight, watching from a window as Killarkin awakened. Smoke curled from chimneys, rising toward a pewter sky. Weak sunlight worked through a smattering of clouds. The quiet beauty overwhelmed to the tipping point of pain.

I dressed, crept downstairs, and started porridge. As I debated whether to eat alone or wake Ciarán, he appeared. After a sleepy kiss on my forehead, he poured himself a cup of coffee and eased into a chair. "You must be back, the table's the right size again. It's too big without you." My heart clutched at his pleased smile.

We made idle, almost shy chat as we ate, then he said, "I'd like ta talk."

I laid folded hands in my lap. Ciarán grew so silent my belly tickled like I'd swallowed a whirring hummingbird. We'd spoken many beautiful words the night before, born of the dark and a three-month separation. Then morning came and with it our reckoning. We stood poised on the edge of a conversation destined to point our course one way or the other, but I didn't press. His cup chinked on the saucer when he set it down. I clasped both his hands and committed to memory the sensation of smooth skin juxtaposed with callused fingers.

"Never having ta consider someone else when I went out before, I didn't appreciate why ya were so upset about my leavin' nor, ta my shame, did I try. It's easier ta indulge in self-righteousness. How could I be with a woman who couldn't acknowledge the importance of my work?"

I chuckled. "Yeah. I wondered why I involved myself with such a selfish brute."

He grinned but hung his head. "How did ya answer?"

"Your leaving dumfounded everyone. It justified my hurt. And never having had a calling, I didn't fully understand yours. But I love the whole

of you, including the passion which took you away from me."
Whiskey nudged my leg with an urgent whimper. "He needs a walk,
and I've missed St. Dall's; come with us?"

Words brimmed within me; no doubt in Ciarán, too. But we
didn't speak. Sleet froze on hills still untouched by sun. The ruins
were crystalline, an ice palace in a fairy story. We paused within the
palpable stillness and the silence entered my marrow.

Ciarán rested a shoulder against a pillar, hands deep in coat
pockets. "We'd been in country a month when one of my colleagues
got word his babby had arrived. It made me wonder what I'd miss
and whether it would be worth the cost."

"Ask your friend."

He pushed away from the pillar, offering a hand. We walked to the
wall and sat. "I did, but ours are different situations. He met his wife
doin' aid work; I first ran ta Cara fleein' the pain of Siobhán's loss
and my own failure. Fear of losin' Ma kept me out. Hidin' behind a
mission, I convinced myself deep bonds were meant for others, not
me. Jaysus, my pride."

"But you had attachments all along."

"Which I tended when it suited me, not realizin' how thick a wall
I'd built around myself until ya started pullin' it away. The wonder
is ya never even suspected the wall."

"It had nothing to do with me. You were ready for it to come
down."

His lips quirked sideways, a contemplative smile. Rather than
interrupt his thoughts, my gaze traveled across the valley, toward
the cottage. Even from a distance, the differences wrought since my
arrival were clear: the fresh paint, moss-free slates, and neat vegetable
beds, black and empty. Graceful, naked tree branches bowed over the
roof, like a mother tucking in a slumbering infant. I crossed chilled
hands over my breast, holding the satisfied joy chuckling through me.

Ciarán's hands stretched wide on his knees. I watched them for the tell-tale restlessness which sent them dancing. Those beautiful, long-fingered hands—skilled agents of work and love—required occupation. When not employed, or when their owner puzzled out a problem, they twitched or drummed. With tender reminiscence I remembered them once braiding grass into a cross.

They lay still now and when he spoke, Ciarán's voice came low, both more and less than a whisper. "Clare, I didn't want ta fear lovin' ya, but the deeper my feelin' for ya grew, the more it frightened me. Ya gave me such delight, but a small part of me hoped I'd get away and find we had nothin' between us so profound we couldn't live without it. And owin' to my cowardice, I hoped you'd realize it first and spare me hurtin' ya. Then ya asked the feckin' question outright."

My hands grasped the icy wall, my breath puffs of cloud on the frigid air. Nothing stirred but the rightness of the moment. Whether the next words brought an ending or a fresh beginning, we'd mark it in the place where we started.

"You're terrible patient with me." He embraced me, his breath warming my cheek. "Stone by pitiful stone I tried closin' the space ya made; smug with the idea I even could. Then, one night, a few weeks after actin' a maggot, I had a dream—more like a visitation—of everyone I ever loved, even folk I helped over the years. They all had your face."

"How unsettling."

"Beautifully so. Clare, there's no savin' the world without savin' myself. The care I give strangers who expect nothin' of me matters little without my bein' decent ta the ones I love. I'm so accustomed ta shorin' my blasted wall, but when I realized it needed ta come down, I turned on it with a fury. I'll keep it down, too, but ya must help me."

The simple words resonated; he'd never asked me for assistance. "How?"

"Love me as ya have done and remind me there's freedom in lovin'. Share your mind with me, as only ya can; it brings me out of myself. Dream and plan with me so I remember ta journey with ya. And when I fail ya, call me on my shite."

The steady timbre of his voice and the untroubled blue of his eyes, clear like a cloudless day, answered the last of my questions. Shivering against him I promised. "We should get back. Paddy's meeting me at The Folly at nine."

"I'll come along."

I tucked my arm in his. "Good. He missed you."

"Well, he has me back. I'll turn my skills ta buildin' actual walls."

Chapter Thirty-Two

"I T'S PELTIN' DOWN," CIARÁN said. He turned from the window, watching me dress for Sunday supper. "Ya wore this frock the first time ya fed me."

"What a random memory."

"A fond one. The blue sets off your hair." He laid a hand on my waist and waggled his eyebrows. "It compliments all your best features. I've suffered many a fantasy of takin' it off ya."

"I haven't worn it since then." He gave me a broad wink and I gaped. "You barely knew me!"

"And yet, I did."

"Play your cards right and, after supper, your dream could come true. Meantime, I have a present." I pulled a case, tied with a bow, from the closet. "Merry belated Christmas."

Ciarán opened it and held the rosewood guitar on his knee, tuning it with harmonics which rang and bounced through the room. "Shite, listen ta the tone of it. It's been years since I played, ya know."

"Is it all right? Declan advised me but trade it for something else if you like."

"It's amazin'." He played a few chords, then flexed his fingers. "I need practice. *Go raibh maith agat, mo ghrá.*"

"You're welcome. Now you and Dec can get the band back together."

He leaned over the guitar for a kiss. "You're relentless and delusional."

Our days were full. While Ciarán joined the crew rehabbing The Folly, I spent every spare minute helping Maeve prepare for the *céilí*. Consequently, we preferred to spend most evenings in the comfort of the cottage. We welcomed people into our home and enjoyed suppers with the family, but throughout January we reclaimed lost time.

One evening Ciarán put aside his guitar and laid his head on my lap, a dreamy smile on his face. I combed his curls with one hand and twined our fingers with the other. "Happy?"

"Content. It's astonishin'. Sure, this cottage is one of the thin places."

"It is magic. But I expect nothing less now."

Magic surrounded and penetrated all my living. It found a restless, aimless American girl and unlocked a Celtic soul which found joy in simplicity and met obstacles with forbearance. Simple tonics like a walk with Whiskey, a cuppa with a friend, or the gleam of my lover's eyes cured the intractable, harsh, or annoying bits of life. In tuning my spirit to glimpse the liminal, the ordinary became extraordinary.

The morning before the *céilí* we arrived at the pub and found it already a flurry of activity. Eamon, Paddy, and Liam erected a large tent in the back garden while Jamie arranged chairs along the perimeter of a makeshift dance floor. Moira and Cathleen swept and dusted, Nessa, now possessed of an obvious baby bump, polished tables. Even aul Tim peeled off his bar stool and helped Eamon unload cartons of whiskey.

I found Maeve in the kitchen, sleeves rolled past her elbows, her plump arms deep in a large bowl of dough. "Thank goodness you're here. Can ya start on the puddin'?"

Cauldrons of stew simmered on the stove. Casseroles heaped with shepherd's pie filled an entire table and oceans of cookies and cakes swamped another. "In the last three weeks we've baked enough dessert to feed the county and the next one over."

"Better too much than not enough. Aideen will arrive soon with her spiced beef, and we'll need platters for Cathleen's ham. I hope she remembers the pickle and cheese." She handed me a wooden spoon. "I'll start on the potatoes."

Winter air through the open windows teased the candle flames on Maeve's altar without mitigating the stifling inferno of hot ovens and steaming stoves. My arms went rubbery from stirring a vat of lemon curd and bowl after bowl of soda bread.

Gerry Fannin arrived with chicken fillet rolls and we stopped for a quick lunch. After Paddy washed down his fourth sandwich with his third pint, he slapped his hand on the bar and released a massive belch. "Off yer arses, lads! Let's hang those lights."

By supper time fairy lights decorated the tent outside and bunting festooned the pub ceiling. The fridges could not accommodate another morsel, and the kitchen tables groaned with food. The other helpers went home for their suppers, and I joined the O'Donnell's at the bar. "You'll soon have your first *céilí*, Clare," Eamon said.

"If I can get out of bed. My muscles are screaming for a massage." Interpreting the statement of fact as a request, Ciarán started kneading the hard knots in my shoulders. I laid my forehead on the bar and made a noise somewhere between an orgasmic groan and a purr.

"We'll sleep like the dead tonight," Eamon said, then with a stern expression for his wife added, "And *you'll* lie abed late tomorrow, darlin'."

Maeve considered with a finger on her chin. "I might make a last batch a meringues tonight."

In unison we cried "No!" and Ciarán added, "Don't make us put a watch on ya, Ma."

"Don't ya dare fuss, young lad." To emphasize her displeasure she snorted, then flounced toward the kitchen. "I do as I please in my own home, thank ya kindly."

Nessa gave me a conspiratorial nudge. "Come along. Follow my lead."

We traipsed into the kitchen, where Maeve studied a large bowl of eggs. Nessa put a hand on her mother-in-law's arm, her smile beatific as the Madonna. "Ma, ya promised you'd come 'round tomorrow and start on the babby's layette."

"I haven't forgotten, darlin' and I'll be there. Do ya believe we have enough, Clare?" She scanned the bountiful tables with a furrowed brow. "Whippin' egg whites takes next ta no time."

"There's plenty, Ma; I'll bet you'll serve nothing but leftovers all next week."

She reached for a mixing bowl and said, "It won't do ta run out in the middle of the *céili.*"

"It's not possible," Nessa replied. "Now, I'll be ready for ya at nine in the mornin'. I intend ta sleep in." She rested a hand on the swell of her belly for emphasis.

I missed my first Irish Christmas, but St. Dallán's Feast ran a close second. Church bells pealed through the morning air as the faithful made their way to Mass. Afterward, knots of parishioners clogged the street, chatting and laughing, their breath like fluffs of lambs' wool on the freezing air. Ciarán and I kept the feast with love making and the ruins. In the late afternoon, he checked in at the pub for last-minute duties while I donned a dress commissioned from Brigid; grass green wool, embroidered with delicate white flowers on the neck and cuffs.

Whiskey gave a joyful yip when Ciarán came home, then the skritch of the dog's nails and my man's tread sounded on the stairs.

"You're a picture," he said.

I twirled and the full skirt of my dress billowed out over a tulle petticoat. "It's ultra-dancy."

He cupped my cheeks with gentle hands. "My beautiful darlin'. Your eyes are shinin' star bright."

With a kiss I urged him to change. "I've heard about this party my whole damn life and don't want to miss a second."

He pulled me close, drawing a finger over my breast. "The entire village will be there, and the pub will be so jammers no one will give a shite if we're late."

"But I will. You promised me a dance."

Holding my hips, he swayed against me. "We can dance here and now."

Instinct and his provocation seduced me closer until I pulled away, laughing. "Ciarán O'Donnell, take me to the *céilí*!"

He let out an exaggerated, aggrieved moan. "Clare Riordan, I'll don the suit and tie and take ya dancin'. Then I'll bring ya home, relieve ya of your fine dress, and commence lovin' ya all night long." He emphasized the point with a kiss, then an intent stare. "It's tradition."

I buried my hot face in his neck. "But no baby come September, OK?"

"Ya best make sure ya took your wee pill."

Birth control confirmed; we stepped out of the cottage into tiny snowflakes wafting through the air. The beauty stopped my breath. The flakes danced in the stream of streetlamps before frosting garden walls and sifting into the corners of windowpanes. Our feet printed the virgin dusting and patches of charcoal slate showed wet where the snow melted near busy chimneys.

People crammed into the pub and spilled out into the tented back garden. The music of the band filtered through the open back door, accompanied by the sedate shuffle of slow-dancing feet.

Distracted by casting around for Maeve, Ciarán had to ask twice for my drink order. "Whiskey, please. Let me confirm your mom isn't roasting a flock of lambs and I'll find you after." I threaded my way through the crowd, but the kitchen contained only the Fannin women, busy with platters and ladles.

"We sent her away, don't ya fear," Cathleen said. "She's banned for the night. We'll see ta layin' out the food."

When I returned to the bar, Ciarán had disappeared. Scanning the room, I spotted Maeve, who fluttered like a nesting bird around Eamon, her sure and massive oak. Declan and Nessa arrived, inclined toward each other in quiet joy. Paddy strode with purpose toward the back garden, fiddle ensconced under his arm, while Liam shyly offered Moira a beer. The pub bloomed with villagers who enjoyed each other and those who didn't set aside their differences for the sake of one dark, wild winter night.

I made my way through the raucous crowd to the back garden and found an empty table near a brazier. Wrapped in a thick woolen shawl I watched, entranced, while three older couples set a perfect hornpipe. Orla sauntered across the dance floor, unconcerned by the threat of dancing feet.

A laughing voice asked, "May I join ya?"

"Thanks, but I'm meeting someone."

"He's a rude gobshite, keepin' a ride like yourself waitin'. I reckon ya could do better."

"Do ya now? And I suppose you'll be after suggestin' an alternative."

"I wouldn't presume." Ciarán slid a whiskey before me, eyed the dance floor, and pulled on his pint.

"I do want to dance, though." I scrutinized my companion and sniffed. "You'll do."

"It's a waltz. I could lead ya if ya care ta follow." I took his hand with an excited squeeze.

After three dances we returned to the table: the snow-flecked air cooling our heated bodies. "I should have trained!" I said, fanning myself. "Why didn't I get dance lessons?"

"Ya have been rather busy."

"I'm slacking. Fitting in here requires more than seven phrases of Gaeilge and two dance moves."

"Now ya mention, the Taoiseach advocates revoking the citizenship of those who can't execute a proper jig."

I snuggled onto Ciarán's lap, wrapping us both in the shawl. "An outdoor party in the dead of winter sounded like madness; I didn't reckon the demands of dancing. Gawd! Why wasn't I born Irish?"

His hands low on my hips he replied, "Ya were, only in the wrong country."

I pouted. "Ness says there's no equivalency between Irish and Irish American."

"She might assess the matter different now. And though some may question my loyalties for sayin' so, I reck you're Irish enough for anyone here."

The dancers cleared and a troop of little girls in matching green velvet dresses took the floor. They stood, backs straight, arms rigid. The bodhrán began its beat and the other instruments joined in while the girls twirled and hopped with precision. "Bet it's too late to learn step dancing, though. Damn."

Maeve sauntered by and paused. "Ya two appear cosy. Are ya enjoyin' yourself, Clare?"

"Very much, Maeve." I accentuated the vee of her name.

She giggled and winked, then in a stage whisper said, "The other name suits better." She led her husband away, calling, "Ya two behave."

"What's she on about?"

"I slipped last night and called her 'Ma.' I hoped she didn't notice."

"Ho! Of course, she did. But it's fittin'. She holds ya dear. Given a choice between us, you'd win."

"Bullshit. She believes her sons are the best who ever lived and would annihilate anyone who said otherwise. But I love her, too."

"Oh, my Clare." Ciarán pushed my hair back and off my shoulders. "*Is tú mo ghrá.*"

"*Mo chuisle.*" Ciarán's pleased grin indicated I managed correct pronunciation. "I asked Nessa for some phrases, in case I ever loved an Irishman."

"Are ya ever caught short?"

I clasped my hands around his neck. "Often. But, oh, nothing could have prepared me for you." I studied his features. "How did I not recognize those eyes? Do you remember what you told me in the secret chamber?"

He pushed a curl from my cheek. "I remember tryin' ta comfort ya."

"You succeeded. You gave me a blanket and a cake and said, 'Ease in, then. You're home here.' Twenty odd years later, I am." The party fell away; dancers and music vanished. Only Ciarán and I existed. "I've had you like a beat on the heart all along. I almost died when Ness taught me *mo chuisle.* You *are* my pulse, Ciarán, and you always have been."

"Over the years I often wondered about the wee *cailín* under the stairs; if her hair still curled around her face and if her emerald eyes ever lost their fear. When we met again, I had my answer." He kissed me, long and lingering, one hand on my cheek. "Thank God I brought ya cake. Thank God ya returned."

Convulsed by laughter, I replied, "Yes, darlin'. The cakes lured me back."

The *céilí* spun back into relief; dancers swirled, the joyous cacophony of flute, fiddle, and dulcimer pumped again into the night air and laughter floated over and through us. I stood, tugging Ciarán's hands. "Dance with me."

He pulled me back on his lap. "In a moment." His lips touched mine again as something cool and heavy slid over a finger on my right hand.

A gold claddagh, with a glowing emerald on the crown and tiny diamonds on the band, shimmered in the fairy lights. "It's on the wrong hand."

"Worn so means you're taken."

"Oh." I examined the ring. "True enough."

"If ya like, wear it as a symbol of all ya love about Ireland."

"It's a beautiful ring, and you are the most lovable of Irish things."

He clasped my ringed hand. "Now, should ya ever consent ta marry me, ya move it ta the left, with the heart facin' out; ya turn the heart toward your own when we wed." He informed me of all this with a casual grin, another tutorial on national customs. But his fire sparkled intense enough to rival the stones on the ring.

"When did you get this?"

"When I came home, before we left Dublin. Declan helped me choose it."

"How did you get the size right?"

"I phoned Edie."

I squinted, suspicious. "Daddy said you two emailed."

"We've stayed in touch since Seamus' funeral."

"Did you ask for my hand?"

Ciarán's laugh trilled with delight. "I asked his blessin' out of courtesy. But it's your hand ta give nor will I accept it from anyone else." The brilliant ring glittered, though I sat motionless. "Make the decision in your own time, darlin'. After what I put ya through, I won't rush ya. But please consider if you'll have me."

I caressed his face, gazing into the cornflower blue I'd known most of my life. "Never doubt this, Ciarán O'Donnell: I love you with everything I am and everything I will be."

"There's an excitin' prospect." He grinned before he lifted me from his lap, set me down, and led me toward the music. "You'll consider?"

"Sure." Then I halted at the edge of the dance floor. "About this offer of yours; how long would I have you?"

He lifted my chin. "I'll content myself with all the rest of our days."

"Here in Killarkin?"

His gentle smile lit my pulse. "Here, where we've come home."

"*Is tú mo bhaile.*" Blushing I asked, "I guessed. Is it correct?"

Ciarán beamed but quirked an eyebrow. "What do ya think ya said?"

"You are my home."

"Sure, and you're mine." He kissed me and tiny tears bloomed in response. Love and commitment were new to me, but I embraced them with every fiber; understanding they were an anchor, not a weight. I lifted my head, tender and grateful, and with a concrete-certain heart, moved the ring to my left hand.

Acknowledgements

The journey began with my G'pa Fraser and my beautiful mother, and many teachers and professors guided my love of story along the way thereafter, but Sanford Yoder, my sixth grade teacher, told me I should be a writer.

All hail, honor, and blessings to my creative mentors Susannah Conway, Jamie Ridler, Meghan Genge, and Caroline Donohue who all in their unique ways laid (and continue to lay) rose petals and magic along my creative and spiritual path.

The YouTube channels and infectious personalities of Clare (Clisaire) Cullen and Diane Jennings have not only brought me a lot of fine entertainment over the years, but their content also enriched this book as regards Irish history, culture, and language. Go raibh maith agat, ladies.

This book would have lived in a cupboard forever without the encouragement, and influence of the dearest writing cadre a woman could ask for and who make weekday morning cozier. Special thanks to Kat Caldwell, Madison Michael, and Nancy Houser-Blum for their nudges, invaluable critique, and unrelenting encouragement as I dusted off the manuscript. What you've done for me, as a human and a writer, goes bone deep.

Tremendous thanks to my gorgeous editor Nicole McCurdy at Emerald Edits, who helped me dig deeper than I believed possible (and who, by the happenstance of being Irish, assured the book's tone didn't come off sounding like a Lucky Charms commercial.) Gratitude to Dahlia Metchis, who offered a steady hand to guide me over a serious hump. Gratitude forever to Kat Caldwell for sparing me from formatting this book. And if the book's cover left you breathless, a) same and 2) it is all owed to the wizard Steven Novak.

Naming every other soul who ever influenced my writer's heart is impossible, but I must mention—in no particular order and for reasons we'll not go into on this day but who are on this list for cause—Lorene, JP, Auld Hat, Michelle, Cris, BJ, Cecelia, Mary B, TH, Chou, the Flamingos, Dana F, Eve, Klaudia, Timofey, and all the Blogtopians from a long-ago era. My wings thank you for the wind.

Love and gratitude to my astonishing daughter Lori for charming my life and my husband Eric who, when I nervously confessed the notion of leaving my job to write full-time replied, "Well, of course you should; you're a writer." Thank you, honey. Now you can read the book.

And finally, to you, dear, dear reader: many thanks for picking up this book and spending a few hours of your life with my characters. Blessings on your head.

About the Author

Raine Fraser started penning stories early, though her first manuscript, *Marshmallows for Mouse Pillows*, is, sadly, lost to time. The dream of being an author never left her, and after trying on various careers and raising a child along the way, she fully committed to writing in 2015.

Where We Come Home is her first novel.

A lifelong native of the soggy Pacific Northwest, Raine holds a BA in English from Seattle Pacific University. When not writing, she is reading, gaming out stories on The Sims 4, and mucking with limited success in the garden.

Follow her on Substack and rainefraserwriter.com to connect and learn more about future books.